THE MOON WILL PAY

Greg Billington

Published by
Time for a Story 2023
Timeforastory.co.nz
8 Bell Bird Rise, Picton 7220
New Zealand

Cover Illustration: Media Production

ONE

A small headline on page six of the Peapod News read, 'Outbreak Concerns.' Dimple Potts, perused the brief article and said to his wife, 'Listen to this. "A new study suggests a possibly serious outbreak of *Alta Stultitia* or Deep Stupidity. Neuroscientist Dr Klas Beekhof says the condition results in thoughts we may think of as common sense, such as 'Dinosaurs helped to build the pyramids – it stands to reason,' and 'I did my own research,' but which are clinically described as cognitive horse feathers. Whilst the condition has been apparent throughout human history, he said that researchers are alarmed to observe the current and rapid diffusion of Alta Stultitia into the general population, worldwide."

Dimple nodded knowingly at his wife. 'This is what I said to the Chair at last week's meeting. I can tell you it's reached our shores.' He continued to read:

"Endeavouring to quantify the trend, Beekhof said that the study asked a broad sample of people across Europe, 'If the moon was to fall, would you prefer it to fall on Africa or South America?' Ninety per cent of people said they would prefer it to fall on Africa."

Dimple gave a short and incredulous bark of a laugh. 'Africa!' he cried. Then reading on. "When asked why, most believed incorrectly, Africa to be wider and therefore less likely to sink, whilst fifteen per cent of these respondents preferred it to fall on Africa because if it fell on the Sahara, which was all sand, it would be hardly noticeable."

Dimple cried, 'Idiots! There are oases – and pyramids.' Then he read, "Beekhof said that when this question was asked ten years ago, sixty per cent had selected the option, 'This is a silly question.' In the current study, this response had dropped to just seven per cent."

'Seven per cent!' cried Dimple. 'We are living in outrageous times…but I can tell you, it's been very obvious to me.' and he took a mouthful of his toast and marmalade. His wife said it *was* a silly question. Dimple replied, 'That's as may be, but I certainly would not have said Africa. I'd have said, if the moon was to fall, we'd need to nuke it. I am wondering why this wasn't an option?'

Dimple's wife offered no comment about this. She sipped her cup of tea and listened with a small smile on her face, to the blackbird singing in the apple tree in the garden. Dimple returned to the article and read, "Beekhof also pointed to alarming evidence of a fall in neuronal connections. In this respect, he said, a significant proportion of the cohort that is defined as 'White older males before actual torpor,' or WOMBATS, said that the moon should be nuked forthwith, *as a precaution.*"

Dimple nodded sagely. 'Prudent,' he observed. 'My thinking, exactly.'

TWO

What had become abundantly clear to Dimple Potts, was that he no longer had a future in politics. Witness the calamity in his previous home town of Brewster's Neck. Just three citizens, including himself and he presumed his wife, had voted for him to continue his short-lived tenure as Mayor. It was preposterous but what could he expect? Hadn't his policies been deliberately distorted and misrepresented by his opponent? For a few moments he allowed his thoughts to contemplate his erstwhile opponent. A Latvian baker. The Latvian baker, Sarah Bumbulis. She had come from nowhere. He had been deputy mayor for twenty-three years and then, a baker who'd lived no more than eleven years in his town, had stood against him and won by a landslide. Humiliation.

The politician, Dimple Potts glanced up and found himself being regarded by himself. He studied the grave image staring at him from the bathroom mirror. He studied the longish but not unhandsome head with its prominent ears; its sombre grey eyes beneath bushy eyebrow and all crowned with a decent head of hair albeit flecked with grey, and considered what word best described that visage. He decided, not for the first time, that it was *dignified*. He raised a hand and took hold of his lapel. It was a dignified posture. It suggested a politician surely, who took things seriously. Not a smirking, flighty, Tik Tok, leotard-wearing and garrulous type, of which there were many, but a man of integrity, indeed, a man-for-all-seasons. He sighed. Three votes. Ignominy. Alta Stultitia. He had departed Brewster's Neck like a dog-shot-in-the-butt, as that dreadful Verbal Pritchard had described it.

3

At the thought of his former PR man, the man-in-the-mirror grimaced. Dimple asked, rhetorically, 'Had I not allowed that charlatan Corker and his vacuous nephew, Verbal anywhere near my campaign, would I not have rebuffed the Bumbulis challenge?' The man-in-the-mirror assumed a most reflective expression, before replying, 'Dimple. You had an albatross around your neck.' Dimple nodded and allowed his gaze to settle on that neck. A solid neck. Not without some wrinkles but nevertheless, not the etiolated neck of a green sprout. It *had* borne an albatross but it was unbowed. The bird-of-ill-omen had been cast off.

His thoughts returned to Corker Pritchard. Founder and owner of the very successful but ultimately infamous business 'Forest Flavours,' bringing consumers a taste of wild venison in its acclaimed sausages and other small goods. Corker Pritchard…not content with making a great deal of money from Forest Flavours, meddled in Council affairs, such that rules always favoured his manifold dealings and schemes. Such as a coal mine. And who had he enlisted to this new venture? The new Mayor, Dimple Potts. And so, when Dimple's fellow citizens and voters discovered that Corker Pritchard's venison sausages also contained various species of vermin as well as a citizen's cherished pet, purely by association, Dimple's campaign sank without trace. Bumbulis triumphant.

Dimple glanced toward the ceiling, 'Was mine not a robust and reasoned policy platform?' The man-in-the-mirror pursed his lips and sucked in his cheeks but made no comment.

'Jobs,' continued Dimple accusingly. 'Everything is about jobs. No jobs? Bottom feeders and chaos. And proper types of jobs that everyone knows about…not the airy-fairy jobs that Bumbulis proposed. Of course, I expected that coal was going to attract some controversy, but didn't I always say it was a transition? I maintained just that, from the beginning.

A temporary gold mine as it were. Then, out with the coal and on with the windmills and so forth. I always said that, but that woman twisted my words. Shameless! And the average punter? Too daft to know the difference, and now we know, getting dumber by the day.' He looked for affirmation but the man-in-the-mirror remained annoyingly silent. Dimple gave him a cold stare.

Perhaps, at the end of the day, Dimple considered, it had been fated. Quite apart from Forest Flavours, there had been the Hemopo problem. Recalling how the uncooperative inventor had derailed the plan for coal, Dimple removed his hand from his lapel and pinched his cheek, quite painfully. The man-in-the-mirror's eyes widened. Both now contemplated Doug Hemopo, who, for reasons to do with a contrarian nature, opposed things – and especially things proposed by the Mayor – on principle. Had Hemopo taken the substantial amount of cash on offer and granted access to the coal behind his land, much that had gone catastrophically wrong, would not have done so. Not only had he obstructed the Mayor and his entrepreneurial sponsor, but he had invented and built that monstrous robot that had quite literally, destroyed Corker's mining equipment. And then what? The iron beast had brought down the electrical trunk lines into Auckland, destroying itself in the process and utterly driving the final nail into the coffin that was Dimple's mayoral campaign.

Dimple said indignantly, 'What would Beekhof make of all that?'

*

These then, were the reflections of a man who had selflessly given twenty-four years of his life to public service. Twenty-three years in Brewster's Neck, and now to the minor political

5

party called the First Union of Conservative Thinkers, here in the leafy and complacent Auckland electorate of Peapod. But what did it mean? To represent the First Union of Conservative Thinkers? Frankly, he did not know. And as the weeks ticked by and the General Election loomed, it became no clearer. And why? Beekhof had confirmed his suspicions. Brain fog abounded and most particularly in the committee for the election of Dimple Potts.

A voice called from another part of the house. Ah, thought Dimple, dinner. Just what he needed. He had detected the aroma of a steak and kidney pie and it was most tantalising. He completed his business, arranged his attire and flushed the lavatory. Then he washed his hands for half a minute. The man-in-the-mirror nodded approvingly. As Dimple exited the bathroom, the man-in-the-mirror inspected his own fingernails and said, 'A man who possesses genius is insufferable, unless he also possesses at least two other things: gratitude and cleanliness.'

Dimple paused in the doorway. 'Do you think that profound? An idiot could pronounce as much.'

The man-in-the-mirror said in his typically offhand way, 'Ich zitiere Nietzsche.'

*

The pie was excellent. The Shiraz was satisfying. But the brussel sprouts were not. Dimple reminded his wife that he did not like brussel sprouts. An expression of distaste came to his dignified face. 'I refuse to eat them!'

Dimple's wife came around the table and taking his knife and fork from his hands, sliced the sprouts and applied a little salt, pepper and butter. She returned to her seat.

In response to her enquiry, he said, 'Yes. I have a committee meeting tomorrow morning. I intend to resign. No more of this shilly-shallying and wringing of hands. I am through with politics. I am through with the First Union of Conservative Thinkers, and I am through with this Peapod electorate. I intend to cut-to-the-chase and brook no argument.' He swallowed the last slice of the sprouts. 'There must be an end to it. I think to become an entrepreneur. Look at Corker Pritchard – made a fortune turning deer and possums into sausages.' He raised his fork and poked the air to emphasise his determination both to resign from politics and to become an entrepreneur. An entrepreneur is the very model citizen, whom everyone wished to be. Hardly anyone wished to be a politician because a politician was held in the lowest regard. Very low. Some of the tweets he had read recently suggested that the authors of those tweets held a cane toad in higher regard. He touched his chest and grimaced. Then he prodded his thigh and said, 'Ouch.'

It had occurred to him that had Corker Pritchard not become excessively greedy and padded his products with pets, he would still be the king of Forest Flavours and the magnate of Brewster's Neck. That was the lesson. When it was discovered that the town's favourite dog, Nostradamus, had been unwittingly eaten by the locals in a Forest Flavours sausage, Corker's days were over. Greed. Or was it stupidity? Or perhaps, just plain carelessness? Perhaps that was the lesson? By some reckoning, it was stupid, certainly, but it wasn't greed, per se, that had led to Corker's disgrace and hasty flight to South America. It was, contemplated Dimple, more akin to carelessness…in which case, the successful entrepreneur's creed must be greed, but with care…

In the midst of these thoughts Dimple prodded his ankle and said 'That hurts too! Perhaps I'm coming down with something.' He poked his chest and cried out in alarm, 'It's everywhere.'

His wife came around the table and took his hand in hers. Then she went to the bathroom and returning, handed him a single band-aid.

'What is the use of this?' Dimple demanded.

His wife advised him to put it on the cut on the end of his finger.

*

In the Peapod office of the First Union of Conservative Thinkers, a meeting was taking place. The subject being debated heatedly, was the party's sole candidate – to wit, Dimple Potts. The debate did not concern candidate Potts's suitability to run for the election in three weeks – the debate was about who might be found to replace him at such short notice. The meeting was characterised by sudden outbursts, with all speaking at once but which clearly boiled down to the sentiment that Potts was a most unsuitable candidate, mixed with not so oblique accusations against those who had brought him into the fold. These outbursts caused complexions to change colour and elicited mutterings beneath the breath – which occasioned sharp questions such as, 'What? What are you saying? Speak up, so we can all share!' These outbursts were punctuated with silences that could best be described as a funk, and in one case, the mysterious demand, 'Who's got the bodgy?' During the funk, eyes were downcast. Fingers fidgeted with pens. Sighs were common, as was the sudden gesture of a hand clapping to a brow. Then a new outburst would begin. 'What I don't understand is how...' and then the question was lost in the cacophony of raised voices.

The meeting proceeded in this vein for approximately an hour. Finally, the Chair was able to make a speech with barely an interruption. 'I think we are all agreed that we've been saddled with an idiot. Yes, yes – let me finish!

Obviously, I take some responsibility for Potts's appointment, but that's water under the bridge. And to be fair, his previous campaign movement, which you may recall was FOKKERS, seemed an admirable fit with our own persuasions. 'Fundamentally opposed to Aucklanders, Kangaroos, Environmentalists, Rivers and Socialists.' I grant you that 'Rivers' was a stretch – but that's the farmers getting their oar in – and of course we're not opposed to *all* Aucklanders – more that we're for ourselves, in a selfless way – but otherwise, Potts's slogan was in pretty decent alignment with the values of the First Union of Conservative Thinkers.' He paused to encourage scarcely perceptible and grudging nods that indicated that indeed, in other circumstances and with a little modification, FOKKERS could easily have been their own.

'What we have since learned, and I'm first to admit I slipped up, but you all know how busy I have been – what we have learned is that Potts was mayor of a village of barely three hundred. In fact, I haven't been able to even locate this huddle of huts on any map I've looked at. And Potts himself disclosed that an Indian, a Pawnee, for Heaven's sake, rode up main street – all fifty metres of it – and shot an arrow into a beggar's throat.' The Chair shook his head. 'Unbelievable, I grant you, but we have to face facts. We're three weeks out from a general election with no other candidate in sight.' Nods accompanied this evident but painful truth.

'What to do? That's our dilemma and that's what we must resolve. We must be of one mind. We must put aside our quite legitimate concerns, and focus on the election. And in my mind, it comes down to this. We either back Potts with everything we've got, or we stand aside for the Other Lot. Now, here's the thing. We're Peapod. And in Peapod, we vote for anyone but the others. It's our badge of honour. It's how we stand apart and frankly, it's why we're the envy of everyone. Peapod would vote for anything that drew breath, provided it opposed taxes and losers. That being the case, I think it more than safe to assume that instilled by us with the correct fervour, Potts could be moulded to become a successful candidate. What happens after, well, that's for the future. But what we must have, is an MP. We must hold the balance of power – and I say, if it must be Potts, so be it.'

The Chair opened the floor for discussion, which occasioned another two unintelligible outbursts, further darkening of complexions and in one case, a body slumping forward onto the table, temporarily indisposed.

'So, I think we're agreed that Potts it is.' The Chair glanced at his phone. 'He's here in ten minutes. We must compose ourselves.'

THREE

Experimentally, candidate Potts poked his bandaged finger into his neck and noted with satisfaction that his neck appeared to be unaffected. He popped into the bathroom and observed in passing that he was presenting his resignation that very day. He said, 'Time to show that the Potts has many strings to his bow.'

With this liberating thought he drove through the elysian avenues of Peapod and wondered what extraordinary and perhaps revolutionary new business he would soon create. He imagined how he would be received. He would enter a crowded room of conspicuous affluence and momentarily, all eyes – envious and worshipping, would be on the Entrepreneur. There would be comments such as, 'That's Dimple Potts, you know...one of the most creative minds in business today...unbelievably wealthy...reinvented the category...revolutionary product...an example to us all...eccentric but a genius...' Indeed, so engrossed was he with his 'new direction,' that when he paused at his favourite café to take a coffee and a croissant, the sudden collapse of the barista; the ensuing kerfuffle behind the counter and the urgent attention of the paramedicals, went entirely unnoticed. With great surprise he replied to the distraught waitress, 'He's dead, you say? Well, well.' And at that precise moment he experienced the frisson of an entrepreneurial idea.

Who wanted to be a pall bearer? How much better if the coffin floated, under a smallish helium balloon and needing only a slight nudge this way or that to be guided to the hearse and thence to the grave site? And once conveniently suspended over the hole, a dart, perhaps, ceremonially thrown by the widow, would cause the coffin to plop to its final resting place without need of any other paraphernalia…The tiresome problem of the overly-tall pall bearer opposite the very short, instantly solved! A coffin that with an adjustment to its balloon, might actually be launched into limitless space and thus solving the worldwide shortage of burial ground. Naturally, there were details to be worked out – but this is where it started, with the entrepreneurial spark and a dead barista. As he drove along the avenue to the office of the First Union of Conservative Thinkers, he smiled and hummed. Approacheth the Great Thinker!

*

At that moment, the Chair was reminding the selection committee that their candidate wasn't *that* bad. They had vented their spleen this past hour, but now it was time to rally around and throw their full support behind their candidate. This is what politics was all about. As much as it might be galling, he reminded them that they had been obliged to swallow frogs of a similar greasiness in the past. He reminded the committee that it was always the lot of the party faithful, regardless of hue, to have to compromise when it came to selecting a candidate. Look at the House! A hodgepodge of tosspots. It really just came down to selecting the least idiotic. But it worked. Even when one of them had taken to appearing in dancing leotards and on occasion, to speaking in tongues, the punters of Peapod had remained staunch and the First Union of Conservative Thinkers had held the balance of power. And that was the point of it all.

*

Candidate Potts pulled into the carpark and adjusted his tie. He knew who would be present. The Chair, who was one of the most self-important buffoons Dimple had ever met. That woman, aptly and frequently referred to by the Press as 'Sniffer.' That ancient accountant who repeatedly demanded, regardless of the issue on the table to be 'shown the money;' that property developer responsible for half of the buildings in Auckland being wrapped in plastic as the only means of keeping the weather out. That ex-boxer whose face was testament to a career that more resembled that of a punching bag, and whose erratic utterances were surely a reflection of too many blows to the head; and that other unbearably condescending woman who was an 'expert in the arts...'

Well, the Potts was prepared. He had decided his speech would start thus: 'Ladies and gentlemen. I'm afraid I must convey sad tidings. After a great deal of thought and soul searching, I've decided that we must part. That is to say, I am resigning my candidacy. I am an entrepreneur by heart and now by inclination. I have decided that at this point in my career, I must do what has become an overwhelming, indeed, an irresistible urge. To unleash my creative and commercial instincts and to create great wealth.'

Dimple glanced in the rear-view and wondered momentarily the whereabouts of the man-in-the-mirror. But no matter. He hastened up the steps, passed down the short hallway and opened the door.

'Ah!' Exclaimed the Chair. 'The man of the hour, no less! Do come in, Dimple. We've been waiting impatiently. Not that you're late, mind, but because we need your sage counsel. Only a moment ago, this committee agreed that we were bashing our heads against a wall and someone said, 'We need our man – we need Dimple.' And here you are. Please, take this seat, at the head of the table.' And because he was a devout lawyer, the Chair added, 'Amen.'

The surprised candidate took his seat. The Chair continued with his effusive welcome and warmed to his theme of how elections were won not by the back-room boys – and girls, but by the candidate, The chosen one – who in the best cases, such as was evident here, had virtually selected themselves by dint of their outstanding leadership qualities and ability to see the Big Picture. A Big Picture that ordinary folk, such as those assembled in this very room, were incapable of seeing. Amen.

During this extraordinary speech, Dimple became aware of something. Teeth. He became aware that the room contained an enormous quantity of teeth. Teeth that rendered the visage in which they existed, a mere backdrop. An unpainted canvas, dominated in fantastic detail by the enamel chisels and discoloured incisors created by God for the purpose of consumption. The teeth, he decided, of ungulates. He permitted himself a gracious smile with the principal purpose of revealing the teeth of a carnivore. Thus, the proper relationship was established. To be sure, this battery of teeth around the table could on a good day dispatch hundreds of kilos of weeds, but only one set of teeth extant, could dismember every one of them, limb from limb. Teeth of the Potts…

In rhetoric worthy of a fire-and-brimstone sermon, the Chair brayed that the Committee was unanimous and committed and without a single reservation, to helping their esteemed candidate to heroically cross the line and to cause mayhem and consternation among his opponents and in government. 'Mayhem and consternation, in the Other Lot, Mr Potts – Dimple. That is our mission. That is our goal, and we know that you have it in you. In spades. Amen.' At this, a clamour of voices called, 'Hear, hear!' and 'Well said, Mr Chair!' and 'Dimple is our Man!' There then came an expectant pause.

It seemed to the Candidate that somehow, at the conclusion of every one of the Chair's acclamatory statements, a commensurate part of his own determination disappeared, until at last, he felt he was in a state of complete bemusement. He tried to recall his prepared speech. It began, he thought, with 'Ladies and Gentlemen...' but beyond that, at this moment, all was blank. Except that there was something to with tidings. He looked from one committee member to the next and as his gaze moved from one to the next, his eye was drawn like a fridge magnet, to molars and incisors. Except when he came to the accountant. Indeed, the accountant's teeth were no longer visible. Instead, Dimple observed that it was the accountant's tongue that was most evident. As it happened, the tongue was lolling out of the accountant's mouth – rather like that of a panting dog, except with much less colour. Indeed, Dimple thought, the accountant has no colour whatsoever. And so, his first words were not 'Ladies and Gentlemen,' but rather, 'I believe the accountant may be dead.'

*

The committee and the Chair agreed that in fact, the accountant was dead and this gave rise to some conjecture and speculation about how long he had been deceased. The woman who was an expert-in-the-arts, observed that however long it was, it could not be denied that the presence of a corpse at the table was aesthetically displeasing. The Chair decided that it was best they adjourn in order to tidy things up. But before he did so, he wanted Candidate Potts to understand that the Committee and the Party, stood rock-solid behind him. They had called this special meeting to say exactly that and to begin the process of refining and formulating the election policy platform – for which purpose they absolutely needed the vast experience and proven acumen of Candidate Potts. As a Committee, he expounded, they were nothing more than a collection of aspirations and ideas of little note. An unguided missile. Amen. What they required was a catalyst. What they needed was the presence of that special chemical that would transform a loose collection of ideas and thoughts into coherent, hard-hitting policy. What they required, indeed, was an alchemist, capable of transforming humble dross into gold!

The Chair was exceedingly gratified at this speech and was particularly drawn to the metaphor of the gold – for if any single idea, or substance, or colour could be said to characterise the First Union of Conservative Thinkers, it was gold. The Chair apologised to Candidate Potts, for having so inconvenienced him with a meeting truncated by the unseemly demise of the accountant – but confided that it was likely the committee would be the stronger for it. The accountant had not been exhibiting very good form for some time, he said. And his tongue? It had been swollen and smooth and resembled if nothing else, a map of ancient lands. 'That,' observed Dimple knowledgably, 'Is a case of geographic tongue.'

The Chair said, 'You don't say?'

Dimple nodded. 'Probably symptomatic of a deeper malaise. I liked your reference to gold, by the way. Very much in accord with my own inclinations.'

The Chair said, 'We will talk further, Candidate Potts. I can see we are aligned. The stars are aligned. I sense it as I sense the presence of greatness.' He bestowed a most winning smile on the Candidate. 'We in the law, Candidate Potts, know a thing or two about gold. Indeed, I know of no other profession that can more quickly sniff out a nugget than my own.' And in this it was clear to Candidate Potts that it was he who was the nugget in question. The Chair continued warmly, 'But you? I sense you too are a digger. A miner indeed. I sense we are destined for great things – with you in the lead – the

16

standard bearer. If it is not taking it too far, the bearer of the golden eagle.'

Candidate Potts said, 'I've heard the call, Mr Chair, and I'm ready.'

The Chair seized his hand and shaking it vigorously, cried, 'Amen!'

*

Candidate Potts mused on his homeward journey. It had been a most unexpected meeting with a most unexpected outcome. The Committee wanted him. The Committee was totally behind him. Far from wanting to tip him out, they expected him to take the lead and to prevail in the hustings. The Chair, who perhaps was not as pompous as Dimple had hitherto thought, envisioned Candidate Potts as the bearer of Aquila – the Eagle. A symbol of speed and power…

'Ah, yes.' Dimple replied to his wife. 'Well, that was my intention – at least, it was an option I had in mind. To resign that is. But that's because I feel this urge to create and innovate in the cause of industry. I feel I've ignored all these years, my true vocation, as it were. I feel most strongly the call of entrepreneurship. So, it had crossed my mind that I might take my leave of politics to pursue my new endeavours. What? Well, that's the thing about being an entrepreneur – you don't necessarily have a business, per se. Anyone can have a business. Look at a plumber – or an accountant. Hardly the work of imagination and innovation. Did I mention that the accountant passed away – yes, actually in the meeting though God knows he may have been deceased days before we even started. How would you know?'

Candidate Potts explained that the Chair had been adamant. The First Union of Conservative Thinkers would be rudderless without the Potts. Indeed, he had suggested that

17

Candidate Potts was none other than the standard bearer. 'Yes, I know. I don't think we'd want to give that metaphor too much currency, but the golden eagle? Majestic and a symbol of speed and power. At risk of being immodest, I like to think that pretty much sums up me, as a politician. Or an entrepreneur.'

Candidate Potts agreed that it was indeed singular, that he had been in the café when the barista died and then, mere minutes later, to be in the same room as a dead accountant. Something to do with the planets, he suggested. As the Chair may have been suggesting at the time. Perhaps aligned, or not, as the case may be. Or the stars? Perhaps both? Perhaps a misaligned star over an aligned planet. Perhaps a cosmic perturbation of some kind…but in the end, just death. And wasn't that Life?

Shortly, after taking tea, Dimple stared thoughtfully at the man-in-the-mirror. It seemed that the man-in-the-mirror was similarly, in a thoughtful mood. He was, Dimple reflected, quite a handsome fellow, all things considered. Though there were times he could be just a little smug. And opinionated. When Dimple mentioned quite casually and as though it was neither here-nor-there, that he had decided to contest the election after all, the man-in-the-mirror had smirked. Just enough to say, 'Oh ho…so much for being determined and uncompromising.'

It was irritating, but Dimple felt he had to explain himself. How he *would* have resigned were it not for the fact that the Party would be as good as dead, were he to follow through. The outpouring of loyalty and support were quite humbling. Had the man-in-the-mirror been present, he would have seen that it was impossible to resign in such a circumstance. Many people would have been devastated. As it was, he suspected that the demise of the accountant was likely because the accountant sensed his intention to resign, and it was simply more than he could bear. And who could be

18

surprised? Of all people, an accountant would understand the value of an asset-in-hand. Candidate Potts was on the balance sheet. Take him off and what did you have? In any event, Dimple expounded, his new direction of entrepreneurship was a very comfortable and complementary fit with the aspirations of the First Union of Conservative Thinkers. What was at the heart of entrepreneurship? Why, it was gold. And what was dear to the heart of the Party – surely, it was gold! And taxes. In the sense that one should have lots of one and none of the other.

The man-in-the-mirror stroked his chin. He agreed that there was a certain synergy. But what, he asked, was the entrepreneur going to *do?* What new business was going to come into being? After all, it wouldn't be convincing to reinvent plumbing, say? Unless one intended to invent a way in which all household wastes disappeared, for example, not down a pipe, but simply into the ether. But one might imagine that though rendered invisible, it might be difficult to eliminate objectionable odours. Or, one might imagine that though rendered invisible *and* odourless, the transformed wastes might cause the atmosphere to become thicker, with the possible outcome that breathing might become more difficult. Perhaps even to the point of suffocation. But assuming that the entrepreneur overcame this problem, was it not possible that the atmosphere could become highly flammable? It would be a most unfortunate outcome of offering a plumbing service that required not a single plumber and thereby avoiding all the mess and pipes and outrageous bills and so forth, if a customer was to strike a match for any reason, and incinerate the entire planet.

Dimple stared at the man-in-the-mirror with an expression of exasperation. 'The reason that I am an entrepreneur and you are not, is that your ideas are ludicrous. Anyone can have a ludicrous idea. The world is over-run with ludicrous ideas. Pick up the newspaper – any day of the week

19

and by the time you've reached page two, you'll have encountered forty-five ludicrous ideas. I can tell you! According to most people, the moon should fall on Africa! That's the fundamental difference between an entrepreneur and the average punter. An entrepreneur, like a politician – and as it happens, I am both, is equipped with sharp teeth. Canines. The average punter, who is also a voter, must make do with a gobful of molars for the purpose of chewing grass. This defines an ungulate. Bovine and an idiot. But necessary. You do not look to an ungulate for entrepreneurial ideas. You look to the ungulate to do mundane work and be eaten. From him, you expect and receive ludicrous ideas, such as you have just offered. I am entertaining a plethora of possibilities. But at this point in time, I am not disposed to share them. I bid you goodnight.'

And with a flick of the switch, he triumphantly abandoned the man-in-the-mirror to many hours of darkness.

FOUR

"The Entrepreneur," Dimple read, "is unconcerned with the humdrum of existence. Instead, the entrepreneur is constantly thinking at a higher plane than the average person. This is frequently manifest in a transcendent state, sometimes augmented with psychedelic substances. This author has instead developed a new, simple and proven technique that requires nothing more than the entrepreneur's native intellect and an appetite for great wealth. The details of this simple technique, which is guaranteed to result in no less than four innovations per session, will be made available to the budding entrepreneur for the give-away price of just Ninety-Nine dollars."

Entrepreneur Potts reflected that this seemed not an unreasonable price, for something new and improved, and read on: "The 'Entrepreneurial Accelerator' will transform the spark of an idea that might otherwise be lost in the phantasms of the mercurial mind, into a concrete concept capable of being commercialised at minimum cost but inevitably leading to extraordinary super-profits."

Dimple paused to gaze at the picture on his living room wall. Entitled "Woman riding a Crustacean," not for the first time he wondered what he had been thinking when he had acquired the piece. Avant garde, he supposed, but really…observing the naked woman astride the large lobster never failed but to engender sensations of an ambiguous kind. Nonetheless, wasn't this exactly what the author of 'Become an Entrepreneur Today,' was referring to? Abstruse thoughts on a higher plane. He read on: "The budding entrepreneur will likely be aware that many economists and bankers have tried to discredit the 'Entrepreneurial Accelerator' on the spurious basis that the number of millionaires it is creating, virtually overnight, is upending economics as we know it. And all for a mere Ninety-Nine dollars, but discounted to Eighty-Nine dollars if you act now! Make your remittance to the bank account below and the 'Entrepreneurial Accelerator' will be with you instantly! Do not delay. The great wealth you desire is finally within your grasp. Act now! A multitude of viable business concepts is waiting only for the key – 'The Entrepreneurial Accelerator.' For the next thirty seconds The Entrepreneurial Accelerator is yours for the absurdly low price of Seventy-Nine dollars. Do it!"

Dimple clicked on the link and secured this astonishing bargain with seconds to spare. Shortly, the link was delivered and he opened it with considerable anticipation.

"Welcome to the Entrepreneurial Accelerator and congratulations! You are now within minutes of learning the secret to creating great wealth from ideas that have passed others by."

The secret, Dimple learned, was to enter into a trance, which could be induced by repeating the phrase, aloud and for no less than fifteen minutes, 'I am a Master of the Universe. Unimaginable wealth resides within me.'

However, he read, whilst this proven method had resulted in various global businesses, it was possible that some individuals may employ, unconsciously, a 'meta blocker,' or that is to say, a collection of negative thoughts that could derail the transcendent experience. If this proved to be the case, then the budding entrepreneur could "absolutely overcome the meta blocker by purchasing the proprietary 'Anti-Meta Blocker,' available on this website and at the heavily discounted price of $999."

*

Perhaps I'm already an inventor, mused Dimple Potts as he emptied the dishwasher. Perhaps I don't need to enter into a transcendent state, after all. Unfortunately, recent experience seemed to indicate that he was indeed one of those rare individuals thwarted by meta blockers and thus causing interference with entrepreneurial inspiration. He had been chanting "I am a Master of the Universe. Unimaginable wealth resides within me," for some thirty-three minutes without a glimmer of an idea, when he was interrupted by his wife. She enquired mildly, if he was a master of the universe, how was it the Party had not seen fit to clean up his election billboard on the corner of such-and-such road, on which had been daubed the word, 'Tosser.'

It was annoying to be interrupted whilst endeavouring to enter a transcendent state, but the large meta blocker – a fatberg, really, was already confounding his creative trance. In any event he said, in some quarters, the term 'tosser' could actually be a term of endearment. Or comradeship. Dimple expanded that had he been a woman – or, say, a youngish woman standing in Peapod, he would not have been called a tosser. Unmentionable terms were typical – accompanied by death threats. To be termed a tosser was tantamount to friendly banter and might easily be considered a compliment.

The Entrepreneur's Guide suggested that a key difference between the average person – who might take to defacing election billboards, and an entrepreneur, was that the latter was constantly examining his or her environment and seeing what others did not. The entrepreneur by dint of curiosity lubricated with a goodly amount of greed, saw how even mundane things that may have been unchanged for a thousand years, could be *improved.* Consequently, Dimple advised his wife, he was even more alert than normal. Indeed, if she went into the pantry, she would see his first invention.

With not a little apprehension, Dimple's wife repaired to the pantry and glanced about. Everything seemed to be in its place. That was a relief. At the precise moment that she was going to request a clue, there it was. The breadboard. But now with something attached to it. She removed if from the shelf and saw that the board now had a crudely formed metal hoop that may previously have been part of an umbrella, secured by a hinge on one side. She raised and lowered the hoop. Clearly, the hoop was intended to seize a loaf of bread whilst a slice was cut. The Inventor explained that the hoop ensured one hundred per cent hygiene. The loaf could not be contaminated because a human hand was not required to hold it whilst a slice was cut. For a thousand years and likely more, people had held a loaf on the common breadboard with their soiled hands and thus, no one could enjoy a slice of bread no matter how fresh, that was safe from cholera or any of a range of other deadly diseases. This, exclaimed the Inventor, was how the entrepreneur thought. Alert to opportunity, his thoughts had bent with laser-like precision onto the idea of *hygiene and cleanliness*.

The Inventor's wife asked whether contaminated bread was a noted source of sickness and was met with a dismissive sound. The 'Breado' was just the beginning. Idea, prototype and proof of concept. These were the terms of entrepreneurship. Not that every idea would be commercialised, mind. Some ideas – like the Breado might remain solely in this pantry. Exclusively, he added with a meaningful nod. But the entrepreneurial process had been proved and the entrepreneur was already onto the next thing. Which was? The Inventor wasn't sure what the next thing might be but this was perfectly normal. Even the most inventive mind needed a rest. And supper.

*

The man-in-the-mirror said that it appeared that Candidate Potts was not taking the Election particularly seriously. It was now barely a week away and apart from receiving the Party's endorsement, what, if it wasn't a delicate question, had been done in terms of policy formulation?

Candidate Potts said, 'If you were a politician, which you are not, you would understand that policy formulation is one of the least important concerns. In any event, I've already decided on my platform. What you clearly do not understand is that the most important goal for the politician is being *aligned*. The average punter does not wish to be led. The average punter wishes most of all to be left alone. It stands to reason that the average punter wants a politician who reflects the average punter's own prejudices. The average punter is most especially unimpressed with grand policy. Grand policy threatens change and for the First Union of Conservative Thinkers, change is anathema.'

The man-in-the-mirror pursed his lips as though to say, 'I'm not sure I'm convinced about that.'

Candidate Potts continued forthrightly, 'No. And that's because you are not a Politician. Which I am. Twenty-three years of experience as Deputy Mayor of Brewster's Neck teaches you a few things.'

The man-in-the-mirror remarked mildly that despite all those years, the newcomer and baker, Sarah Bumbulis seemed to have been rather better aligned, to the extent she took the mayoralty in a landslide.

Candidate Potts said impatiently, 'You really can be a negative force. I would challenge anyone to maintain alignment once the town discovered it had eaten a well-known dog! Anyway, I'm not interested. It's ancient history. I'm the candidate for Peapod and that's an entirely different kettle of fish. This electorate has just two values – money, and something else...but here's the thing, which if you had any

25

understanding of politics, you might have grasped. This electorate and this Party are motivated by greed, because greed is what propels progress. If we had no greed, we'd still be wondering what that round thing is.'

'A wheel?'

'No. A gold coin. Gold is at the heart of greed and as you know, the eagle, Aquila, was gold and I am the standard bearer. That's perfect alignment. Greed, gold, speed and power. That's my policy platform. Cut-through. That's good policy. And what you do not seem to understand is that my new direction of entrepreneur is more than perfectly aligned with Peapod. That is why I am focusing on invention. Shortly, I have no doubt, through superior insight and the fact that I have canines, I will create a breakthrough that will lead to a great deal of gold. As a matter of fact, I made a start earlier. My wife now has the world's first Breado. I don't intend to commercialise it, at this point. I'm already thinking about other things. I have a restless mind. But understand this, Dimple Potts, Entrepreneur will be worshipped in this electorate and quite possibly beyond.'

Candidate and Entrepreneur Potts cleaned his teeth, which were not the blunt grass grinders of the ungulate, and refused to engage in further conversation. In fact, giving way to slight pique he flicked his brush at the mirror and scored the man-in-the-mirror's right eye with a blob of toothpaste.

＊

Candidate Potts's wife said at breakfast that she wondered how effective the Breado would be, since unless she wore gloves, it was difficult to avoid handling the loaf either before or after cutting a slice.

Dimple looked up from his newspaper and said, 'It says here that the accountant may have succumbed to a kind of dormancy. I can't say I'm surprised. Quite the opposite temperament of an entrepreneur, which as you may know is very much alive to the moment. The entrepreneur's constantly active mind, means nothing escapes him.'

His wife passed him a cup of coffee and mentioned that she wasn't certain that the Breado would help with bread hygiene, unless it was meant to be used with gloves only, in which case the hoop for holding the loaf might be redundant?

Dimple said, 'You know? I recall one time that the accountant suggested that *he* was an entrepreneur. Astonishing really. One of the things I've noticed about entrepreneurship, is that many aspire but few have the native aptitude. Take me. Until now, I've focused on politics. And politician that I am, constantly creating new things – improving things, is what I do. And when I say *politician*, I mean someone with my kind of qualities and not those who are simply pretenders. Vanity. That's what drives most of them. Vanity and ego. Not a creative bone in their body. And what have you seen already? Most people would look at a breadboard and say, that's a breadboard. But what did I say? I said, no, that's not a breadboard – that's a device for the hygienic slicing of a loaf of bread. Presto! The Breado. But I've moved on from that and that's because of the restlessness of my mind. Never goes to sleep, my dear.'

His wife said, 'Would you mind awfully, if we took the hoop off the breadboard? I find it really makes slicing bread a bit of a task. And have you seen the umbrella?'

Dimple said, 'Many people like to think they are entrepreneurial, but they're all talk. When you ask what they've invented or improved, they say, oh, it's a work in progress. Died of apathy? I'm not the slightest bit surprised.' The Entrepreneur sipped his coffee and then added, 'And I can tell you – the worst case of geographic tongue I've ever seen. For once I agreed with that woman who fancies herself as an art expert. The accountant didn't improve the aesthetics of the place – dead or alive.'

Dimple put down the newspaper and folding it thoughtfully. Thinking about his next-door-neighbour, he said, 'You know Mildred Titsman's dog? Well, I had a thought, in the small hours. I believe I may have come up with a rather singular idea. I shall be in my office. I have thinking to do.'

*

The fact was, Dimple Potts had never been a 'hands-on' person. He was not in the DIY mould. But it didn't matter. He would make use of that-boy-two-doors-down-on-the-left. That-boy-two-doors-down-on-the-left was very adept with his father's tools. Dimple had observed various go-karts – one of them motorised; a Trebuchet that could launch a missile across the street, and had; and the father of that-boy-two-doors-down-on-the-left, had proudly mentioned that his son had built his own workshop.

It said as much in The Entrepreneur's Guide – that the entrepreneur didn't need to actually build anything. That was for those who could do helpful things with tools and was a decidedly lower order of skill, compared to the creativity of the entrepreneur, whose curiosity and natural greed, drove him or her to conceive of *better* ways. And that was what presently exercised Entrepreneur Potts. Consequently, he remained in his office for two hours and a bit, doing numerous sketches and diagrams, full of arrows and annotations. Some aspects of his final design were a tad vague, but the thing was, when you involved someone with mechanical aptitude, a way would be found.

The Entrepreneur advised his wife that he would be out, down the street for an hour but he would be home in time for dinner. 'Hygiene and cleanliness!' He exclaimed. 'That's my current theme. I am alert to the possibilities,' and waving his diagram in the air, he cried, 'Nietzsche!' and headed out the door.

That-boy-two-doors-down-on-the-left was surprised. He recalled how Mr Potts had roundly berated him for the noise of his go-kart and had threatened him with a decent term of imprisonment if another piece of concrete, launched from the "infernal Trebuchet," came anywhere near his property again. That-boy-two-doors-down-on-the-left also recalled how Mr Potts had seemed to find it greatly amusing that time when the Trebuchet had inadvertently scored a direct hit on a passing Volvo. And yet, here he was, with a crude plan of some kind and asking if it was possible to build a prototype. That boy declared that it was, and he appreciated the offer of ten dollars for his time. They shook hands and Dimple returned home in high spirits.

FIVE

Meantime, the election drew near and the Chair called a special meeting, attended by everyone except for the one whose funeral had passed largely unnoticed, and who's cause of death was recorded by the coroner, presciently as we will find, as 'Irregular Dormancy. Or Torpidity.'

Privately, the Chair had confided in the Committee that it would be best if Candidate Potts said nothing prior to the election. What the Party didn't need, was any reference to the mud-hut hamlet of something-or-other Neck, where Potts purported to have been mayor, but which Google had still been unable to locate. Certainly, the Party did not want to be linked to Candidate's Potts's previous campaign movement, the FOKKERS or to a sausage company of any sort. But one thing the Party could be most grateful for at least, was that Candidate Potts had declined to don leotards.

Despite all this, the Committee had struggled to formulate a clear policy direction. They all agreed, naturally, that they were conservative. But not too conservative. Except when it came to taxes or wage increases when they were extremely conservative. Or new public holidays, which had been suggested by the Other Lot and which was a terrible handbrake on business and self-made folk generally.

It was at this moment that Candidate Potts arrived and was welcomed, with great warmth on the part of the Chair, to a meeting in which policy and strategy were the subject.

'Excellent!' cried Candidate Potts. 'Bread-and-butter to me. Policy. In fact, I've been giving some thought to a manifesto. And as it happens, most timely since I've been invited to be interviewed on tomorrow's news. TV. Jolly good exposure in the run-up.'

The Chair privately thought this the worst news he had heard for many months. He said, 'Wonderful! Splendid timing indeed. Well, we're all here in support, one hundred and ten percent.' He enquired after the *manifesto.*

Candidate Potts indicated that he had yet to write it up, because he had been deeply involved in the development of an innovation that he was confident would have wide commercial application. He advised that he had been thinking about the subject and more importantly, the practice of hygiene and cleanliness of late, and because of his entrepreneurial nature, he had already invented two remarkable technologies.

The Chair said, 'Fascinating! Exactly what this electorate admires most. But it might be best not to labour that – in the interview? Stick to the policy platform?'

Candidate Potts agreed that if he mentioned it at all, about him being an entrepreneur, it would be in passing and couldn't be more because the essence of entrepreneurship, was secrecy. Until such time as one hit the market. Privately, Candidate Potts lamented that he was encumbered with such a truly pedestrian bunch of nincompoops, who had been unable to develop a policy worthy of the name after all these years. Small wonder they stood in awe of their new candidate…Candidate Potts offered to share a little of this thinking, re the manifesto, if the Committee wished.

The ex-boxer thought privately, 'I'd take him out with one punch to his glass jaw,' and the woman who was an expert-in-the-arts thought, 'I believe that is a grease-spot on his tie,' and she shuddered. Nonetheless, the Chair welcomed the opportunity to be inspired by the Candidate's ideas.

'You may recall,' began Candidate Potts, 'that I made mention of greed. As you will be well aware, in some quarters greed is seen to be a sin of some sort.' He gazed thoughtfully at the ceiling. 'But we must challenge this misguided contention. For I will argue that without greed, we would all still be carrying clubs and have brains the size of a walnut. I have come to the view that greed is the driving, evolutionary impulse that distinguishes us from the dumb beasts. Just look.' And the committee looked. The Chair looked at the Candidate and wondered whether they might not yet hear words that would prove beyond a doubt, that Candidate Potts was a lunatic. The woman who was expert-in-the-arts looked at the Candidate's tie and concluded that even if it did not carry the grease from some awful repast, the tie was so vapid as to make her feel faintly ill. The ex-boxer looked at the wall and flinched at the sudden vision of a large glove coming at blinding speed and remorseless heft to flatten his nose, again. The property developer looked at his Rolex and wondered why they had to listen to a buffoon who would win the Peapod vote if he never uttered another word in his life.

Unconscious of these less than charitable thoughts, Candidate Potts continued to develop his theme. 'In the absence of greed, you will see a large number of animals that are stupid to say the least. Take the dog. Man's best friend, some say. I say, a creature whose aspirations never ascend above the base impulse of wanting to sniff the other fellow's parts. Imagine how different this animal could have been, had it been motivated as we were, by the insatiable thirst of acquisition? Even so, I am the first to admit that greed in the absence of circumspection, you might say, is not a good thing. For this reason, I have been playing around with the idea – a slogan really. 'Greed-with-Care – it's how we get ahead.'

The Chair observed, cautiously, 'Profound.'

The Property Developer said with some irritation, 'Why are we talking about dogs? Tax is what we don't like.'

The Chair said, 'Let us hear our Candidate out. I believe he may be conceiving a more…expansive vision.'

Candidate Potts continued, 'Yes. Greed-with-Care, is entirely consistent with our general philosophy of keeping the government's hands off what is ours. But note that I am not promoting the crude and careless greed, such as we commonly see in everyday life – wherein, for example, a dog might end up in a venison sausage. No, the concept I am conceiving, might be thought of as a kind of benign greed. Even a compassionate greed...in fact, the slogan might also be expressed as 'Compassionate Greed...'

The Chair said, 'I detect wisdom in these words, Candidate Potts.'

'I have yet to fully develop these ideas, but I hope this Committee can see that it quite neatly dovetails with entrepreneurship, which as it happens is second nature to me. We must deliver sound bites that capture the idea that is dearest to the average punter's heart – self-interest.'

The Chair said, 'Compassionate Greed...wonderful.' Perhaps, the Chair mused silently, Candidate Potts had hit the nail on the head. Perhaps, by sheer accident, they had found the right man...The Chair said, 'Candidate Potts, I congratulate you! As I am sure my fellow Committee members also congratulate you. You have presented a profound ideology that will inspire glee in the electorate. Greed, gold and glee! How about that?'

But it was clear that Candidate Potts was not enthused about having 'glee' introduced into his manifesto. Privately he thought, 'Amateurs.' He said, 'At this point in time, we'll avoid diluting the message. We can be gleeful afterward, perhaps.'

The Chair apologised for offering up trivial ideas. But it couldn't be helped, given the enthusiasms aroused by Candidate Potts's inspiring ideas! As Candidate Potts left the room, the Chair cried, 'Hail Aquila!' and laughed mightily at his wit.

SIX

Dimple said to that-boy-two-doors-down-on-the-left, who had been tasked with building a prototype 'Doggo Cleano,' 'Cleanliness, young man. That's the thing. That's what inspired me. For thousands of years, what have we done? When the dog needs a bath, we fetch a bucket or a hose. And what's the result? The owner ends up as wet as the pooch and fed up to the back teeth. I believe that this device will do for dog owners what the automatic washing machine did for the housewife, or husband as the case may be.'

Dimple was impressed with the craftsmanship apparent in the prototype Doggo Cleano and said so. He also said that indeed he did have a vacuum cleaner. In which case, said that-boy-two-doors-down-on-the-left, the prototype was ready for a trial. At which the entrepreneur and his mechanic repaired to the Potts front garden and the prototype was made ready. The entrepreneur indicated that now they must find the subject, which was the dog going under the name, 'Doc Cod' and owned by Mildred Titsman. The dog, he explained, was named for Mildred's deceased husband, who was Doctor Codalink Titsman, but Mildred shortened it for ease of use, and as it happened created a palindrome. As in, the Entrepreneur explained, 'Too bad I hid a boot,' or, come to that, 'level,' or 'civic.' Same word, or words even when read back-to-front. But enough of that, said Entrepreneur Potts, indicating that it was the further task of that-boy-two-doors-down-on-the-left to fetch up the palindrome, who he would find snoozing on the front porch next door.

Shortly, Doc Cod, who was a very gentle and aging hound, was inserted into the Doggo Cleano. When the lid was closed, only his head was visible, protruding dolefully through the aperture at that end. The garden hose was connected to the inlet valve, and employing an extension cord, the small motor that would drive the rotating cleaning brushes was ready to start. Into a small funnel on top of the Doggo Cleano, the Entrepreneur poured a quantity of dish wash. He then fetched his vacuum cleaner and this was plugged into the evacuation port near Doc Cod's rear.

How splendid it was! Entrepreneurial inspiration transformed into the first working prototype, and now, the first trial of a device that would surely earn the Entrepreneur the world's thanks and decent riches. The Entrepreneur pointed out how, with Doggo Cleano (and what did that-boy-two-doors-down-on-the-left think of the name? He liked it? Jolly good!) the dog owner could flick the switch and then go make a cup of tea whilst the device went through its cycle. Which is what Dimple intended to do. The garden hose was duly turned on and in moments, water filled the Doggo Cleano and poured as intended, out the overflow. At the sudden ingress of cold water, Doc Cod's eyes widened and he emitted a most peculiar sound that indicated at the least, bemusement. Then the motor was turned on and the array of paddles, the design of which had been inspired by a carwash, commenced to give Doc Cod a strenuous scrubbing, at which the peculiar sound that dog had been making went up several octaves.

'Take no notice,' cried the Entrepreneur, 'He'll get used to it.' But his assurances were belied by the strident and agitated trumpeting now emanating from the front end of the Doggo Cleano – though due to the copious amount of foam squirting from several places,
the front end of Doc Cod was no longer discernible. Across the veldt, Doc Cod's distress carried to the ears of Mildred Titsman. It was no use. Nothing that Dimple could say would placate his neighbour, and nor could he make head-nor-tail of what it was she was trying to say. Nevertheless, there was the

35

possibility that through her emotional exertions she might pass out, and that, the Entrepreneur concluded, would be inconvenient. That-boy-two-doors-down-on-the-left turned off the motor and Mildred fell to her knees, sweeping aside the foam to reveal, as Dimple remarked, a perfectly intact dog that was now also a clean dog. But he did not listen to the cautions of that-boy-two-doors-down-on-the-left before turning on the vacuum cleaner to actuate the drying part of the cycle. Consequently, the vacuum cleaner ran for about five seconds before emitting a plume of blue smoke and a vile electrical smell, because, as that-boy-two-doors-down-on-the-left explained, there was water in the Doggo Cleano and the vacuum cleaner needed to be set to blow, rather than suck.

Meanwhile, Mildred Titsman had extracted Doc Cod and was carrying the senseless animal off the property whilst crying out, far too loudly, 'I'll sue, you swine!'

That-boy-two-doors-down-on-the-left said he needed to do his homework, and the Entrepreneur repaired to his office to reflect on the learnings from the first trial.

*

With a frown the Head of News read the schedule. He asked, 'Who the f*** is Dimple Potts?'

The Senior Reporter said that she thought it advisable to hear from the First Union of Conservative Thinkers at least once before the election, since it was entirely possible the Party could be a king maker. And Dimple Potts was the Party candidate in Peapod. The Head of News asked whether Potts had said anything of note and the Senior Reporter replied that to the best of her knowledge, he'd not uttered a word. The Head of News asked what they had on file and the Senior Reporter said that that was the thing – Potts had simply appeared from nowhere. Which was intriguing in itself.

36

However, there was a short note attached that indicated Potts had been the mayor of a place she had been unable to locate, and that somehow, he may have been connected to that incident when a very large robot took down Auckland's power supply.

The Head of News pursed his lips. He said five minutes was too long. Two-and-a-half would suffice. The Senior Reporter stood her ground and said she had a couple of angles in mind and needed the extra minutes. The Head of News relented but with the firm admonition that she had better get something of real interest, and he departed to his office to pore over ratings and lament that the opposition channel had picked up that shock jock beloved of bigots – which was nearly everyone – but hated by the rest.

Meanwhile, one of the Senior Reporter's team said he might have a new angle. He passed the Senior Reporter a note, which she read and then said, 'Well, that's something! Well done you!'

*

Candidate Potts was on the phone to the Chair. The Chair had felt moved to call because he was suddenly filled with misgivings.

The Chair said, 'Just called to wish you luck. All prepared for the interview?'

Candidate Potts said that he was. There was a pause before the Chair ventured, 'If they ask you about your previous political experience…' He felt it better to leave this question open lest it become pointed. 'Though I daresay you'd pretty quickly tell them you're along to talk policy, not history. And in terms of policy, I daresay you'll just refer them to the main message. We're a bit more conservative than the Other Lot. Sensibly, against tax and profligate government

37

spending, and so forth. I'd imagine that would just about cover it.'

Candidate Potts said that was much as he saw it though he was ready for anything they might throw at him.

The Chair said, 'But if they mention that robot thing…best to deny all knowledge, really.'

Candidate Potts said, 'Oh, I know all about the robot. Know the fellow who built it. Exchanged the odd head-butt with Doug Hemopo. I sacked him, actually. Had to. He was obstructive. Stood in the road of progress.'

The Chair's heart sank. 'Quite. But if they come at you about your links to that chap who minced pets into sausages? You'd want to steer clear of that. Flat denial would be best.'

Candidate Potts said, 'Corker Pritchard! Now, there's an example of greed but *without care*. You'll recall that's my main policy idea. If they raise that it will be the perfect opening.'

The Chair squeezed his forehead with his eyes clenched tightly closed. 'You won't mention the Doggo – what was it?'

'The Doggo Cleano? I should think not. Still in the prototype stage. I don't want to give the competition a heads-up.'

The Doggo Cleano, the Chair reflected, as he had when the entrepreneur had first described it, was surely one of the more inane ideas he had heard in a lifetime of practice. It was certainly up there with dancing in tights. 'Quite right,' he replied with relief, 'Keep it under wraps. But me? No need to mention me, at all. I mean, best to keep the spotlight on *you*. Don't want to dilute the message.'

Candidate Potts said he couldn't think why he would need to mention the Chair, but he was always prepared to put in a plug.

The Chair rang off.

Candidate Potts liked the Senior Reporter. She asked if he was going to emulate Ronald Reagan? Reagan, she said, had said to a reporter, 'Before I refuse to take your questions, I have an opening statement to make.' Candidate Potts observed that this was a most amusing anecdote. 'Is that what he said?' and they shared a chortle at Reagan's temerity.

The red light came on and the Senior Reporter made a brief introduction. Turning to Candidate Potts, she said, 'Mr Potts – Dimple…I have here,' and she waved a piece of paper, 'Advice that you are being prosecuted for cruelty to animals. In fact, your neighbour's dog. Can you comment on that?' She smiled an earnest and sympathetic smile, and in his lounge, the Chair slumped and cried, 'Ambushed!'

Candidate Potts stared at the piece of paper as though it were instead, a condom, perhaps. Seconds ticked by. Candidate Potts felt unnaturally hot and silently cursed his tie. Silently he also cursed Doc Cod and most especially, his litigious neighbour.

Feigning concern the Senior Reporter said, 'Mr Potts…would you like some water?'

Seconds ticked by. The Senior Reporter said, 'Are you able to tell us anything about this accusation, Mr Potts?'

In her ear, the Head of News said, 'That's more like it!'

In his lounge, and mesmerised by the horror unfolding, the Chair stared at his screen with open mouth whilst shaking his head. He muttered, 'Down at the first jump. Down at the water, you horse's ass.'

Candidate Potts coughed and then said, 'Ahem…before I refuse to answer your questions, I have an opening statement to make.'

The Chair sat bolt upright. 'What's this?' he cried. 'The Phoenix?'

The Senior Reporter said, 'That's a good line, Mr Potts, but unoriginal. Can we address my question?

Candidate Potts said, 'I'm here to talk about the policies of the First Union of Conservative Thinkers. And my party won't be side-lined by false accusation – on unrelated matters. I'm here to talk about how my Party can make this country great again. By reducing taxes. By applauding greed, but not greed that comes at the cost of others. I'm here to talk about the *Greed-with-Care*. What we in the First Union of Conservative Thinkers also refer to, as Compassionate Greed.'

The Senior Reporter tried to interrupt but the interviewee was having none of it. He continued, 'In some quarters, greed has a bad name and deservedly so. But my Party, the First Union of Conservative Thinkers understands that without *greed-with-care*, we will make no progress. Not to put too fine a point on it, we will collapse to the level of dumb beasts.'

In his lounge, the Chair had risen and though speechless, his spirits, like the legendary bird, were rising rapidly.

Via her earphone, the Senior Reporter was deafened by the Head of News.

The Senior Reporter said, 'Mt Potts! I'm sorry – Mr Potts – are you going to answer my question – *are you guilty of cruelty to animals?'*

'Mt Potts!' Shouted the Head of News. 'You half-wit!'

Candidate Potts continued serenely, 'My contention and that of my Party, is that greed per se, is much and unfairly maligned. It is greed, with care that motivates the entrepreneurs among us. The people who, through their unceasing drive to make things better, generate the wealth that pays your salary. Indeed, I would characterise the idea of greed-with-care, as *Moral Money.'*

In his lounge the Chair cried, 'Bullseye!'

In the Senior Reporter's ear, the Head of News bellowed, 'What a f***-up!'

And at that precise moment, the cameraman slipped from his stool and crashed to the floor. The interview was at an end. Shortly after Candidate Potts had taken his leave, it was ascertained that the cameraman was not unwell. He was dead.

*

The-man-in-the-mirror said, 'Moral Money? That was clever. Facile. She was going to skewer you but you outflanked her. With your Greed-with-Care…when did you come up with Moral Money?'

Candidate Potts said, 'If you must know – at that exact moment. But this is about experience. The cut-and-thrust of politics and as you know well, I've been in the thick of it for a very long time. Put it down to experience. Knowing the moment. I must say…It did come off rather well. Did you see her face?'

The man-in-the-mirror conceded that the interview had gone passably well, which observation Candidate Potts suggested stiffly, was 'magnanimous.' Then he added that he had more important things to think about. He reminded the man-in-the-mirror that as a standard bearer for the First Union of Conservative Thinkers, he was equally, a standard bearer for Entrepreneurship. 'Rust never sleeps,' he said, referring to the unceasing vigilance of the entrepreneurial mind. Then he repaired to his office and hung a note on the door handle, purloined from the Bayview Hotel reading, 'Do not Disturb.' To which he had added, 'Inventor at Work.'

SEVEN

The Chair spoke to the woman-expert-in-the-arts. The woman-expert-in-the-arts said she wouldn't go so far as to say brilliant, but she certainly agreed that Compassionate Greed, which was an idea, coincidentally, she had had some years before, was exceptionally good. But 'Moral Money?' The woman-expert-in-the-arts paused before saying she thought that a truly wonderful idea that entirely summed up the Party's raison d'etre. The Chair was experiencing a long overdue sense of euphoria. Since he had first entertained the most unpleasant notion that the candidate he had selected might actually *be* an imbecile, to discover now, in the red-hot crucible of a live television interview the imbecile, or rather the standard bearer, could go the distance, was an enormous relief and vindication.

The property developer with whom the Chair spoke next was more enthusiastic. Candidate Potts had said exactly what most people thought but were constrained by wokeness from expressing. 'Changed my mind,' he said. Greed, he reminded the Chair, 'is good.' Gordon Gekko, he cried, made one of the most important speeches of the twentieth century, 'But look. Our own candidate has trumped Gekko. Greed-with-Care? Moral Money? It's ballistic!' And he congratulated the Chair on his perspicacity. The Property Developer didn't mind admitting when he was wrong. The Property Developer didn't mind owning that he too, had thought their candidate a waste of oxygen. But the Property Developer was big enough to say he'd made a mistake and now let's move on. He for one, was more than ready to get onboard!

The Chair called Candidate Potts but Candidate Potts was not taking any calls. His voicemail said, 'This is not a suitable time. I am inventing. Please don't leave a message.'

The Chair shook his head. He said, 'Brilliant, but eccentric.'

*

Entrepreneur Potts sipped at his seventh short black. He was feeling uneasy and wasn't sure if it was due to the coffee or a growing sense of annoyance that he had been quite unable to produce that single idea that would mean the road to riches. To be frank, he had lost interest in Doggo Cleano. Titsman and Doc Cod were suing him. In any event, dogs, he concluded, were hardly worth his effort. They were dirty by habit and nature. And without a doubt Titsman lived up to the old truism, that the owner resembled her hound. The Entrepreneur needed to move on – to come up with something big. Neither Breado nor Doggo Cleano were big. In fact, the Entrepreneur was feeling mildly embarrassed that he had ever conceived of them.

But the Big Idea was nowhere in sight. After three and bit hours he had crossed off his brainstorm list, 'Possum milk,' 'Rabbit patties,' 'Rabbit flour (from the bones),' 'Stuffed Possum Pudding,' 'Kangaroo Walking Service,' and 'Possum Safari,' and revisiting his theme of hygiene and cleanliness, 'Self-cleaning underwear,' 'Self-cleaning self,' 'Automatic horse cleaner,' and 'Automatic barber.' Of these, only the last idea caused him to pause. He considered his barber. His barber was a garrulous nincompoop who drank excessively. Not only was he tiresome company, but as it was with every barber of Dimple Pott's experience, he ignored the customer's description of what he wanted and did the exact opposite. Customer Potts would say, 'Just a light trim,' and the barber

43

would give him a Number One. If he said, 'A little more off the sides,' the end result made his ears look like the deck of an aircraft carrier. And that time he'd wondered aloud that premature greyness was unhelpful, his barber had dyed his entire head as black as the inside of a pitch-pot. A barber, Dimple reflected, was a menace. A public nuisance who one was actually obliged to pay. How much better if one could take one's seat and simply say, 'A light trim thanks,' and voila – a light trim one would receive and without tiresome observations about the barber's favourite rap music, reality television or most recent sexual experimentation.

'Dimple,' said Dimple, 'There's something in this.' And the previous sense of uneasiness was replaced with a new surge of entrepreneurial excitement.

*

'Have you seen the poll?' cried the Chair. Candidate Potts admitted that he had not, since he had been busy with other business. The Chair said that everyone was talking about it. Everyone was saying how much they liked the way Mount Potts told the reporter he was going to refuse to answer any of her questions. Everyone loved that bit, said the Chair and indeed, the Chair loved that bit. Everyone had longed to hear someone stand up to those pigeon-heads of the Press and to say what they all wanted to say. 'Sod off!' And that's what Mount Potts had done. And had he been cruel to animals? No-one cared a jot. If he had, well, that was no more than God's punishment for an animal being so stupid. It was a red-herring, such as the Press were constantly bandying about. They loved red-herrings, but the serious voter did not. The serious voter was interested in hearing about what the candidate was going to do for the serious voter's pocket. The serious voter could care less that the candidate had dropped a baby on its head –

shit happens – what the serious voter wanted to hear was what the candidate was going to do about money – and more specifically, to ensure that the serious voter had more of it, which could mean by way of zero tax, preferably, or by creating wealth. Obscene riches were also fine.

The Chair rejoiced, 'A surge, Candidate Potts! The First Union of Conservative Thinkers has overtaken the Sprouts.'

'The Sprouts?'

'The Greens, Dimple. But that's only the half of it. Mount Potts is now rated as a preferred PM.' The Chair was elated. The Committee were elated. Was Candidate Potts elated? Of course, he was, the Chair exulted. And to think that some had wondered whether Candidate Potts was the man for the First Union of Conservative Thinkers? Not himself, mind you. The Chair had known from the first time they had met. The Chair had said to himself – 'A fine chap. Pragmatic. The opposite of a sprout, which as everyone knew was a truly dreadful vegetable that should have been banned long since.'

Candidate Potts said, 'My opinion exactly. I'm constantly telling my wife.'

But the Chair was not concerned about vegetables. The Chair had said to others, from the very beginning, they should have no concerns about Candidate Potts. Still waters and all that. A dark horse if ever you were going to see one. That is what the Chair had said, 'Amen!'

*

Candidate Pott's wife had not seen the interview. She had been in town purchasing a new vacuum cleaner, which she sincerely hoped would not be used for anything other than its designed purpose. She sincerely hoped that it would be possible to mend the rift with their neighbour, Mildred

Titsman. Was Dimple aware that Mildred had made a complaint to the Police? He had. Well, she had accused Dimple of deliberate cruelty to her dog, Doc Cod, and theft, on the basis that he had stolen Doc Cod off her own front porch. What was he going to do about that?

Still mildly disappointed that she had not witnessed his television triumph, Candidate Potts said that he was now rated as a preferred PM. Was that not more significant than a mean-spirited complaint by a frankly sociopathic neighbour who took umbrage at a genuine attempt to make her life easier? In Candidate Potts's view, it was a great deal more significant and, if he *were* to be PM – and he was speaking hypothetically, but if he were the PM, he would see to it that a charitable gesture such as his, could not be subject to the petty complaints by the Titsmans of this world. There would be a new law.

As it happened, the Constable was sympathetic. When Mr Potts explained his entrepreneurial intentions and with nothing but goodwill towards Doc Cod, the Constable said, 'I can see, Mr Potts, that this is likely what we in the Force term a *vexatious* complaint. That is to say, a complaint made by a member of the public, be they man, or woman or otherwise, but a complaint that is made for reasons other than the remedying of any harm done. And indeed, it might be that an examination of the evidence showed no harm whatsoever, other than perhaps some emotional distress, which was a matter not for the Police but for a psychologist. That is to say, the complaint is designed primarily, Mr Potts, to vex the accused and in disregarding the trouble it caused the Police when they had many other important crimes to solve – the complaint served to vex the Police also. It certainly appeared to this Constable, that Mildred Titsman was making what he felt he would be obliged to report to his superiors, was a vexatious complaint. And what happened when a complaint was so classified? Well, the Police would notify the

46

complainant, who in this case was Mildred Titsman, that the Police could find no grounds for proceeding further. Indeed, the Police might chastise the complainant and point out that she was in danger of maligning the excellent character of a politician of considerable standing, who now rated as a preferred PM. In which respect, the Constable offered his congratulations and especially for the way in which Mr Potts had seen off that reporter. If the Constable might offer an opinion, it was long past time that the Press received a knock on the snout and it was a pleasure to see a politician with the strength of character prepared to do just that.

Candidate Potts was most appreciative of the Constable's eminently reasonable assessment of the situation, and he assured the Constable that not only was he done with Doc Cod and indeed all dogs, but when and if his Party held the balance of power – and who knew, perhaps more, that this politician would take a good hard look at the Police Pension Fund, which in this politician's view had been disgracefully underfunded.

The Constable was most appreciative of this gesture of support for the Force and promised that on the matter of a certain vexatious complaint, he would hear no more.

*

Candidate Potts munched a scone and sipped his cup of tea. He pointed out to his wife that things had turned out exactly as he expected. Nevertheless, his wife said that she would take Mildred some scones, as a peace offering.

Candidate Potts said that he had wasted enough time on his neighbour and that went for Doggo Cleano, which he now consigned to the metaphorical bin of promising but failed ideas. That caused the Entrepreneur no concerns whatsoever, since the lifeblood of entrepreneurial endeavour, was constant experimentation. And as it happened, he was well-advanced in his conceptualisation of a new idea – a revolutionary innovation he might say, that required his urgent attention.

EIGHT

It was an extraordinary triumph. The President of the Society of Entrepreneurs, Liars and Fools, or SELF took his seat and pressing the button on the arm of the chair, allowed the Automatic Barber to descend to fit neatly over his head. And comfortable? The President of SELF exclaimed that he could hardly feel the large silver helmet placed just so, by the Automatic Barber's robotic arm. By way of explanation, the President of SELF said they included Liars and Fools in the Society because there simply weren't a sufficient number of true Entrepreneurs to make up the numbers. The President of SELF said 'Potts. Genuine entrepreneurs are hen's teeth. Hen's teeth! But wannabes – liars and fools we call them, are-a-dime-a-dozen. A dime-a-dozen, Potts! Should be on salary. Should be in the warehouse, or the back office, Potts. That's where they belong. Not an entrepreneurial bone in their bodies. *No bone,* Potts – that's my guess. They're like goddamn jelly fish. Boneless!' And the President of SELF roared with laughter, 'But we're happy to take their sub. Happy for them to be paying members, though most of them couldn't invent a tooth pick, Potts. Not if their lives depended on it.'

Entrepreneur Potts laughed with the President of SELF. After all, Entrepreneur Potts had invented and successfully commercialised the Automatic Barber and the franchise, 'Barbomatic,' with the tagline, 'Get the cut you want. No inane chat.' And here was the President of SELF himself – inventor and billionaire owner of the world's first consumer nerve-gas company, that had utterly transformed the urban environment all around the world. The President of

49

SELF had given teeth to Neighbourhood Watch, and made the police redundant. And he was impressed with Barbomatic. Indeed, he was beyond impressed and wanted to buy the company. This very day, he told Entrepreneur Potts – for a pile. Was Entrepreneur Potts interested? Then he touched the start button on The Automatic Barber's arm and said, 'A light trim. Leave a bit over the ears. Sideburns to the mid-ear and take a fraction of weight off the top.' Then he pressed the 'Go' button and within thirty seconds the cut was done, the silver helmet lifted off and without a loose hair to be seen, the President of SELF admired himself in the mirror and cried, 'Absolute genius. I'd come close to killing my barber, Potts. It was all I could do. But now he's gone - fired. I'll have the Automatic Barber installed immediately. Three. At home, the boat and the villa. Three everywhere!'

And whilst the Potts considered the ludicrously large sum offered by the CEO of 'Acme Home Security Inc,' the money rolled in. Moral Money, derived directly from Greed-with-Care and best of all, tax-free, due to the rampant success of the First Union of Conservative Thinkers, having become the major party and effectively the Government, over which, naturally, Entrepreneur Potts presided, as Prime Minister Potts – or, as he was affectionately known, Mount Potts. Though of course, there was little enough to distract Prime Minister Potts since in the absence of tax, which had remained Moral Money, there was no government expenditure of any kind.

Good days indeed! But then the Founder of Barbomatic received an ominous call. Something untoward had occurred. Something very untoward, it might be said – at a franchise in Glasgow. There appeared to be a bug in the software. Had it been hacked? Perhaps, but regardless, the bug appeared to be directly related to and confounded by the incomprehensible Glaswegian accent. Fortunately, there was a CCTV clip that showed exactly what happened.

Unfortunately, the clip had now received just over a billion views on Facebook, alone. The Founder of Barbomatic was alarmed. The Founder watched the CCTV clip, taken that previous afternoon – even as the Founder considered the offer from the CEO of SELF. But such was the volume of cash rolling in every day, from the millions of punters who revelled in the cut they wanted without the banal wittering's and gingivitis of a live hairdresser, the Founder of Barbomatic couldn't quite bring himself to accept. And now, the Founder watched a video showing a Glaswegian gasfitter, as it transpired, taking his seat in the Automatic Barber. He spoke something completely unintelligible and pressed the green button. The Automatic Barber did not respond. How could it, the Founder asked himself. How could any person, let alone a machine, understand that gibberish? The gasfitter persevered and quite quickly, became agitated and the Founder gathered, largely from the gasfitter's gestures, that the gasfitter was threatening the Automatic Barber with a good bottling.

At his last attempt to give instruction, which entailed much shouting, repeated jabs of the button, and at one point, several severe whacks to the helmet, the Automatic Barber shuddered. The gas fitter's eyes widened unnaturally and then he emitted a blood curdling, Scottish cry. 'Good God!' cried the Founder of Barbomatic. 'The Hound of the Baskervilles!' The Founder could not believe the amount of *blood* that poured down the shoulders of the tormented customer. The Glaswegian gasfitter had become a Glaswegian Singing Fountain! Mercifully, as his torso slumped, the shrieking stopped. The Automatic Barber raised the silver helmet from the customer and the Founder of Barbomatic observed that the customer no longer had a head.

The Founder of Barbomatic sat bolt upright and emitted a terrible cry that would have done justice to the noise of the deceased gasfitter. The Founder's pyjamas were soaked in sweat. The wife of Entrepreneur Potts also sat bolt upright.

51

Entrepreneur Potts said hoarsely, 'Bad dream.'

The wife of Entrepreneur Potts suggested that he should try his summer pyjamas.

Entrepreneur Potts said, 'I've decided against the Automatic Barber.' Then he fell back, trembling, and stared sightlessly into the darkness. 'I foresee pitfalls,' he said.

*

The Police Constable filed his report. His senior complimented him on his clarity and the concise nature of his prose. His senior said that if all police reports were as breviloquent, police productivity would escalate. He glanced down at the Constable's report. "Following an interview with the complainant – the shrew Mildred Titsman – and examination of the object of the complaint, the hound Doc Cod, and an interview with the subject of the complaint, the honourable Mr Dimple Potts (who is now reported to be a preferred PM), this officer discovered no evidence whatsoever of malice on the part of Mr Dimple Potts who appeared to this officer to be the owner of an admirably good nature, and nor was there any evidence of wilful mistreatment. It was this officer's view that a thorough cleaning by the Doggo Cleano may have at most, dislodged some loose hair about Doc Cod's buttocks. In the considered opinion of this officer, and given that Doc Cod's behaviour suggested only that Doc Cod was likely senile, the complaint should be regarded as vexatious and dismissed."

The Constable's senior said he was particularly pleased that the Constable had placed some emphasis on assessing the 'natures' of the parties involved. Too often, he said, police officers focused solely on the tangible evidence – blood and hair and so forth. But the good type of officer understood that the police were dealing with the trickiest of animals, and he wasn't referring to the likes of Doc Cod, though goodness knew, dogs could be tricky animals. No, he was referring of course to the human animal – and he used the term most advisably, since good police officers knew damned well from long experience in the field, that shrews, like for example the Titsman woman, wove webs of deceit and mayhem for reasons that challenged even the police eggheads, or psychologists as they were also known. Webs of deceit and mayhem, continued the Constable's senior, were the hallmark of the very tricky animal that was otherwise known as a human. But the good police officer, and God, knew only too well, a human was nothing more than an animal disposed to lie, cheat, invent and abuse simply in order to get to the front-of-the-line, and not to mention the animal's general proclivity to do-the-other-man-down, which behaviour had only recently been exemplified in all its beastliness, when the politicians had voted to reduce the Police Pension Fund. At which point, the Constable mentioned that the honourable Mr Potts said that if he were to become part of the Government, he would be taking a close and positive look at that very thing.

The Constable's senior said, 'There…a most edifying outcome to an exemplary investigation. And I must commend the use of the term, *shrew*. In itself, as you have apprehended, the shrew is an unimpressive animal. An oblong animal, with a rodent-like body; sporting greyish brown fur; a small head with a pointed snout; and small and untrustworthy black eyes.' The Constable's senior paused as he contemplated this unimpressive but distasteful animal. 'Do you know, Constable, that foul-smelling secretions from special scent glands are supposed to help to protect the shrew from predation? It is not uncommon, that another animal may kill a shrew only to refrain from eating it because of the strong odour. Which shows, among other things that the shrew is also a stupid animal, since special glands that work only after death are pointless to say the least.'

53

The Constable was unaware of these facts. The Constable's senior was surprised, since it used to be an important part of Police Training and in fact had been written by himself. But never mind. The Constable's senior enquired whether, in his dealings with the complainant Titsman, did the Constable detect a foul-smelling secretion? The Constable apologised that he had not detected a foul-smelling secretion or indeed an odour of any description. The Constable's senior seemed to be mildly disappointed at this, but then he brightened and asked whether the complainant possessed a pointed snout, and was greatly cheered when the Constable confirmed that the complainant Titsman, did indeed have a somewhat pointed snout. Not a sharp snout, perhaps, but definitely somewhat pointed.

The Constable's senior quickly made a sketch on his pad and asked if the Titsman snout was similar to the snout in his sketch. The Constable felt that perhaps, it was not quite so upturned. If the senior didn't mind? He took the pencil and altered the snout a little and declared that the Titsman snout was more like this.

The Constable's senior considered the sketch and with an 'Ah ha!' declared it to be very, very interesting. He said that what the Constable had encountered was somewhat like a shrew, but it might more accurately be likened to the snout of a pigmy vole. Was the Constable aware that two pygmy voles could produce up to 100 offspring in a single year? This meant, the senior observed, that an unchecked population of pygmy voles could grow quite out of hand, in a very short period, which was clearly problematic for an already over-stretched police force. The pygmy vole, the Constable's senior added, is a very randy animal. He asked if he had noticed anything about the complainant Titsman, that might suggest an inclination to randiness? No? Well, no matter. The case of a vexatious complaint was well established and would be dismissed. The Constable's senior might even write a formal note to the complainant to caution against the further wasting of police time. Or not.

*

The Chair was very excited. For years, the First Union of Conservative Thinkers had been regarded as something quaint on the fringe of real politics. For years, the Party had been dismissed by commentators as a clique of privileged twats with no ideology except money. But change was in the air…television wanted another interview. Media of all kinds wanted an interview, with Candidate Potts. The Chair positively glowed with satisfaction. Who had *discovered* Candidate Potts? Who had seen the potential? Who had been able to put aside natural misgivings about the candidate's aptitudes, not to mention the candidate's resemblance to an Easter Island monolith? The Chair carefully wiped the butter that had squelched from his toast to dribble down his chin. The Chair said, 'I saw the gold beneath the dross.' And he felt considerable satisfaction at this metaphor, as even further evidence that all these years of presiding over a committee of frankly pretentious and privileged beakers, were about to be rewarded. The Chair's wife did not bother to ask what gold her husband had seen, or indeed, what dross. Indeed, she did not wish to know anything about dross. That it existed was beyond question. It was everywhere. Bottom feeders they were and best not thought about. Indeed, best not encountered at all and a terrible shame that they existed, but there was the human dilemma. The Chair's wife shivered. Fortunately, there was plenty of gold – though there could be more. That was the thing about gold. It was always good to have just a bit more. The Chair's wife surmised that her husband had found yet another way to secure a little more gold. Well and good! The Chair's wife excused herself, since she was playing tennis

55

with the girls. Thank God for the girls! What a great pleasure it was for all of them, to be away from their husbands for a morning of pleasant goss. Whilst it was true that their husbands were very effective miners, or thieves, in most other respects they made the most tedious company. That was the only fly in the ointment. But compromise was the name of the game. The Chair's wife would much preferred to have run off with the gardener, but where would that have ended? Adventures and great sex undoubtedly, but virtually no gold of any description. The Chair's wife sighed as she went out the door. She wondered where the gardener had ended up and wished for a moment that he might drop by – for a brief visit.

The Chair waved his hand as his wife departed. For a moment he wondered how much her Botox cost. Whatever it cost, it wasn't worth it. Not that it mattered – in terms of the cost. Inconsequential really. Likely quite a bit less than what he spent on his secretary. At which he thought that he might take his secretary to the Party conference. Incognito, as it were. That would make that tedious affair much more fun. But wait, he reminded himself. That was before Candidate Potts! That was the First Union of Conservative Thinkers, *before* CP! Now, they were in the new age. They were in AP. The Chair beamed and wondered whether he might use the analogy in his conference speech.

The Chair reflected on his conversation with the television reporter. The reporter had said they had no interest in any accusations about cruelty to animals. They knew that the Police had treated the whole thing as a vexatious complaint and that was water under the bridge. And yes, the reporter was quite agreeable to apologising to Candidate Potts, if he would appear for a second interview. And no, the Senior Reporter would not be doing the interview. The studio agreed that she had not taken a proper line and had been, one might say, even disrespectful of Candidate Potts, and the studio was most disappointed. So, if Candidate Potts agreed to another interview, the Chair could take it as read that the interview would be undertaken by this reporter, and would be properly respectful. The sole focus of the interview would be on this exciting new policy platform referred to by Candidate Potts as 'Greed with Care,' that had ignited great interest across the entire electorate and in fact, across the entire political spectrum. Whether it was true or not, no-one was the slightest bit concerned about a dog, and it was the opinion of this reporter, and totally aligned with every social media thread she had reviewed, that dogs were more trouble than they were worth. Did the Chair know, by the way that the name of the dog, Doc Cod, was a palindrome? By accident, she understood. But of course, the Chair would have seen it instantly. But wasn't it hilarious?

The Chair certainly agreed that it was hilarious and since he liked the sound of the reporter, suggested they had lunch, some time. Discreetly. Experienced as she was in the ways of politics and so forth, the reporter did not say yea or nay to this invitation, but in a coquettishly evasive kind of way, left the door open.

The Chair said that he was entirely happy with the proposed interview and that he would arrange for it with Candidate Potts, who the reporter might not know had been personally selected by the Chair. The Chair explained that he had a 'nose for quality.' He gave the reporter to understand that this nose had clearly also detected the quality of the reporter and thus, a fruitful relationship was possible and indeed, to be welcomed by the Chair.

NINE

Entrepreneur Potts wasn't entirely happy. He had come up with a good number of entrepreneurial ideas but frankly, had had to accept that they were more likely embarrassing as well as useless, without being simply useless but commercially viable. In this respect, he had approached the wife of the neighbour-four-doors-down-on-the-right who had recently severed his left arm and dislocated his neck whilst in the act of DIY home maintenance. Following the advice of the Entrepreneurial Guide, Entrepreneur Potts wanted to gain some customer insight as to the potential commercial viability of his latest concept of a red circle with a diagonal bar across the acronym, 'DIY.' Accordingly, he had presented his diagrams of several of the proposed innovations to the wife of the neighbour-four-doors-down-on-the-right. He showed her a rung-less ladder. 'Two poles,' she said. 'Whatever for?' When it was explained that this was the ideal ladder to prevent the DIY man, such as her husband – when he returned home, from ever climbing an oak again, she added, 'What a silly idea.' And when Entrepreneur Potts showed her a hammer without a head, she suggested that he might like to talk to someone. A professional, she meant. Someone more than a doctor.

It was a bit dispiriting. Entrepreneur Potts had created a new vision. In this vision, he was the Founder of a vast enterprise employing hundreds, if not thousands and making pots of money. Entrepreneur Potts and now Founder Potts, would be regarded as a business guru. But what, he asked himself, was he the Founder of, and the answer that came back was, 'You are not the Founder of anything. You owned a small, second-hand motel that barely made ends meet. What if they ask you about that?' Clearly, the candidate's credibility could be seen to be slight, if the candidate's entrepreneurial activities were limited to a poorly patronised motel in a hamlet that not even Google could locate.

And now what? A great many people were head-over-heels about Greed-with-Care and Moral Money. It was being talked about in cafes and online. It was being talked about in share clubs, book clubs, tennis clubs, rest homes and even in schools. Headmasters were reportedly asking that certain curricula be upgraded and updated to incorporate this thoroughly modern but overlooked philosophical foundation of a forward-looking contemporary society.

But this was of passing interest to Entrepreneur Potts. He frowned.

The man-in-the-mirror did not frown. The man-in-the-mirror said, 'Perhaps you are more of a politician? Perhaps, you are a thought leader – in public policy and so forth? Perhaps you are diluting your energies when they could be focused on the development of your new political philosophy?'

Candidate Potts completed his shave and wiped the remaining foam from his cheek. He asked himself why he listened to such nonsense. Entrepreneur Potts said, 'I'm already a political thought leader. But so what? I could as well say, let's ban plumbers, or replace doctors with crystals and I would be deemed a most astute policy wonk. In fact, I may do so. No, a zombie can be a political thought leader. I believe I am by nature, a Founder. And a Founder I shall be.' And with that pronouncement, he dismissed the man-in-the-mirror, who was of little account, and departed the bathroom.

*

The Head of News demanded to know the angle. What he didn't want, was a repeat of the fiasco he had witnessed this past week. What he didn't want was having some twerp of a politician given a free-ride on his show. What strategy had the news team come up with that would avoid a repeat fiasco and a free-ride for Dimple Potts? Before the reporter could begin to explain the strategy for the interview, the Head of News vented his considerable disquiet about the so-called 'Potts Paradox,' as it had been described by a rival channel – which also made the Head of News damnably annoyed. Why, the Head of News demanded, had his team not come up with the 'Potts Paradox?' It was smart journalism. It was a clever way to describe an ideology invented by a political twerp that had, against all logical thinking, captured the popular imagination. And what did the Potts Paradox reveal about the average punter? It revealed, said the Head of News answering his own question, that the average punter was self-absorbed, shallow and concerned above all, with his hip pocket. And what had this News Channel done? This News Channel had given Potts the conch. And what did this News Channel need to do now, today? It needed to take that conch away. It needed to show that Potts was an empty vessel of even lesser import than the rest of them. So, demanded the Head of News, what was the strategy for pulling the rug?

The reporter and her team knew better than to interrupt the Head of News when he was venting displeasure. It was always best to allow the vent to run out of steam. It could take some time, but it was always for the best. Consequently, even when the Head of News appeared to have finished, the reporter carefully gauged the landscape for signs of steam elsewhere. Deciding at last that it was geothermally safe, she outlined the strategy. It was simple but she believed it would achieve the objective. The Head of News calmed. He liked the strategy. He said so. The reporter and her team beamed.

*

The Chair had told Candidate Potts that he had thoroughly briefed the reporter. The Chair said that he had laid out the ground rules in unequivocal terms. The reporter, said the Chair, was under no illusions about what this interview was about. This was an opportunity for Candidate Potts to fully enunciate, for the layperson, what the new ideology of the First Union of Conservative Thinkers – to wit, 'Greed-with-Care,' actually meant. And in a respectful way. Indeed, Candidate Potts should be unsurprised, but magnanimous, when the reporter apologised for the shameful way he had been treated at the previous interview. But at which event, needless to say and through superior wit, Candidate Potts had turned to advantage. Tonight though, in part, and certainly in significant part, it could be said, the efforts of the Chair to lay down the ground rules would be most evident.

Thus reassured, Candidate Potts suffered the make-up artist to apply various powders and ointments to his face to, as she described it, 'To bring out the full majesty of your unusual physiognomy.'

Candidate Potts liked the reporter. She was younger than the Senior Reporter and friendlier. She told him how impressed she had been at the last interview. She said that many politicians lacked his calm composure and assurance and she admired that facility. She told him that she was impressed with the new concepts that he had introduced and which were creating such widespread interest.

With several minutes to spare before the interview, the conversation turned to personal interests and Candidate Potts declared his great interest and initiatives in invention and entrepreneurship. The reporter's eyes narrowed momentarily. Then she laughed when Candidate Potts recounted his bizarre dream about the Barbomatic. She agreed that even in a

61

nightmare, seeing a customer's head removed by one's invention would be at the least, unsettling. But, she said, wasn't that the nature of invention? Hadn't the famous Thomas Edison, inventor of the light bulb and the phonograph and who had a prodigious number of patents to his name – a thousand at least. Hadn't he said, when challenged about his apparent failure to find a suitable filament for his lightbulb, that he hadn't failed at all – he had found ten thousand ways that didn't work? The reporter and Candidate Potts laughed about this witty anecdote and Candidate Potts thought privately, how well-informed this young woman was, and he looked forward to magnanimously accepting her apology for the disrespect he had been shown by the Senior Reporter.

The Chair lounged comfortably in front of his television. He had learned that the Prime Minister was also to be interviewed this evening – but after Candidate Potts. Indeed, after the ad break…the Chair chuckled. This was as it should be. What would the PM be spouting off about? Likely another ludicrous impost on business. Likely an extension to her pet project to cripple businesses with even more paid parental leave. The Chair scowled. This is why it was imperative that the First Union of Conservative Thinkers needed to get firm hold of the reins. The horse was bolting. Only last week the PM had been blathering on about how in the first three years of life, a child's brain formed one million neural connections per second. She had been boring all-and-sundry to death, about research that suggested that paid parental leave was the single-most important policy lever for giving a child a head-start. The Chair shook his head. He seriously doubted that any brain had a million neural connections. Where would they all be? And who ever understood what she was talking about? Did the average punter have the faintest idea what a neural connection was? No! What the average punter understood, and this is what Candidate Potts had so cleverly revealed, was that the average punter understood greed. The average punter had been liberated by what the Chair had seen referred to as the Potts Paradox. The Chair suspected that the media, as usual were trying to undermine a brilliant idea, but no matter. The average punter was onto it and wanted more. Candidate Potts was revealing what the First Union of Conservative Thinkers had always known, that Gordon Gekko had simply stated what the average punter understood only too well – Greed is Good. But Gordon Gekko had failed to see what Candidate Potts had seen. An insight into human nature of stunning import – that Greed was good, if greed was *made* good, with care…

The Chair sipped his beer and noted with relish that Candidate Potts was in the studio. The candidate…who resembled something…it came to the Chair that he had seen a likeness of Candidate Potts…on that island, somewhere. Easter – that was it. Well, no matter. At least he wasn't bald. What Gordon Gekko had not seen, was that you could not overturn centuries of religious twaddle about greed, by simply saying that greed was good. He might as well have said murder is good. No, it had taken candidate Potts to turn Gekko's rather rudimentary idea into a philosophy. What Candidate Potts had done, and it was a masterstroke, was to acknowledge implicitly, that greed per se, might *not* be good. What Candidate Potts had suggested, was that if allowed its head, but properly reined, then greed was a horse of quite a different kind. Greed was not a draught horse, with clumsy hooves that crushed everything in their path. Instead, the Potts kind of greed was a high-stepping thoroughbred that minced and pranced with uncommon beauty, and then dashed off to win the race! At the end of which awaited the winner's prize – accolades and most importantly, a decent pot of gold.

The Chair sighed. He wondered momentarily whether he should do some speech writing. The ideas, the metaphors and the inspiration were flowing freely. Perhaps he would discuss this with Candidate Potts. But now, the interview was about to begin. The Chair noted that the reporter was as attractive as she had sounded. He really must have her for dinner.

The reporter introduced the subject of tonight's leading item. She recounted how the new policy platform of the First Union of Conservative Thinkers, first revealed on this show, had stimulated the greatest interest from one end of the country to the other. Consequently, Candidate Potts had been invited back to discuss further, the inspiration and import of his concept of 'Greed-with-Care.'

The camera switched to the visage of the Potts. 'Dignified,' thought the Chair. Certainly, it was a longish head, but it was dignified. And at least it wore a tie. When did the PM wear a tie? She didn't. How could anyone take seriously, a prime minister moins tie?

The reporter smiled sweetly at Candidate Potts. Then she said, 'Mr Potts…may I call you Dimple? Thank you. Dimple, your resume says that you are an entrepreneur. But we can't actually *find* anything that suggests you have actually *invented* anything. Or produced anything. Can you explain to us how you are an entrepreneur?'

The Chair sat bolt upright, spilled his beer and cried, 'Delilah!'

Candidate Potts had been on the point of replying, 'Thank you. I appreciate your apology but let's call it water under the bridge.' But there was no call to say that, since there had been no apology. Silently, Candidate Potts again cursed his tie and the unnatural wave of heat that engulfed his body. Seconds ticked by.

The Chair said, 'Underhanded swiper! And he clapped his hand, painfully, to his forehead.

The reporter showed growing and sincere concern. She asked whether Dimple would like some water? In her ear the Head of News said, 'Spot on! You've got the twerp now…'

The seconds ticked by and the Chair closed his eyes. All was undone...but what was this?

Candidate Potts coughed, 'Ahem...You know, that's an interesting question. I daresay you are acquainted with the story of that greatest of inventors, Thomas Edison?'

The reporter opened her mouth but Candidate Potts pressed on. 'A reporter, somewhat like you perhaps, asked Mr Edison whether he regretted his long history of failures, in being unable to find a filament suitable for his new electric light. Do you know what Mr Edison said? He said, "Oh no, I haven't failed. I've discovered a thousand ways that won't work."

The Chair stood with an expression of amazement. The Head of News shouted in the reporter's ear.

The reporter said, 'But Mr Potts, you're not Thomas Edison? Are you suggesting-

Candidate Potts continued imperturbably, 'Am I Thomas Edison?' He smiled winningly and for several moments resembled less the stern countenance of an Easter Island monolith and more the benign kisser of a parish priest and continued, 'Good Lord no! But I walk in the footsteps of the great man. We all do. In the shadow of course, but following his example. Constantly seeking new ideas and ways of doing things. That is what characterises the entrepreneur and I am proud to describe myself that way.'

Desperately, the Head of News bawled in the reporter's ear, 'You're losing it! Ask him if he's ever buggered a dog!' But the Programme Editor cried into the reporter's other ear, 'Don't ask him that!'

The Chair waved his arms and cried, 'Brilliant!'

The reporter capitulated. She asked, 'Mr Potts, perhaps you can tell us a little more, about how Greed-with-Care might...about how it could be...'

The Head of News shouted, 'You lame brain!'

The reporter finished, 'About how Greed-with-Care might translate into policy?'

Candidate Potts resumed his expression of quiet dignity and earnestness. He said, 'I'm glad you asked me that.' And then Candidate Potts went on to explain how, in essence, Greed-with-Care meant that ordinary people could also become enormously wealthy, with a clear conscience. What Greed-with-Care meant, was that the pent-up aspirations of ordinary people to be rich, but which were improperly restrained by parsimonious vicars and so forth, could be properly unleashed. Gone would be the moralistic carping about the ills of greed – and Candidate Potts was the first to acknowledge that there could be ills – but only if that greed wasn't exercised with care. What did the ordinary punter want? The ordinary punter wanted a great deal of money. The ordinary punter was tired of window shopping. The ordinary punter wanted to buy the shop. Was that bad? No, that was just human nature. Would it hurt anyone? No, observed Candidate Potts firmly, it would make the ordinary punter feel like someone. And wasn't that just natural, human nature? To want to feel like someone? The First Union of Conservative Thinkers was all about helping the ordinary punter to feel like *someone*, and the mechanism by which this laudable and lofty goal could be achieved, was through Greed-with-Care.

The Head of News had departed the studio. He had gone directly to his office and picked up a tray full of documents, and hurled it into the wall. Passing by the reporter's desk he snapped the stem of her potted plant. Then he had departed the building.

The Chair was hugging himself. He shouted several times, 'Ha!'

Candidate Potts told the reporter that she was welcome.

TEN

Candidate Potts swung into his driveway and noted that there was a protest of some sort outside. He saw that the sign read, 'Dog Abominator,' with an arrow pointing downwards at the sleeping hound Doc Cod. The sign was held by Mildred Titsman.

Dimple's wife said she had seen the protest and wondered if it was linked to the graffiti on his election billboard, with the original 'Tosser,' now being accompanied by, 'Beastly.' She observed that whilst Mildred had accepted the plate of scones, it appeared she was not placated and continued to bear her neighbour, the entrepreneur at least, some animosity.

Candidate Potts dismissed all this with a wave of his hand. The cut-and-thrust of politics, he replied. It knew no boundaries. On the face of it, Mildred Titsman was protesting about him cleaning her dog, but in reality, she hated what he stood for. No, not greed, but success. Success in others simply magnified their own abject failure. That was what he was striving to change – to help the average plonker shed the chains of their own flunk.

Undoubtedly, Mildred had seen him on the news, ahead of the PM, by-the-way, and making mincemeat of the reporter – had Dimple's wife seen the interview? No. Well, that was less than edifying. Not the first one and now, not this one either. One wondered whether one's wife even supported one in one's quest for power and influence. But no matter. Mildred had seen the interview and was consumed with envy.

Dimple's wife said that she felt that was somewhat harsh, and that it appeared to her that Mildred was chiefly concerned about how Doc Cod had lost all the hair on his hindquarters. Dimple rolled his eyes. He cried in some exasperation, 'He's old. He's going bald! We all do. And is he cleaner than he was? Yes. Mildred is concerned with very small things. I am concerned with big things.'

*

In her office, the Prime Minister put down the newspaper and sighed. After all the effort the PM had put into improving teacher training, pre-school education, breakfast-for-kids, and not to mention parental maternity leave, it had come to this. A new Outbreak of Alta Stultitia was on the cards. The Director General of the WHO was concerned. Society at large, it seemed, was becoming measurably more stupid. Indeed, only the previous evening on television, she had tried to put the case for extending maternity leave, but no-one wished to hear. Not even the reporter, who had the gall to interrupt to ask her about Dimple Potts and his new and exciting policy platform, 'Greed-with-Care.' Later, the PM had asked her Chief-of-Staff, who on Earth was Dimple Potts? She was incredulous when her Chief-of-Staff had mentioned that Potts had just polled as a preferred PM for seventeen per cent of voters. Just five points behind the PM. She was even more incredulous when her Chief-of-Staff explained that 'Greed-with-Care' was a leading topic on social media. And the Election was on Saturday. According to the polls, said the Chief-of-Staff, the First Union of Conservative Thinkers was polling at nineteen per cent.

ELEVEN

In a dimly lit corner of a poorly lit café in Auckland, a plumpish fellow sat reading his newspaper, with a small torch. The fellow, who was attired in a colourful Hawaiian shirt and blue shorts and with red jandals on his feet, raised his rubicund face from the paper and said, 'Percy. This is an opportunity. This is big.'

The man sitting opposite, who was attired in a dark suit and whose complexion was as pale as pastry dough said, 'To what do you refer, Corker?'

As it happens, the man called Corker Pritchard was well-known to Dimple Potts. In a previous existence, Corker Pritchard had been the owner of 'Forest Flavours,' a large, small goods meat company based near the village of Brewster's Neck, and where Dimple Potts, after serving for twenty-three years as deputy mayor, had by dint of the tragic death of the previous mayor, Georgy Pruitt, succeeded to Georgy's position. However, in the first local body elections, which came just three months after his elevation, Mayor Potts was deposed in a landslide by the Latvian baker, Sarah Bumbulis. This unexpected and unwelcome downfall had three causes. First, Corker Pritchard had stumbled onto a remarkable secret, courtesy of the town mendicant, Homeless Hauptmann, who, whilst stumbling about in the hills with a geologist's hammer, discovered a seam of gold.

The exact location of the gold was ascertained by Corker Pritchard when he secured the map drawn by Homeless Hauptmann, shortly after Hauptmann was killed by an arrow to the throat. After a lengthy investigation, it was established by the local constable, Herb Hikaka, that in fact

69

Hauptmann had not been shot by a Pawnee, but rather, had accidentally shot himself with the weapon he had purloined from a visiting Pawnee tourist, named Jim. Be that as it may, Corker was determined to mine the gold, but he encountered a difficulty. The difficulty was that the gold was located beneath land belonging to Doug Hemopo. Coincidentally, on the adjacent land, there happened to be a seam of coal, fortuitously exposed by the torrential rains that accompanied a once-in-a-hundred-year storm – such event having last occurred two years prior. Being of a most entrepreneurial and enterprising nature, Corker and his younger brother, Percy, with whom he was presently sitting, conceived of a plan whereby they would mine the coal, which was not on Hemopo land, but surreptitiously send a shaft from the coal mine, beneath the Hemopo boundary to access the gold, unseen and unnoticed.

It was an excellent plan but for two things and those two things were Hemopo and Bumbulis. Doug Hemopo was an inventive and eccentric engineer, who at the time, was designing and building New Zealand's largest robot, which he named Roboman. Doug did not like the idea of a road across his land for the purposes of extracting coal, and sided with the baker, Sarah Bumbulis who was opposed to the mining of coal on the basis that it was the worst kind of fossil fuel. Indeed, so opposed was Sarah Bumbulis, that she stood for Mayor.

In a very small and naturally parochial town with very few employers, it was likely that her campaign would have failed, except for the disappearance of a popular dog by the name of Nostradamus, who was known to most, as Nostril. The campaign manager for Sarah Bumbulis, the local beekeeper Porterhouse Johnson, discovered that Nostril had been inadvertently incorporated into a batch of Forest Flavours sausages and subsequently consumed by an unknown number of townspeople. This was not well received. But the inquisitive Porterhouse Johnson also discovered that

Corker Pritchard was deliberately procuring possums, rats and other forest creatures, to supplement the dwindling supply of venison for Forest Flavours small goods.

The third thing that had confounded Corker's plans, pertained to Roboman. Roboman wasn't simply large, it was intelligent. It will never be known if it was sentient, but through ingenious modification of the artificial intelligence that Doug obtained from Mitsubishi, Roboman showed all the signs that it was learning and developing a sense of 'self.' In any event, Roboman somehow understood that Corker and Percy were creatures of the Empire, with which he had become familiar during his programming. Consequently, when Corker found a way to access the coal using the riverbed that was the boundary of the Hemopo land, Roboman engaged in a violent confrontation with Corker's earth-moving and mining machinery. The outcome of this Herculean battle between mechanical behemoths, was the total destruction of Corker's Coal Ltd.

Unfortunately, Roboman needed a great deal of electrical energy and again, on his own initiative, decided that he would obtain that power from the nearby pylons that carried electricity from the south to the city of Auckland. Perhaps because his battery was so low, when he had climbed the pylon to reach the live wires, Roboman inadvertently created a short and in a spectacular explosion, ended its own existence and plunged Auckland into darkness.

These misadventures caused Corker and his brother to flee to South America, and the campaign of Dimple Potts, who had argued strenuously for the economic good that would surely flow from Corker's Coal, to crash miserably to the sum total of three votes.

*

Corker Pritchard did not like Venezuela. Consequently, having had Percy ensure that a good deal of their funds was safe from the purview of Inland Revenue, he decided to return home, pay the not insignificant fine for misrepresentation of his small goods, and to seek new opportunities. It is for this very reason, that on this particular morning in this dingy café in downtown Auckland, Corker's small blue eyes gleamed with entrepreneurial triumph.

Corker said, 'Listen to this. "A new study suggests a possible outbreak of Alta Stultitia, or Deep Stupidity. Endeavouring to understand the trend, researchers asked people, 'If the moon was to fall, would you prefer it to fall on Africa or South America?'" Corker laughed, 'What a bloody silly question. You'd nuke it. And it says here, Percy, that the WHO fears an Outbreak and possibly even an Epidemic.' Corker shone his torch into his younger brother's eyes.

Percy said, 'Do you mind?'

Corker said, as he turned the torch onto his own face, 'What affect do you think this study, and this article will have on your average punter?' Percy remained silent and expressionless. Percy was the accountant, and the implementer. And when necessary, the enforcer. Which is why Forest Flavours had had no competition within one hundred kilometres of Brewster's Neck.

Corker wagged a finger. 'I'll tell you what will happen – and you can bank on this. There'll be a general panic. Mothers will be thinking their sprogs are going to fail at school. Men will think they're losing their edge in bizzo. The government will want to be seen to be doing something. Doctors, will want to prescribe something. Do you see?' Corker stared keenly at his brother, who stared inscrutably in return. Finally, Percy said, 'We're not short of funds.'

Corker said, 'Funds, Percy, come in two sizes. Not enough, and not nearly enough. And now the thing is, do we have enough to kick-start a global bizzo – before any other bastard thinks of it?'

And already knowing the answer, the Pritchard's got down to business.

*

Meanwhile, and not seeing the business opportunity that had leapt from the page at Corker Pritchard, Entrepreneur Potts repaired to his office, hung his sign, closed the door and then opened it again, to return to the kitchen to remind his wife that he was not to be disturbed, and then again repaired to his Place of Inspiration. This was one of the Big Things, according to The Entrepreneur's Guide. Deep, undisturbed lateral-thinking time. It was analogous to powering up a jet engine. The entrepreneur would focus on an object with such intensity, that it might spontaneously combust, and indeed, it had happened that a handful of nascent entrepreneurs of a rare and particular kind, had spontaneously combusted. Barring that misadventure, at such times, ideas of exceptionally profitable provenance might appear in the entrepreneurial night sky like a blazing comet. This method of brainstorming, said the Guide, was only to be used if the chant, "I am a Master of the Universe, etc," had not produced the desired results. Only the truly stout of heart should attempt this method, advised the Guide.

Entrepreneur Potts considered his focus-up object. It could be his pen. But then, why not the pencil? Or, the painting of a naked woman dancing with a platypus. Now that he was looking at it again, Dimple wondered what had induced him to buy it. Clearly, it was a physical impossibility for the platypus to be in that position. The creature was flat and designed to stay flat, and to the best of his knowledge, rather less than a metre-and-a-half long – or tall. What was the

73

woman thinking? Life was indeed, full of mysteries. His eye wandered and was caught by his wastepaper basket. Instantly, he felt this a most suitable focus-up object. It was an heirloom. Part of a meagre legacy bequeathed by his grandfather, Dimple understood that his grandfather had shot the elephant that had owned this foot, that was now his waste-paper basket, whilst on safari in darkest Africa. The details were hazy. It was difficult not to suspect that the elephant in the photograph on which his stern-faced grandfather sat, had been dead for at least a month already. But his family put that down to the quality of the photograph.

Entrepreneur Potts placed the elephant foot on his desk. To avoid any untimely restriction of blood-flow to the entrepreneurial brain, he removed his tie. The technique, he read in the Entrepreneurial Guide, was to clasp the focus-up object – since the physical connection was important, and then to fix the gaze on one to two hundred points on the object, since a very broad depth of field was paramount, and thence to 'cast oneself adrift in the Entrepreneurial Cosmos.'

Entrepreneur Potts placed a hand on either side of the elephant foot, and wondered idly whether the elephant had a name. Not an English name, of course, but in his elephant language. Was he known to other elephants as 'Oowoombe,' for example? But no matter. Water under the bridge. It was the future that needed to be contemplated. Entrepreneur Potts began the task of fixing his gaze on more than one hundred points on the foot, and found he wasn't progressing beyond two, and really, that was only one. For several minutes, he strove unsuccessfully to bring in more points. He held his breath until he could hear the pulse in his ears. He widened his eyes until he felt the eyeballs might pop. He increased his grip until he felt cramps developing. And then, a breakthrough! A sudden soaring of the number of points. Dozens of extra points were appearing until, he was certain, he had exceeded one hundred. No longer was he conscious of his office. No longer could he feel his chair, or his knuckle-white hands. He was entering a new domain. The mists were clearing. A wave of exultation enveloped him. He cried out, as required: 'I cast myself adrift in the Entrepreneurial Cosmos! Speak to me!'

Something was there! Something was materialising from the vapours. Incandescent – an idea was about to be born. The road to riches was about to be revealed. In ecstasy, Entrepreneur Potts cried, 'Come forth. I command you to come forth! Make yourself visible! Come! Come now, I say!'

The Entrepreneur's wife said, 'There's no need to bellow, you know? I thought you didn't want to be disturbed.'

Entrepreneur Potts stared wildly at the naked woman dancing with the platypus. Speaking in tongues, he cried, 'Oowoomba! Bawana mo kawanka!' And then he fell, quite senseless, from his chair.

TWELVE

Election Day dawned like any other day. Partly cloudy with some showers but otherwise sunny, if a storm didn't eventuate, and with a few sea breezes, if there was no gale. At the residence of the Candidate for the First Union of Conservative Thinkers, a small but vocal protest was taking place. The shrill cry of 'Dog Destroyer!' could be heard behind the placard held by Mildred Titsman, which read in red, 'Potts is a Pig.'

Dimple's wife observed over breakfast that it was unlikely he could count on Mildred's vote. Candidate Potts observed that he didn't believe their neighbour even realised there was a General Election. Candidate Potts wondered aloud just whose vote he *could* count on? Bearing in mind that at the local body elections of Brewster's Neck, he had secured just three votes. Himself, he didn't mind saying, and who else? Candidate Potts's wife said that was the wonderful thing about an election, wasn't it? That every vote was confidential. And she smiled a mysterious smile.

But the polls were auspicious, replied Candidate Potts, so it didn't matter if those one might most like to think *would* vote for one, did not.

In the residence of the Chair of the First Union of Conservative Thinkers, the Chair was in his basement cycling for all he was worth. His complexion was puce and his lungs heaved like the bellows in a foundry. The Chair was getting fit. Momentous things were afoot, he told his wife. His candidate might well deliver something the Chair had only dreamed of – real power and influence. And if the candidate delivered real power and influence, then the Chair, as the real power behind the throne, needed to be in high state of battle readiness. His wife said that she had a game of tennis with the girls and asked if he might bring home some milk. He asked why she didn't bring home some milk. She said that she could hardly be expected to stop by a common dairy in her tennis outfit, which whilst not intended to be so, might be viewed by some as exceedingly provocative. The Chair acquiesced but privately he thought that the likelihood of the man-in-the-dairy leaping over the counter to take advantage of his wife – even were she naked and carrying a sign saying, 'Open for business,' was about the same as the moon falling onto the Earth. Which, when he thought further, he had come across somewhere. A peculiar notion but in any event, the Chair concluded as he pumped at the pedals, the best thing would be to nuke it.

*

The PM pushed aside her muesli and declared that she simply didn't have much appetite this morning. A General Election could do that to you. Her husband agreed that it certainly could as he bounced their giggling daughter on his knee. The PM thought that watching her husband and her daughter play, was a much better thing than voting, even if people were voting for her. But many would not. She sighed. Many would rather cast a vote for a dead buck-rat. That was the odd thing about politics. The moment one became a candidate was the moment one created implacable enemies who suddenly discovered all manner of objectionable things about one. Indeed, so objectionable that they would happily boil one in oil. What one needed to keep uppermost, was that it wasn't personal. It might look personal. When one read comments such as, 'I do not like you. You make me feel violently ill most of the week. The colour of your eye is disgusting and when

77

you speak, I am reminded of a Komodo Dragon, and I am hoping and praying that your life will be short,' – this could *feel* personal, and hurtful.

A Komodo Dragon couldn't help what it was. True, the way it hamstrung its prey with a poisonous bite and then remorselessly tracked the afflicted animal for days, which finally escaped its agony when the dragon fell upon it with ravenous maw – none of this was attractive. Nature could be cruel. Nature wasn't just roses of many hues, and small birds singing, and sparkling streams…indeed, the PM reflected ruefully, it was a challenge to find a sparkling stream below a thousand metres, on account of that being the altitude accessible to the average cow. Nevertheless, the PM had long-since become inured to insult and venom because that was the politician's lot. Unless…the PM pondered how it was that a white, middle-aged male, or older, in a suit and tie, seemed to escape the opprobrium she had experienced. Her thoughts turned to the Candidate for the First Union of Conservative Thinkers. According to her Chief-of-Staff, there was a real possibility, if the election was as close as the polls seemed to suggest, she might find herself having to negotiate with Dimple Potts. What would he want?

The PM had requested a dossier that would explain the detail and import of his concept of Greed-with-Care, and a solid description of Dimple Potts. She had been surprised to find that the dossier contained one sheet of paper and comprised two paragraphs. The first read, "Unfortunately, we have been unable to find any documentation describing what 'Greed-with-Care' actually means, or how or what the First Union of Conservative Thinkers, think it will bring to wider policy considerations." That was the first paragraph, which in fact was just one sentence.

The second paragraph read, "Dimple Potts was, for three months, Mayor of a small village called Brewster's Neck. Our researchers are endeavouring to discover where this place is but it is assumed to be somewhere in the Waikato. As Mayor, he contested an election in support of a proposed coal mine, but was soundly beaten by a Latvian baker who was opposed to the mine. Potts reappeared soon after as the candidate for the First Union of Conservative Thinkers. What does seem apparent, is that despite there being no policy as such, the idea of 'Greed-with-Care' has resonated with a significant number of voters."

The PM shook her head and hoped that a negotiation with Mr Potts would not be necessary. She held out her arms and her daughter climbed gleefully into her lap. The PM said, 'It's a big day for Mummy, sweetheart.' Her daughter said, 'Can we get an ice-cream?'

*

Candidate Potts cast his vote at mid-day precisely, down at the mall. He was surprised when he appeared at the polling booth, to be greeted with many cheers and cries of, 'Good on you Pottsy,' and 'Up with Greed!' One woman even cried above the tumult, 'You have a lovely long head, Dimple!' And one prominent placard said, 'Peachy Potts Pelts the Press Properly!'

A television reporter, whom Candidate Potts did not recognise, thrust the microphone toward him and asked how he felt his campaign was going. Candidate Potts replied modestly, that it appeared to be going passably well, but he wasn't counting his chickens and would wait with magnanimity, on the verdict of his fellow citizens. Then the reporter asked if he had seen the study by Dr Klas Beekhof that suggested that human evolution had gone into reverse and people were evolving backwards towards the apes? Candidate Potts laughed indulgently and said that yes, he had, and he added that had *he* been asked, he would have given the obvious answer that *were* the moon to fall to Earth, and who could know – stranger things had happened, then why, we'd simply have to nuke it. Indeed, he added, it might be prudent to nuke it anyway.

*

On the day of the General Election, far across the Pacific, the General looked at the wall. Then he looked at his shoes. Which gleamed like sleek black seals. Shortly, he looked at the Secretary-of-State.

The Secretary-of-State found it remarkable that regardless of where the General looked, or indeed, regardless of the subject at hand, the General's expression did not change. The Secretary-of-State assumed that this must be a characteristic of the military nature. The outward projection of very great stoicism, which made sense to the Secretary-of-State, since one did not want one's generals to become excitable in testing times. One wanted a phlegmatic disposition and a steady hand that did not reach, at the least provocation, for the button, or the trigger or the firing pin or whatever other mechanism resulted in the unleashing of mayhem. Despite these thoughts, the Secretary-of-State was disturbed. The General appeared to be seeking support for the practical application of a nuclear bomb. That is to say, the General wasn't happy that the only tests that he could do, were simulations. The Secretary-of-State had asked as light-heartedly as possible, the very obvious question, of where the General thought an actual detonation of a nuclear bomb could take place, without upsetting quite a number of people. Our people, as well as theirs…after all, the Secretary-of-State thought as she asked these questions, perhaps the General has a sense of humour. Perhaps he is testing me. And the General didn't appear to have a plan, which fact also suggested to the

Secretary-of-State that shortly, the General's face might crack into a smile and he would say, 'Just a little joke, Ma'am.' And they would share a little chuckle.

But the General replied only that *options* were being considered. In the absence of further input on his side, the Secretary-of-State cautiously wondered why the General was broaching the subject. Were we under threat? The Welsh, perhaps? The General did not so much as smirk. Were we, she continued with just the slightest sense of exasperation, unhappy that simulations, which currently cost in the vicinity of fifteen billion at Livermore, could not guarantee that when push came to shove, our bombs would actually go off? The Secretary-of-State was beginning to wonder whether she should just say, 'Ok. Enough of the nukes. Let's get on with the agenda.' But she did not say that because there wasn't a hint in the General's demeanour to suggest he was not serious.

The General said that he did have doubts. He had doubts about the Russians. He had doubts about the Chinese. He had doubts about the Greeks. He most particularly had doubts about the viability of his bombs. 'Our bombs,' the Secretary-of-State corrected. He said that that is what he meant. He said that the boffins advised him that the probability that any given bomb would go-off when required, was just 99.98 per cent, which clearly, left room for doubt. The Secretary-of-State observed that it didn't seem to leave very much room for doubt, at which he asked, whether she would want any doubt whatsoever, when push-came-to-shove? When the enemy's bombs were laying waste, would the Secretary-of-State be happy that our bomb landed with a dull thump and just sat there, like a lemon?

The Secretary-of-State thought it uncanny that the General could describe such a disastrous scenario with a face as immobile as a plaster-of-Paris. Admirable self-control! But what did she think? She decided to play for time by suggesting a coffee break. The General politely declined and continued to stare at her with an expression that she really couldn't decide was inquisitorial, bumptious or totally insouciant. She thought that he would be a very difficult fellow to come up against at the poker table – or in a trench.

At last, she said with as much equanimity as she could, that she wasn't opposed to the idea of a real test, *in principle.* But she would certainly need to see a very detailed plan with every contingency accounted for. The Secretary-of-State privately assumed that her request would cause the issue to disappear without trace.

The General agreed that this was the correct course of action and he would see to it that his people were onto it. At which he stood, saluted and departed. The Secretary-of-State lifted the phone and sought advice. She was wondering whether the General had been subject to any psychological testing, say, in the last three months. She was informed that he had not and was not due for a test for another nine months. The Secretary-of-State wondered whether there was any way – any pretext that might be used to hasten such a test, into, say the next two weeks. She was advised that this was not possible without demonstrable cause. The Secretary-of-State rang-off and sat for some time, wondering whether a request to detonate a nuclear weapon, anywhere, was not adequate cause for hastening a psychological test. But finally, she had to acknowledge, reluctantly, that anything less than a one hundred per cent probability of a successful detonation of one of her bombs, when push-came-to-shove, was less than satisfactory.

THIRTEEN

The Chair of the First Union of Conservative Thinkers was ecstatic. Giddy, was not too strong. Candidate Dimple Potts had secured sixteen per cent of the party vote and won Peapod with the most crushing majority, ever. The thing is, the Chair told the Party Committee, the PM has to do a deal with us – and we'll go for broke. Finance, at the least. Time at last to get our hands on the Treasury. Our natural home, he told the Committee and nothing less will do. 'My goodness!' Exclaimed the Chair, 'We'll get among those taxes! We'll trim the fat. We'll keep what we earn and do government as government ought to be done. On the sniff of an oily rag.' This strategy was met with acclaim in the Committee and the Chair conveyed these exact sentiments to Candidate Potts. But the Chair was decidedly miffed when he learned that the negotiation between Candidate Potts and the PM, would not be including him.

The negotiation that did not include the Chair, took place the very next morning, in the Office of the Prime Minister. Candidate Potts admired the view and mentioned that it had been a surprising election, but it soon became clear that the PM was in no mood for small talk. She had a number of other parties to talk to, in order to cobble together a new government.

Candidate Potts accepted a cup of tea and sitting across the coffee table from the PM, reflected on what a strange world it had become. Sarah Bumbulis, a Latvian baker was the preferred Mayor of Brewster's Neck – albeit that there were extenuating circumstances – and here, the country was governed by a youngish woman, who without doubt was intelligent, but really, and when all-was-said-and-done, surely to goodness, a mature businessman was the ticket?

Across the coffee table, the PM glanced quickly at the dossier, to which there had been a recent addition, which read, "Potts is on record as having supported a coal mine, but there is reason to believe that he is essentially a pragmatist."

The PM had given this matter some thought, even as she had been thinking about why it was, that middle-aged men and older of a certain kind, assumed they had a divine right to rule. It was particularly ironic when the majority of those she had encountered were more-or-less characterised by a paucity of imagination, virtually no principles to speak of, and no apparent ideology beyond the acquisition of money. She gazed steadily at Dimple Potts and wondered just how pragmatic he was, and more importantly, how biddable, and then, how likely to upset the apple cart with a slavish adherence to the ghastly motivations of the First Union of Conservative Thinkers.

At last, the PM said, 'I understand that in your last political capacity, you were a champion for a coal mine?' She smiled.

Dimple Potts thought, 'Blast! She knows. Of course, she knows. Head of the Secret Intelligence Service. What else does she know?' A fleeting image of Nostradamus in Corker's mincer came into his mind. He said, cautiously, 'Ah, yes. I do seem to recall a proposal to mine coal. Mind you, Prime Minister, it was merely a proposal…'

The PM said, 'I suppose you were attracted to the employment opportunities – jobs, in a small rural community – it's important, isn't it? Despite the other issues…'

Dimple Potts thought, 'Have to be careful here. She's bound to hate coal.' He said, 'I couldn't agree more, Prime Minister. But you know, I asked the community to give it *consideration.* That was the main thing. The coal was there. We needed jobs. I felt it my duty to be put on the table.' When she didn't respond but kept her rather unsettling gaze fixed upon him, he added, 'Personally, I'd prefer just about anything else. I've always liked windmills...'

The Prime Minister had seen the new attachment in the Candidate Potts dossier, which quoted Mayor Potts saying that "Coal was the future of Brewster's Neck and that opposition from the likes of Sarah Bumbulis, was the kind of thing that could be expected from someone intent on taking us back to the Stone Age." The PM said, 'So, you weren't really a strong proponent for a coal mine?'

Dimple Potts thought, 'Got her now. She likely thought I was a coal man, but now she's thinking I was simply doing politics. Must press my advantage.' He said, 'Nail on the head, Prime Minister. It was all just politics. You would know.'

The PM thought, 'Totally biddable.' She said, 'Yes. In this business one must be prepared to make compromises. But let's get to the point. I want to give you an important portfolio. I think you've got that kind of capability. My advisers say you're a person I could rely on – to do a solid job and to bring credit on this government and the country at large.'

Dimple Potts said, 'I'm flattered, Prime Minister. But yes, I think you could be sure that I would be someone you could rely on – loyal – can I say that I was thinking that Finance-'

But she interrupted, 'Excellent! I had a feeling, Mr Potts, may I call you Dimple? I had a feeling that you were someone who would be an asset. You've all that local body experience, and I understand you're an entrepreneur...that's a perfect background to really make a difference, in Foreign

Affairs. Probably the highest profile in Cabinet and the face of our international diplomacy. I think you'll fit the role hand-in-glove.'

Dimple said, 'Ah, but I was thinking, the Treasury-'

The Prime Minister interrupted, 'I'd thought about Finance, but it's not *you,* Dimple, and it's much less important, in the wider scheme of things. Foreign Affairs is what I suspect you were born for. Few politicians have the requisite *worldliness.*' And she smiled in such a way that the soon-to-be-Minister of Foreign Affairs, found simply irresistible. It occurred to him that they were all wrong. All his colleagues who derided her femininity and so forth. This was a formidable woman who could see in an instant, what a man actually was. She was absolutely right. He had considerable personal charm. He looked dignified and acted with dignity. His commercial experience meant he would dive into trade deals like a duck into water. How insightful and thoughtful she was? Anyone could count beans, but only a special kind of chap could represent his country to the world.

The PM thought, we'll send him on a regular junket to Tonga, and perhaps Samoa. Can't do any harm and out of the way. She said, 'I'm delighted we've been able to sort this thing so quickly, Dimple – but then I'm unsurprised. You've got a reputation for clear thinking and no procrastination. Would that the others were as dynamic.' She added with a most conspiratorial smile. 'So…' she wrote a note and then continued, 'I'm sure I can persuade my colleagues that you are far and away the obvious choice.'

The new Minister of Foreign Affairs said, 'I shall look forward to being of service. I thought we might touch on my new concept, Greed-with-Care-'

The Prime Minister said, 'Yes. Very interesting.' She rose and extended her hand. The new Minister of Foreign Affairs and the Prime Minister shook hands and she said she would be in touch. His experience and expertise would soon be required.

*

The Head of News smirked. Dimple Potts had been given Foreign Affairs. Side-lined. Very clever of the PM. But the new Minister of Foreign Affairs was on the record only the previous day, of saying if it was up to him, he would 'nuke the moon.' The Head of News smirked again, and then called his Senior Reporter.

*

The Chair was speechless. Potts actually thought he had pulled something off. The man actually thought that Foreign Affairs was important. The Chair saw it all in an instant. That damned woman would put him on the first plane to the outer Cooks. The man had been played like a fish and was too damned daft to know it! But what was to be said? The Chair offered his congratulations. Then he called each Committee member and told them through clenched teeth, when he wasn't shouting, that Potts had sold all their hard work down the road for a bauble, and their chances of getting their hands on the books were zero. Taxes for public hospitals. Taxes for public education. Taxes for cycleways. Taxes for sewerage treatment. All would remain. It was enough to make anyone feel ill.

*

In the flickering light of a candle, Corker Pritchard and his brother Percy talked business. The plan, devised by Corker,

87

was, in his words, 'A bloody cracker!' They had designed the product and the pricing strategy. They had worked out the manufacturing. They had gotten on top of distribution – domestic first, but quite quickly into export markets. But there was a significant fly in the ointment. Corker Pritchard's record. He told Percy that it would be hard, if not impossible, to go to market with the new product, when punters knew about the fate of Forest Flavours. Punters, he told Percy, usually have very short memories, but on something like this, even that short little attention span would range with unjustified indignation over the perfectly safe practice of incorporating other denizens of the forest, into a sausage. After all, it was just bloody protein in the end. In other countries, you'd get a medal. And as for that blasted dog, who could have known it would turn up at the Forest Flavours plant and fall into the chute carrying carcasses to the mincer? Served the damned thing right – paid a price for its own greedy guts and sheer carelessness. And what did all this mean? It meant, he told Percy, that he, Corker, could not be the front-man. Corker Pritchard would have to adopt the role of 'silent investor.' Invisible, even to the Companies Office. Percy said that this at least, would be easily arranged, with trusts and so forth. Corker said he was quite aware of that. What Corker wanted to know was how they would solve the problem of the front-man? Who would be the Founder of the new company? Who would speak authoritatively for the new product? As it happened, he continued, he had invited his nephew, that media man, Verbal Pritchard to join them to discuss that very issue. And it was a blasted nuisance that Verbal was late.

In fact, Verbal Pritchard was delayed by an altercation. Not with a listener on his talkback radio show, called 'Flog it with Verbal,' but with the manager of his radio station. The show had begun, uncontroversial enough, with Verbal's view that liberals belonged in the same biological family as the rodent naked mole rat, whereas conservatives belonged to the far more noble family of lions. New evidence for this difference, Verbal said, had been recently uncovered by scientists doing autopsies on liberals, which had shown that liberals, just like the mole rat have a high affinity for oxygen, which is why they are so keen on reducing carbon dioxide in the environment. At the very same time, another group of scientists had found that the courage and majesty of the lion was identical to that found in the genes of most conservatives. Verbal's first caller said that he had real doubts that liberals were actually human, as we know it. 'Bingo!' cried Verbal. 'My friend, you have stated what many *knew* but were afraid to say, and I for one, am momentarily overcome at your courage in saying what nearly all scientists and left-wing politicians know to be true, but which they deliberately conceal from us, the average punter.' Verbal added that if you looked at a typical liberal through half-closed eyes, you could actually see the resemblance to the aforesaid rodent and he invited his listeners to find a photograph of the Prime Minister to try this experiment themselves. Within a few minutes, dozens of callers had confirmed that they had done the experiment and sure enough, the PM bore an uncanny resemblance to the naked mole rat.

This was all splendid talkback, said Verbal's manager, but he had to draw the line when Verbal had asked listeners about the idea that elderly people might prefer to be put in a freezer, when the time came, rather than ending up wasting their own time and that of others in some ghastly rest home that was a financial burden on the rest of us. Eskimos, Verbal declared, had been doing this for centuries – except they didn't need a normal freezer, since they lived in a bloody big natural one. But the principle was the same. The old person simply passed out from the cold and didn't feel a thing, which was extremely humane. And then they were eaten by a wolf or suchlike, which was pretty noble, and also meaning they were recycled in a pretty cool way.

Verbal's manager said that whilst he was absolutely the champion of free speech, Verbal needed to remember that old people made up thirty-three percent of the station's audience and accounted for over fifty per cent of its advertising revenue.

Arguing principle, as the manager knew he always did, Verbal said that it was simply impossible to do a show that was free and frank and unfettered by woke nonsense, and cleaving to the highest levels of integrity, such as he strove tirelessly to do, without treading on a few toes. After considerable and quite heated to-ing and fro-ing, Verbal agreed that in tomorrow's show, he would say that the idea of putting old people into freezers was in fact a secret government policy and was the brainchild of the PM herself.

*

Having borrowed a torch from the barista, Verbal found his two uncles, in the opposite corner of the café to the one in which he found a lady who was perfect example of someone who should be in a freezer, who was feeding nuts to a huge parrot that cried, 'Piss off! What's that sound? Piss off!'

Verbal blinded the old lady with his torch and whacked the parrot off the table with his newspaper, where it continued to repeat its shrill cries and adding, 'Bring me a cuppa!'

He told his uncles that birds and parrots in particular, had always made his skin crawl, and then recounted his argument with his manager. Corker said that he was in total agreement about parrots, and also about Verbal's principled stand on the aged, and that it had just given him an idea for a new business. But that would have to wait, since he had another marvellous enterprise, all set to go – as soon as he could sort out certain aspects relating to the branding and so forth, which was where Verbal came in. It had been Verbal, after-all, who had come up with the concept of FOKKERS, for Dimple Potts's mayoral campaign – standing for Fundamentally Opposed to Aucklanders, Kangaroos, Environmentalists, Rivers and Socialists, and had it not been for *those* circumstances (which they needn't go into again), that concept would have had Dimple bolting across the line. As it happened, it was because of *those* circumstances, that Corker could not be anywhere to be seen, in relation to his new venture. What he needed was the right name for the product, which was revolutionary, and a 'clean' stooge who could be persuaded, for a minor shareholding, to lend his or her name to the business. That was what he wanted his nephew to consider.

The media man, who was thinking that people should be paid to keep cats to get on top of the bird problem, hardly interrupted as Corker described the new business and the avalanche of profits in waiting, once they had the final piece of the jigsaw in place. 'And you, my boy, will be the marketing guru.'

Verbal said he was onboard, and then he said, holding out a copy of the morning's news, 'Have you seen this?'

Corker hadn't. He said, 'Is that Potts? Is that old Dimple? Minister of Foreign Affairs?' Corker guffawed. 'Anything is possible!' But almost instantly his expression became shrewd. 'Are you thinking, Verbal, that Pottsy could be our man?'

The media man winked and tapped his nose.

Corker continued, 'The Minister of Foreign Affairs endorses our new business? Indeed, *is* the Founder of our business? Highest levels of Government, backing me.' Then he reflected, 'But we didn't part on the best of terms, exactly. I think Dimple blames me for his loss. Bloody unfair but that's the way people are. Always want to find someone to blame for their own shortcomings.'

Verbal said, 'He's describing himself as an entrepreneur...'

Corker snorted. 'An entrepreneur? Did you hear that, Percy?'

Percy said, 'Credibility, isn't it? He wants credibility.'

Verbal said, 'Got it in one, Uncle Perc. We set Dimps up as Founder and we've got a front man, and he's got credibility.'

Corker said, 'A Minister of the Crown to boot. Brilliant!'

It was agreed that the concept was more than brilliant. It was agreed that the marketing guru would develop some creative concepts, about the brand and so forth. And it was agreed that they needed an urgent meeting with the Minister of Foreign Affairs, which they all agreed, was best left to Verbal Pritchard to arrange.

As they departed the café, both Verbal and Corker shone their torches into the opposite corner. Corker said, 'A certain type of freezer...not your typical whiteware. You'd make it comfy. A pink cushion. Maybe some scent, like flowers...probably have a fake window showing a field, with sheep, or something like that.'

Verbal said, 'Oldies like gardens. And some music. Mozart and so forth. But no wolves.' At which the Pritchard's laughed heartily and the parrot cried, 'Piss off! Bring me a cuppa!'

FOURTEEN

The man-in-the-mirror said, 'So, are you going to meet with them? After what they?'

Dimple brushed his hair. He cleaned his teeth. He paused to stare at the man-in-the-mirror with an expression that might say, 'That'll be the bloody day,' but then turned into an expression that might say, 'Possibly. Or, not. But maybe...' Then he said, 'After what they did to my campaign, I should like to have told Verbal to take his permed hair and his snakeskin pants and chuck himself in the river.'

'But you didn't? Are we being weak, or have we detected some advantage? Though I must say, I cannot see how a Minister of the Crown would gain anything but further calamity from any association with the Pritchard's.'

Dimple said, 'You might well think that. But you are not a wheeler and dealer. You do not have a nose for the main chance. I do. And unless I miss my mark, I'd say there's something afoot. Of course, they'll be wanting something, but I'm alert to that. They'll have seen my rapid rise and now I'm someone they want to get alongside. But things will be different this time. No more being at Corker's beck-and-call. I'll be calling the shots.'

The man-in-the-mirror made no further comment.

*

The Director General of the World Health Organisation was troubled. He had on his desk a copy of the study that seemed to suggest that humanity was going backwards, or more

93

precisely, that people of all ages were becoming measurably more stupid but that white, middle-aged males seemed to be significantly more affected than other cohorts. The DG had discussed the study this past week with his team. They had been unable to decide whether they were looking at an isolated outbreak or something more challenging. They had pondered whether there was a possibility that the outbreak could become an epidemic – or worse…

And now, this very morning, he had received an addition to the original report that had put him completely off his breakfast. The study had been extended across the African continent, the Middle East and Latin America, and in all of these areas, the percentage that said they would prefer that if the moon was to fall, it should fall on Africa or South America, mirrored the Eurasian result except that Latinos, unsurprisingly opted for an African disaster, and vice versa. That was bad enough. That alone added fuel to his worst fears – a Pandemic of Stupidity, to which there was no known antidote. Almost as bad, where the original study had shown that those who were in favour of nuking the moon, despite that this wasn't an option in the study, were white, middle-aged male – the extended study showed quite conclusively, that it was middle-aged males, period. Ethnicity made no difference. Religious beliefs were of no consequence. Even political ideology and socio-economics made no material difference. Communist or Capitalist. Christian, Buddhist, Hindu, Muslim, Atheist…middle-aged males everywhere, overwhelmingly, were in favour of nuking the moon. Soon.

Embarrassed even to ask the question, none-the-less, the DG shortly confirmed that there was no evidence that the moon's trajectory had changed one bit and nor was it expected to. Immediately, the DG convened a high-level working group with experts from every relevant discipline. The DG reminded the team of just how serious the situation was. The world was facing crises in every direction. Every one of these crises

94

required clear thinking, great expertise, and international collaboration. In a word, *intelligence*. In these perilous times, a Pandemic of Stupidity was the DG's nightmare. And here, the world order, with one or two exceptions, was governed almost exclusively by middle-aged men. And what did we now know? That middle-aged men were perfectly prepared to nuke the moon – *as a precaution*. The DG paused and for a moment rested his head in his hand, and at that precise moment, thought '*I* am a middle-aged male…' and coincidentally, he envisioned the moon, on a very bright night, hanging in the heavens with all its ghostly beauty, and then a magnificent explosion occurring…a truly towering mushroom, smack in the middle. So overcome was the DG, he was unable to stop himself exclaiming, in a manner which suggested considerable excitement, '*¡Dios mío!*' Instantly, he apologised and muttered about having had a late night, too much black coffee, and stress. He assigned investigators. He issued directives. He exhorted the team to do whatever was required to bring this thing to heel. Most particularly, he wanted to know where the Epidemic had originated. Had it leaked from a lab? And if so, whose?

The DG returned to his office and closed the door. Silently, he interrogated himself about the nuking vision and why he had experienced a sudden and powerful impulse to press the launch button, and the answer that came back to him repeatedly, was that it was no more or less than because he was a *middle-aged man*. Confused and contrite, the DG sat on the floor behind his desk and assuming the position of the Lotus and commenced a most determined meditation.

*

The Minister of Foreign Affairs made his way to the gaslit corner of the café, where he espied three familiar forms. It

95

would have been considerably better to have had them ushered into his grand office on the sixth floor, but this meeting he decided, should remain clandestine until he had a better idea of the lay-of-the-land. As he approached the Pritchard's table he was startled by the shrill cry, 'Piss off! I'll grab your nuts!'

The Minister cried, 'What in the blazes!' and then espied the large parrot sitting on the table of an elderly woman who wore an expression of complete indifference at her companion's intemperate language. Indeed, the Minister discerned that her eyes were closed.

The Minister said, 'That is a very unruly beast. I shall make a complaint.'

Percy replied, 'I may wind it up.'

'Put it on the list, Percy,' cried Corker, rising from his chair to seize the Minister's hands in effusive greeting. 'How wonderful to see you again, Dimple, my friend and colleague. It truly gladdens my heart! Do sit.' And Corker pulled out a chair for Minister Potts. The Minister of Foreign Affairs could recall no such prior deference or warmth. Not one time had Corker suggested that it was wonderful to see him. He did recall statements such as "Do your job right, Dimple, and we'll see eye-to-eye." But none of that today. Instead, it was, 'What an honour, this is, Mr Potts. A man with one of this country's most important portfolios – a man with weighty matters on his mind that we punters can scarcely imagine, lowering himself to come to meet his old friends and business acquaintances! Humbling it is. Percy, fetch the Minister a coffee. And a bun! Isn't this just a Red-Letter Day, Verbal? Even for a high-profile media man,' he waxed, 'who by comparison is no more than a pimple on my arse, if you'll excuse the expression, Minister. Ha! Ha! Forgetting my place. But this will be a day for Facebook – it most certainly will!'

The Minister found it hard to imagine Corker Pritchard putting anything on Facebook. He could imagine Corker

96

firing off a barrage of colourful tweets licensed by a very broad interpretation of freedom of speech. But he was indifferent. Today, the boot was well and truly on the other foot. And if there was one thing that the Minister had learned in his brief tenure, and it must be said, largely from the PM, it was the value of keeping your counsel so that the other fellow could make a complete fool of him, or herself. So, he said no more than, 'Oh yes,' and 'All's well,' and 'In your court, Corker.' So circumspect was he that afterward, Verbal remarked to his uncle that Dimps had become as tight as a clam and about as readable as The Guardian.

However, when Percy had materialised with a coffee and two buns, Corker made a further abject apology for taking the Minister's valuable time and begged his indulgence such that Corker might *put something on the table*, as it were, that Corker was thinking that the Minister, being also a businessman and an entrepreneur, of note, mark you, might find of at least passing interest. And if not, well, who could blame an old friend wanting to do another old friend a favour. And when in recorded history, and likely even back in the days when a man lived in a cave with bats and so forth – when didn't old friends look out for one another and most especially when it came to the subject of greed and consequently, truly unspeakably large profits – but not your old type of greed. No sir! The only type of greed that Corker, and indeed Percy, and indeed Verbal entertained, nay, were *committed to,* was greed-with-care!

The object of this impassioned and enthusiastic sales pitch remained unnervingly distant.

Corker said, 'Not a moment to waste. You see Percy, Verbal – the Minister is not only the visionary of the wonderful concept of greed-with-care, he's a cool and calculating businessman, such as we'd seen way back in Brewster's Neck, where we forged a friendship as stout as…a very stout thing.'

97

The Minister glanced at his watch, as though to signify that he must remain aware of the time to the minute, in order to keep to his over-booked schedule, when in fact his day was otherwise as clear as the blue sky outside.

Corker said, 'Minister, I've asked Verbal, our media man, to give you a quick run-down on an idea. You see, we're very aware of your entrepreneurial disposition and talents and so forth, and though we've got the *kernel* of an idea, we realised that nothing was likely to happen unless we got a chap with real insight and entrepreneurial ability onboard. Do you see?'

The Minister did see.

Verbal asked if the Minister had seen the study that proved once and for all, that humanity was going backwards, in the sense of being dafter? The Minister had seen some reference. Verbal asked, in a very general way, whether the Minister – but more as Entrepreneur Potts, had considered whether there might not be a solution? An antidote, as it were? Which might represent indeed, an opportunity?

The Minister had not, but thinking quickly, he said that perhaps a vaccine…

Verbal and Corker uttered exclamations of amazement that Entrepreneur Potts had so quickly hit the nail on the head. Verbal said that a *vaccine*, in the generic sense might possibly be several things, but the purpose was to create, or devise or conceive or confabulate, if he might say, or otherwise bring into being, some means by which to counter the rising tide of stupidity. You didn't need to be an egg-head, to see that therein lay a prodigious if not to say a most colossal or indeed, an astronomical business opportunity, whilst being rooted in the inestimable if not to say compassionate concept of greed-with-care.

And Corker cried, 'The name of the game, Minister, is *moral money!'*

Considerably impressed, Entrepreneur Potts recounted that the majority of punters had thought it better for the moon to fall on Africa – rather than, as he personally proposed, that the moon should be nuked forthwith. Evidence enough, that the majority of punters were indeed, imbeciles.

Corker cried, 'Eye to eye, Minister!'

And Entrepreneur Potts began to think that perhaps he and the Pritchard's might share some common something-or-other – though at this point it still seemed somewhat vague. With sudden inspiration, he said, 'A pill?'

Corker pushed back his chair with an expression of amazement. He said, 'Verbal? Do you hear that? Percy? The Minister has just shown us the way. Here were we, thinking that perhaps a vaccine or some such…but a pill! Brilliant! Imagine,' he cried, 'Imagine hopping into your dairy and being able to pick up a packet of pills that would make the average punter smarter? No need for school or intellectual mumbo jumbo that no-one wants. No more Africa – just nuke the problem out of the sky. Who'd miss it? No…simply pop a pill and watch TV. Minister, Dimple, that's why we wanted to plug into your entrepreneurial savvy. Verbal…'

Verbal said, 'Dimple. In our simple and you might well say naïve way, we've been toying with some ideas. Some conception, or intellection, you might say. And one of those theories or hypotheses as an egg-head might say, and just as you've said, is a pill.' Verbal proceeded to open a large pad to display a diagram, which Dimple traversed with his torch. The diagram depicted an oblong pill with one half coloured blue, and the other half red. Above the pill, in speech marks was the word, "Brainee." And beneath the diagram of the pill, were the words, "As taken by Einstein." And beneath that again, the words, "Beat Stupidity with Brainee. Proven by experiments to make a rat as brainy as a horse." And beneath that, "The every-day pill favoured by quantum physicists." And beneath that again, the words, "Contains Brain Booster XL8™"

The Minister of Foreign Affairs and Entrepreneur Potts stared silently at the diagram. Corker Pritchard stared silently at The Minister of Foreign Affairs. Percy Pritchard stared at the nails on his right hand. Verbal Pritchard stared silently into the gloom and thought that a good talk-back topic would be the stupidity of liberals. Indeed, he wondered whether one of the product claims might be, "Experiments show no effect on reptiles and liberals," but perceived that this might unnecessarily limit sales.

The Minister of Foreign Affairs was a little troubled. Had *he* conceived of this pill? He had said that a pill might be the way, *before* Verbal showed him this diagram, so in that sense, it was Dimple's idea. And it came to him that when he had thought of a pill, the words, "Beat Stupidity with Brainee," though not perhaps explicit, were, more-or-less circulating in the back of his mind. On balance then, it could be said that this *was* the idea of Entrepreneur Potts...and that was a very good thing. He said, 'Ah...' and paused.

Corker said quickly, 'Yes, Minister? Dimple?' His hand outstretched in invitation, 'Your initial thoughts? About your brilliant concept?'

Dimple said, 'Yes...I am thinking that the pill is a good idea – a sound idea, with commercial application...'

Corker said, 'Yes. And?'

Dimple said, 'But I don't think we can say that.' He pointed. 'I don't think this would be acceptable. Not at all. People won't want to hear about a rat and a horse. People would think they were being compared to a rat or that they might become as smart as a horse. I believe that people want to be smarter than a horse.'

Corker shook his head in admiration. 'Minister – Dimple, mind like a steel trap. Razor sharp and absolutely on the money. Verbal, cross that off. Rats! Horses! Lunacy! We've got to be a business of integrity. That's what we're about. Greed-with-Care. To be sure, Founder Potts will be making a pile, but why not? He's doing it for the *right* reasons. He's doing it because he cares, about people. About saving themselves from their own dumbness. That's what Founder Potts would be saying. He conceived of this brilliant product out of a deep sense – a deep well of concern for his fellow human – lest his fellow human continues to go backward until his fellow human has a tail. And then who would we have to talk to?' Corker beamed and in further expression of his great esteem, he clasped the Minister's hand and shook it vigorously. 'I hope you realise what you've done, Minister – Dimple. In just a few minutes, you've come up with an innovation that might change the world! And we…' and he gestured toward Percy and Verbal, 'We've stumbled around thinking may be this and may be that, and then you come along, with your entrepreneurial acumen and simply say, that's it. It's a pill and it's Brainee. And not just a pill – a red and blue pill – a bipartisan pill! This is why we needed you, Dimple!'

Entrepreneur Potts was most gratified. He said, 'When do we start?'

Corker cried, 'When do we start? Do you see, boys? This is not a Founder who waves his hands about in some airy-fairy way and then heads off to the bar. This is a Founder who wants to roll up his sleeves and get his hands dirty. Well, Dimple. Welcome aboard. We have our Founder. The man who has created the vision. The man who says, we're on a mission. In this together. And we…your servants, Dimple, we've been muddling about with a bit of plan. Full of holes, but you'll soon put that to rights. But a bit of a look at manufacture, distribution, promotion and a few other things, Crude at this point, though I can say we've got a nice little plant ready for you to just give the word and the pills will start rolling. And as it happens, we've got a couple of major buyers lined up – but nothing's set in stone. The Founder's oversight is required. My word, it is. And a few formalities, Dimple, if we may. Percy?'

Percy opened his briefcase and extracted a sheet of paper and laid it in front of the Founder.

Corker said, 'This makes it official. See, here it says that you are the Founder of the company 'Brainee Ltd,' and here it says that as Founder you have a shareholding of five per cent...hang-on, that's not right, Percy. Five per cent is generous, to a fault you might say, but this is our old friend, Dimple, without whom none of this would even have been conceived. I'm going to take an executive action...' Corker produced his pen and crossed out 'five' and wrote 'ten.' He said, 'I know you'll be thinking I've gone mad, Percy, but it can't be helped. I won't be part of an enterprise, as huge and as successful as it will undoubtedly become, where our Founder has less than ten per cent! There, it's done. And here, Dimple, is where you sign and then we're good-to-go.' He placed his pen in Dimple's hand.

Entrepreneur Potts was astonished. That he had thought Corker Pritchard a charlatan? How uncharitable he had been. Ten per cent – of stupendous profits...Entrepreneur Potts signed on the dotted line. Percy slipped the shareholding agreement into his briefcase, and with a round of handshaking, slaps on the back, and avowals to get the wheels in motion, the entrepreneurial meeting came to a close.

The barista uttered a strange sound of astonishment and dismay. Then he said, looking around helplessly, 'I think this old woman may have died!' The parrot was leaning towards the slumped form and studied it with a beady eye. It said, 'Let's have a cuppa.'

Corker said, 'We won't be back!' And hastily ushered his business associates out the door.

FIFTEEN

The PM stared at the front page of the newspaper with astonishment. The lead article, covering the top half of the page, was dominated by a large photograph of her new Minister of Foreign Affairs and the headline, 'New Minister Proposes Nuking of Moon.' The PM studied the photograph. It reminded her of something. That longish, heavy face. That beetle-brow. That blunt top-of-head with its dense thatch of hair. That grave expression that suggested, what? She wasn't sure. But the whole…conveyed a somewhat monolithic appearance. But never mind – many of the businessmen and indeed, several politicians of her acquaintance were of similar countenance. The PM returned to the article, which made reference to Dimple Potts being the architect of the revolutionary policy , 'Greed-with-Care.' The PM paused and pursed her lips. She recalled very clearly, asking Dimple Potts what his greedy concept meant, in real-life and from a political perspective, and it was quickly apparent that he had not the faintest idea. He waffled for a short-time about greed with integrity and the 'good face of greed,' and then suggested with a distant expression, that the idea was still being developed. The PM had asked by whom? and Potts had stared vacantly for a moment before saying, his Party…

The article quoted several commentators who enthused that it was the most creative idea they had seen in contemporary politics, and they couldn't wait to see how Potts would use it to get this witless Government back on track. The PM sighed.

The article took a different turn. What, it asked, were the foreign policy implications of Potts declaration that in the

103

'right circumstances,' such as in a 'precautionary sense,' it might make sense to 'nuke the moon?' The PM was normally a calm and quite composed sort of person. Ordinarily, she could contemplate inane ideas, of which she saw on average, ten every day, with equanimity. But this was different. This was her new Minister of Foreign Affairs, pedalling not just a bizarre notion that however it was dressed up – greed in any respect was just plain old greed, but now, apparently suggesting that it might be worth contemplating firing a nuclear weapon at the moon. Why? She rose and began pacing her office. She never rose and paced her office. But this was different. Her phone rang. Her Private Secretary said the American Ambassador was on the line. The PM took the call and listened with the feeling that she was trapped in a narrow vertical pipe in which the water was rising up to her neck. The Ambassador said that his Administration was interested in the idea reported today, in the newspaper. The Ambassador said that his Administration would have preferred to have been consulted before a policy announcement of this kind were made publicly, but they understood that this was likely a mere slip-up, what with the Minister of Foreign Affairs being new to his role and so forth. The Ambassador said that Minister Potts's proposal had particularly resonated with the American military and most particularly with a certain General. The Ambassador and his Administration understood that Minister Potts was not proposing some unilateral action – since to the best of the Ambassador's knowledge – and he allowed a little chuckle – the PM did not have nukes at her disposal. But here's the thing, said the Ambassador, the General had said that having this proposal come from such a respected and independent source as the PM's Government, could be the perfect catalyst for advancing a plan currently in consideration in the Pentagon.

The PM wondered whether the call was a spoof – perhaps by one of those child-men who styled themselves shock-jocks. She digressed. She asked about the Ambassador's holiday – where was it again? When she was satisfied that it was indeed the ambassador, she asked what he meant by a 'catalyst exactly.'

The Ambassador said, 'Madam Prime Minister, I wonder if we might arrange a meeting? Soonish? Perhaps tomorrow?'

The PM said that she felt that was more than possible. Privately, she considered that such a meeting was extremely urgent indeed.

*

Founder Potts looked at the door. In particular, he gazed at the discreet, but not too discreet metal-plate on the door. The plate announced, 'Founder.' The sign on the outside of the building, above the entrance, said, 'Brainee Ltd. Smarter People Tomorrow.'

Corker said, 'Enter, Mr Founder, it's your office.'

Founder Potts opened the door and regarded the large office, dominated by a large, dark wooden desk. Corker encouraged the Founder to try the executive chair. Founder Potts found it to be very much to his liking. He swivelled the chair towards the large window and the view towards the park. This was indeed an exclusive address. Corker Pritchard sat in the visitor's chair. He looked up to the Founder and the Founder looked down on him. It was an aspect very much to the Founder's liking. The Founder enquired what title Corker had? Was it CEO? Was it President Pritchard? No, cried Corker emphatically. Corker was Nobody. No-one would even know he was here. A back-room man, beyond even the back-room. A total nobody and why not? The company had its Founder and frankly, under the Founder's leadership, they needed only a handful of rather minor functionaries, such as a bean counter, in which capacity Percy would serve admirably, and a marketing guru, which would be Verbal; and a chemical whizzo, who was a woman by the name of Aretha Titsman – indeed, Doc Titsman.

The Founder started. 'Titsman, you say? Do you know anything about her? Do you know, my neighbour carries that very name? And she's tried to sue me? A woman who possesses a blasted hound called Doc Cod? Titsman!'

'What a coincidence, Dimple! Another of life's funny little mysteries – six degrees of separation and all that. But our Doc Titsman has just arrived from Albania, and she has no family here. Knows her chemistry though – my word, she does. Knows how to bake a cake and so forth. Very sophisticated. Had to leave Albania I believe, but everyone deserves a second chance. Where would we be if no-one could have a second chance? You'd have no Government for starters. And half of industry would close over-night. The clergy would be gone and so would the Queen, most likely. Not to mention yours truly. Am I to be cast out forever? No – and why not? Because we give punters a second chance. That's the way of a civilised society, Dimple.' Corker paused to allow the Founder to digest the truth in these earnest sentiments. Then he added, 'That's progress, isn't it? I won't be surprised if the eggheads discover that trees misbehave.'

But Corker had had enough of Doc Titsman and the coincidence and trees, and the necessity of allowing a second-chance. He glanced around the bare walls and apologised that they had not introduced any suitable decoration for the Founder's office. Time was of the essence, he said, and the Founder agreed entirely that time was indeed of the essence. The focus, the Founder said, having also moved on from the Titsman coincidence, and with a most determined expression, must be on *action*. The focus must be on the *means of production* and not such frippery as the decoration of the Founder's office. Nonetheless, he wondered whether that

106

large wall-space, over there, might not be greatly enhanced by a large landscape of some sort. Or an abstract perhaps? Had Corker Nobody seen the painting of a woman riding a crustacean, by the way? But not to worry about that now, since time, and the means of production were of the essence. Even so, replied Corker Nobody, and agreeing one hundred per cent with the Founder about time and all that, even so, getting the Founder's work-space – the place of brain-storming and creativity, leadership and new thoughts and so forth – of a kind that would undoubtedly drive this company forward, why, that was equally, if not more important. Indeed, Corker Nobody would insist that the marketing dork, Ha! Ha! would make space in his terribly busy day – and too bad that the marketing dork was on a terribly tight deadline to get their first marketing brochure out – he would find time this very day, to acquire some suitably inspirational art, for the Founder's office wall. He would instruct the marketing dork to look out for a painting of a woman riding something…

The Founder felt well-pleased and mentioned that he already had the platypus, but insisted that the means of production be attended to first. After-all, observed the Founder most sensibly, 'No pill, no bill!'

'Ha! Ha!' cried Corker Nobody. 'I like it! No pill, no bill. Percy and Verbal must hear about this. A pearl of wisdom from the Founder – on the very first morning. One would expect no less.' He paused to compose a tweet.

Corker Nobody led the way down a long corridor, past the small offices of minor functionaries that as yet had no name-plates at all. Through another door and down some steel steps they came into a large white-panelled space in which there was a confusion of stainless-steel piping and vats and screw-drives and pots and conveyors and fillers and so forth. And moving in and out of this confusion, ghostly masked figures, all in white moved silently here and there – turning this dial, pushing this button, adjusting this thermostat or

107

control, and examining this or that mechanical process as the whole intricacy emitted hums and hisses and clanks and other sounds of industry. Founder Potts was agape – though the casual observer would not have apprehended that he was agape since the Founder resembled more a monolith in a meditative state. But agape he was. He nodded approvingly and said, 'Good work, Corker. You've certainly got things moving along…but I wonder if that light…' he gestured at a spotlight that shone onto a large vat. 'I wonder if that light might not be better pointing a bit to the left?'

Corker Nobody pursed his lips and squinted and then exclaimed, 'Why didn't I see that! My word, Dimple, an eye like an eagle!' He seized the arm of a passing ghost and passed on an urgent instruction, and the ghost hastened to find a ladder to execute the Founder's astute idea about the light pointing a little more to the left.

Founder Potts walked around the conglomeration of steel and paused by a chute from which spilled a continuous stream of red and blue pills. Bipartisan pills! Corker Nobody laughed and made it very clear that it was permissible for the Founder to take up a pill. Handfuls of pills if he so wished. They were, after-all, the Founder's pills!

Founder Potts examined the oblong pill closely. Corker Nobody observed that everybody loved pills. Two-tone pills, he said, were better than those that were of one colour. People understood that two colours denoted higher functionality than single-colour and therefore lesser pills. Founder Potts agreed that this pill looked to be a very serious pill. Which is what one would expect if one was looking to gain more intelligence. How could anyone expect to properly counter stupidity with a pill of just one colour?

Corker Nobody congratulated the Founder on his perspicacity. The Founder asked wherein was the special ingredient, Brain Booster XL8? Was it in the red part or the blue part? Personally, he would most expect it to be in the red part.

Corker Nobody clapped a hand on the Founder's shoulder and cried that the Founder second-guessed everything at a glance. Of course, Brain Booster XL8 was in the red part! And why? Because the chemical whizzo had already suggested that the Founder would want the special active ingredient not in the blue, but in the red! That, added Corker Nobody with great warmth, is the conservative end of the pill! And how much the Founder's vision infused every aspect of the Founder's brainchild. This, cried Corker Nobody waving his arms at the hissing and humming production line – this was Founder Potts's Brainee Ltd, in production!

For a brief moment, Founder Potts reflected on his previous entrepreneurial ideas. He briefly recalled Doc Cod running through the hole in the fence, minus the hair on his hindquarters. He shuddered momentarily as the image of a headless Glaswegian emerged from beneath the Barbomatic. He dismissed instantly his recollection of the wife of the man-four-doors-down on-the-right, disparaging the visionary ideas of the ladder with no rungs and the hammer without a head. But now? Here was the fruition – the pinnace of his entrepreneurial talents and drive and determination to rise above the average punter – that truly ordinary plonk who was content to be told what to do, day-in and day-out as he raised his family. Just as these nameless ghosts tending to his machinery of production, here in Brainee Ltd, were doomed to clock-in and clock-out. This, the Founder reflected, was their fate for simply being lesser kinds of beings. The Founder meanwhile, moved on a higher plane invisible to the lesser kind of being, and enjoyed the deserved fruits of his vision. A torrent of riches. Such were the thoughts of Founder Potts as he admired the apparatus that was his modest contribution to Changing the World.

How could it be? Asked Dimple over dinner, that the protesters outside his residence, could be so unaware that they were protesting against the Minister of Foreign Affairs and the Founder of Brainee Ltd? What did Mildred Titsman and Doc Cod think?

Dimple's wife suggested that perhaps if Dimple were to apologise...

'Apologise?' cried Dimple. 'I cleaned that woman's dog. And now what? She holds a placard saying, 'Potts is a Phoney.' That, by the way, is a most unprepossessing sort of dog. Frankly, I had to advise that-boy-two-doors-down-on-the-left, which end was which. In my opinion, the end that now has no fur is the better-looking part – but he insists on sitting on it. Is that my fault?'

It was hair, rather than fur, Dimple's wife corrected, and suggested that perhaps Mildred felt aggrieved, not so much at the cleaning and perhaps not even so much about the loss of hair, but that Dimple had snatched Doc Cod off her veranda without asking. Dimple rolled his eyes. What was Dimple's wife suggesting? That Doc Cod preferred to be an unclean dog? That Doc Cod could not have exercised his right to be left alone? Did Doc Cod bite the arm of the boy-two-doors-down-on-the-left? No, he did not. Anyway, Dimple declared, with finality, right now he was concerned with higher things – much higher things. The fact was, he concluded, that Doc Cod was likely more intelligent than many of the people who were in desperate need of the pill he was currently making. He added that the kindest thing anyone could do for Mildred Titsman, was to prescribe her a course of Brainee. Perhaps Dimple's wife could offer – free-of-charge, which was magnanimous by anyone's reckoning.

Dimple's wife had no comment about that, but she expressed surprise that the Minister of Foreign Affairs might have anything to do with Corker Pritchard. She was also surprised that Corker Pritchard might make anything for anyone, that could be beneficial and safe.

Dimple shook his head sadly. 'I can understand, at one level, why you might think that, but you are not privy to the information that I am privy to. And nor is yours the mind of an entrepreneur. I do not mean to diminish you, we are what we are, but you must be aware that the entrepreneurial mind, such as mine, looks past the obvious. And in fact, when I look back at the events in Brewster's Neck, I have asked myself, was Corker unjustly maligned and the answer that comes back, is that yes, he was. How could he be expected to keep out a nosey dog? Dogs are naturally nosey animals. This is the way it is for dogs. And if that busy-body of a beekeeper hadn't told the entire town that Nostril had gone into Forest Flavours sausages, none would have been the wiser or worse off. It is true that Corker likely should have noted possums and suchlike, as ingredients on his labelling, but show me the company that's perfect? And he's paid his fine and everyone deserves a second chance. That's my philosophy. So, you know, I look past these trivial concerns. I look at the bigger picture – which happens to be a global outbreak of stupidity. It has a medical name, you know? *Alta Stultitia.* And I conceived of a pill that contains a secret active ingredient that Corker discovered in the darkest jungles of the Amazon. Brain Booster XL8 it's called. So, you see? My entrepreneurial vision and Corker's ingredient, and the pill, Brainee, will help to shift the bell curve to the right. The dunce will become normal. The normal may become a genius. Even Mildred...'

Dimple paused to sip his coffee and at the moment his wife opened her mouth to speak, he continued, 'And we will become rich.'

Dimple's wife replied as she passed a cup of coffee that the PM's office had called, because he hadn't answered his phone. Dimple checked his phone and said it was on silent because he had been on more pressing business down at his factory. At which place, he added, he had a larger office than the one assigned to the Minister of Foreign Affairs.

*

The Head of News denounced his colleagues in The Press. He waved the newspaper at his team. He exhorted them to consider the free-ride that Public Potts received from the journalists at The Press. Where, he demanded, were the searching questions about why it might be a good idea to nuke the moon? Nowhere to be seen. Where, he cried was the in-depth interrogation about the entrepreneurship espoused by Positive Potts? And, neatly sidestepping, again – he added darkly, staring at his Senior Reporter – the denuding of the hapless hound, Doc Cod. The Head of News fell into a fug. He wondered silently why it was that reporters these days were such patsies. In his day, a chap asked the hard questions. A chap didn't just accept whatever piffle was thrown out by the likes of Piffling Potts. A chap demanded evidence, reasoning and straight answers. The Head of News wondered suddenly, whether he was witnessing symptoms of the Outbreak of Stupidity referred to by the World Health Organisation, here in his own studio. It was an unpleasant thought. He glanced around the table. Not one of them had spoken up. Why? In his day, a chap would speak up and hang the consequences. Surely to goodness he wasn't already a victim of Staff Stupidity?

The Head of News said, 'I want a hard-hitting interview. Live at Six. I don't want to witness another game of dodgeball. I want Peripatetic Potts put on the mat.' He stared hard at the Senior Reporter.

The Senior Reporter said, 'I'm on it.'

SIXTEEN

The Minister of Foreign Affairs was ushered into the Office of the Prime Minister. The PM introduced the Minister to the American Ambassador. The PM said that the Ambassador had been interested in something the Minister had said. The Ambassador said that his Administration looked forward to a warm and productive relationship. The Ambassador was silently impressed. There were too many politicians with weak chins and big eyes. Minister Potts did not have a weak chin. This man had a chin you could trust and eyes that could reduce to slits in an instant. Minister Potts looked like the Ambassador's sort of chap. Not too bright, possibly, but when push-came-to-shove, you didn't need a boffin. You needed an immovable object with a firm jawline who could laugh when a bridge collapsed.

The Ambassador began by explaining just how impressed was the Military, with the Minister's proposal that the moon should be nuked. Flattered though he was, the Minister began to say that it wasn't a proposal exactly, but more of an off-the-cuff…

But the Ambassador waved away the Minister's modesty. The Ambassador leaned forward as though to express a great confidence. The thing was, the Ambassador said in a lowered voice, such that the PM wondered whether she was meant to be privy to this conversation, the thing was, that the Military knew that the Chinese had had the exact same thought. And, the Ambassador added, so too, the Russians…

The Ambassador left this implication dangling. The PM said, 'Ambassador? Surely you are not suggesting, seriously, that anyone should fire a weapon at the moon?'

The Ambassador sat up with a mildly pained expression. He had been forewarned, of course, that this woman would likely try to interfere. It simply proved the point, about jaw-lines and so forth. The Ambassador assured the PM that this was not about war or anything like it. It was the opposite. It was about all the nuclear-armed nations openly and honestly, testing their weapons in a totally safe and open way – to keep the World safer. The fact was, he continued, that several companies were close to initiating mining operations on the moon. Private companies funded by various billionaires. And what that meant, was that there was a rapidly closing window of opportunity. Clearly, the Prime Minister would understand that it would be difficult – nay, impossible to nuke the moon if there were people mining there? It stood to reason.

The PM was silent for a moment. She felt, suddenly, light-headed. She felt somewhat like she did, those many years ago when she had smoked a joint. Momentarily, she wondered whether the Ambassador had been smoking a joint – this morning. The PM said that she found it impossible to imagine why anyone would want to nuke the moon, whether there were mining companies there or not – and by the way, what international understandings were there about mining the moon, let alone committing wilful acts of violence against a celestial body? The moon, said the PM quite forcefully, belongs to us all – it belongs to humanity. It is central to the cultures of many peoples. How could anyone seriously entertain nuking what was a revered by children and people of all ethnicities and persuasions?

The Ambassador massaged one of his fingers as he listened to this impassioned speech. He glanced at the Minister of Foreign Affairs and exchanged a knowing look. This was the thing. Certain types of chaps simply knew when they were on the same page. They didn't even need to speak. Certain types of chaps could be in great pain, and certain other chaps simply understood and there was no need for all that sympathetic twaddle. This was the kind of knowing glance exchanged by the Ambassador and the Minister of Foreign Affairs.

The Ambassador said evenly, 'All excellent points, Prime Minister. But we're in the twenty-first century. Worshipping a nearby rock isn't part of the twenty-first century. And in the twenty-first century, well, the fact is that big is generally better. And in this case, the biggies, as it were, are of a like mind. And with the greatest respect in the world, Prime Minister, your country is not one of the biggies. But…' and the Ambassador paused to ensure that his next words conveyed proper emphasis, 'Your country nonetheless has a very important role to play. And that's because your Minister of Foreign Affairs has hit the nail on the head. Nuclear weapons must be tested. For far too long now, we've relied on simulations. The fact is we need a live test, and I'm absolutely certain, Prime Minister that you would not condone for a moment, a live test here on Earth. Who would? It would be madness! No, that's why your Minister's proposal is both incredibly astute and timely. We need to act soon and our information is that it's not just the Chinese and the Russians onboard – the others – the Brits, the North Koreans, the Indians…they're all onboard. So, what we're looking for, from our new friend, Minister Potts, is a forceful declaration that a controlled nuking of the moon, quite properly under the auspices of the United nations, is in the world's best interest.'

The PM felt numb. She felt numb in her fingers and her legs. She felt numb in her mind and even in her tongue. She felt as she sometimes had, as a child, caught in one of those unpleasant dreams when she was about to fall off a cliff. The PM thought with great alarm, 'I'm paralysed.'

*

What the PM experienced at that moment, was what the Director General of the WHO had been apprised by his immunologists and other medical experts, as a little-known condition called Torpor. That the PM hadn't slumped to the floor, was testament to her very robust immune system, which in this case, the experts believed, was linked to the degree of strength of her mind. For victims with lesser strength of mind, Torpor generally proved to be instantly fatal.

The Director General's experts were still endeavouring to define the true nature of Torpor, but they had concluded that the condition was directly linked to Alta Stultitia, and that it required a Vector. The Vector, they surmised, might be virtually undetectable. The Vector likely suffered from Alta Stultitia but unlike those who simply displayed increasing symptoms of stupidity, was able to transmit Torpor to others, whose unique susceptibility frequently resulted in their untimely death. Cases of untimely death with no obvious cause, were being notified to the WHO from all over the world. The only common factor that the Director General's experts had thus far identified, led the Director General's experts to suspect that the Vectors of Torpor were, more likely than not, to be that cohort comprising older males of all ethnicities and persuasions.

*

The Chair asked sniffily, when he might have an audience with the Minister? Since the election and elevation of Candidate Potts, the now Minister of Foreign Affairs had disappeared – from his Party. But here he was on the front page of The Press and making strange statements about the moon. What had the bloody moon got to do with tax? The moon was irrelevant. Taxes were here and now and frankly,

117

everywhere! Taxes were the surest way to degrade gold. Taxes were a liberal disease expressly designed to suffocate the honest endeavours of those who understood how important it was to be rich. And not just rich. Bloody rich. Wasn't that what Greed-with-Care was about?

The Chair stared balefully at the newspaper. Potts had barely mentioned the Party's new and revolutionary policy platform. The Chair had a sudden and unpleasant thought. Perhaps Potts had pulled the rug over his eyes – the Chair's eyes? It was easy enough to pull the rug over the eyes of the Committee, but the Chair? Perhaps Potts was a Pretender, who had played the Committee like a fish, to get their endorsement. To stand on the proud ticket of the First Union of Conservative Thinkers, but with no real intention to crash headlong into the wall of taxes that threatened decent people like a tsunami? The Chair shuddered. And now, that bastard wasn't returning his calls. What was he up to? What little game was Potts playing? Well, the Chair wouldn't have it. He turned on the News. He did not like the look of the News Anchor. She reeked liberal from every pore.

The Chair sat bolt upright. He cried, 'Good God! It's him!'

Indeed, it was the Minister of Foreign Affairs, sitting with one leg crossed over the other, hands gently clasped and with a dignified expression, giving way to a slight but dignified chuckle in response to some off-air remark by the interviewer. Then, the Senior Reporter turned to the camera and welcomed viewers to this special edition of 'News-Blast-it-All,' and then with a warm smile, asked the Minister of Foreign Affairs, why it was that a country with no nuclear weapons, was promoting that they be fired at the moon? The Minister was grave. The Minister was suitably reflective. The Minister said that in his capacity as Minister, there were certain things about which he could not speak. He was sure the Senior Reporter would understand. 'That, said,' continued the Minister, he realised completely that the honest and hard-working people at home, deserved some insight into the heady nature of international politics and diplomacy. The Chair was mesmerised. The Chair wondered how it was that the ex-mayor of a hamlet no-one could locate, could now be beaming into his living room and speaking of international diplomacy. The Senior Reporter replied that she understood, but believed she had an obligation to the honest and hard-working people at home, to ask whether shooting things at the moon was Government policy? The Head of News said in her ear, 'Good question. Ask him about the PM's agenda.'

The Minister hesitated. He did not hesitate because of the gravity of the question. He hesitated because he had just seen one of the grips, slide to the floor and remain there completely motionless. The Minister wondered whether he should say something, but he didn't wish to interrupt the interview, so he made a small pointing gesture in the direction of the grip. The Chair saw this small pointing motion and shook his head slowly with an expression of resignation. The Senior Reporter saw the gesture and thought that her subject was cracking – which was an excellent sign. She repeated her question. The Minister looked up as if in surprise and said, 'Government policy? Goodness, no. How could the Government have a policy to nuke the moon when as you observe yourself, we have no nukes.' The Minister glanced back at the recumbent form at the rear of the studio. No-one seemed to have noticed. The Minister again tried to make a surreptitious gesture that might draw someone's attention to the ailing grip. The Chair groaned. The Senior Reporter asked if it wasn't Government policy, what were the PM's views?

The Minister wondered whether the grip had had a heart failure, but she looked to be little more than twenty. Heart failure would be a very strange thing, and he said so. The Senior Reporter was excited. An enormous scoop might be happening this very instant. She said, 'Pardon, Minister? Heart failure? Are you sure?'

The Minister said that he was no expert, but the way she had collapsed – just a short time ago…

The Senior Reporter was very excited. The Head of News shouted in her ear, 'Terminate the interview. We'll cut to the Hospital,' and then he shouted at the backroom team, 'Dig up the PM's eulogy. I want it ready to go to air within ten minutes. Get the PM's Office on the line.'

The Minister was shepherded quickly out of the studio. As he passed down the corridor, he said. 'Quite extraordinary. She's so young!'

The Chair was stupefied. What a way to announce the PM's predicament – indeed, possibly, her death…Potts was nothing if not a loose cannon. First, shooting the moon and now this. But here, on his screen, was the PM. Smiling and very much alive. No, she said firmly, she had not collapsed and as far as she knew, she was in robust health, thank you. Did Minister Potts say that? Perhaps he had been misunderstood. He was under considerable pressure at present. It was a big portfolio and he was still getting his feet under the table.

The Chair wondered if the Potts was having a breakdown of some kind. It would not be surprising. Most likely he had never had to deal with anything more significant than a blocked pipe.

The Head of News shouted, 'What a monumental cock-up! That bastard's wandered off having implied that nuking the moon is an international issue and you…' he pointed at the Senior Reporter, 'You let him go! We know nothing about the PM's view on all this and we learned nothing except what everyone already knew – the PM is in good health.'

The Senior Reporter said, 'But you told me to terminate-'

The Head of News cried, 'Of course I told you to terminate. Your interview led the entire country to believe the PM was down. Did you not think to look where he was pointing? He was *pointing,* for God's sake!'

The Senior Reporter knew it was entirely useless to argue, but she felt she must make some effort. She said that the *way* he was pointing, was not a normal way of pointing. The Head of News cried, 'What's a normal way of pointing. Like this? *With a finger?* Wasn't that what he was doing?'

The Senior Reporter agreed that that was the *normal* way of pointing, but the Minister hadn't pointed quite like that. The Senior Reporter did her best to emulate the way in which the Minister had pointed. She assumed a meaningful expression and repeated the gesture. The Head of News watched with incredulity. Feeling decidedly foolish, the Senior Reporter said, 'I actually wondered whether he was trying to… scratch himself. And I didn't want to draw attention to that.'

Once again, the Head of News fell into a fug. In his day, even if a chap suspected that the interviewee was trying to scratch his nuts on prime-time television, he would have looked, carefully. As a consequence of this journalistic diligence, in his day, the grip would have been discovered more quickly. Not necessarily before she passed away, but certainly before a chopper had put another reporter on the front steps of the Hospital to make ludicrous statements about the PM's plight. And certainly, before the PM had come on-screen in a most jocular mood to make the channel look like a troupe of gibbering baboons. The Head of News-Blast-it-All, decided to call it a night.

The Chair sat in his favourite chair with a whisky to hand. His expression was sober and reflective. What, he asked himself, was Pott's' game? Was he so overweeningly ambitious that he would seek to publicly create doubt in the punter's mind, about the PM's health? It was a clever tactic.

Once the punter had it in his mind that the PM was ailing, the PM would never be able to fully refute it. The punter was a firm believer in no-smoke-without-fire. The average punter would instantly begin to think about who would be the *next* PM. And who might they think of – a Minister of Foreign Affairs who was becoming the international spokesperson for a tactical strike on the moon? A notion that like Greed-with-Care, was finding rather broad appeal. A man of action, they might be thinking. If there was anything the average punter liked, it was a *Man of Action.*

The Chair found himself to be impressed once again. He had misjudged. Potts was already manoeuvring to oust his boss. Clever...

The Chair turned his thoughts towards the moon. He mused as he sipped his whisky, about nuclear warheads crashing into the moon. A novel idea to be sure, but without a doubt, it would be quite something to see. And what would it matter? Once the mushroom clouds had subsided, who would be able to tell the difference? The moon was already covered in holes. The Chair idly imagined the mushroom clouds. Given the moon's very thin atmosphere, presumably the mushroom clouds would rise faster and much further...it was an intriguing thought.

SEVENTEEN

The Secretary of State looked up from the dossier on her desk. The General gazed at the wall over her shoulder in that unnervingly stolid way that the Secretary was beginning to understand was the military way. Idly, she wondered what it would be like to *live* with a Five-Star General, and instantly vanquished the thought as completely preposterous. The Secretary gathered her thoughts. This thing seemed to be gathering unstoppable momentum. This dossier implied that to naysay the proposal to nuke the moon would be tantamount to treachery. Indeed, the dossier explicitly stated, 'The benefits to the international community of cooperation and mutual management of complex systems and outcomes are such that the Pentagon believes the proposal should be implemented with all possible speed.'

Where did that leave one, the Secretary mused? However, needs must. The Secretary said, 'General, the proposal is persuasive.'

After a decent interval the General said, 'Madam Secretary. We believe it is in the best interests of our great country.'

The Secretary said, 'The necessary agreements seemed to have been reached...' Privately she thought, why didn't I know that the Australians had become a nuclear power? 'Yes, so, the Chinese are all for it...'

The General said, 'The Chinese especially. We know they've been wanting to test their newest bomb for some time. The Russians are set to go. The North Koreans. Pretty much everyone.'

The Secretary said, 'But the French...'

The General said dismissively, 'The French are maintaining that the proposal is an act of international vandalism and won't participate. In some quarters it's believed that they're simply not ready and don't want to be embarrassed. That is not a view I hold. This is a bare-faced attempt to take the moral high-ground. Trying to curry favour with the Africans and to get one back at the USA. But they'll line up.'

The Secretary said, 'Is that something that we've canvassed…thoroughly – the ethical aspects…'

The General said, 'With respect, Madam Secretary, ethics are the bottom-line here. It is the view of the Pentagon, and myself, that it would be distinctly *unethical* to continue to maintain a defensive arsenal that we could not assure our constituents, and our enemies most particularly, and not to mention our allies, that our arsenal is not ready and capable at all times.'

The Secretary said, 'Well, when you put it like that…' She glanced again at the list of recommendations and immediate actions. She continued, 'This Minister of Foreign Affairs…Dimple Potts. I take it we've met with him and his Government?'

The General said, 'Our Ambassador had a fruitful exchange. We believe this part of the program is ten-ten.'

The Secretary assumed from his manner, though that hadn't changed discernibly, that ten-ten was a good score. She said, 'So, he will put the proposal at the Security Council, as an independent spokesperson with no vested interest? And the Council will, as you say, gratefully acknowledge the good sense of the Minister's proposal and will accept it. Yes…' The Secretary wondered silently, why it was that she simply couldn't can this absurdity, right now. She said, 'There's a reference here to 'Big Boy…' The Secretary was aware that the two bombs dropped on Japan, were Fat Man and Little Boy. She wondered how it was that the military mind could apply with such insouciance, such familial names to the most brutally destructive weapons humankind had ever produced.

For the first time, the General's demeanour changed. It wasn't animated exactly, but there was a flicker of something. Almost sly, or supercilious, perhaps. Or pride…

The General said, 'Madam Secretary, not even our friends know about Big Boy. The Chinese and the Russians certainly don't. The others…they can create craters. In the case of the Chinese and the Russians, pretty big craters. But Big Boy…' For a moment the General seemed lost for words. 'Big Boy, Madam Secretary, will take out a mountain. In fact, that's our intention. Our rocket will be the last up there. We're planning to run the program alphabetically. That means the Aussies will go first. The Chinese think they're going to give us a surprise but we'll have the final word.' To the Secretary's surprise, there came a flicker of a smile to the General's lips, but it vanished so quickly she wondered whether she had detected it at all. The General continued, 'We don't doubt, Madam Secretary, that they'll move some rock – but we know *how much* rock. They have no idea what Big Boy will move. That's part of our strategic mission. To scare the bejesus out of all of them.'

The Secretary examined her nails. She examined the veins on the back of her hand. She removed her spectacles for a moment to massage the bridge of her nose. For no reason she could think of, she had a sudden vision of playing on her family's farm in Montana, with her beloved dog Betsy. She recalled rolling on the grass with Betsy and both of them laughing. The Secretary reluctantly forced herself to concentrate on the dossier. Scaring the daylights out of one's enemies is what the US did best. She reached for her pen and signed her authority for the program, "The Moon will Pay." She wondered what the moon had done to offend the military. She wondered further, whether it was because the military had failed, in 1959, for Heaven's sake, to gain support for an enterprise just such as this. Surely, it was a long time to hold a grudge against an inanimate object? The Secretary passed the dossier to the General.

The General rose, saluted and departed the Secretary's office.

The Secretary of State stood motionless for some time. Then she returned to her chair and picked up the phone. She said, 'Hi Mom. Just wondered how you're getting on?'

*

In the War Room of the WHO, a most significant conference was taking place. The DG had called together Field Operatives from all over the world. Such a gathering was unusual, for it was both difficult and expensive to assemble one hundred and ninety-two, at one time and in one place and consequently, a meeting of this kind was called only when the DG and his senior team considered that they were on the brink of a crisis.

The DG did not stand on ceremony. He said, 'Welcome. We're on the brink of a crisis. But we don't want to create panic. We must communicate our advice to world governments extremely carefully. And ironically, it is the nature of this crisis that makes what we say and do, all the more sensitive.' The DG paused to scan his audience. Black faces. Brown faces. Yellow faces. White faces. Concerned faces. Apprehensive. Attentive. Determined. Agitated. Distracted...as well they might be. But with growing consternation, the DG apprehended several expressions that could only be described as bovine. The DG felt a sudden flush such that he must loosen his collar. The DG thought, 'I must think...are any of these people Vectors...' He said, 'At this point, I think we will take a tea-break.'

The moment he said this, the DG caught himself. Why did he call a tea break two minutes after the commencement of the conference? Was he giving the Field Operatives time to digest the gravity and import of his words? But what had he said beyond that they could be facing a crisis? What kind of crisis? He hadn't said. The DG was bemused and increasingly embarrassed because he sensed that somehow, he had just done something that was remarkably witless, at which thought he uttered an involuntary groan. Fortunately, the field operatives were queuing for coffee, which of course was not ready since the caterers were not expecting a coffee break for another hour and a half. Which was normal. But this was not normal. This was a crisis.

The DG asked an attendant to ring the bell. The Field Operatives were confused. First, the DG had called a tea break, and now, two minutes later the bell rang for proceedings to recommence. Only four Field Operatives had managed to secure a lukewarm cup of coffee. In several places this caused some mild resentment, which in one case, resulted in the Lithuanian Field Operative having his elbow accidentally jolted, and consequently, much of the coffee was spilled. A brief altercation occurred in which the Field Operative from Wales, was berated as a poksi mažas skaičius, which translates roughly as a 'poxy little number.' But the satisfaction of having deprived the Lithuanian resulted only in the Field Operative from Wales giving up a self-satisfied smirk.

When once again he faced many seated faces, the DG said, 'As you now know, we have on our hands what we in the WHO, call a Crisis, which is just one step below an Epidemic. You will all recall what happened with Covid. We were circumspect. We were perhaps, unduly cautious. In our concern not to create panic we succeeding in creating panic. You will recall that we listened to the Chinese. With the greatest respect to our Chinese Operative, we listened rather than acted perhaps, for too long.'

The Field Operative from China was about to leap to his feet and to shout with great indignation that this was a grave insult to the People's Republic. Such comments were disrespectful of the Chinese leadership and a typical Western slight and an example of wrong-thinking that would cause loss of face. But he didn't leap to his feet and he didn't say anything, because at that moment he was overwhelmed by Torpor and without the slightest of movements, he expired. And this was not discovered until sometime later, by the Field Operative from Northern Ireland.

Meanwhile, the DG was reflecting about the criticism levelled at the WHO, and himself over the whole Covid debacle. Declaring an Epidemic, let alone a Pandemic, was an extremely serious thing. The DG wanted evidence and lots of it. He was still assembling that evidence when it became apparent without need of any formal declaration, that the Covid horse had bolted. The DG did not like seeing a bolting horse in any circumstance. A horse was a big animal and a horse could be clumsy. If you put big hooves together with a not very big brain, a bolting horse was not a pretty sight.

The DG gazed gravely at his audience. He said, 'What we don't want to see is a bolting horse.'

The assembled Field Operatives digested carefully the DG's words. There might possibly be a crisis. There was an early tea break in which virtually no-one could get a coffee and the Field Operative from Wales was still smirking. And now, the Field Operatives were made to understand that they needed to be particularly alert to the possibility of, and the desirability of stopping, or at least avoiding, a bolting horse. These words resonated very strongly with the Field Operative from Iceland who had never seen a horse, except in movies, and he wondered whether the spectacle of a bolting horse should not be on his bucket list.

The DG said, 'The WHO needs to act pre-emptively. The WHO needs to be *seen* to be acting pre-emptively. This is the reason I have called you all here now, and not next week, or next month for that matter. Though had I called this conference next month, we would have achieved a considerable saving on airfares. The reality is, we were gouged. Airlines everywhere gouged us because we made these bookings at the last minute – and because we're the WHO. It's outrageous but it's the way of things and I invite you not to be upset. I myself, *was* upset but only for a short time. I am sure that you can all imagine how much better we would all be, in all countries, of all races, ethnicities and persuasions, if we weren't constantly gouged by airlines. I'll not single anyone out, but suffice to say that the cost of getting the Irish Field Operative to this conference, was about the same as setting up a field hospital in Mali.'

The DG paused to regather his thoughts. He felt that he may have wandered from the point. He gazed at the assembly and it came to him that it looked not unlike the assembly at his old school. Indeed, in a rush of nostalgia, it was on the tip of his tongue to ask the assembly to join him in a joyful rendition of 'Here I kneel before you,' but reminding himself sharply that he had been an atheist ever since school, caught himself in time. It occurred to the DG that had he not caught himself, he would have been guilty of a rather stupid thing and that reminded him, with another jolt, that that was exactly why this assembly was here.

The DG said, 'The reason we believe we may have a Crisis, is that it appears we may be seeing the first evidence of an outbreak of *Alta Stultitia* – commonly known as Deep Stupidity. Although Alta Stultitia is known to us, this outbreak may be the worst we've seen for nearly ninety years. There have been lesser outbreaks. Field Operatives will recall Y2K. I myself waited until midnight at the turn of the Century to see if my computer would crash. I was not alone. Certainly, we at the WHO were alert to the possibility that a new strain of Brain Fog was abroad, but thankfully, though near global in effect, the outbreak disappeared and our medical experts concluded that the outbreak was a direct result of allowing tech-heads to speak to the media. I am pleased to say that on the recommendation of the WHO, most tech companies now have a policy whereby tech-heads have no access to a phone or if they do, media contacts are blocked.' The DG raised his hand in appreciation of the applause at this win for the WHO. He continued, 'Which brings me to this present outbreak, which in some ways is more insidious. As you know, the first manifestation was the international study that showed that a majority of people think that if the moon were to fall, it would be best to fall on Africa, because Africa would be less likely to sink than South America, and if it fell in the Sahara, it would hardly be noticed because that's dry sand and so on, like the moon.' The DG paused before continuing, 'This comes within the standard guidelines defining stupidity. Clearly, it is stupid to answer a question about something you do not have the faintest notion is remotely possible. To wit – the moon falling. On the other hand, the Sahara is large and it is mostly barren, so, it is not unreasonable to speculate that it might be better for the moon to fall there, rather than elsewhere. However, the Sahara is only 1800 kilometres wide, which would not accommodate the moon, and thus, stupidity rooted in ignorance may be denoted. Or possibly an optical illusion with regards to the Mercator projection and so forth. But mainly, we think, this is evidence of ignorance. Ignorance is important, because it muddies our definition and measurement of stupidity. Which leads us to the other major and disturbing finding. The study showed that nearly all middle-aged men of all colours, creeds and educational backgrounds, ignored the options re Africa versus South America, but nor did they select the third option, which was that the question itself is silly. Instead, the majority of middle-aged men and older, volunteered that it would be best to nuke the moon. Immediately. What does this tell us? Clearly, if the moon were to fall, nukes might be a means to deflect the moon from a direct hit on Earth, and though we have no data to suggest the outcome one way or the other, it might be conjectured that a sufficient kilo-tonnage of nukes might actually destroy the moon before it could make Earth-fall, in which case, speculating about whether Africa or South America might be the better, would be redundant. This suggests that the response from middle-aged men may be neither stupid nor ignorant. However, the question that arises is, why did those men not qualify their opinion with a statement such as, 'Of course, such a drastic remedy would only be countenanced in the event we had irrefutable evidence that the Earth was actually threatened by such a catastrophe.' Had they done so, we might regard the idea of nuking the moon to be an astute response. Had middle-aged men suggested something along those lines, then according to our experts, this would most definitely not be a stupid response to the question put in the study. However, middle-aged men did *not* so qualify their response. Instead, the majority proposed that it would be best to nuke the moon *as soon as possible,* in order to prevent the moon from falling in any direction at any time. Our experts advise us that in this, there is no mitigation due to ignorance. Our experts conclude that this view renders the response from middle-aged men and older, to be a classic example of deep stupidity. Further, our experts, including Dr Klas Beekhof, tell us that this study has confirmed what many researchers have suspected for some years now, and that is that middle-aged men of all nationalities, are prone to the dangerous self-delusion that not only are they smarter than everyone else, but that they live in an alternate reality in which there are two species – men, on the one hand, and what could be described clinically, as *other life forms*, embracing women, children and irregular animals.'

131

The DG observed that his words were causing a considerable reaction. Quite a number of younger Field Operatives were nodding and many were glancing askance at their older, male colleagues. Was it significant, the DG wondered, that those older male colleagues were staring straight ahead, and indeed, with expressions that incorporated no more than the pursing of lips and some other indications of either a coma, or supercilious indifference?

The DG raised a hand and said, 'I can see that people are disturbed. As am I. For days now, I've been wondering about how best to categorise the different groups. Those whose stupidity is mitigated by ignorance, and those who are simply, middle-aged men. I have been thinking that the first group might be described as 'the misguided.' But the second? How does one best described this cohort, which when all is said and done, essentially governs most countries and controls ninety per cent of the world's wealth? I welcome your suggestions.'

A hand rose half-way back on the left.

The DG said, 'Ah. There's someone. An American Field Operative, I believe.'

The American Field Operative, who happened to be a young black woman said, 'Black or white doesn't matter. I've met plenty of middle-aged man. I call them a jackass.'

With a smattering of exceptions, the conference participants burst into enthusiastic, foot-stomping applause.

At that moment the Field Operative from Northern Ireland leapt to his feet and cried, 'I think this Chinese f****** here, is dead!'

EIGHTEEN

Corker Pritchard raised his glass of beer. He proposed a toast. 'To our Founder, Dimple Potts! And to our first million pills!' Corker Nobody was very pleased. Sales of Brainee were up three hundred and twenty-three percent. Domestic orders were strong, and Brainee Ltd had just taken its first export order from Australia, which was, Corker observed, only as might be expected. And enquiries from eighteen other countries were in the pipeline. The pipeline, Corker said, was getting bigger every day. Nordstrom gas, he suggested, would be like a strand of vermicelli compared to the Brainee pipeline. When all glasses had been raised and the Founder and the million pills had been suitably toasted, Corker said that he had asked Percy to look at putting in a second production line. Percy indicated that he had requested pricing from several suppliers.

The Founder was feeling most gratified at being toasted and he was feeling most gratified at the prospect of ten per cent of the profits. However, he felt that something had been overlooked. The Founder said, 'All good, Corker. All good. But I'm just wondering, you know, about the second production line. In the sense that, shouldn't the Founder be consulted about that kind of decision? After all, being more or less my enterprise, I might have a view about the timing and suchlike?'

Corker Nobody clapped a hand to his forehead with an expression of horror. 'Dimple,' he cried. 'Of course, you must be consulted! This is one hundred and ten per cent a decision for the Founder. Surely you read my email? Where I suggested that due to the exponential increase in demand, actual sales and so forth, that you, as Founder might like to consider directing your team to undertake a preliminary exploration of options and so forth?' And it was clear as he spoke, in his abjection that had he a strand of barbed wire to hand, Corker Nobody would have instantly commenced a self-flagellation of the most severe kind.

The Founder was embarrassed. The Founder coughed and frowned and squinted and made a certain sound that did not resemble any known word.

Corker Nobody stared incredulously, 'You didn't receive it? I can see instantly, Dimple, that damned email never arrived. Because I know you. You'd have been on the phone in a second or two. Mind like a razor and asking what the sales projections looked like and with what confidence could that bean counter Percy make such a projection? And you would have instantly asked, was Percy asking two suppliers of production lines, or three – and likely Dimps, you would have demanded three.' Corker Nobody shook his head and muttered, 'That damned Google. Probably put some fantastic filter in place that simply took out a straightforward communication from a minor functionary to his Founder.'

The Founder was mollified. The Founder agreed that Google could be very high-handed and might be the cause of quite a few problems around the world. But never mind, the Founder said that he thoroughly approved of the actions taken by his team and let's get on with it.

The Founder added, 'By the way. You'll have to do without me next week. I must wear my other hat. I am required to address the Security Council.'

Corker Nobody shook his head in admiration. 'Dimps. I've always said you were top draw. Absolutely top-draw.' He reflected a moment and then said, 'Just a thought. I don't suppose you could slip-in something about Brainee?'

*

The PM put down the phone and called her Chief of Staff. The UN Secretary would have loved to have had the PM speak to the Security Council, but the Council was unanimous in its determination to hear solely from Minister Potts. The Chief of Staff agreed that the situation was inexplicable and advised that in that case, the PM must write the Minister's speech. The PM agreed. The PM had in front of her the note from the US Ambassador. The Ambassador stated that the Security Council wanted to hear from Minister Potts – representing as he did a largely non-aligned country with no-axe-to-grind – a ringing endorsement of the proposal to nuke the moon. The Ambassador said that the key points the Council would appreciate hearing were: That the integrity of Mutually Assured Destruction could only be preserved by actual tests of nuclear weapons held by all countries in the Nuclear Club. That the Minister's country was entirely neutral in all this and understood that such tests were both desirable and not possible on Earth. That the moon was an ideal testing ground since a) it was a long way off; b) no-one lived there; c) the results of each test could be observed by all parties; and d) it would be a warning to the Moon not to fall on the Earth.

The PM poured herself a whisky. It was the first occasion on which she had poured a wee dram for three years but suddenly, it seemed essential. She cancelled her appointments and asked that she not be disturbed. The PM wrote:

"Members of the Security Council. It is a great honour to be asked to speak to you today. My Government fully appreciates both the privilege this represents but also the grave responsibility. On behalf of my Government, I have been requested to put our position on the proposal to fire nuclear weapons at the moon. I must commence by saying that we fully understand why this might seem to be an idea worth considering. However…" And thence, the PM went on to emphasise the cultural significance of the moon. She stressed the 'ownership,' in a metaphorical sense of the moon for all peoples throughout the ages. She put great weight on the rights of labour, worldwide to have a stake in humanity's relationship with the moon, since it was self-evident that without the efforts of labour, space exploration could not even take place. The PM drew the Council's attention to the current dilemma, whereby a handful of billionaires were changing humanity's interface with space and not necessarily in a good way. She observed that astronomers, who were the source of all our knowledge of the Cosmos, could not properly view the night sky and thus were being hampered in their endeavours by the arrays of satellites being launched by these few companies. She drew the Council's attention to the fact that it would be very confusing and likely unsettling for a member of the Baniwa or Kuripako in the deepest Amazonian forest, to see a string of new 'stars' appear in the night sky – let alone a conflagration on the moon. She pointed out that this present, unregulated near-space activity was having the profound effect of changing the eternal night sky into something that more resembled a district in downtown Tokyo.

The PM pointed out that the moon was a mere 3500 kilometres in diameter and accordingly, scientists had no way of knowing just what effect a nuclear bombardment might have. The PM urged the Security Council to consider these different aspects that clearly suggested that nuclear weapons were best left where they were – in their silos, or better still, the Council could lead humanity in a better direction by agreeing to begin the urgent elimination of all nuclear stockpiles. The PM stressed that the idea of a live test was a need unproven and frankly, was the flimsiest of justifications for unleashing such a holocaust, since any uncertainty about the viability of bombs affected all equally. The PM concluded her draft by saying that if the Council decided to approve the proposal to nuke the moon, then it would be remembered for having encouraged middle-aged and older men in one of the greatest follies in humanity's history.

The PM deliberated on this last point for some time and then crossed it out. Instead, she wrote, "Should the Council decide to oppose the proposed nuking of the moon, it will be remembered for having taken one of the most enlightened and responsible stands in its history, and middle-aged and older men will be congratulated for their profound wisdom."

When he returned, the Chief of Staff agreed that this was the only way. Then he hesitated. The PM asked why he hesitated. The Chief of Staff said, 'Well, Prime Minister. I think you have made the case well. Very well...'

The PM said, 'But?'

The Chief of Staff said, 'Well...I just wondered, if the bit about the live test...' The Chief of Staff appeared distinctly uncomfortable. 'Perhaps, it might not be quite *that* flimsy. But it's up to you of course. I just wondered...'

The PM regarded her Chief of Staff a little more closely. She noted his quite large jaw. And his quite long brow. She guessed he was in his early fifties. The PM said, 'Thank you Chief of Staff. But I'm happy with it as it is.'

The Chief of Staff said, 'Quite so, Prime Minister,' and added as he closed the door behind him, 'I don't know what I was thinking.'

*

Corker Pritchard said, 'I'm not surprised. Scientists! What do they know about marketing? The average punter knows this is an ad. The average punter knows that all adverts are shite. The average punter knows that Einstein is dead. We all know! But so be it. We'll take it off the labels and so forth. But no rush, Verbal. If that damned Advertising Standards comes at us, just remind them that we're a business and you can't just change all your packaging and promo material overnight. Remind them that we're a business, risking our all and struggling to create jobs and so forth, for the good of the economy – for the country, so that bozos like them, can be paid. But don't call them bozos.'

Verbal said, 'Fear not, Unks, I've come up with a new slogan.' He produced his pad and showed it to Corker, Percy and the Founder.

Corker shook his head in admiration.

The Founder stared at the pad. The Founder studied the words that read, "As endorsed by Darwin." At length, the Founder said, 'Isn't Darwin also dead? In which case, won't the Academy of Sciences come at us again?'

Corker smiled winningly. 'Dimple, you've never said a truer word. And your word is gospel around here. There's not a shadow of a doubt that they'll be tearing at their white coats and shouting theories and so forth as quick as a flash. But you're already several jumps ahead of us. The Advertising Standards bozos will have to look at the claim and then they've got to come to a decision, and then some bozo will have to write their opinion, which will have to be vetted by their file whacker, and that will go back to their head honcho, who may or may not sign off in the first-instance, but if she does, it will come to us. And what will we do? We'll tell them we've received their opinion and we'll respond ASAP, because we're a struggling business, doing our best and so forth, and that for obvious reasons their complaint will need to examined by our file whacker before we can respond, officially and all that. And what does that mean? It means that we'll sell another thirty million Brainee pills before we have to change our packaging and so forth.' Corker pointed his finger at the Founder knowingly, 'I knew you'd show the way, Dimple. So that's settled.'

The Founder was about to say something, but Corker continued, 'And did I mention that we took orders for twenty million pills this week? A biggie from France – for rest homes I understand. That's a market segment we've only just begun to tap, and what could be better than an endorsement from the man who discovered the difference between apes and us? Not a lot, if what I've read is to be believed. I'm wondering, Verbal, if we might not fetch up an illustration of a punter with a tail? Just blowing smoke, but we could say, "If your grandad lived in a tree, get Brainee." Just a thought.'

It was evident that this thought wasn't immediately catching on with the marketing guru, so Corker moved onto 'Other Business,' and perceiving that nothing was arising, began to declare the meeting closed, when the Founder coughed. An 'ahem,' sort of cough.

Corker's eyes widened. Mystified, Corker said, 'The meeting was closing. You all saw that I expect? I said, 'Any other Business,' and on hearing nothing I was already saying, this meeting is closed. I daresay that was already being entered into the minutes? Percy?' But it seemed that Percy had not recorded that the meeting was closed.

Corker said, 'Blow me down. You understand a meeting protocol to be of a certain nature and then what? Your understanding is turned on its head. What you thought was a meeting closed, it turns out is a meeting open. For how long? That's what anyone would ask. For another hour? Until midnight? Anyone would feel bamboozled when they thought business had been duly dealt with, the meeting was finished and done and dusted, you might say, but no – quite the opposite of their quite reasonable expectations, the meeting it seems has taken on a life of its own. No longer the bailiwick of the Chairman – no, the Chairman it seems has been rendered redundant. The Chairman thought he was in control of the meeting but he finds quite differently that in fact, he has never been in control of his meeting.' Corker shook his head at the mysteriousness of it all whilst staring down at the desk whilst shuffling papers fitfully.

The Founder made a small apologetic cough and opened his mouth but before he could speak, Corker said, 'It's not as if we didn't have a full agenda. That's what baffles me. Production issues – none. Sales issues – none. Marketing issues – boffins complaining about Einstein and dealt with. And new marketing slogan vigorously debated and approved. And then, 'Other Business' and where this Chairman thought there was none and was ready to go attend to some other very pressing matters, which demanded his attention even before this meeting commenced, this Chairman finds he cannot go and attend to certain pressing matters because *after* he had commenced to close this meeting, having canvassed a wide variety of issues, in the proper manner, someone – not being personal, but someone coughs after the proceedings are in the process of closing as though to say that this meeting isn't closed.'

Corker Nobody shook his head again with an expression clearly indicating how much this conundrum was vexing him, though not in a personal way. The Founder again opened his mouth, but the Chairman cried as though he had discovered floodwaters at the level of his bed, 'What to do? That's what anyone would ask. Where will it end? That's just a natural and logical question from your average and your above-average punter, come to that. And the Chairman has to make a decision. The Chairman is called upon to make a decision. Does he simply say, No, this meeting was so close to being formally closed that to back it up would be to breach all normal meeting protocols, and so constitute a disruption of a serious kind, whether in a democratic or a communist state; or, does the Chairman decide that his own standing as Chairman is of no consequence, none whatsoever, and that the ignominy, the sheer humiliation the average punter might say, of having to say, no, this meeting was being closed but having detected a cough at the very last instant and just as the door was about to be closed to keep out a bloody cold draft, or a rat, you might say, this Chairman will abase himself before the meeting and say. Well, what is it? But not being personal about it.' At which Corker fastened his bewildered blue peepers on the ceiling. At which the Founder said that he had simply coughed and had not meant anything by it. At which the Chairman cried, 'In the absence of any Other Business, I declare this meeting closed.'

NINETEEN

It was more than apparent that the General was discomforted. It was possible that he might even be angry. He sat in his chair opposite the Secretary of State in a posture so erect it caused the Secretary to feel exhausted at the mere sight. And there was just a hint of colour in a visage ordinarily as pale as a pinewood plank. The Secretary made the General wait. She pretended to be reading the papers on her desk, but instead was thinking about preserves. The Secretary liked preserves. It was what her mother had done, and to remember preserves was to instantly conjure images of her childhood on the family farm, which altogether seemed infinitely saner than most things that came her way. Like these papers. The Pentagon was seeking her opinion about its proposal to call for contractor bids on a 500-ton battle tank. The Secretary tried to imagine a 500-ton battle tank. The diagrams did not convey this perspective. The file in front of her, which she had stopped reading at this point, said that the Leviathan was designed to inspire such fear, even before it got onto the battlefield, that enemy troops would simply flee in terror. The Leviathan could destroy four city blocks with one salvo. Of course, it was perfectly apparent to the Secretary that the Pentagon wasn't really seeking her opinion. It was telling her what it was doing.

The Secretary looked up at the General, whose posture had not changed a fraction since he had sat down. The Secretary assumed her most business-like expression, which she knew was an exercise in futility because she was a woman and it was not possible to look like a middle-aged businessman, let alone a General. Dammit, she thought. She excused herself for a moment and reaching into one of the draws in her desk, she produced a mask, which she fitted to her face. She adjusted the mask behind her ears until she could see clearly through the eyeholes. The mask looked like a middle-aged man with just a hint of a smile. The jaw was strong and the nose forthright. The colour was sufficiently pale that the face might belong to a Caucasian, but sufficiently tinted that it might also be Latino and at a pinch, a Black. In any event, she observed that instantly, the General felt more comfortable. His posture softened and the fidgeting of his thumbs ceased. The Secretary invited him to proceed, and made a mental note to again ask her Chief of Staff to see what could be done about the mouth, since it was smaller than hers and consequently, her voice sounded a little muffled. This was due in part because the teeth in the mask, contained a device that dropped her voice a couple of octaves. This too, had a calming effect on the General and it must be said, most other male officials regardless of age. The Secretary had wondered whether perhaps she might not have the boffins make a full body mask, as it were, with suit and tie and a quite masculine physique, that she might sit behind but without having to actually don the disguise. She speculated whether the General might continue to address the dummy, even were she to stand and quietly leave her office – for a coffee. It was possible and might be worth the experiment at some future time.

At her invitation, the General said that the French were shilly-shallying. The General did not like shilly-shallying. If a critter said one thing, he said with disdain, whether that was in English or some other lingo, then he expected that that was it. If that critter then said another thing, he suspected he had encountered a mangy dog. The General was most concerned because the Security Council had agreed that a decision to proceed to nuke the moon, must be unanimous. The General suggested that the Secretary might be able to use her authority to bring the shilly-shallying French back into line. Quick smart.

The Secretary adjusted her mask and wondered whose voice her digital teeth were emulating. It sounded a bit like Morgan Freeman. The Secretary said that she would do what she could, but she reminded the General that when the French declined to back the Iraq War, 'French fries' were renamed 'Freedom fries.' Patriotic Americans stopped buying French products, although a later study revealed that most of the brands that consumers identified as French, were not, which translated into tens of millions of lost sales for American companies. Be that as it may, the Secretary said, the French were known to be obdurate. Nonetheless, she would have a word.

The Secretary then asked how things were progressing on the 'catalyst' front, being the New Zealand Minister of Foreign Affairs? The General said that he had to block an attempt by the Prime Minister to address the Security Council, who Intelligence described as being virtually a Commie. Fortunately, the biggies had already indicated that the invitation was exclusive to Minister Potts, and he expected Minister Potts to be on hand shortly.

The Secretary glanced down at the diagram of the Leviathan. The proposed battle tank weighing in at the size of a small ship, appeared rational compared to the adventure which was, "The Moon will Pay." The Secretary brought the meeting to an end with a promise that she would speak with the French. She removed the mask and turned it towards her. She decided that whoever had designed the mask had been inspired by The Terminator.

*

The Director General of the World Health Organisation was struggling. The DG had become aware, because they shared a love of preserves, that the Secretary of State in America, was also struggling. We are the leaders, he mused whilst thinking about his country Spain, together with Greece, in the production of fruit preserves in Europe. We export almost half a million tons. Peaches, which were the DG's favourite and which his mother had preserved in abundance, came first. But apricots, pears, strawberries and cherries…on the other hand, the DG knew that apples – and especially Honeycrisp, and Damson plums were the favourites of the Secretary of State. Only two years ago, when he had accepted his present position, the DG had exchanged several jars of Spanish Calanda peaches for Montana Damsons.

The DG liked the Secretary of State and was honoured to receive her call. After an exchange of pleasantries, the Secretary of State admitted to feeling out-of-sorts. No, it wasn't anything in particular – but yes, it was. The Secretary had seen the international study, which suggested a sudden spike in Stupidity – had the DG seen it? Of course, he had. The DG said not only had he seen it but he was presently engaged in a special conference with all his Field Operatives to consider the scope and scale and the spread of the outbreak. And, as it happened, he was as troubled as she. At his recent conference, his Chinese Field Operative had succumbed to Torpor. The Chinese were demanding an apology.

The Secretary wondered privately how much she should divulge about her reasons for falling into her present funk. And privately, the DG wondered how much he should share his present indecisiveness, which had led to his own falling into a considerable funk. He ventured that he also was feeling somewhat out-of-sorts. There was silence for several seconds as both wondered whether and how much they should elaborate. The Secretary asked the DG whether he could pinpoint the cause of his current state-of-mind, beyond the obvious implications of increased global stupidity. Taking the bull by the horns, the DG said that the spike in deep stupidity was alarming enough, but it was that part of the Study that indicated a congenital predisposition to stupidity in middle-aged and older men of all nationalities, that was his greatest concern. According to Dr Klas Beekhof and others, this predisposition could lie dormant in most men – but for reasons still not well understood, at the age around forty-two (which number had previously been described as the Answer to Everything) could suddenly be activated in the great majority. And worse, some individuals who were carriers of Alta Stultitia, could also be Vectors of the mysterious Torpor that could kill at a distance. The DG was extremely worried.

The Secretary decided she must be frank.

'What I am about to say must stay strictly between you and me.' Then she told him that the Security Council would be voting in three days, on whether or not to nuke the moon, and there was a high probability it would decide to do so.

The DG was stunned. Intuitively, he had suspected that middle-aged men and older, might do something stupid of truly epic proportion, and here it was, and imminent. After several seconds of silence, the Secretary continued to say that only the French stood between the moon and a holocaust. She added, that she had spoken to the French President. The French President had confided that the French had many reasons to oppose the plan, at which the Secretary was greatly heartened. He said that the matter of calling French fries, 'Freedom fries,' still rankled with many French people. And had French people boycotted American goods? By-and-large, no. The French, he said were big-hearted, but there were limits. Did the Secretary have any suggestions about how this grave slight might be remedied?

The Secretary promised the French President to give this utmost consideration, but, the Secretary said to the DG, the French were unreliable. She had never warmed to the

French habit whereby men kissed each other on the cheek, and nor did she appreciate the way the French took an hour to drink a coffee. The DG agreed that these were not desirable habits and they did not reflect well, on that nation. The DG added that he was glad that the Pyrenees stood between his country and theirs.

In any event, this exchange did little to lift the spirits of either the Secretary or the DG. Finally, the Secretary decided she could share one last piece of vital information, but the DG must swear on his mother's preserves, not to breathe a word of it. The Secretary said that she had spoken to the Prime Minister of New Zealand. As it happened, the Secretary and the PM had a 'solid relationship.' And the PM had shared the speech that her Minister of Foreign Affairs was going to make to the Security Council. The Secretary said that this speech was their last and only hope that an act of lunacy might yet be avoided. The DG thanked the Secretary for her confidence and indeed, he felt that he was rising, just a little, above the enervating fumes of the funk. Moved by something — perhaps the circumstances, perhaps because of the confidences shared with the most powerful woman on the planet, perhaps because they had talked briefly about childhood and preserves, the DG ventured to offer an invitation. To his hometown of Malpica, on the coast. With small fishing boats in the tiny harbour and rocky gardens where, nonetheless, his family grew peaches. He said, 'My family home is still there. I would be most honoured if you would visit. We could share a madeira and a cherry pie.'

The Secretary said, 'I can think of nothing better.'

This exchange did much to lift the spirits of both the Secretary and the DG and the Secretary concluded the call by saying she was going to send over a couple of jars of Damsons.

The DG sat at his desk with his head resting on his clasped hands and recalled Malpica. He recalled his

147

grandmother drying him with a towel when he emerged from swimming in the rock pools. He recalled his father and mother dancing the Fandango together in the front room and laughing all the while. He recalled playing football with his two brothers and occasionally connecting with one of the chickens foraging in the yard. These were very pleasant reminiscences.

The DG picked up the newspaper and idly cast an eye over the headlines. But only one article drew his immediate attention. Near the bottom of the page, he read a small header, "Last elephant departs." Something lurched in the DG's chest. Almost a sharp pain. He read, "The WWF announced yesterday, that the last known wild elephant, called Oowoombe, died in the Kruger on Tuesday. The WWF believed that the pair of tusks auctioned on eBay Wednesday, belonged to Oowoombe. The tusks fetched a record ten million, four hundred thousand and fifty dollars. It was reported that the new owner of the tusks tweeted that he had no intention of allowing Oowoombe's tusks from becoming curios of various sorts. He intended to have the elephant's name tastefully inscribed into the tusks. 'Oo' on the left tusk and 'woombe' on the right."

The article concluded quoting the CEO of the WWF, who said, "Of course, we are disappointed. An elephant is a particular kind of animal. Just as the lion, which ceased to exist in the wild last month, and I should mention, the hippopotamus last year, are particular kinds of animals." The CEO of the WWF also said that the WWF was winding up its operation in June, since there were no significant particular kinds of animals remaining outside zoos. Zoos, he added, did an excellent job of reminding people everywhere, that particular kinds of animals actually exist. Otherwise, no-one would believe that an animal could have a trunk.

*

The Head of News was moderately confused. This was not customary, for the Head of News had a most astute nose and very strong convictions, and a tendency to caprice. If the Head of News had been a dog, he would be a Rhodesian Ridgeback – known to be loyal and intelligent the Ridgeback is nonetheless, inclined to be aggressive and is acknowledged to be a poor choice of dog for the inexperienced. In this regard, his staff and others, incorrectly described the Head of News as a Rottweiler – since this is a dog that is typically good-natured, placid in its basic disposition, very devoted, obedient and biddable. Consequently, when they referred to 'Rotty', they perpetuated an unintended compliment, where they should really have been saying 'Ridgy, is in one of his moods.'

Presently, Ridgy was confused by the Minister of Foreign Affairs – who was also the representative of the First Union of Conservative Thinkers and who had recently been accused – perhaps falsely, of cruelty to a dumb animal by the name of Doc Cod. But now what? It appeared, that Minister Potts was also the entrepreneurial brains behind the fastest growing business in the country, to wit, Brainee Ltd. And to add even further to the confusion experienced by the Head of News, he had just learned from his source in the Beehive, that Minister Potts had been invited to address the UN Security Council. Why? The Head of News shook his head. The Head of News had been certain he was going to prove that Dimple Potts was an empty vessel – an end-of-pier clown, who was therefore, a singularly inappropriate appointment to any Ministerial portfolio. His source had advised him that the PM had been turned down by the Security Council. The Council was only interested in Potts.

The Head of News gazed at the photograph of Founder Potts receiving an export award. In a little over two months, Brainee Ltd had gone from nothing to a twenty-million-dollar enterprise. And here was the French Ambassador congratulating Founder Potts because already in French rest homes, an uptick in intelligence had been observed. Of course, these results were still somewhat anecdotal, but the information had come from many rest homes across France. Residents deemed too stupid even to find their teeth on the bedside table, had been reported to suddenly be expert in Wordle and suchlike. It was a wonder, a testament to science and evidence if ever the French Ambassador had seen it, of Greed-with-Care, which the French called "Gourmandise avec Soin," in action.

Founder Potts was quoted in the article as saying, "Yes. It's true that we're generating very substantial profits. But 'obscene profits' really is not our way. My vision was a bipartisan pill at a fair price, to reverse the known outbreak of stupidity. I can only point out the great good that Brainee is doing." The adjacent photograph showed a very elderly, beaming French woman, standing alongside three geeky and crestfallen youths – the woman apparently having trounced all in the local annual chess tournament. The woman, who was described as having not uttered a word in the past two years, had only ever played bingo, was now eloquent, and after managing to lose her teeth on her bedside table every single day for longer than anyone could remember, had taken to ordering new sets on-line.

Minister Potts was indeed a mystery, and the Head of News felt a slight, grudging respect. Potts the Entrepreneur and Potts the célèbre at the UN. But there was the question about Darwin…The Academy of Sciences was complaining about "false and misleading advertising." Of course, it was false and misleading – but scientists made for very boring news, The real question, he decided, was what the UN wanted of Minister Potts? And the instincts of the Ridgeback told him that therein was the story and by God, if needs be, he would maul it to death.

TWENTY

Dimple asked if he should wear his blue suit, or the grey? After some consideration, his wife suggested the blue. Dimple said that he felt the grey might convey a more pronounced air of gravitas and was perhaps more suited to the occasion. His wife replied that the grey would indeed, be fine. Dimple said, but on the other hand, a blue suit might be described as being more optimistic in nature – more in line with the entrepreneur's 'blue sky' thinking, which would be appropriate when one had to present something of a visionary kind – which was why he had been invited to the UN. His wife replied that the blue suit was certainly consistent with the making of a visionary statement. Dimple thoughtfully, and slowly munched his toast. He asked, if he wore the grey suit, might not members of the Capitalist States think he was somewhat aligned with the Communist States? His wife said that she assumed that was possible. But, continued Dimple, if he wore the blue suit, the Communist States might conversely feel that he was sending a subtle signal that he was against them. Might they, and the Republicans for that matter, not think, that he was siding with the Democrats? His wife replied that his choice of suit was indeed, politically fraught. Perhaps he should wear the blue trousers, with the grey jacket and a red tie? Dimple nodded appreciatively and remarked that his wife was as always, a very reliable source of wisdom.

Dimple's wife enquired how his meeting with the PM had gone. Dimple's wife liked the PM. Dimple said that his opinion about the PM was changing. To be sure, she didn't look like one expected of a PM. Oh, said his wife. What should she look like? Well, said Dimple blithely, more like a man. Dimple's wife regarded him with that expression that said, 'Surely you didn't just say that?' It was an uncomfortable expression. Dimple added hastily that he was absolutely fine with a woman being the PM, it was just that *other* people expected to see a suit and tie and an experienced and affable face – all of which pointed towards a man. A businessman – that is what most people expected. He was just saying that that was what people expected, and he wasn't expressing a personal opinion. Indeed, he now thought the PM a most competent person. She had helped him with his speech and it all made a great deal of sense. To be totally frank, he said, he had been wondering what on Earth he was going to say to the Security Council. To be even more frank, he was still wondering why they had invited him. Of course, he was a successful entrepreneur – had he mentioned that they had just taken another order from Spain for twenty million pills? No, well they had and even now, Corker was planning a third production line. Had he mentioned that school children were the second-fastest growing segment, after octogenarians, who just exceeded middle-aged men? The segment that seemed to be the late adopters, were women – and especially Millennials. According to Verbal, Millennial women seemed to be rather sceptical about Brainee – except when it came to their kids – when reason prevailed. But never mind. Overall, sales were very strong.

Dimple's wife observed that perhaps it was because women were very conscious about chemicals, but that they were devoted to their children?

Dimple said, 'Pah! The world is awash with chemicals. Why, I asked our Chemical Whizzo about this very thing and she said that if you worried about chemicals in your life, you might as well stop living. And that columnist, Dave Barry made the excellent point that without the chemicals hydrogen and oxygen you wouldn't have water, which happens to be an essential ingredient in beer.' Dimple paused. He asked, 'Where was I?'

Dimple's wife said he was wondering why he had been invited to speak to the Security Council. Dimple said that that was what *he* had been wondering. He doubted that he had been invited because he was a successful entrepreneur. He glanced at the Export Award on the mantle. It represented an eagle soaring through what he assumed to be industrial piping, and thereby capturing the spirit of the entrepreneur and the fruits of his vision being an industrial complex from which flowed innovation and great wealth. Or, was it a duck? He stared intently at the Award and then rose to take it in hand. He said, 'Surely this isn't a duck?' Then he sat down and though mildly troubled, he continued to speculate and said that the American Ambassador had said it was mostly about his remarks concerning the moon, which had impressed many people. Fortunately, the PM had written an excellent speech. He hadn't studied it closely, but the gist was that though there was merit in considering nuking the moon, perhaps there were equally, if not more weighty considerations that might suggest it wasn't such a great idea as had been first thought. The PM said that this point-of-view was easily reconciled with the point-of-view put by the American Ambassador, in the sense that the Ambassador perceived in Minister Potts, a chap of independent mind and great integrity. The Ambassador and the Security Council, clearly wanted to hear an objective and clear-sighted perspective that might help them to make a proper assessment of the proposal. The PM said that in her estimation, they had chosen the exact right person to deliver this very important message. The PM had said that she herself, was glad it was not her who had been invited. She was of the firm opinion that only Dimple, could represent this country and the World, on this critically important matter in a manner befitting. The PM had even suggested that if he performed this duty in the manner that she fully expected he would, there was the question of the role of Deputy Prime Minister…It was becoming apparent, said the PM that for health reasons, the incumbent may well have to relinquish the role. The PM said she needed to be thinking about who best to fill those shoes. She said that someone who had proven commercial experience but who, most especially could prove the staunchest loyalty in carrying out a crucial assignment – which as it happens, an address to the Security Council would certainly be – well…

Dimple said that the PM had shaken his hand and that to his surprise, it was the kind of handshake he might have expected from a chap of a particular age – but there it was and simply reinforced his growing view that the PM was the equal of many chaps of his acquaintance and frankly, and he didn't mind owning that he had thought differently at one point, the PM was *better* than many chaps of his acquaintance.

Dimple's wife said that that was certainly an astonishing revelation, and excused herself that she might attend to pressing matters. Her clinic was full this morning.

*

Corker Pritchard, silent investor and invisible fixer for the enterprise Brainee, regarded the official with astonishment. Corker was astonished if not a little dismayed that the Department of Health was curious about Brainee. Surely, Corker said, the Department of Health would be over-the-moon about the wonderful effect that Brainee was having on the plague of Stupidity that was afflicting modern society? Surely, the Department of Health had seen the evidence, from France no less, that proved that the aged and decrepit and who, Corker cried, were waiting with dull resignation for their final curtain call, had turned back the clock. Dullards had become players of chess and suchlike. Certified morons had written novels. Dangerous imbeciles were out on the streets doing charitable works. The incontinent were mastering the high jump and so forth. Surely, the Department had seen the Export Award? 'The Golden Goose,' no less?

The official said she was impressed with the evident accomplishments of Brainee, and she was of course, aware of the standing of the Founder, being also the Minister of Foreign Affairs. However, the Department had a responsibility to protect consumers and in this it was the Department's role to enquire into the nature of business enterprises that produced substances of an allegedly therapeutic kind.

Corker's jaw dropped. Surely, cried Corker, the Department didn't suspect anything of an untoward nature. Goodness Gracious! Corker promptly produced a packet of Brainee, took three pills and swallowed them and then offered the packet to the official, who politely declined. Corker shook his head vigorously and then his shoulders and then his torso and finally, with his eyes bulging, he slapped his cheeks until they assumed an even deeper shade of pink. Corker apologised and explained that whenever he took Brainee, it had this instantaneous and highly stimulating effect, and he asked the official whether the official had an interest in quantum physics, which subject had engrossed Corker from the day after he commenced his consumption of Brainee? He said that he had zeroed in on the arcane field of quantum effects in the area of pygmalion and hypersonics. The official said that she was unfamiliar with quantum physics, in any detail. The official explained that she was a chemical engineer by training, and in that capacity, she wished to interview the Chemical Whizzo.

Corker Nobody pursed his lips and sighed. Would that that were possible, said Corker, but unfortunately, the Chemical Whizzo had just left on a lengthy trip to the Amazon Rainforest, from which dark, mysterious and wonderful place the essential, active ingredient – the Brain Booster XL8, was sourced. Discovered by Corker when he was…holidaying, in South America. The official made no immediate comment on this, but she was aware that Corker Pritchard had fled New Zealand for South America, presumably to escape prosecution for misrepresentation of product labelling, and to escape the ire of a small town that had discovered it had eaten its favourite dog; and that he had been subsequently fined on his return.

Corker leapt to his feet and began to write a formula on the small whiteboard on the wall behind his desk. Corker scribbled for a moment and then with a sound of exasperation, rubbed the formula off with his sleeve and declared that ever since he had taken Brainee, it was a challenge simply maintaining one's equilibrium, when the formulae were literally coming like a volcanic eruption. But he assured the official, the moment the Chemical Whizzo returned, the official could count on being notified instantly.

The official said that was most helpful, and wondered whether it might be possible for her instead to meet with the Founder? Ah, said Corker, sadly, that too was impossible for the Founder, in his other capacity of Minister of Foreign Affairs, had only just this morning departed for New York on matters of national security and suchlike. However, Corker said, he was certain that the Founder would be only too willing to find time – in his immensely busy schedule – to help the official with her very important work. The official said that she would not like to be seen to be imposing. She asked whether she could be shown around the production facility.

Corker Fixer assumed an expression of utter remorse and concern and chagrin and sorrow. How he would have liked to have shown the official around the Brainee production facility! Nothing would give him more pleasure – but he was simply too embarrassed to have to say that the plant was currently inaccessible due to its lockdown for the purposes of hypersonic cleaning. Such had been the production demands,

156

and such were the rigorous quality control standards – standards that far exceeded those of the most tyrannical bodies – such as the EU, that Brainee disciplined itself to deny the needs of clamouring customers, to harden the corporate heart to the plaintive cries of the afflicted, simply to ensure, and despite a painful loss of profits, that Brainee pills were the cleanest pills in either hemisphere. Corker said that he was sure that the official would understand completely, the Brainee commitment to health and safety and the highest ethical standards of commerce and so forth.

The official took up her briefcase. The official did not shake the pink hand proffered by Corker Pritchard. The official said that she would be reporting the results of the interview to her superiors and that Brainee Ltd would hear from the Department shortly. At which she saw herself out.

*

In fact, the Founder and Minister of Foreign Affairs was about to depart.

The man-in-the-mirror said, 'Well, well. From Mayor of Brewster's Neck to the UN...who would have thought?'

Dimple said, 'Yes, yes, you've already said that. I daresay you're envious and I can't blame you. Once, you know, I answered the call to step-up when Mayor Georgy Pruitt was knocked down – by that bus. Little did I realise that that was a poison chalice. What with Corker off to South America as fast as his legs would carry him, and that lunatic Hemopo and his robot taking down half the national grid, I was up against it. Mind you. Did I let it keep me down? I should say not.' He paused to fix his eye on the eye of the man-in-the-mirror. 'A man must always be ready to step-up-to-the-plate. Corker said that you know? When I was called to replace Georgy? He said that any chap not prepared to step-up-to-the-plate was a chilblain and did not deserve the vote. I agreed with him then and I still do. Corker and I see eye-to-eye on many things. Like myself, a man of action.'

Changing the subject, the man-in-the-mirror said, 'I wonder if you have a preference – one way or the other? Vocationally, I mean? Politician or entrepreneur?'

Dimple considered this question for a few moments and paused in the brushing of his hair. 'I believe I am one of those truly ambidextrous people. When I am in Ministerial mode, I find that all my faculties are directed at foreign policy. But when I am wearing my entrepreneurial hat, why, it's the same. I can see only innovation and new products and markets and so forth. I simply won't be distracted. I believe I may be a polymath. Though I concede that it can become a little tiring – being expert in so many things. I rather doubt that you have any real conception of how much energy and drive is required to do what I do.' Dimple replaced the hairbrush in its drawer and glanced at the time. 'Time to go.'

The man-in-the-mirror said, 'Bon voyage!'

Dimple said, 'What? Aren't you coming? Oh well. I don't want to be held back by anyone who might be afflicted by doubts.' At which he departed the bathroom and went in search of his wife.

TWENTY-ONE

The Senior Reporter said that her source in the Beehive, indicated that Minister Potts was talking to the Security Council, but the subject was top secret. The Senior Reporter began to say that she had worked out a line of questioning about the Minister's intentions, when she was interrupted by the Head of News.

The Head of News said, 'This international study...people becoming more stupid...we haven't really covered this.'

The Senior Reporter reminded the Head of News that she had suggested they do a piece but that he had said it wasn't important. The Head of News said airily that it wasn't particularly important, *at that time.* The Senior Reporter observed, cautiously but not without a mite of satisfaction, that that was at the time he had insisted they do a piece about Doc Cod. The Head of News scowled and said that sometimes, there was a wrong and a right time to run a piece and as far as the international study went, this was the right time. In any event, it was always the right time, to run a piece about a dog.

Privately, the Head of News was thinking, the Senior Reporter could be quite a pain. Self-righteous, if not to say smug.

The Senior Reporter said, 'I was wondering, if we should do a piece about the loss of the last wild elephant?'

'What do you mean?'

'I mean, it's just been reported, but not widely, that that elephant called Oowoombe, was shot by poachers last Tuesday.'

159

The Head of News paused. 'What's the angle? Kruger goes out of business?'

'I was thinking, more about how children have always loved elephants. Everyone does, really.'

'And? The zoos are full of them. Punters would rather see stories about dogs, and cats. Ideally, an old person whose pet has been electrocuted by a municipal blunder. Put the mayor on the mat – incompetence and so on – that's a good story.' The Head of News dismissed this time wasting with a wave of his hand. He continued, 'Now, I think we should tackle Potts about both the UN address, *and* the activities of his own company, Brainee.'

The Head of News wondered this in a way that indicated to the Senior Reporter that elephants were out. And given that Brainee was explicitly claiming to reverse stupidity, he added, what did the public actually know about this wonder drug, and more particularly, how it was that an ex-mayor of a hamlet at some indeterminate location in the Waikato, could develop something so sophisticated, so quickly? Was he a chemist? Had he ever started a business of any description? Warming to his theme, the Head of News asked rhetorically, who did the clinical trials? And who had sought verification of the cases from France, including ancient women who were apparently transforming into chess champions and novelists. And who had talked to the Department of Health? The Head of News cried suddenly, 'Get on it!'

*

The Director General of the WHO swallowed an anti-depressant. He had no appetite. He had slept badly and at one point found himself dreaming about an elephant standing proudly and trumpeting on the top of a hill, silhouetted against the African night, moments before the animal was blown away by a bazooka. Now, he had viewed a clip of an ancient Frenchwoman transformed. There was a photograph of the woman, who appeared to be all of ninety-five, lying in her bed and to all intents and purposes, with mouth agape, no teeth, and ghastly pallor, could be dead. Then there was a video clip of the same woman, apparently, but now she was spry and appeared to have more hair. She was walking around a room in which four young fellows were sitting at their chess boards, deep in anguished concentration. When one of the young men made a move, the woman glanced at the chessboard for mere moments before moving one of her pieces, which evidently caused immediate shock to her opponent. The ancient woman, who now looked to be more like fifty, gave a small and modest smile and a fellow in a white coat said to the camera, "It is hard to believe that Madam Hortense had never played chess until last week – but here she is taking on and beating four junior chess champions, simultaneously." He turned to Madam Hortense, who had just made another stunning move such that her opponent, with a small cry of desperation, tipped over his king before allowing his head to fall into his hands. The fellow in a white coat asked Madam Hortense to what did she attribute her truly remarkable reversal from clinical dementia to chess master – or mistress?

Madam Hortense said, "Two weeks ago, I was dumb as a rabbit and getting dumber. Then I discovered Brainee." She held up a blue and red pill. "This wonder pill has changed my life. It will change yours too!" And she turned away and the clip faded out the words remained on screen: "Brainee. The Wonder Pill to Change your Life!"

The DG gulped at his coffee, too soon and burnt his lip. He cried out to his otherwise empty hotel room, 'How can anyone believe this?' But they did, for he had seen a news item that said that all the rest homes in France were being

161

supplied with Brainee and that the Germans were trying to out-bid the French to secure their own supply.

The DG made his way to the War Room of the WHO. He looked out upon the sea of brown, white, yellow and black faces. The DG tried not to stare at the face of the Field Operative from Texas, but the expression on that man's face was disturbing. It wasn't the colour – which was no more than might be expected of a being that consumed beef three times each day. It wasn't the neck, though in its width it more resembled a trunk. The DG forced his gaze away, but he had already concluded that the outbreak of Stupidity was present in this very room. If that were so, then he must also assume that here was evidence of the widespread nature of the disease. And if he and his senior team reached that conclusion formally, they must communicate that decision to world governments. And they must recommend a strategy to be adopted by governments, to stop an Epidemic or worse.

With these very sobering thoughts, the DG advised the conference that together, they would create a virtual map of the Outbreak. They would do this by comparing and contrasting the various experience and data that could be provided by each Field Operative from every area of the world. They would do so alphabetically. Consequently, the FO from Afghanistan commenced. He said that some people had heard that there were living things on the moon.

Instantly, there were muffled sounds of amusement in the War Room – but not just amusement, but bemusement also, and in some cases, the DG detected murmurings of agreement! The FO from Afghanistan continued. 'Sir, it's been reported. On the moon, there are creatures like us, in some respects, except that they have wings.'

A voice called from somewhere in Eastern Europe, 'That's right. Batmen! It's known.'

From around the War Room came numerous voices of assent and the nodding of heads. The FO from Texas rose and said, loudly, 'In Texas, we're going all out to help these folk. They may have wings but otherwise, they're pretty much human.'

A voice from somewhere in Asia – perhaps it was Laos – cried, 'Those batmen are fornicators.'

The DG looked from one to the other and back to the FO from Texas, who cried, 'Fornicators and what else? We don't know. But we do know they fornicate openly and without shame, in the streets.'

Voices rose all around the War Room. There were expressions of disgust, such as, 'Animals! They may look a bit like us but they're obscene beings.' And expressions of amazement, such as, 'You don't say. I must say I'd wondered. But why didn't our astronauts see them?' And forthright responses such as, 'But they did! The government has been keeping it secret. That's why we haven't been back. The batmen fly like a bat and they're vampires.' Which occasioned remarks like, 'I've been wondering whether we've ever landed on the moon...why would you, when you can see vampire batmen fornicating everywhere...'

Voices rose and fell for several minutes and the DG wondered whether he had woken this morning. Perhaps he was still in the elephant dream.

The voice of the FO from Texas, who was still on his feet, rose above the clamour. 'In my State, we're doing what must be done. We're fixing to send these fornicating heathens, the Holy Bible. We're going to fire a rocket of peace and the Good Word right smack into the heart of Beelzebub!' This pronouncement was met with some acclaim and some dismay. Voices cried, 'And the Koran. The Koran must also be fired at the batmen.' And other voices rose with the words such as, 'And Twitter! We must educate these primitive beings.'

The DG raised his hand until silence returned to the War Room. The DG felt that he must handle this startling development very carefully. He said that the disclosure by the

FO from Afghanistan was most interesting. He now wished to gauge the *currency* of this unusual story. Consequently, he invited the Field Operatives to hold up one of three paddles that indicated their view of the notion…the idea that Batmen inhabited the moon. Each Field Operative selected a paddle, though it was apparent that many were having difficulty choosing one over another. After a minute or two, most had raised a paddle. At a glance, the DG could see that the majority were showing the paddle marked with the numeral '1.' The DG's heart sank. A smallish number held the paddle displaying the numeral '2' and just one held the paddle marked '3.'

How could this happen, and so quickly, the DG wondered. Only the Field Operative from Horodger, which was not yet actually a country, held the number three paddle that indicated 'Seriously Stupid Idea.' Perhaps twenty held aloft the number two paddle that indicated the view, 'Possibly Stupid.' But here, the DG was confronted with a sea of number one paddles that indicated, 'Smart As.'

The FO from Texas, who was still standing, bawled, 'The Holy Bible will smite the Batmen!'

The North Korean FO cried that the Dear Leader was already in correspondence with the leader of the Batmen.

*

The Chair was incredulous. How could it be that the first item on prime-time news, was once again, Minister Potts? And was the Chair alerted beforehand? No, he was not. Was the Committee of the First Union of Conservative Thinkers given even one opportunity to instil its collective wisdom into its political representative? No, it was not. Had the Chair heard the rumour that the PM had Minister Potts around her little finger? Yes, he had. Was Minister Potts introduced by the

Senior Reporter as the face of the First Union of Conservative Thinkers? No, he was not. The average punter, whom the Chair knew was as thick as two short planks – *before* the Outbreak – might think that Dimple Potts was a member of the *Other Lot*. And the Other Lot were dangerous. Did the average punter have any idea of just how dangerous the Other Lot were? No, they did not.

The Senior Reporter said that Minister Potts was about to depart on his first overseas mission as Minister of Foreign Affairs – and what could be more important than addressing the Security Council of the UN?

The Chair cried, 'What the F***?'

The Senior Reporter asked the Minister about the purpose of the visit, but as she expected, the Minister said that he couldn't disclose any detail on account of national security considerations.

The Head of News said in the Senior Reporter's ear mike, 'Now hit him!'

Without changing her innocent expression, the Senior Reporter said, 'Minister Potts – I understand that you are the Founder of the company, Brainee Ltd? Yes. And your company sells a pill that purports to increase IQ? It does. And is it true that you claim that your pill contains a special active ingredient called…Brain Booster XL8? Minister Potts, can you also confirm that your company claims that Brainee has transformed an elderly Frenchwoman, incapacitated and possibly even close to death's door, suddenly – within a week or two, into a chess master?'

Minister Potts said, 'I'm afraid I cannot speak for any individual. Brainee may have different effects for different people. It has much to do with a person's inter-normative and pre-colonic neural modality.'

The Senior Reporter hesitated.

The Chair said, 'Good God!'

The Head of News shouted, 'Don't just sit there!'

Minister Potts continued, 'You see, what we know is that there is an Epidemic of Brain Fog. Some experts describe it as stupidity, which who knows, it may yet prove to be? In any event, certain sinosinclastic aberrations occur in the submorpheous apparentinka that can be altered through the administration of a perischolastic rudimatarium, such as the Brainee pill, containing, as you correctly point out, Brain Booster XL8.'

'But Minister-'

'I am sure you will understand that we are dealing with neurological and spasmological concerns well-beyond the reckoning of your average person.' Minister Potts paused to smile indulgently, 'Is it reasonable to expect your average person to truly understand the putaspheric subjunctivorpal of his or her cranial locus? No. And why, because if the average person was to focus his or her neuropedantic faculties on this kind of abstruse matter, he or she might experience a dangerous and potentially fatal spasm of brain fog.' The Minister removed from his pocket a red and blue packet and held it such that the brand, 'Brainee' could be seen quite plainly. 'I would like you to have this pack of Brainee, with my compliments.'

The Chair was on his feet. The Chair cried, 'The man's a genius, or a full-fledged swivel-eyed loon. But who cares?'

The Head of News bawled in the ear of the Senior Reporter, 'Say something, or you're fired!'

The Senior Reporter said, 'That was…at least…well, Minister Potts. I think…We wish you well on your trip.'

In the corner of a certain café, barely visible in the half-light, Corker Pritchard said, 'Percy. You know, I really must congratulate myself for securing the services of a Minister of the Crown. Look at this.' And he held his phone towards Percy, and they watched the local market online orders for Brainee appear at a rate of about one per second.

166

TWENTY-TWO

The Secretary General of the UN was extremely pleased to meet the Minister of Foreign Affairs, Mister Dimple Potts. The Secretary General was pleased to hear that the movie selection on the flight had been good. Though unfamiliar with the movie, she was very pleased that the Minister had particularly enjoyed, 'The Day of the Jackass,' and enquired whether the name was not 'The Day of the Jackal?' It wasn't. The Secretary General observed that the idea of a donkey becoming President was novel – and amusing. Was it amusing? It was – but not especially so, said the Minister, since it was more of a thriller.

The Secretary General was surprised the jackass had received an Oscar. She surmised that this may have been more for the actor who provided the English voiceover? It wasn't? It was actually *for* the jackass, who spoke good English. How surprising, the Secretary General agreed. The name of the jackass was Ralph.

Nonetheless, the Secretary General couldn't help wondering, how it was, despite that President Ralph wore a pinstripe suit, no-one noticed his ears, or his teeth? And why for that matter, did they not notice his feet, which she assumed would be hooves?

Coffee was delivered to the Secretary General's office. Her guest took two lumps of sugar and a peanut brownie, and then explained that because Ralph was nearly always seated, and wore gloves as well as shoes, his hooves were mostly invisible, and he had the habit of wearing a red baseball cap, which concealed his ears. Large teeth, he added mildly, are not so uncommon. The Minister recalled a certain accountant of his acquaintance…

In any event, he explained, the only time he had really noticed was when Ralph was running down a marble corridor to escape the FBI, and had forgotten in his haste to put on his shoes – at which time the clip-clopping was audible. And the thing was, observed the Minister, was that after five minutes you simply forgot about the large nose and so forth, because Ralph was dealing with matters of State and suchlike including what was, more-or-less, the End-of-the-World. Unfortunately for Ralph, he was assaulted by a terrorist with a machete, before he could be apprehended by the FBI, and before the End-of-the-World occurred. And frankly, had the Minister been in Ralph's hooves, he would have preferred to have been snuffed by the End-of-the-World. Indeed, if he had a criticism of the movie, it was that Ralph's demise was a quite unsettling scene that at some twenty minutes in length, in the Minister's view, was considerably more graphic than was strictly necessary. Apart from that, it was dramatic and the Minister recommended it.

The Secretary General sipped her coffee and listening to this candid review, wondered how it was that certain types of people, and most particularly, men, got into positions of power. Two days prior she had met with the Secretary of State and the General. The Secretary General and the Secretary of State were on good terms but the former gained the feeling that the latter was holding something back. The Secretary General noticed that Madam Secretary was avoiding her eye and seemed to find the rather dull landscape on her wall of singular and fixed interest. The General had said that the Security Council would be swayed by the views of Minister Potts, because he represented a country of no account. The General said that the Minister's declared support for a careful program of nuking of the wasteland that is the moon, would be, 'Ad rem,' or relevant.

The Secretary General expressed her concern that even the most careful program to nuke the moon must surely constitute an act of unmitigated vandalism? She was unsurprised that the General's expression did not change. She was surprised that Madam Secretary made no comment when the General said that that view was straight out of the French playbook and consequently, was immaterial.

And now, here in her office was that very Minister, who was apparently supportive of quite the most horrible proposal she had heard of in her long career in diplomacy. And what did she see? Yet another middle-aged man whose stolid features, large forehead and prominent jaw – and nose, come to that – and ears, reminded her of something. The Secretary General bit her lip and momentarily glanced at the summer seascape on her wall and found her equanimity quickly restored. Nevertheless, the Secretary General made a mental note to watch the movie, and then gave a little cough. She asked politely, why the Minister was supporting the unleashing of nuclear weapons at the moon?

The Minister said that he wasn't really supportive, in that sense. Indeed, more-or-less to the contrary. The Secretary General was nonplussed. But wasn't that why he was here – to lend strength to the bow that was even now, half-bent and armed with numerous deadly missiles?

The Minister said that he personally, wasn't very interested in missiles, but one must acknowledge that missiles of various sorts were part of a man's heritage, as he understood it.

The Secretary General agreed with the Minister but added, most warmly, that whilst they were part of humanity's heritage, she saw no need to cling to old and outmoded ways of thinking and doing things – and in this she personally saw missiles as outmoded. Did the Minister not agree?

The Minister did agree. To some extent. He agreed that missiles could be dangerous, but, he emphasised, that was

169

really if they fell into the wrong hands. If missiles were in the *right* hands, then the Minister had nothing much against them. Personally, if he was asked, he would have to say he leaned towards larger missiles – or rockets, in the same way that one preferred to watch a volcanic eruption hit the stratosphere. A lava flow by comparison, was a bit of a damp squib. Was the Secretary General aware, by the way, that when a Saturn 5 was launched at Cape…yes, Canaveral, that the vibration was detected on various forms of scientific instruments, right here, in New York. It made you think.

The Secretary General said that indeed, it did make you think. The Secretary General suggested that the Minister was in the truly unique position of being able to influence the Council in a way even she could not. It could even be said that the Minister had it in his powers, to cause the international community to act in an ethical and honourable way. It was, she said, an astonishing privilege and opportunity. If the Minister said the *right* thing, he would be remembered as a statesman of real stature.

Did the Minister permit himself a little smile? He did. Minister, Founder and Statesman…the Minister wondered what that Latvian baker, Sarah Bumbulis – Mayor of that town that wasn't even a town, would think of that?

The Secretary of State probed a little further. She presumed that the Minister had a very carefully prepared statement to make to the Council. Knowing that he would have a very restricted time to say his piece?

The Minister nodded gravely. 'Oh, yes. The Prime Minister most kindly put my thoughts on paper. You know, I'm really beginning to think that she's not such a bad egg.'

*

170

The PM observed gloomily, 'I really don't know how it came to this.' The PM was ordinarily most charitable – even concerning ideologs at the outer ends of either spectrum. The worst she had been guilty of was to most accurately describe an opponent as 'an arrogant prick.' But this was different. This was a matter of national importance first, and undoubtedly of international importance second. She added, 'We've sent – no, let me correct myself because we would never have actually *sent* Potts. Potts has been *demanded,* by the Security Council. What I should say is that we are represented at arguably the World's most important forum, by an idiot. Do you think that's unkind? I suppose I should say, we're represented by someone of prodigious naivety. That's not his fault. Mine, I suppose. I thought it would be a role in which least harm would be done.'

The Deputy Prime Minister, who at the age of ninety-two, was contemplating bringing his own political career to an end, was sympathetic. The Deputy PM reminded his boss that she had scripted his speech. Even a clown might deliver a scripted speech without doing harm. But the PM was not to be mollified. What, she said, would Potts say if he was subjected to questions? She shook her head and gave a sigh of resignation.

The Deputy PM said, 'Did you see Potts on the News? I hadn't realised that Brainee was his company. But he handled himself pretty well, I thought. Saw off the question about the UN without hesitation. And then the interviewer tried to pin him down about the pills and he did it again. All sounded pretty scientific and everyone's using them. Matter of fact, I've got some myself. Thought I might as well try them. No longer a spring chicken and all that. And especially as it's one of our colleagues making them.'

The PM fixed her stare on her Deputy. He had once confided that he had aspired to be the PM from the age of twelve. How could any properly balanced child, aspire to be the PM? What on Earth did a twelve-year-old boy think the PM did? What sense of aggrandisement accompanied such an aspiration, when his young friends would have been thinking they might like to be a pilot, or a truck driver or perhaps a deep-sea diver? And now? His long and undistinguished career in politics was coming to an end. How would he be remembered? As affable, perhaps? A safe pair of hands on the Horse Racing portfolio.

The Deputy PM continued, 'Apparently, a French woman, my age, as it happens and close to death, and unable to even find her teeth in the morning, has become a chess master. Remarkable. Apparently, and Potts was describing this in the interview - though naturally, he couldn't be too specific because of commercial sensitivity, but the Brainee pills contain a secret active called…Brain Booster. Something out of the Amazon rainforest.'

The PM laughed unhappily. 'We've let loose a plonker who is also a scam artist!'

The Deputy PM was affronted. He said, 'It's said that Big Pharma want him out of the way.'

The PM said, 'Pardon?'

"Yes. I read it somewhere. He's cutting into their profits something terrible. They can't stand the competition. I notice by the way, that you didn't refer to the Batmen…'

The PM, who was still digesting the news that Potts might be in danger from pharmaceutical companies, looked up sharply, 'What?'

'The Batmen. Apparently, there's a community of Batmen on the moon. Like us, I understand, but with wings – like a bat. And I've heard they are not shy about…certain things…' He allowed a small, knowing smile.

The PM thought, 'He's got to go.' But she said, faintly, 'Things…'

'Well, not to put too fine a point on it, they roger each other in the streets. A bit like bonobos and so on.'

172

The PM had an impulse to lift the phone and call for emergency assistance. But she continued, 'Are you serious? Batmen? On the moon?'

The Deputy PM bridled at her rather aggressive questioning. 'Yes, I am serious. It's quite well-established. In the New York Times, apparently.'

The weariness the PM had been feeling became suddenly more pronounced. She replied that she would have her team find out what they could.

The Deputy PM departed but as he went through the door, he paused to say, 'We wouldn't want to be nuking aliens, would we?'

TWENTY-THREE

The limousine pulled up outside a most exclusive restaurant. The General's Aide said, 'Le Bernardin earned four stars from The Times just after opening, and you know, Minister Potts, it has never dropped a star since. I believe it is the only restaurant to do so. It has also won the James Beard for Outstanding Restaurant in America.'

The General said, 'You have something like this at home?' But the General didn't wait for his guest to reply because he knew he didn't.

The concierge led the General and his guests to the staircase. When Minister Potts paused to gaze at an enormous depiction of a turbulent sea that covered most of one wall, the General's Aide laid her hand lightly on the Minister's sleeve. 'Quite a sight, isn't it? Magnificent décor, is it not?'

Minister Potts turned to agree but was rendered speechless by the proximity of the deep blue and sparkling eyes of the General's Aide. She smiled and Minister Potts placed a hand on the banister to steady himself. The General's Aide said, 'We're taking you somewhere very special! I think you will love it!' Minister Potts gave a modest smile. He was certain he would love it The dinner party continued up the staircase and the General's Aide welcomed him into one of the private Salons Bernardin. She said, 'The Zagat Guides have named Le Bernadin the Most Popular Restaurant in the city, for years. Frankly, Minister, we couldn't have brought you anywhere else!'

Minister Potts savoured a glass of Clos de Vougeot, which the General casually observed, was among the world's most expensive pinot noirs. The General's Aide glanced at the etched glass windows and then read from the menu, 'A great pairing doesn't just emphasize the wine or the food, it transforms them both and elevates the partnership to a perfect harmony.' She smiled winningly. That's what they say here, at Le Bernardin. It seems so appropriate for this meeting...of friends. Don't you think?'

Minister Potts agreed that it seemed most appropriate.

The General's Aide said, 'Yes, 'Elevating a partnership to the perfect harmony.' I think that is a wonderful sentiment. Don't you agree, General?'

The General agreed that it was a most wonderful sentiment by saying, 'Yes.'

Minister Potts thought his caviar, which the General said offhandedly was a snip at $145 an ounce, quite the most delicious he had tasted, without mentioning that it was indeed, the only caviar he had ever tasted. The Minister indulged himself with many inward chuckles. The Minister recalled his many meetings, as deputy mayor of Brewster's Neck, at which the standard fare was a cheese scone and a cup of tea, until the last meeting before Christmas, when the Council let loose with a bottle or two of Cold Duck...he recalled his business meetings with the Pritchard's in the darkened corner of a certain café where he scoffed a lemon muffin. Even the Cabinet's inaugural dinner, which at the time had seemed very grand, now seemed quaint. And the General's Aide...the Minister brought to mind his ministerial colleagues. Lumpen fools all. It was uncanny, the Minister mused, at how the General's Aide seemed to have an almost visible aura – a glow of soft light that became even brighter when she leaned close, as though every word was a very special confidence.

The Minister agreed that his lightly Smoked Sea Trout Tartare with Meyer Lemon Jelly Black Pepper Crisp, and Vodka Crème Fraîche, was simply the best choice. And yes, he was quite content to continue with the Clos de Vougeot, though he was not at all averse to sampling the 1973 Chateau

Montelena Chardonnay, which the General said was a collector's item and went for around $11,000 per bottle. But the occasion *merited* this little indulgence. After all, the General opined, how often did allies – indeed, *friends* the General's Aide enthused – how often did friends, the General continued, get together to jointly plan one of mankind's greatest adventures. One of *humankind's* greatest adventures, added the General's Aide, pointing out that women too, were excited about the prospect of the spectacle of the world's nuclear powers all testing their arsenals in this spirit of collaboration and friendship.

The Minister said that his Caramelized Puff Pastry, Whipped Milk Chocolate Ganache was undoubtedly, the most delicious he had encountered. The General's Aide was most complimentary about the Minister's choices. She could see instantly, that the Minister was an epicurean and likely, she cried gaily, placing a hand lightly on his, and with a twinkle in her deep blue eyes, a true *bon vivant*. Minister Potts was not exactly sure what a bon vivant was, but he owned, with a knowing chuckle, to being one all the same.

The conversation turned to the meeting with the Security Council.

The General said, 'Don't want to talk shop, but just a little curious, Minister Potts.'

The General's Aide said with mock reproof, 'Oh, he shouldn't be *Minister* here. Dimple is such a lovely name.'

The General continued. 'Ok…Dimple. So, tomorrow. You're all set to get them all aligned?'

Dimple said that he would certainly do his best. To get alignment. The General gazed steadily at his guest. 'We're counting on you.'

The General's Aide cried, 'Oh, I'm sure that Dimple knows that. Don't you?' And Minister Potts wasn't entirely certain but he thought for a fleeting and wonderful moment, she had given him a little pinch.

176

The General said, 'Got your speech all set. All written out?'

Dimple agreed that he had. In fact, he had it here – and he patted his jacket pocket. The General called for a bottle of the finest tawny port in the House. He briefly referred to his favourite Cuban cigars and lamented that they couldn't share that experience right now. Perhaps later, he added. Then he said, 'Look…Dimple. I know you've got a ton of experience in addressing conferences and so on, but can I give you a tip? The Security Council is a big deal. I know you know that. Well, experience has shown us that even the best orators – they like the Auto Cue.'

The General's Aide agreed most fervently, that even the best speakers ever, in a forum like the Security Council, why, they all used the Auto Cue! Wouldn't Dimple like to use the Auto Cue? It was just so much better than trying to read from a piece of paper, which after all, and she was certain that Dimple would agree, could look a little amateurish?

Dimple did agree that looking amateurish was not the right look, and he enquired how he might avail himself of the Auto Cue.

The General's Aide said that was easy and that she would be delighted to personally set it up for him. If he gave her his speech, she would see to it that it was loaded into the Auto Cue and that would be that. Nothing could be simpler and he would be simply commanding.

Momentarily, Minister Potts wondered about parting from his speech, but he was also certain that he should not like to look the slightest bit amateurish when making his historic presentation. In any event, the Minister would have entrusted his life to the General's Aide, so he passed her the speech and immediately felt that it was a splendid thing to be in such safe hands. And he smirked inwardly at the thought of Mayor Bumbulis, cracking a bottle of Cold Duck at the Brewster's Neck Council meeting and thinking she was living it up!

Abruptly, the General declared that he must leave. He had been buzzed. Minister Potts began to thank his host but his host made a small wave of his hand and was gone.

The General's Aide said it was one of the trials of being at the *heart of things* – but she was sure that Minister Potts knew all about that. Then she glanced at her watch and said with surprise and evident regret, that she too must leave. Her priority was to ensure that Dimple's speech was on the Auto Cue at UN Headquarters, and she wouldn't sleep until that was taken care of. But she would escort Dimple to his cab. Where she bade him a wonderful night and playfully kissed him on the cheek.

At her departure, the lights on W 51st Street seemed to dim, but the world's most expensive Chardonnay and Pinot Noir, and the most exquisite cuisine at Le Bernardin – and not to mention the truly delightful company, easily conspired to engender a sense of voluptuous wellbeing. Indeed, shortly after, as the Minister slipped between the sheets in his very comfortable bed, and in the moments before he fell into a deep sleep, he felt that he had acquitted himself remarkably well in this first major diplomatic assignment. He recalled how the Chair had wanted him to get on the Treasury benches...well, the Chair was an ass.

Downstairs, in the hotel foyer, paramedics lifted the concierge onto a stretcher. There was little need to be delicate for the concierge was evidently dead.

*

The Brainee gopher knocked at the door whose nameplate said, 'Nobody.' He waited until the small light alongside the door lit up and then he entered. He walked the approximately fifteen paces that was the distance between the door and the two chairs in front of Corker Pritchard's desk, and sat. He noted that two new messages, or slogans he supposed, had been added to the wall on which were already displayed the slogans, 'As used by Einstein,' and 'As endorsed by Darwin.' The new slogans said, 'Banish Brain Fog with Brainee,' and 'Certified Idiot becomes Doctor.'

Corker Nobody looked up and pursed his lips. He said, 'What do you think? Which one rings the bell? Yes, well, I think I'll go with the second. Verbal's work.' Then he held out his hand, 'Come on. What have you got?' He received the letter, perused it quickly and then emitted a braying laugh. 'Ha! Ha! Speaking of certified idiots. It's the Royal Society again. They object to our reference to Darwin. Ha! Ha! I'll change it. It will be, 'Certified idiot becomes Scientist.' Send the usual letter. Our humble apologies for causing consternation and so forth and humbly beseeching a little patience vis-à-vis Darwin and so on, and we'll change our advertising as quickly as possible etc. Ha! Ha!' Corker picked up the phone. He instructed the marketing guru to add another five or six slots for the Darwin ad for the next three days. Then he said, 'Anything else? Oh. That reminds me…' He tapped furiously for a minute. 'Don't know whether the Founder will see this in time – very busy man, our Founder, but worth a shot.' In fact, the Founder saw the email almost immediately. Sitting as he was outside the UN conference hall, he read, 'Know you're up to your gills, but if you can get a plug in for Brainee, it'll be worth gold! Corker. PS All good here. Big sale to Walmart.'

A jingle of awful carnival music interrupted Corker mid-way through instructing the gopher to set up a meeting with the Head of the School Principal's Association. Not for the first time, the gopher wondered why his boss had selected what he felt was quite possibly the worst advertising jingle he had ever heard.

Portly
Skinny

Portly
Skinny
Portly? Skinny
Portly Portly Portly
Skinny Skinny Skinny
Cooky all a chicken after catchy

However, the jingle put Corker Nobody in very high spirits. He sang, 'Cooky all a chicken! Ha! Ha!' And he pointed to the digital real-time sales display on the opposite wall which now showed that one hundred million Brainee pills had been sold. Then he said, 'Anything else?'

There wasn't, so the gopher departed, carefully closing Nobody's door behind him.

TWENTY-FOUR

In the offices of the UN, the assistant to the Secretary General invited the Minister of Foreign Affairs to come this way. The Minister followed the assistant down the corridor, through a vestibule and then onto the podium where sat the Secretary General. The Secretary General rose and extended both hands to clasp those of the Minister. Then she turned to the members of the Security Council and introduced their esteemed guest from New Zealand. She said that it was a great honour, to have Minister Potts join the assembly to offer a point of view on the grave matter lying on the table. The Minister, she said, had been the first politician to publicly refer to the possibility of discharging nuclear missiles at the moon. The Minister had quickly seen that this concept had resonated with people all over the world and now, here at the highest levels of government, Minister Potts's prescience was borne out in the Motion lying on the table, to wit, that the Security Council might approve a program in which all nuclear capable nations could take the opportunity to launch one missile at the moon, in order to verify the efficacy of its nuclear arsenal. The Secretary General said that if the proposal was accepted by the Council, it was suggested by the sponsors of the Motion, that the integrity of Mutually Assured Destruction, would be strengthened. However, the Secretary added, there also existed a view that perhaps alternatives might be considered – even, she added gravely, the idea that all nuclear weapons be decommissioned, forever. But she was not here to present an argument one way or the other. That was up to the Council members and no doubt, they would find the views expressed by Minister Potts on behalf of a small, independent nation with no stake one way of the other, to be a very valuable, if not deciding contribution to the debate. But that was enough of an introduction. It was now her privilege and honour to ask Minister Potts to address the Council.

The Secretary General took her seat and silently prayed that the French dug their toes in and that Minister Potts's message in favour of nuclear disarmament found a favourable reception with at least one representative. In confidence, the Prime Minister had shared the speech that Minister Potts was about to deliver. The Secretary General was delighted. She told her that it trod a very difficult line with delicacy and erudition and they could at least hope.

Minister Potts thanked the Secretary General and took his place at the podium. One of the Chinese representatives whispered to a colleague that whilst he approved of the grey trousers worn by the Minister, he did not like the blue jacket. His colleague agreed and whispered in return, that had the jacket been grey, that would have been much better.

The American Ambassador whispered to her colleague that it was truly one of the worst outfits she had seen, but at least the jacket was blue. Her colleague smirked behind his hand and whispered that the Republicans would be pissed.

Minister Potts waited until the Auto Cue showed the beginning of his speech. Nodding once to the Secretary General, he began to read. 'Madam Secretary General and honourable members of the Security Council of the United Nations. I am humbled to be standing before you today, to offer a perspective on behalf of my small and insignificant country, that hopefully, might also be seen as a contribution on behalf of all insignificant countries.'

The Minister thought what a truly wonderful device was the Auto Cue. How easy it made it all. What a wonderful person was the General's Aide! He continued, 'I and my Government, fully understand and appreciate what a grave and very important subject is to be debated and decided by the Security Council today. Naturally, I and we fully understand that you might choose to ignore the thoughts of a small and insignificant country, such as mine – but we crave your attention for these brief few minutes.' The Minister was a little surprised that the Prime Minister had twice characterised her country as insignificant, in just two paragraphs, and in point of fact, he had not remembered that she had said anything of the sort. He read on, 'As you know, there are some parties that wonder if the Proposal might not in some minor way, be seen by certain backward indigenous people, whose numbers are now so inconsequentially small that they are no longer included in any global census, as interfering with primitive superstitions about the moon. We in New Zealand understand primitive superstition. But as Council members know better than any, and especially better than those who inhabit small and insignificant countries, we are in the Twenty-first Century. As charming as old myths and quaint rituals may be, we are now fairly and squarely in the Age of the Algorithm. We are the Masters of Technology and that is the reason you are gathered here today. To consider how best to verify one of our most important technological advances – the nuclear weapon.' Minister Potts struggled to recall how these words could be at all consistent with the Prime Minister's views.

Minister Potts continued, 'Clearly, the Global Strategy of Mutually Assured Destruction must be preserved and strengthened. Nuclear scientists of all colours and creeds in the Nuclear Club, are of one mind. Simulations are no longer regarded as the gold standard for nuclear weapon operability. Nuclear scientists are unanimous in their view that it is time for a 'levelling up.' And this levelling up can only be attained by an actual test firing.

However, both scientists and members of this Council understand full well that the time of atmospheric and underground tests on this planet Earth – our Home – can no

183

longer be considered an option. It is this understanding that has led to the proposal to implement the proposed program to detonate weapons on the moon.' Minister Potts paused to extract his handkerchief to quickly wipe his brow. The Secretary General was no longer gazing at the Assembly through hooded eyes. Instead, her head rested, face down, in her hands.

Minister Potts continued, 'I now turn to the matter of environment. You will be well aware that there are certain parties that are concerned about environmental damage...' As these words appeared in the Auto Cue, Minister Potts felt a wave of relief. Of course, the PM had sacrificed the cultural perspective. Of course, the nuclear powers wouldn't give a fig about indigenous or cultural or romantic connections with the moon of any sort. They didn't give a fig about indigenous, cultural or romantic connections here on Earth. But the environment...even the nuclear club was forced to confront the reality of environmental degradation. That was a Twenty-first Century issue. That was why they wanted to take their testing into Space. The Minister entertained a fleeting but profound admiration for the PM's realpolitik. The Minister continued to read with renewed confidence.

'So, let us consider what the impact might look like. The moon is characterised by craters. We have been advised by NASA, that there are around 5,185 craters on the moon that are at least twenty kilometres in size. Scientists also estimate that there are roughly one million craters bigger than one kilometre across and more than half a billion larger than ten metres. But then, there is The South Pole-Aitken basin. On the far side of the moon, the South Pole-Aitken is one of the Solar System's biggest known impact craters. Ladies and gentlemen, I invite you to imagine a crater with a diameter of roughly 2,500 kilometres and a depth of up to 6.2 kilometres...' At this statement, a spontaneous round of applause occurred. Minister Potts continued, 'Ladies and gentlemen, I also invite you to consider how a handful of additional craters, such as we might expect would result from the proposed program, none of which could even begin to rival the South Pole-Aitken, would affect the appearance or indeed, the topography of the moon.' Again, a round of applause was forthcoming and the Russian ambassador whispered to the attaché on his right, 'Comrade, this Potz may have made a terrible mistake in wearing a blue jacket, but his analysis is very smart.'

Minister Potts read on with entirely mixed feelings. The unexpected applause was most gratifying, but the PM's environmental message was not as he expected or remembered. 'Further, ladies and gentlemen, I hardly need remind you that a new impact crater occurred even within the last thirty-eight years. Did we hear environmentalists complaining about this impact? Did we hear primitive tribes bemoaning this natural change in the appearance of the moon?' Several delegates rose to applaud this observation most enthusiastically and there was a furious nodding of heads and several cries of 'Quite so!' and similar pronouncements in other languages.

As the applause subsided, Minister Potts concluded, 'I believe I do not need to take any more of the Security Council's time. I believe that members will see that we, in our small and insignificant country firmly believe that the Council has not just the right but the *duty* to proceed with the proposed program – for the advancement of all humankind!'

The Minister offered his humble thanks for the honour of being able to offer a small and insignificant view that nonetheless, he hoped and prayed would be helpful.

It is true to say that Minister Potts had never experienced a standing ovation. It was, he decided, the most energising of moments. Raising his hand in acknowledgment, and in passing, he silently wished that the Latvian baker who had usurped his position as Mayor of Brewster's Neck, could have witnessed this extraordinary occasion.

*

It occurred to the Secretary General that the Director General of the WHO, did not look particularly well. She wondered if her own visage appeared as pale. She *felt* pale. She felt drained of resilience. The DG squeezed his brow as though to expunge a painful intrusion. He asked the SG, what had gone wrong. The SG said that she realised they were lost, just a minute or two into the Potts speech. To say she was flabbergasted did not begin to describe how she felt at that moment. Betrayal, wasn't too strong. I realised, she said bitterly, that I was in the presence of a charlatan. I realised that I had been deceived by the New Zealand Prime Minister. What she sent me and what Potts said were completely different. And when he exhorted the Council…that it was not just their responsibility but their *duty* to nuke the moon…The SG shook her head sorrowfully. She described the standing ovation. She described the various degrees of glee – it was the only word, on the faces of the Council members. She described how she felt ill as she watched several delegations shake Potts by the hand and slap him on the back. She recounted how the Chinese ambassador had completed his congratulations with that ancient proverb, which the SG knew well: 'A single conversation with a wise man is better than ten years of study.'

The SG lamented, 'A wise man? Could there ever have been a more inappropriate circumstance? The French simply rolled over when the Americans said they were renaming 'Freedom Fries' as 'Fabulous French Fries.' The only debate was about the order of launching of rockets. Who would go first and who would go last? It's to be alphabetic. Australia will go first. *Australia?* Who knew? And the US last.' The SG

186

lit a cigarette and coughed. 'I know,' she said, 'I haven't smoked for thirty years, but there it is…' The DG nodded sympathetically. The SG continued, 'But know this? This is not simply a nuclear test – multiple nuclear tests in fact – no…this is going to be a 'Nuclear Festival.' The SG emitted an hysterical laugh of a kind the DG had never heard in the several years they had been acquainted. It was a laugh that spoke of a deep depression of spirit. Yes, the SG continued bitterly, the Council was so pleased with itself, they decided it should be a spectacle for all humankind. They would phase the tests over three weeks, allowing a day between launches. Each missile strike will be clearly distinguishable. 'Clearly distinguishable!' she cried, drew heavily on her cigarette and then impulsively extinguished it by savagely thrusting it into her desk and absently took another from the packet.

For several long moments, the SG and the DG gazed at one another without expression. Each contemplated the outcome of the Security Council meeting. Each contemplated a Nuclear Festival. The DG recalled the last session of his conference and in particular, the description by the Field Operative from Canada of his country's decision to annex the Niagara Falls. He recalled the fracas that had shortly thereafter broken out between the Canadian and the Field Operative from the US, that had rapidly degenerated into a brawl when the FO from Mexico had shouted that the Mexicans intended to reclaim New Mexico. On the other side of the WHO War Room, the Australian FO suggested that plans were advanced to finally make New Zealand the Seventh State of Australia, as had been the intention from the beginning, and the Singapore FO said that his country intended to 'take Malaysia' since the Singaporeans were tired of paying the Malaysians for fresh water. The DG recalled his utter amazement when the badly bruised Canadian and Mexican Field Operatives had later admitted that there were no such plans, but that they seemed like they *should* be good plans,

187

and the Australian FO said through substantial bandage around her head, that she was just joking and the Singaporean FO said he was feeling most unwell and had departed, only to become another victim of Torpor before he reached the street. And now…a Nuclear Festival.

At last, the DG said, 'Did you see the protest outside the UN? They say there were at least several thousand there. "Save the Batmen." The DG shook his head. 'The government is accused of concealing the existence of the Batmen for well over one hundred years. Since 1835!' The DG shook his head. 'It was a hoax. A satire published by The Sun, in New York. But here it is again. There are Texans who want to fire Bibles at the moon.'

The SG said, 'Better than nukes.'

The DG replied distractedly, 'I believe I am going to have to declare a Pandemic.'

The SG nodded and coughed. 'Guidelines and so forth?'

The DG said, 'Yes. There'll need to be warnings, descriptions of symptoms and associated ailments – who's more vulnerable and suchlike. Underlying conditions etcetera.'

The SG added, 'And remedial measures? Antidotes?'

The DG said, 'Yes. I've got a team on it now. But who knows? Some of our researchers may succumb, if they haven't already. One of them – one of my best ecologists – suggested to me that we need to find a way to get a specimen of the Batmen, before they're wiped out. I've not the faintest idea what she's thinking. And it's apparent we have at least two Vectors in the building.'

The call lapsed once again into gloomy silence, then the SG said, 'What do you suppose the explosions will look like?'

The DG said, 'I guess they'll be pretty bright. Depend on the yield, I suppose. I daresay the Russians, the Chinese and the Americans will put on a pretty good show.'

The SG said, 'But you wouldn't want to count the Brits and the French out. Or the Indians for that matter. National pride and so on. A lot of competition to be best and biggest.'

The DG said, 'I've a brother-in-law whose got a decent telescope.'

The SG said, 'That'd be good. But I believe there will be public mega screens. Time Square, Tiananmen, Trafalgar, Red Square and all that, showing each blast in real time. I believe the idea is a kind of celebration of technology and our willingness to work together.'

The DG said, 'That's the beneficial side of things.'

The SG and the DG gazed into their computers silently. The SG thought that the DG was perhaps looking a little less depressed than when they had begun. The DG thought something. But he wasn't absolutely sure what it was. In one moment, he imagined a stupendous flash, on the moon, and in the next, he found himself wondering whether it really mattered if the Batmen were exterminated.

*

The PM was furious. She caught herself muttering. She never muttered. She broke the first pencil she had ever broken in her life. She had taken one sip of her morning coffee and then tipped the cup out. She realised when she went to her private bathroom in the Beehive, that she had forgotten to brush her hair. She never forgot to brush her hair. The PM had taken a call from the Director General of the WHO. The WHO had just issued its first alert advising all governments of a Pandemic of Alta Stultitia. The DG explained, confidentially, that the decision of the Security Council regarding the proposal to nuke the moon was a deciding factor. But even before the Council decision, he knew that the WHO must act. The DG described the evidence of outbreaks of Stupidity as evinced by his Field Operatives from around the World. They were many and growing. The DG said that even in the conference, he had witnessed previously unimaginable folly. At that time, he said, he and his senior team were of a mind that they were seeing the early stages of an Epidemic. But then – the Security Council's unanimous and evidently enthusiastic decision to implement a nuclear weapons test on the moon made it abundantly clear that the Epidemic must be upgraded.

Had the PM seen the outline of the proposed test? She had. She was aware that the proposed test was to be communicated as 'The International Nuclear Validation Festival.' The 'INVF' had a tentative commencement date in just two weeks – beginning with Australia.

The PM was still stunned. She had seen the media release from the UN that had begun: "The Security Council of the United Nations is gratified that it is able to advise that it has come to the unanimous decision supporting a proposal to carry out a nuclear weapons validation program on the moon. The Security Council believes that this program will materially strengthen the World's commitment to Mutually Assured Destruction. The Security Council has established a management team for this 'The International Nuclear Validation Festival (INVF)' to be headed by Dr Hank Titsman, who will develop the Program and Festival, with the objective of arranging sequential validations in alphabetic order of nuclear armed nations…The Security Council sees the INVF as a positive and proactive means to drawing the peoples of the World closer together. Acting as both a reminder that misunderstandings could lead to Armageddon, and providing an opportunity for all peoples to celebrate together and especially at a time when many other issues vex policy makers and ordinary citizens alike…"

The release ended with the light-hearted observation by the UN Secretary General that the INVF would likely become "The Greatest Show on Moon," and an assurance that Batmen did not exist.

The PM read this release over her breakfast, which this morning had comprised her favourite Eggs Benedict with Hollandaise. Except that she ate just one mouthful. In a separate note from the Ministry of Foreign Affairs, she read that her Minister's address to the Security Council had been "forthrightly supportive of the Proposal, and highly persuasive and had resulted in a standing ovation."

The PM had shouted, loudly, 'Stupidity!' Her partner and daughter had been alarmed. They could not recall seeing the PM or 'Mummy' in this case, in such high colour. The PM had cried, 'It's a plague!' And she had left for the office in such a hurry she forgot to pick up her satchel, or kiss her family.

And now, she was told that Australia was to be first out-of-the-blocks.

'When did Australia become a nuclear power?' cried the PM. 'The deceit! And right next door! What madness is this?'

The PM asked what was the WHO's advice? What did the WHO suggest that governments do?

The DG said that his team were still working on this. They were urgently researching vaccines. Victims of Alta Stultitia would be described as having symptoms such as brain fog, confusion, belief in UFOs, Batmen and/or the inability to finish one coherent sentence, and/or ignorance of such standard ideas as a round Earth. These victims, for the purposes of medical treatment would be termed, 'Fogged.' His team was also, as a matter of great urgency, striving to find a means to identifying Vectors of the closely linked and

191

frequently fatal Torpor. Curiously, observed the DG, it appeared that victims of Torpor had simply given up – as though overwhelmed by a toxic gas of some kind. But as yet, no gas had been detected. The DG said that some of his experts were working on the idea that somehow, the victims came into the presence of an intensely sapping force, that at best, caused a kind of temporary paralysis, and in others, the loss of the will-to-live. The DG added that his experts were hypothesising that sudden exposure to an intense episode of stupidity, may well be the trigger…

But there was some good news. Whilst her Minister of Foreign Affairs may have appeared to have gone badly off piste in his address to the Security Council, the DG was having second thoughts.

The PM frowned. Surely, she said, her Minister was guilty of subterfuge at the least? Were it not for the fact that he was being hailed in the media everywhere, she would have summarily sacked him.

The DG thought, 'What a passionate woman! She could be Spanish!' he said, 'I understand completely. But think on this. Had he spoke *against* the Council, there may have been no unanimity. And I suspect that certain nations would have proceeded to attack the moon regardless. We may have seen acrimony and enmity developing. Acrimony and enmity, when it comes to the Nuclear Club, are not good. Instead, your Minister Potts brought all the parties together. The Americans were only too happy to concede on Fabulous French Fries. And did I mention the impact that your Minister Potts had through his remarkable choice of suit? No? Well, half loved his communist pants and half loved his capitalist jacket. Goodwill, Prime Minister. The Secretary General told me that there was largely goodwill everywhere, with the exception of the 'Save Our Batmen,' or SOB movement. Even he, who was devastated at the time, is coming to see that your

Minister Potts may have played a very clever hand indeed.'
The DG grinned.

The PM said faintly, 'I'm not sure I understand any of this.'

TWENTY-FIVE

The Head of News wore a jubilant smile. Indeed…it might well be described as a merciless or even, in certain lights, a ravenous smile. It was the smile of a Rhodesian Ridgeback. And what had provoked this unnerving expression? It was the video clip of an elderly Russian woman, by the name of Olga Bogdanov – who was also a life-long and skilled (though unrecognised) chess player – admitting that she had been paid to lay in bed with the appearance of a senseless stiff, and then to do what she was perfectly capable of doing, beating several school boys simultaneously at chess. And yes, she was fluent in French because she had spent much of her life in Nantes. And yes, she agreed that a video showing her as being death's door and then due to the miraculous intervention of a drug, become a rejuvenated being, could appear to be somewhat misleading – but one had no family and so one did what one could to make ends meet. And what was the name of the drug that was purported to have accomplished this miraculous renewal? She did not know and nor did she know the name of the fellow who had arranged for the misleading, if not to say fraudulent video to be made. But the Head of News did.

*

The light outside the door of the office bearing the nameplate, 'Nobody,' glowed red. From inside the office came the cry, 'Enter!'

Founder Potts entered the long office of Corker Nobody and found himself in an enthusiastic embrace. And then he found himself in possession of a cigar.

Corker cried, 'An El Rey del Mundo, Dimple! A light but rich tobacco and a cigar known as 'The King of the World! What could be better? For a Founder and Minister who has taken his creation to the World.' And even as Corker pointed, the digital display sang its carnival jingle and Corker cried, 'Cooky all a chickens!' And the display showed that sales of the Brainee pill had just passed one billion. Corker exclaimed, 'You dark horse, Dimps. You cunning devil...who would have suspected? Why, me! I knew from the beginning, when you had your idea of developing a pill to counter stupidity, that you were the man to launch it. Your vision and inspiration, Dimps – that was what I saw from the beginning. And now look – we've taken an order from the World Health Organisation for two hundred and fifty million pills! And more to come! We're rich, Dimple! You're rich! And what did you call it? Greed-with-Care. You guru. You Top Entrepreneur and what else? A Minister of the Crown who receives a standing ovation from the Security Council! Here, sit down, sit down. Allow me.'

And Corker Nobody took the Founder's cigar and cut the sealed tip, explaining that the way in which the cut is made, determined the quality of the draw, the subtlety and intensity of the cigar's aroma, whilst assuring that the cigar remained evenly lit. 'You see, Dimple, the head of a handmade Havana is sealed with a cap of tobacco, like this, which helps to secure the wrapper leaf in place. Before we light, we must create a broad opening, to permit a proper draw. Like this.' And he took up cigar scissors and made just such a cut. Then he sat in the chair opposite the Founder and took up a box of matches. He said, 'I have saved this for you, dear boy. But we must take care. You might think that I might just light and suck – but that would be a travesty! There are two simple rules…' and he winked, 'Take your time, and do a thorough job. A thorough job, Dimple, such as you have done with Brainee. You see? The whole of the foot of the cigar must be alight before we settle back to enjoy. We do not want the El Rey del Mundo to burn down unevenly. And being a little fatter, the more time we must take to light it.'

Corker struck the match and held it where the flame barely touched the cigar. He held the cigar just above the flame, at a 45-degree angle so that the heat, not the flame, caused the combustion. He carefully rotated the El Rey del Mundo so that the outer ring of the foot became evenly lit. He brought the cigar to his lips and with eyes closed in dreamy appreciation, rotated the cigar through the first few puffs.

Corker paused to lay his cigar on the tray. He said, as he cut Dimple's cigar and handed it to him, 'Dimple, the appreciation of an El Rey del Mundo, is like the appreciation of the finest wine. It is an exceptional form of art – a sophisticated pastime for the true connoisseur and frankly, for the rich. There. We do not 'smoke' the El Rey del Mundo, we *savour* the El Rey del Mundo.' He took up his own cigar and drew. Founder Potts also drew. Corker continued, 'Every draw, Dimple, is an experience of succulent pleasure to the palate, as the rich bouquet of varied tobacco flavours in the El Rey del Mundo bloom. Bloom! Just as Brainee, your brainchild, Dimple, blooms and grows!'

Founder Potts was startled and flattered. Indeed, he had been startled and flattered ever since he had delivered his address to the Security Council. No, he thought on reflection, he had been startled and flattered ever since his dinner engagement with the General and his Aide at Le Bernardin. That he had been instrumental in the decision to proceed with the International Nuclear Validation Festival, was a considerable accomplishment – as had been pointed out to him by the Americans, and the Russians and the Chinese and others…unanimous in their praise of his far-sighted vision of a World at Peace because the INVF would eliminate uncertainty about MAD. Minister Potts would long be remembered for being the catalyst and the visionary, said the French. Wonderful speech and superb delivery, said the Americans.

Founder Potts contemplated these wondrous events as he savoured in the proper fashion, the El Rey del Mundo and basked in the praise showered upon him by his colleague – nay, good friend, Corker Nobody, who, even as Founder Potts gave a slight cough, reminded him not to inhale the smoke. The true pleasure, cried Corker, was to be found in appreciating the finely balanced blend of tobacco flavours, which Dimple would detect on his palate through his refined sense of taste. And who has a refined sense of taste for an El Rey del Mundo? Only those who can afford it! And Corker laughed uproariously.

Founder Potts did as he was instructed. He relaxed and mulled the flavours. He ensured that his El Rey del Mundo did not even begin to dampen, lest it offer only a disappointing mixture of hot air and thin smoke. Founder Potts glanced at the wall on which the large banners were displayed' 'As used by Einstein.' 'As endorsed by Darwin.' 'Banish Brain Fog with Brainee,' and 'Certified Idiot becomes Doctor.' With 'Doctor' being crossed out and 'Scientist,' inserted. Founder Potts enquired about the campaign. Corker waved a hand dismissively. The Royal Society had objected to the first three slogans and the Advertising Standards bozos were coming at them about the 'Certified Idiot,' but the marketing guru was busy developing new material all the time. Anyway, now that the Founder had captured the WHO, who cared? And Coker went very pink with satisfaction. For some time, they savoured their cigars in silence.

Then, the light on Corker's desk lit up and Corker scowled. 'What does that bozo think? I'm sharing a moment with my boss, and he dares interrupt!' He cried, 'What?'

But it was not the gopher who popped his head around the door.

'Marketing dork!' Cried Corker. 'Well?'

'I come with *certain* news...' With a sober expression, Verbal Pritchard strolled into the office and eased himself, uninvited, into the chair alongside of the Founder. 'As a matter of fact, certain news that concerns our Founder...'

'Certain news?' Corker sniffed, drew on his cigar and then smirked at Founder Potts, 'Here is our Founder. Behold! Sharing a well-earned moment with Nobody. Ha! Ha! In quiet contemplation of his raging success. Entrepreneur extraordinaire! International diplomat, adviser to the Security Council, and purveyor of the world's most valuable therapy. Here he is, marketing dork. Fit as a fiddle and ready to approve the expansion of Brainee into China. Certain news? Our Founder is the source of *all* the news! Ha! Ha!'

Founder Potts chuckled. The source of all the news...indeed. The media everywhere wished to interview the Entrepreneur and Diplomat. Some wanted to know why and how he had persuaded the Security Council. Was he concerned about the Batmen? Some wanted to know what was the secret ingredient in Brainee. Was it a gift from a grateful indigenous people? Some wanted to know what his next foreign policy initiative would be. Would New Zealand respond to a nuclear-armed Australia and how? The questions went on and on.

Corker waved a hand at the digital display. 'Over a million dollars a day, nephew. Certain news? Who cares? But okay. What have you discovered? That our Chemical Whizzo did time? They were test subjects. Likely enough they'd have croaked anyway. No? Well, what?' Corker rolled his eyes in the direction of Founder Potts. 'Get to the point, man, the Founder and I have matters to discuss.' And he winked at the Founder, who returned his wink whilst emitting another indulgent, managerial chuckle.

'I have reason to believe that our Founder is a target for assassination.'

Founder Potts dropped his cigar and lurched forward in his seat.

Verbal Pritchard continued, 'I believe that Big Pharma has put out a contract. Brainee is too successful. They want us gone and taking out Founder Potts is the perfect way. Poison…'

Founder Potts's eyes widened and he cried, 'Poison?'

Verbal replied, 'I believe they're bringing a law suit, accusing Brainee of peddling a pill that is poisonous. Pure character assassination.'

Corker Nobody leapt to his feet and drew furiously on his cigar in a manner not recommended, and blew a huge plume of smoke. 'I foresaw this. Didn't I say? Well, I did. Big Pharma? Big Losers more like!' He rounded on the bearer of certain news. 'So, what are you doing about it? What's our campaign? Rebuttal, refutation, counter law suit and so forth? What are you doing? And don't say nothing. You're overpaid as it is. Let me tell you…' he levelled a finger at his nephew, marketing dorks are a dime-a-dozen. 'If you think you can come bearing certain news, that Corker Nobody has already foreseen, without a campaign up your sleeve and ready-to-roll, then you're on the slippery slope to the back door. And just remember, we don't pay a cent of redundancy. Well?'

Founder Potts gasped, 'Assassination? They mean to kill me?'

Corker Nobody replied, 'Exaggeration, Pottsy. Scare tactics and so forth. They could use a gun, or a knife, but what they really want is to drive us out of bizzo with untruths and sleight-of-hand and such like. Misinformation. It's the way they work. Why, if they'd wanted to top you, you wouldn't be sitting here this very moment. Could have done it yesterday. Any day. No, Just want to unhinge you – but they've picked

on the wrong man. No-one puts the fear up Founder Potts!'
Corker Nobody drew on his cigar and then cried, 'Well?'

Verbal tapped his nose. 'I've formulated a plan.'

'Of course, you have! I wouldn't have thought otherwise. Would we Pottsy? We wouldn't have thought otherwise. Well?'

'We expose them. We put it out that Founder Potts has been targeted by Big Pharma, to strangle the competition. We put it out that there's a whistle-blower, and the whistle-blower has revealed a conspiracy, at the highest levels, to strangle Founder Potts.'

'Strangle?' Cried Founder Potts, clutching his throat.

'Figure of speech, Pottsy.' Replied Corker Nobody. 'So, a whistle-blower? I'm not surprised. Will he say more? Which reminds me of that book – "Who Flung Dung."

Wiping his brow with a handkerchief, and preoccupied with the threat to his life, Founder Potts asked incredulously, 'Who Flung Dung?'

'By Willie Throw More. Ha! Ha! But will he say more? That's what I'm asking. Deep Throat and so on. Will he leak like a city water pipe? Will he-'

Verbal looked surprised, 'No.'

'No?'

The marketing guru said, 'We in marketing don't need *actual* sources. We need sources who if they existed, *would* have been whistle-blowers. In that circumstance. Which gives us a perfect marketing boost.'

'Do we need a marketing boost?'

'No.'

'I would have thought not.' Corker Nobody settled back and drew on his cigar. 'But we'd never turn one down. So, how will we use this conspiracy? Posters?'

The marketing guru winked. He opened his folder and displayed the statement, "Genius Founder fears for Life.

Brainee too effective. Whistle blower describes Big Pharma Conspiracy."

Founder Potts, who had been distractedly contemplating his own end, perhaps by knife or strangling or poison, read the words and cried, 'What are we going to do?'

The marketing guru turned the page to display the words: "Brainee throws 24-hour security around Founder Potts." And beneath that, "Founder Potts scorns Big Pharma Threat." And under that again: "Brainee says it won't be intimidated by Big Pharma Assassination Threat."

Founder Potts was gratified to see that he would not be cowed, but where, he demanded, was his security guard. How many were there and could we trust them? The marketing guru replied that the best type of security, was the *covert* kind. An invisible wall of steel. The marketing guru glanced over his own shoulder, and then over the shoulder of the Founder and gave an almost imperceptible but meaningful nod.

Founder Potts said, 'You mean, they're here?'

The marketing guru put a finger to his lips.

The Founder continued, 'Even when I leave?' He gestured towards the door and perhaps spaces beyond. 'Everywhere I go? Even when asleep?'

The marketing guru said, 'A ring of steel.'

The Founder said, 'I must go. This has come as a shock. But I won't be intimidated.' He leaned toward the tray and was instantly intercepted. An El Rey del Mundo was never stubbed, cried Corker. It should be laid thus...he said, gently laying the El Rey del Mundo to rest, in which position, he added solicitously, it would simply self-extinguish.

The Founder started toward the door and noticing a slight bulge in the drapes, paused to cast a questioning glance at the marketing guru.

The marketing guru returned an almost imperceptible nod.

The Founder returned a slight narrowing of his eyes, and departed.

*

The Secretary of State said that it had gone well. This was not her private opinion. Her private opinion was that she rather wished she had never left the family farm in Montana. Her private opinion was that a life with her folks, and her friends, including her beloved collie and her equally beloved pony; growing and harvesting crops and making preserves – all of that, which she had been in such haste to leave when she was young, now seemed the best thing in the world. Now, she was saying to the General that the decision of the Security Council to proceed with the International Nuclear Validation Festival, was the 'right' outcome. It was not the right outcome. It was an act, she had silently and privately bemoaned, of sheer lunacy. Nonetheless, she had been disturbed and rather taken aback, when she had detected another private thought, and indeed, she had wondered where it had even come from, when momentarily and with a sense of childlike wonder, she imagined a gigantic flash on the moon as a very large nuclear weapon detonated...

This thought led the Secretary to ponder the roles of the brain stem versus the prefrontal cortex. The Secretary was well aware that the prefrontal cortex was where many important functions took place. Such as controlling one's behaviour and impulses. Or, delaying instant gratification and regulating one's emotions. Not to mention planning and seeing and predicting the consequences of one's behaviour. The Secretary understood that while this neurological centre of reasoning could moderate and keep behaviour under control, it could not entirely suppress the basic instincts, sometimes described as the crocodilian instincts, generated in the brainstem.

The Secretary was reflecting on these ideas even as the General said, with evident satisfaction, that the Chinese and the Russians had 'fallen into line.' This meant, she understood, that they would take their place in the alphabetic queue and that they would specify in advance the yield of the weapon they proposed to test. The Secretary agreed that that was sensible and presumably in-line with the intentions of the USA. When the General did not respond, the Secretary made clear that this was not a rhetorical question. The General replied that the Secretary's understanding was 'largely correct.' The Secretary asked if she was largely correct, where was she not correct? The General assumed an expression of just the slightest indication of abdominal pain. The General said that the Secretary was correct in that the USA was aligned with an alphabetical launch sequence, but not entirely correct regarding the disclosure of yield. The General added, evidently reluctantly, that 'Big Boy' had a yield some distance beyond that which US Intelligence knew either the Chinese or the Russians could 'put in the field.' The Secretary enquired what the General meant when he said, 'some distance beyond?' The General pursed his lips and the Secretary, still reflecting on the nature of the human mind, wondered whether the recently announced Pandemic of Stupidity might not yet be linked to some measurable degradation of the prefrontal cortex, or, alternatively, to an expansion of the brainstem. It had not escaped the Secretary's attention that the General had a slightly receding forehead and a particularly solid neck. Indeed, she found that she was contemplating the necks of several of her middle-aged and older male colleagues and remarkably, she could see a pattern. A straight, vertical line from the shoulder to the top of the head. She decided that she must have a discreet conversation with the Secretary of Health.

The Secretary said, 'I believe you mentioned that we might use the test as a demonstration?'

After a pause, the General said, 'Ma'am. The RDS-220 hydrogen bomb, also known as the Tsar Bomba, was the biggest thermo-nuclear bomb ever made. Soviet. Exploded in October '61 over the Russian Arctic Sea. Dropped by a Tu-95 bomber using a fall-retardation parachute.' The General stared at the wall as though even at this moment, he could see the Tsar Bomba on its way down. His eyes just ever so slightly narrowed. 'Detonation 3 miles above the ground. It produced a yield of 50 mega tons.'

The Secretary said, 'Forgive me. But I don't really understand what that means.'

The General said. 'It means that it was equivalent to the explosive power from the simultaneous detonation of 3,800 Hiroshima bombs.'

The Secretary suddenly held her breath. She couldn't help it and indeed, she found that she had to force herself to continue breathing. At last, the Secretary was able to ask, 'But we've never let off something...that huge?'

The General said a trifle sharply, 'Ma'am, we don't *let off* nuclear weapons. Excuse me. No. We built the B41. Half that yield – but we built 500 of them.'

The Secretary's insight was that for the General and she presumed his colleagues, this enormous number of American bombs, simply did not compensate for the fact that the Soviets had built the Tsar Bomba.' She said, 'But now...'

The General allowed himself that slight, constrained smile, 'We've got 'Big Boy.'

The Secretary said, 'And Big Boy, is bigger? A lot bigger?'

The General said, '100 mega tons'

The Secretary said, scarcely believing what she was saying, 'So, we could destroy Hiroshima 7,600 times over, with one bomb? Big Boy?'

The General considered this for a moment. 'Yes, Ma'am. More or less.'

The Secretary gazed at the General's neck because he was gazing at the wall. She found she was fascinated and afriad, as she might be if she instead beheld a puff adder. She felt that her hypothesis about an expansion of the brainstem, possibly at the expense of the prefrontal cortex, was a most plausible explanation for what she was hearing, and indeed the events of the past few days. In her mind's eye she saw Minister Potts and recognised the similarity. Not as pronounced as the General, but his neck too, she recalled to be not far short of the width of his head. Minister Potts had not seemed so…committed, as the General clearly was, but he was not a military man, and perhaps his condition was not as far advanced. Even so, he had urged the Security Council in its decision to undertake the INVF.

The Secretary said, 'How many Big Boys do we have?'

'Just one. That's all we need.'

'So, the Festival and Big Boy is really an exercise in intimidation? Only no-one knows? And then we'll have bragging rights and the Tsar Bomba will be relegated to nuclear footnote?'

The General said, 'Your understanding, Madam Secretary, is right on the button.'

The Secretary did not wish to be 'right on the button.' She felt that no-one should be 'right on the button.' The Secretary remembered, almost painfully, how wonderful was a dessert of preserved Damson plums, with sweet shortcake and ice-cream. She wondered whether the General had ever had such a dessert. Had he done so, perhaps Big Boy might never have been conceived…

The Secretary of State said, 'General. The speech that Minister Potts gave at the Council…was not the same as the speech he described to me.'

The General's gaze turned slowly from the empty wall to the Secretary of State. In a tone that he might have employed had he been asked to give an opinion about the colour of the Secretary's wall, he said, 'I presume his thinking advanced. Afterward.'

*

The Prime Minister regarded her Minister of Foreign Affairs. The PM's intention had been to deliver an excoriating reprimand. Her intention had been to reduce the Minister to an abject doohickey of no consequence. The PM had it in mind that the Minister would leave her office stripped of his portfolio and relegated to the risible position of assistant minister of Horse Racing and never in her political lifetime, to be heard from, or of, again.

But the PM had spoken to the Director General of the WHO. And the PM had seen the entirely favourable headlines, acclaiming the only known antidote to a Pandemic of Stupidity – the Brainee pill with Brain Booster XL8. And now, the PM was the recipient of a letter that rendered her previous intentions quite redundant. The PM read the letter and found that her hands commenced to shake and her breathing to become an effort. The PM discovered that an unpleasant drumming was occurring in her left temple. She glanced down at the letterhead of the United Nations and the signature of the Secretary General. The letter said that unfortunately, Dr Hank Titsman, who had been designated to lead the International Nuclear Validation Festival, had disappeared. Consequently, the UN wished to appoint Minister Potts, as the Director of INVF. The Security Council members were of one mind, that Minister Potts – by dint of his exceptional grasp of the issues and MAD, and by dint also of his exceptional abilities as an entrepreneur; and by dint of his position, representing as he did a small and insignificant nation with no vested interest; then Minister Potts was the perfect person to assume this prestigious role.

The PM studied her Minister of Foreign Affairs. Her intention had been to begin by demanding an explanation for the astonishing and unauthorised changes he had made to the speech she had written. Instead, the PM was forced to smile.

Minister Potts observed the small smile and was relieved. For a minute or two, he had actually wondered whether the PM was angry and he felt most uneasy. But she had smiled and his considerable apprehensions rapidly evaporated. He took the initiative and offered that 'Things had worked out well.'

The PM pinched the inside of her left forearm. It was extremely painful but it had the desired effect. She congratulated the Minister on a job well done, and welcomed him home. She said that it appeared they needed to make an immediate media release. No, not just about the Security Council decision – and she held out the Secretary General's letter – but about the UN's invitation for Minister Potts to become the Director of the International Nuclear Validation Festival.

Minister Potts listened to the PM and read the brief letter. He paused with some alarm on reading of the disappearance of Hank Titsman. However, it was likely, he mused silently, that Titsman was not surrounded at all times, by a covert ring of steel. And surely Big Pharma would not dare threaten a man appointed by the UN...Minister Potts looked toward the window. The media release came to mind. 'Minister Potts becomes Nuclear Czar.' Or perhaps, 'Well-known Entrepreneur and Minister of Foreign Affairs, appointed to high UN position.' Or perhaps, 'UN grateful for far-sighted Potts finding solution to MAD.' Minister Potts imagined such a headline on the front page of the 'Brewster News.' The fake mayor – the Latvian baker, Sarah Bumbulis who had stolen his mayoralty, would read how Dimple Potts had taken the Security Council by storm. Bumbulis would be rendered so humble she would become invisible, perhaps even to her husband, Herb Hikaka. Not that Dimple had anything against Herb. But did he really warrant his promotion to Sergeant for having uncovered Corker's indiscretion? When all was said and done, what real difference did it make what was in a sausage? But that was another matter. Bumbulis would read that Dimple Potts had been appointed to a very high position in the UN. Minister Potts permitted himself a small smile.

The PM said that the Secretary General had extended the invitation. It was for Minister Potts to make the call. Did he want to take on this very large, extra responsibility, particularly given that the PM had been thinking that the Minister of Foreign Affairs had an important assignment, building a new understanding and trade deal between New Zealand and Tasmania, entailing a lengthy, on-the-ground visit? Perhaps the Minister might like to give this some thought – for a day or so.

But the Minister didn't want to give it more consideration. The Minister wished to accept the position. Well, said the PM, that was fine and she would advise the Secretary General accordingly. She assumed that the Minister understood that he would likely have to undertake some arduous international travel – dealing with, if she could be frank and in strictest confidence – some really quite tricky customers. She was referring to the Defence Departments of countries in the Nuclear Club. Not to put too fine a point on it, did the Minister feel he had gained sufficient experience in international diplomacy to address the many complex issues he would be likely to encounter?

Minister Potts understood that the PM was endeavouring to be helpful. It was, he thought, extremely decent of her. Another type of PM might have simply tipped him in the deep-end, but she was not that kind of person. Minister Potts thanked her for her concern but said that his career in politics was long. Minister Potts said cheerfully, 'You can imagine what a local body Council is like, Prime Minister.' And he had in mind Old Fred Witherspoon and Ted Potross as he added, 'Mad as fruit-bats – all of them.'

TWENTY-SEVEN

The Chief Executive of the Department of Health frowned. The European Medicines Agency wanted to know what the active ingredient called Brain Booster XL8 was comprised of. The CE took up the other letter on his desk and read again the urgent request from the US Food & Drug Administration, for details concerning the formulation of the therapeutic drug, Brainee. The CE glanced at the Department's Chief Chemist and shook his head. The CE drummed his fingers on his desk and then sighed. And though he knew pretty well where they were on this, at last he said, 'Where are we on this? On Brainee?'

The Chief Chemist appeared to be a little uncomfortable because he also knew pretty well where they were on this – which wasn't very far at all. His official had made no progress whatsoever in her investigative visit to the production facility of Brainee Ltd. The factory had been in lock-down in order to undertake intensive cleaning. And the Founder, who also happened to be the Minister of Foreign Affairs, was overseas. The Chief Chemist supposed that the CE had seen the outcome of the Minister's visit to the UN?

The CE had seen the headline on the front page of the morning news: "Minister Potts to Attack Moon!" With the sub-head, "Acclaimed Minister of Foreign Affairs, Dimple Potts is appointed to prestigious position, as Director of the UN's International Nuclear Validation Festival." The article continued, "Deftly traversing the dark woods of international politics, Minister Potts proved that he is no bunny when he led the Security Council towards a major international collaboration to validate the nuclear arsenals that keep the peoples of the Earth, safe and secure. As Director of the INVF, Minister Potts will oversee the development of the Festival, which he said will bring people closer together in a celebration of humanity's ability to not just develop new technology, but to ensure that the technology actually works. Minister Potts said that more and more people, all around the world had begun to question whether the nuclear weapons held by their governments, would actually do the job if 'push came to shove."

This questioning, said Minister Potts, led to people living in a state of continual anxiety, which could exacerbate brain fog and confusion and so forth, and in this, he had a most personal interest, as the Founder of Brainee Ltd. The Minister said that the recent international Study that showed that Stupidity was on the rise, had just this week been elevated by the WHO, when it declared a Pandemic. Minister Potts said that out of his great concern for his fellow humans, the Study had inspired him to create Brainee with Brain Booster XL8, which had now sold more than a billion pills world-wide. Questioned about his commercial motives, the Minister said that while it was true that Brainee was returning strong profits, this was entirely consistent with the Minister's personal values, as well as being the political philosophy of his Party, the First Union of Conservative Thinkers, promoting the very worthy ideal of 'Greed-with-Care.' Minister Potts added, 'Who could not feel compassion for those less well-endowed? Personally, I feel a grave responsibility do what I can.'

The Minister pointed to a new purchase order from the WHO for a very large shipment of Brainee, which he understood was to be prioritised for what the WHO regarded to be the most vulnerable group – middle-aged and older men – of all nationalities. Did the Minister take Brainee himself? The Minister laughed, and his photograph, which accompanied the article captured that very moment, and said that naturally, as one falling into that vulnerable group, he

211

took the recommended dose of Brainee twice each day. And had he noticed a difference? The Minister had. Since taking Brainee he had, with laser-like clarity, visualised the flaw in one of his previous innovations that had removed a considerable amount of fur from the hindquarters of the test subject, Doc Cod and consequently, he was considering renewing his interest in the development of the 'Doggo Cleano.'

The Chief Executive of the Department of Health frowned again. He said, 'This is awkward.'

The Chief Chemist said, 'It's very awkward.'

The CE asked lightly, 'Do you take them?'

The Chief Chemist nodded. 'Thought I'd better give them a test.'

The CE said, 'But we'll have to respond, to the EU and the FDA.'

The Chief Chemist nodded.

The CE said, 'Do we have any idea about the active ingredient?'

The Chief Chemist said, 'It's a trade secret. They haven't applied for patent so we're going to have to do chemical analysis. Take quite a bit of time. Two to three weeks.'

The CE said, 'I'll go back to the EU and the FDA and say our information isn't yet complete. Probably two weeks?'

The Chief Chemist nodded.

There was a lengthy pause. Then the CE said, 'What do you think about the Festival? Nuking the moon?'

The Chief Chemist said, 'Big call. But at the end of the day, the moon's just a rock. Thin atmosphere so radiation isn't going to be a problem.'

The CE said, 'No. Those are my thoughts. They'll be different sized weapons, one supposes…some small but likely some pretty big. The Americans and the Russians…and the Chinese…they'll likely go for something bigger.'

The Chief Chemist nodded. 'I read that each test will be streamed real-time, right around the world. Quite a spectacle.'

The CE said, 'I remember the early footage of nuclear tests. Awful of course, but you couldn't help being impressed by the size of the cloud and so on. Remember Bikini? All those ships – just disappeared. Damned impressive. Awful, of course.'

The Chief Chemist nodded. 'Most people will have forgotten. But this Festival could really bring it home – except entirely safely. It's a pretty smart idea. Apparently, there was a substantial number of people in that international Study who thought of it – quite spontaneously and independently. Makes you realise that as humans we have far more in common than not.'

The CE said, 'Yes it does. But our Minister was actually the first politician anywhere to say that we should take a good look at it. We're a small and insignificant country, but by golly, we punch above our weight – and now look – Potts is the head of the whole thing.'

The Chief Chemist said, 'You won't need binoculars to see the big ones. The naked eye will be enough. There'll be a helluva flash, before the cloud.'

For a few moments the CE and the Chief Chemist sat silently and imagined privately, what that helluva flash would be like. Perhaps it would appear as wide as the moon itself? That would certainly be a once-in-a-lifetime sight.

The Chief Chemist said, 'But what about the Batmen?' And the Chief Chemist and the CE laughed uproariously.

'No more fornicating in the streets!' cried the CE.

*

213

The Minister of Foreign Affairs, Founder of Brainee, and Director of the International Nuclear Validation Festival, glanced out the window of his chauffeur-driven limo. The face of his neighbour, Mildred Titsman was obscured by the placard she held, which read, "Poison Potts." The Minister's driver said, 'A bit on the nose, Minister? The Police should move her on.'

The Minister said, 'I ask you, driver, is that Doc Cod's face or his butt facing us?'

The driver glanced swiftly toward Doc Cod but he was driving, so it was a fleeting glance and he said so. Nonetheless, he was confident that that was Doc Cod's face.

The Minister snorted, because he said that was Doc Cod's butt. Which just went to show. Did the driver notice that Doc Cod's name was a palindrome? The driver had not and was pleasantly surprised. Had the Minister mentioned the Doggo Cleano? He hadn't – so the Minister described the prototype Doggo Cleano and the initial trial in some detail and explained why it was that Mildred Titsman had developed such a snitch. The driver agreed that Mildred was being a bit precious and it was hard to understand why she should bear such a grudge. Was Doc Cod's hair growing back? In part. It seemed that some affected areas might be forever bald, but did that really matter on a hound as ugly? In any event, the Minister's entrepreneurial endeavours had long since moved on from dogs and hygiene.

The driver said that coincidentally, he had been thinking about a business concept related to dogs, that he called the Dogomatic. Would the Minister like to hear? The Minister didn't, but he said that he did. He had no interest in the fantasies of a driver, who would always be a driver who would dream endlessly of inventing something wondrous that would make pots of money. He would likely entertain such futile dreams to the day he was nailed into a box. It was a very strange thing, the Minister mused, that those least equipped to invent anything, harboured such a strong desire to do so. It was vanity, he supposed. How did a man, or a woman measure the value of their life? Of course, they might think of the children they had dragged into this world, or the garden in which they had grown bushels of potatoes, or their ability to stump up a dreadful tune on a piano accordion, or this job or that. But in the end, they knew that there was only one measure that truly counted – the money they made. And not just the money that paid a power bill or the rent or bought new shoes – no, the measure was money in excess. More money than anyone could ever need to live and very comfortably at that. No, what this driver wanted was so much money he could throw handfuls into the street just for the pleasure of watching others run for their lives to catch it. And what ludicrous fantasy was going to bring about this miracle? A Dogomatic…The Minister reflected for a moment on the millions of Brainee pills being sold every day. A small smile came to his lips and he closed his eyes. If he wished, he could open the car window and throw handfuls of cash he'd never need, into the street. That was the measure.

The driver said that for as long as anyone could remember, dogs failed to come when called and many dogs – sometimes the same animal, habitually left a deposit in the middle of a nicely mown lawn. What did the Minister think this behaviour could be attributed to? Well, never mind, the driver said. The dog was by nature a wilful animal that liked to think it was higher up the pack. After many years of observation, it was the driver's view, that many dogs with bad habits were the kind of a dog that thought they should be the Alpha male when in fact they were as dumb as lard and were properly the Dogsbody, as it were. The question is, what can be done?

The Minister most definitely didn't want to hear what could be done, and hoped that his silence might suggest just that. However, the driver persisted because he dearly wished

215

to share his brilliance with the Minister. Finally, the Minister said, 'Do tell.'

The driver said that most dog owners simply put up with these vexations, and thereby allowed the dog to supplant the owner as the Top Dog. A crazy outcome, the Minister might think, but the Dogomatic would change all that. The Dogomatic, continued the driver, warming to the subject, would be a robot in the form of a dog. When the real dog failed to come when called or made an unwelcome deposit, the owner would direct the Dogomatic to carry out corrective action that would make it very plain where the real dog was in relation to the Alpha male. The Dogomatic would bite the offending animal without fear of being bitten in return, since it had no nerves and the real dog would know that it would likely break its own teeth on the titanium from which the driver intended the Dogomatic would be made. What did the Minister, who was also a highly successful entrepreneur think? Did the Dogomatic have legs?

The Minister thought the Dogomatic quite the most absurd idea he had heard for years, but he said, 'The idea has some merit. Require a great deal of development, but some merit.'

The driver was gratified that someone as clever as the Minister, who was also a renowned Entrepreneur, could see some merit in the Dogomatic concept. He was in fact, building a prototype out of wood. But the teeth were steel and the Minister might be impressed to learn that the jaws of the Dogomatic were modelled on those of the Tyrannosaurus. Changing the subject, he said that he had been reading about the International Nuclear Validation Festival. He was very impressed that Minister Potts was the Director. He was also very impressed that the Minister was the Founder of Brainee and he wondered whether the Minister – or Founder more likely, could give him some advice. The Founder would have preferred to disembark, but he said he would be happy to offer advice if he could.

The driver explained that just last week, he had been driving the Minister of Housing to an important meeting. Halfway across town, the driver had suddenly felt awfully hungry, even though he had had his usual breakfast. He liked sausages, eggs, tomatoes and toast. And a coffee. Quite often, he had some extra toast with marmalade. Did the Minister like marmalade? The Minister hesitated, because he liked some, but not all marmalade. Some marmalade was too sharp for his liking. He said that he preferred the sweeter, orange type of marmalade. The driver exclaimed enthusiastically, that so did he. And wasn't that a coincidence. The driver lapsed into silence and they passed through several blocks. At last, the Minister asked, was the driver going to say something about the Minister of Housing?

The Minister of Foreign Affairs asked because privately, and frankly he did not like the Minister of Housing. The Minister of Housing reminded the Minister altogether too much, of his latter-day enemy and nemesis, the Latvian baker, Sarah Bumbulis who had stolen the Mayoralty of Brewster's Neck and usurped his rightful position. The Minister had learned that the Minister of Housing had been against his appointment as Minister of Foreign Affairs, and it had come back to the Minister of Foreign Affairs that she had described him as a 'duffer.' And now, she had stated publicly that the INVF was immoral and reckless, and that the role that certain persons in this Government had played in its conception was to be greatly regretted. Naturally, the PM had had to step in and state that whilst she had some sympathy with the Minister of Housing's views, that was not the view of the Government and that Ministers needed to focus on their own portfolio.

The Minister repeated, 'You were going to ask my advice?'

The driver's head started, since clearly, he had fallen into some kind of reverie. At the Minister's words he exclaimed that so he was. But added nothing further.

The Minister said, 'You were mentioning your breakfast, and how hungry you were?'

The driver said, 'Ah, yes.' He said that he felt this overwhelming hunger – so much so that all he could see in front of his eyes, was a fried sausage. For some reason, and though he liked them a great deal, he didn't see eggs – just the sausage. He shook his head in wonder.

The Minister prompted, 'And?'

The driver started again, since he was apparently absorbed in his vision and memory of the sight and fragrance of a sausage done to a turn. He said that instead of driving the Minister of Housing to the Beehive, he drove the Minister of Housing to his own home. The Minister of Housing asked why they were at this address, and not at her destination? The driver told the Minister of Housing that his wife was ill and he needed to check on her. It had come to him suddenly that she desperately needed his help.

Minister Potts said, 'So, nothing to do with breakfast? The sausage was actually your wife?'

The driver cried, 'That's it!'

Minister Potts rolled his eyes and said, 'The Minister of Housing? Did she cut up rough? Give you an unfair reprimand perhaps?'

The driver said that on the contrary, the Minister of Housing was most sympathetic and insisted on coming into his house to help. Minister Potts was mildly disappointed at this but thought how like Sarah Bumbulis – election thief as she was – how like the Minister of Housing. But never mind. Was the driver's wife in dire strife? Did they get her to hospital on time? What was the matter with her?

The driver said, 'That's the peculiar thing, Minister. I don't have a wife.'

218

The Minister contemplated this disclosure for two blocks before asking, what advice the driver had thought to obtain.

The driver said, 'Advice?'

The Minister said, 'Yes. You were going to ask my advice?'

The driver was silent but the Minister could see in the rear-view mirror that the driver was frowning fiercely, evidently struggling to recall what kind of advice he wanted.

The Minister said, 'Driver…let me ask you a question. If the moon was to fall onto the Earth, would you prefer it to fall on South America, or Africa?'

The driver thought for a moment and then said, 'I think, if the moon was going to fall, I'd want it to fall on Australia.'

The Minister rummaged in his briefcase and said, 'I'm going to give you a packet of Brainee, free. I suggest you take four immediately, and then two in the morning and two at night.'

TWENTY-EIGHT

The Head of News said, 'Seriously. Are we playing whack-a-mole? '

The News team hung their heads. They did not want to whack-a-mole, but privately, they admitted that their previous interviews with the Minister of Foreign Affairs, the Founder of Brainee Ltd, and the leader of the First Union of Conservative Thinkers, had not gone at all well. They had held post-mortems. And what had the News Team concluded? The News Team concluded that Precious Potts was deceptively slippery. The News Team concluded that in Precious Potts, they were dealing with a Master of Disguise. A man who appeared to be most evidently, a middle-aged buffoon, but who, in the heat of the moment, became a wizard in a cloak of many hues.

The Head of News said, 'Potts is a charlatan peddling a vegetable in a pill and his advertising is fake. And at the same time that he's espousing his mealy-mouthed political philosophy about Greed-with-Care, he's becoming obscenely rich by taking advantage of the great unwashed. And now what? He's lauded internationally as the architect of the Nuclear Festival. He's a hero. It makes me feel ill. You make me feel ill. Our job – your job, which hangs by a thread, is to expose him for what he is. It's our last chance – it's *your* last chance…'

The Senior Reporter maintained her bravest face. 'We've got this.'

The Rhodesian Ridgeback's lips curled. Words were unnecessary.

*

Corker Pritchard motioned the Chemical Whizzo to sit. He said, 'Don't give them a thing. It's a trade secret.' He pursed his lips and scowled. 'I braved the wilds of the rainforest – creatures – carnivores and parasites and so forth.' He waved his arm so that the Chemical Whizzo and Percy might better visualise the carnivores and so forth. 'Steaming and nasty jungles I battled, for weeks, like a lost soul, but finally, and close to starvation I was – near death, that's when I stumbled onto the secret ingredient. And do you know how I knew I'd made the discovery of the century?'

Having heard several times already, the Chemical Whizzo and Percy knew how Corker Nobody had made the discovery of the Century, but they listened patiently.

'Well, I'll tell you. I found an old man. They said he was around one hundred and twenty-six. That's over a hundred!' he added unnecessarily. 'But no-one was absolutely sure since everyone else who'd been around when he was born, was dead as a nail – which makes sense. And here, in the deepest, darkest depths of the Amazon, and me at death's door, and here's this ancient man who could speak not just his lingo, but English, and French…and Latin, and some others I can't remember, and he was performing open-heart surgery on a chap half his age. No scalpel as we know it. No drugs or what not, such as we have. Just the cunning stuff he'd gathered from the jungles, and the thing was, he'd never left his village in his entire life!' Corker's eyes widened at the recollection of the astounding savant. 'Told me which valve was which. Which tube did what. Course he didn't use our medical jargon. He said, "Here's the thingamy that goes into this thingamy, and out of this thingamy this stuff comes and goes down this thingamy." As expert as you'd ever see. And just goes to show you don't need a five-year medical degree and so on. If I was down for a heart job, I'd be calling for that man. Tell her Percy.'

Percy said, 'I wasn't there.'

Corker said, 'No. That's right. It was just me. Risked my life and so forth, but got the reward. By jiminy, I struck the jackpot! That man had been eating a particular herb – a plant, from the jungle, for his entire life. And, he told me that only he ate this stuff, which was why the others were so dumb. And he was so grateful to have an English-speaking chap turn up and pass the time of day and so forth, and he agreed to show me that plant. And what a plant it is! You'd never know, just to look at it.'

Percy said, 'What kind of plant is it?'

Corker squinted as he brought that plant to mind. 'It's small...and greenish...and it has a tiny little flower...pinkish...or maybe white...'

The Chemical Whizzo asked, 'What do I do if the officials want to see that plant?'

Corker scowled, 'You don't show them anything. That's what I'm saying. You say it's an *extract*. And at present, due to the sheer demand for Brainee, we're currently out of it. And we're sourcing some more – as fast as we can, from the Amazon.'

Corker gazed at the wall to which Verbal's latest campaign slogan had been added. 'Family of six with total IQ of 93 joins Mensa.'

Corker said, 'I don't know about that slogan. Who knows what Mensa is? You, Percy? Sounds like a club for men but the last letter's been dropped off. Should be, 'Mensay.' That's two words. Men say. That makes sense and people would understand that because it's a proven fact that men always say. Except you wouldn't *join* 'Men say.' Unless you realised that it was better to be Men, say, than something else. You wouldn't want 'Chemical Whizzo say,' or 'Accountant say.' Who cares?' Corker made a mental note to mention it to Verbal. Verbal, he said, could get a bit high-brow and then no-one understood and wasn't that what Brainee was all about. As they became dumber, people could understand less and less, high-brow stuff and that was why Brainee was going through the roof. Some doctors, Corker expounded with evident scorn, were suggesting that exercise, diet and some proper reading would be the best antidote to stupidity. Corker laughed. 'Doctors should be the first to take Brainee. You really would wonder how a person who has studied and so forth, to become a doctor, could be so dumb as to think people will exercise – or read.'

Corker returned to his original point. 'So, Chemical Whizzo, the Department of Health can go whistle. If they want to go on a dangerous trek into uncharted jungles and can happen upon an ancient surgeon, totally self-taught, then good luck to them. But they're not having us tell them what's in Brain Booster XL8. That's commercially sensitive information.' Corker had another idea. He would mention to Verbal that they should be saying something about how dangerous it had been, discovering the jungle secret that lay behind Brain Booster. But without mentioning the ancient surgeon. Whose English name, Corker added reflectively, turned out to be Ralph.

TWENTY-NINE

The Australian Nuclear Validation Launch Team (ANVLT) said they were chuffed to be first-out-of-the-blocks. This they said, was the Aussie way.

The ANVLT explained that they had 'borrowed' the British plans when the Brits were testing bombs in the Aussie Outback. Which seemed fair. After-all, the Brits let off 12 bombs during the 1950s and 1960s, along with hundreds of smaller trials. And the fact is, since they were granted access to the land again, the local indigenous folks had faced a lot of problems. Like? Well, for starters, the food grown near the Maralinga site is too dangerous to eat. And? Well, now that you ask, many different plants can't even survive in soil that's as sterile as a dead dingo's donger. All of which went to show that the INVF and the plan to validate bombs on the moon, was just smart thinking and the ANVLT took its hat off to Minister Pottso for persuading the Security Council to get off its hands and get on with it.

Was the ANVLT ready to launch? Director Pottso could make a safe bet that the ANVLT was ready to launch at the designated time of 0900 Thursday, Sydney Time. Was there anything else that Director Pottso wanted to know? No? The leader of the ANVLT offered the Festival Director and his Technical Adviser a couple of cold ones, and said they would throw a few snags on the barbie. Whilst they drank the beer and ate a barbecued sausage, the leader of the ANVLT said that the rocket would travel at 58,536 kph, which wasn't a bad rate of knots, and would take 8 hours and 35 minutes to the target destination, which was the Mare Serenitatis or Sea of Serenity, which seemed a very good choice given the peaceful nature of the Validation Festival, and being close to plumb dead centre of the near side of the moon.

Director Potts said that the Australian missile looked very professional and his Technical Adviser confirmed that everything seemed set for a successful launch of both the missile and the Festival.

Director Potts returned to Sydney and was similarly impressed by the enormous outdoor screens, recently erected, where large crowds could watch each rocket's launch and impact in real-time. On the steps of the Opera House, a small but vocal "Save the Batmen" demonstration was taking place, alongside a slightly larger, "Save Our Moon," demonstration. The leader of SOM approached the other demonstration and using a loud hailer, shouted, 'You people are an embarrassment. Bugger off!'

The response from those demonstrating on behalf of the Batmen, was a kind of eery wailing and flapping of large black wings. Director Potts was advised that the peculiar sound was the language of the Batmen, apparently.

Director Potts said, 'Am I mistaken, but are those Batmen...?'

'Yes. They're fornicating – identifying with the Moon Batmen.' The Director's Assistant added, 'That's what they do, mostly. On account of the moon being more-or-less a dull place. It's all rock and all the same colour. So, when they're not flying about, they do this.'

Director Potts said, 'Does anyone know if they can read? Not much use sending Bibles otherwise.'

At that moment, the leader of the SOM who had just shouted through his loud hailer, 'Batmen have gone Troppo,' stumbled to his knees. His voice greatly weakened, he cried, 'Bats have more...' Then he pitched forward and lay quite still.

'Crikey!' Exclaimed the Director's Assistant. 'Looks like Torpor. There must be a Vector here. We should go!'

225

Minister Potts flew onto Beijing and was accorded a State Welcome. The Chinese Nuclear Validation Launch Team (CNVLT) said that their Ambassador at the UN had been very impressed with Minister Potts's address. Most professional. Highly independent and not influenced by Other Parties, and with suitable grey trousers. The CNVLT was ready to launch the day following the Australian Validation. The CNVLT would have liked to have been first and should have been, were it not for the rather sly entry of Australia to the Nuclear Club. The CNVLT wondered whether the Australians had any real expectation that their bomb would work, since they had been unable to test here on Earth. Minister Potts reassured the CNVLT that the Australians were good to go and that since they had simply borrowed a set of plans from the British, who had after-all made quite a radioactive mess in someone else's country, then there was no reason to expect that the Aussie bomb would not work.

The CNVLT wondered whether the Director of the Festival could shed any light on the plans and intentions of 'Others?' Did the Director, for example, have any information about the exact type of bomb that the Russians, say, or the Americans, intended to launch? They enquired only out of a natural curiosity about what to expect. And naturally, the Director would understand that there might be some prestige attached to some aspect of the Validation...like, for example, the yield...

The Director was obliged to apologise and say that the bomb each country chose to test, was up to them and if one looked at it in the sense of being a Festival, then a surprise was the best possible thing. Rather like waiting to see what firework would go off next.

The Director inspected the Chinese rocket and said that it made the Australian missile seem like a bit of a small willy, which remark greatly encouraged and amused his hosts. But still, if the Director, had any inkling about the missiles of

Other Parties, the CNVLT would be very grateful for his advice.

The Director flew onto the Guiana Space Centre in the northwest of Kourou in French Guiana, where the French Nuclear Validation Launch Team (FNVLT) kissed the Director on both cheeks 18 times, and then took an hour and twenty-three minutes to have a coffee. However, the Director was impressed with the French missile and his Technical Adviser confirmed, through his interpreter, that the FNVLT was prêt à viser la lune. The Director asked why the FNVLT was 'shooting *for* the moon,' rather than shooting *at* the moon. The Director reminded the FNVLT, through the interpreter, that the whole point of the INVF was to shoot *at* the moon, with a high degree of certainty that the moon would be hit. The Director said that shooting *for* the moon fell some way short of the declared objective and indeed, the rules of the INVF. The Director said that he would be most sorry if he felt that he had to report to the UN Secretary General that any party, French or otherwise, was planning merely to shoot for the moon. The Director was confident that the FNVLT would understand that such an intention left open the possibility of a damp squib. The Director explained that a damp squib meant a debacle, and was sure the FNVLT would not want to be guilty of a debacle? The Director added that should the plan of the FNVLT maintain as its principal objective, 'shooting for the moon,' then the involvement of the FNVLT might be questioned at the highest levels.

At the end of this speech, the leader of the FNVLT established through the interpreter that the Director of the INVF could not speak French. He then said 'Vraiment, vous êtes un idiot, directeur.' And then with a winning smile, said in English that the Director's words were indeed, very wise words and that his team would forthwith, change their operating objective to 'Shoot at the moon.' He then insisted that the Director remain for another coffee, which social occasion persisted for two hours – kissed him on both cheeks sixteen times and bade him bon voyage.

As they flew toward India, Director Potts remarked to his Technical Adviser that the French meeting had gone well, and especially since he had ensured that the French were 'on track.' The Technical Adviser, who was fluent in French, had no comment to make about the French being brought back on track.

The Technical Adviser advised the Director that shortly, they would be taken by helicopter out to Dr Abdul Kalam Island in the Bay of Bengal in the vicinity of Odisha, which he explained, is the main Indian missile test site. The Technical Adviser mentioned that the Indians might be a little prickly, because they had wanted to fire their rocket after the Pakistanis. The Indian Nuclear Festival Launch Team (INFLT), had said privately, to the UN Secretary General, that coming before the Pakistanis would not be well-regarded by India generally. The INFLT did accept that one team must bat first, but whomever batted first was always decided by the toss. Consequently, the INFLT proposed that India and Pakistan tossed a coin, in the time-honoured, cricketing way, to see who would bat and who would bowl, with first to bat being first to launch. This was the way on the sub-continent and given that India was now the acknowledged World Power in cricket, this surely was the splendid way. The Secretary General acknowledged India's supremacy in cricket but regretted that the rules had been agreed by all members of the Security Council, including as he recalled, India, and that they must abide by the rules.

As it turned out, the meeting with the INFLT went very smoothly. This was due in no small part to the early disclosure by Director Potts that he had once bowled a decent googly and on one memorable occasion, had taken a hat trick. Consequently, Director Potts joined the INFLT for an excellent cup of tea and a discussion about the upcoming

World Test Cricket Cup. The leader of the INFLT was most complimentary that New Zealand had won the inaugural Cup, but suggested, without wishing in any way to offend, that he believed the Indian team might have prevailed had the final comprised of best-of-three matches. Director Potts agreed, but observed that both teams had ample opportunity over the five-day duration of the contest to seize their opportunity. The leader of the INFLT suggested that perhaps the Indian team had underestimated their opponent…silly…but he was sure it would not happen again, and Indian cricket supremacy would be reaffirmed next time. Director Potts and his Technical Adviser departed amicably and without receiving one kiss.

THIRTY

The Senior Reporter complimented the Director of the International Nuclear Validation Festival. She said that it was amazing, if not awesome, what Director Potts had achieved – literally bringing the world together at a time when there were some pretty disconcerting things going on. Did the Director hear that the very last glacier in the Himalaya had melted? Well, it had and there was now not enough ice in those mountains to grace one gin and tonic. The Director agreed that this was lamentable and that any mountain looks better with snow. However, being absorbed in organising the Nuclear Festival, the disappearance of the last glacier had escaped the Director's attention, but he agreed that it did indeed, make you think.

Meanwhile, the Senior Reporter *was* thinking. She was thinking about a red herring. She said, 'We'd like to talk about the Nuclear Festival. What's involved and so forth.'

The Director nodded approvingly. He was happy to share what little he could, without, as the Senior Reporter would appreciate, divulging any State secrets. They both chuckled knowingly in that way that said, 'We do understand each other.'

The Senior Reporter glanced at the time. Four minutes to live. The Director sat silently and solemnly. The Senior Reporter wondered yet again, though silently, how someone so...ordinary, could have accomplished so much and so quickly. The Director was without doubt, a chameleon. By way of small-talk and to relax her guest, the Senior Reporter asked, 'Director? Would you prefer I call you that? Rather than Minister, or Founder?'

The Director said, 'Perhaps, Minister, might be best. Although Founder is equally important. But yes, Minister.'

'Minister, I assume you are familiar with Keynes? Maynard?'

The Minister vaguely recognised the name. Silently, he wondered whether that was the name of the chap who repaired his car that time – or was that Keen? Fred Keen? He nodded in a vague way that might be interpreted as 'Absolutely. Isn't everyone?' Or, if he was pushed, it might mean, 'Somewhat familiar, perhaps…but do go on.'

The Senior Reporter went on. 'It quite intrigues me that nearly one hundred years ago, Keynes predicted that about now, technology would so have advanced that human labour would be transformed if not made irrelevant.'

The Minister thought that this certainly didn't sound like his mechanic. He said, 'Did he indeed?'

'Yes. He also said that this would mean that humanity would come to realise that the pursuit of money, the love of money, he said, would be recognised for what it is – a somewhat disgusting morbidity. Those were his very words.'

The Minister raised his eyebrows. 'An intriguing view…'

Since the Minister offered no further comment and noting that she still had two minutes before the interview commenced, the Senior Reporter smiled and added, 'He actually said that the love of money would be seen as a semi-criminal and semi-pathological propensity.'

'Really?'

The Senior Reporter nodded. 'I was an Economics student. Keynes was my favourite. He was a great economist, but I don't think he was a great prophet.' She smiled conspiratorially, 'It is too bad, isn't it? He said that when the accumulation of wealth is no longer the central impulse of humanity, we would discover in ourselves, the much better aspirations that have lain dormant. And where are we?'

231

The Minister also smiled a conspiratorial smile. 'A very good question…where are we indeed?' But he proffered no answer to this very good question since he had no idea where we were.

The Senior Reporter was about to say that in her view, humanity was nowhere near Keynes vision and was perhaps going backwards, but she saw the interview was about to go-live. She indicated as much and the Minister composed himself, thinking that the Senior Reporter was a much more interesting young lady than he recalled.

*

The Chair of the First Union of Conservative Thinkers settled back in his easy chair with a glass of chilled Tio Pepe, to watch the evening news. To his astonishment, as the programme commenced, he saw that none-other than the Leader of the First Union of Conservative Thinkers was in the studio. But he was not introduced as the Leader of any party. He was introduced as the Minister of Foreign Affairs and the Director of the International Nuclear Validation Festival.

'Bugger me!' Cried the Chair. 'Here he is again!'

The Senior Reporter introduced her 'most illustrious guest,' and described how he had virtually single-handedly brought the World's nuclear powers together for a Festival that would soon make the World a safer place, by reassuring those whose fingers might be poised above the button, that if push-came-to-shove, the nukes would actually work. It was an astonishing accomplishment, the Senior Reporter said, and she said that already there was talk of the New Year Honours List – perhaps even a knighthood…

The Chair lurched in his chair and spilled his Tio Pepe. 'Knighthood!' he shouted.

The Senior Reporter advised her audience that they had invited Minister Potts onto the show, again, because it was clear that Minister Potts had very rapidly become one of Aotearoa New Zealand's most influential people. She smiled winningly at the most influential person, who as it happened was thinking that the interview was going particularly well.

The Senior Reporter reminded her audience that the Minister was also the Founder of the Company that was literally turning the tide against Alta Stultitia, or as it was known, the Pandemic of Stupidity.

In her ear microphone, the Senior Reporter heard the Head of News, 'Good. Keep it going. Make sure you tease out the human suffering thing.'

The Senior Reporter reminded the audience of the dreadful symptoms of the disease. She quoted Dr Klas Beekhof, who said that on its current trajectory, the Pandemic would cause most people to become so stupid, they would no longer understand the significance and application of even the most mundane of technologies, such a toothbrush or toilet paper. At that point, Dr Beekhof said grimly, humanity could literally, kiss its ass goodbye.

'That's it.' Said the Head of News. 'Now, go for the jugular…'

The Senior Reporter fixed her gaze on her guest. 'Minister, or I should say, Founder Potts, your company is making the only known antidote?'

The Founder nodded solemnly but wondered silently, when they would get onto the International Nuclear Festival.

'And having a virtual monopoly, I understand that Brainee Ltd is now worth around five billion dollars?'

The Founder frowned and said, 'Ahem…yes…but-'

The Senior Reporter cut in, 'Can we just look at this Brainee advertisement…' and the Senior Reporter cued the video of the elderly French woman near-death, who then defeated a group of junior chess champions. The French

233

woman attributed her remarkable transformation from brainless human vegetable to Chess Master, to a two-week course of Brainee with Brain Booster XL8.

Founder Potts agreed that the advertisement was compelling and likely to induce many sales. But could they turn to the International Nuclear Festival? Apparently, they could not, since the Senior Reporter insisted that they watch a further video in which here was the same elderly French woman disclosing that she had been paid by someone to pretend she was at death's door and that she had never played chess – when in fact she was a master. And in point of fact, she had never eaten a single Brainee pill.

The Head of News cried, 'Got him! Nail him down!'

The Chair cried, 'There goes your knighthood, you pilchard! And there goes the Party…' and he clapped his hand to his brow with such vehemence the remainder of his Tio Pepe flew across the room.

The Senior Reporter asked, 'Founder Potts – this seems to be the most…shameless and unethical deceit.'

'Ha! Ha!' cried the Head of News.

The Senior Reporter pressed, 'And aren't you the architect of the ideology adopted by the First Union of Conservative Thinkers, of…what is it called? Greed-with-Care? And yet, you are becoming hugely wealthy on the back of advertising that is evidently a complete lie and a fraud, and…' the Senior Reporter pretended to read her notes, 'And with a pill in which the secret ingredient, is in fact a vegetable that most people hate?'

'Ha! Ha!' cried the Head of News, 'We've got the f*****!'

'The Chair rose from his chair and bawled, 'You hopeless pillock!'

The camera zoomed into the face of the hopeless pillock and f*****, as the Minister, Founder and Director was known in some quarters. The lips of the hopeless pillock were pursed. The eyes of the hopeless pillock were narrowed. But the teeth of the hopeless pillock were not the weed-grinding teeth of the ungulate. The teeth were the canines of a carnivore.

After what seemed an interminable pause, in which the Senior Reporter, the Head of News, the Chair and the entire audience expected to witness an abject meltdown and capitulation and perhaps a humiliating mea culpa, the hopeless pillock began.

'I'm very glad you raised these points. I hoped you would.'

Dumbfounded, the Chair crashed back into his chair.

The Head of News cried, 'Stab him!'

The Senior Reporter said, 'You're glad, Minister? You're-'

'Oh yes. Very glad. You see, the Pandemic is very complex. You will understand that. As does Dr Beekhof. The world is on a very slippery slope. We are, as a species and even at this moment, falling backwards – evolving backwards, you might say. Imagine were we not aware of the meaning of toilet paper? A social disaster, I'm sure everybody would agree. What must we do? We must clutch at straws, if that is all that comes to hand. We-'

The Senior Reporter interrupted, 'But we have just seen a monstrous lie. We've-'

The Minister continued, 'We are weak creatures, you and I. Are you familiar with Keens? I believe you are a student of economics? It is over a hundred years since Keens suggested that we would realise that our love of money was blinding us to our true and noble selves. No longer, Mister Keens said, will we pursue our semi-criminal lust for gold and so forth.'

The Head of News said with frightening intensity, 'Either he dies, or you do. It's your choice.'

The Chair poured a large Tio Pepe and once again stared with amazement at the pillock.

The Senior Reporter said, 'Minister Potts-'

But the Minister continued, 'We at Brainee are well aware of Dr Beekhof's research. We are aware of the great concern of the WHO. We are driven by our ethos, which as you point out is Greed-with-Care. Greed-with-Care, Shannon – may I call you that? Shannon. Greed-with-Care is a simple summation, I might say, of Keens prophecy. It is our humble attempt to reconcile humanity's natural love of gold, but with noble compassion and higher things and so forth. So, what must we do? In the dire circumstance in which humanity now finds itself, we must use every means at our disposal to persuade those already afflicted, women and little children – the aged and demented, to avail themselves of a treatment endorsed by the WHO. It is not what we prefer to do, but it's our *duty of care* that drives us. And a vegetable?' Minister Potts gave a most avuncular and indulgent chuckle at this silly suggestion. 'I'm afraid you are unaware of the secret and miraculous Amazonian herb that we know for a fact, has kept the most remote tribes in the most robust health. That is the essence, if you will, of Brain Booster XL8.'

The Minister gazed earnestly at the camera. 'We make no apology for our deep concern for humanity. If we use some…creative thinking to help bring our fellow citizens along…then yes, we are ready to plead, guilty…'

THIRTY-ONE

Director Potts glanced out the window of the aeroplane and made out the Israeli Spaceport at the Palmachim Airforce Base. The Director said, 'By the way, did we inspect the Indian rocket? We did? Jolly good. I thought it quite a good idea – tossing to see who batted first.'

The Technical Adviser said that he didn't mind one way or the other. Frankly, he found the game of cricket incomprehensible. How, he asked, could a game go on for five days and still end in a draw? People could die in that time. The Director observed that people were always dying. The Director observed that death was the ultimate antidote to all ills – including stupidity. It did not matter how stupid anyone was, or became – the instant they died their stupidity died with them.

The Technical Adviser begged to differ. There were surely acts and results of great folly that remained long after those whose stupidity had given rise to those acts and results, had passed on. As the aeroplane circled, and continuing in the taxi that transported them to their meeting with the Israeli Nuclear Validation Launch Team (IsNVLT), the Director and his Technical Adviser considered examples of acts and results of great folly that crossed all nations and stretched as far back as one could go, all of which lent strength to the Technical Adviser's view. There was some indecision about Brexit, and the Wall between America and Mexico, which though both agreed were acts of great and enduring stupidity, those who had conceived of these acts of folly had yet to die. But should do so as soon as decently possible.

Nonetheless, the Director said that his original point, was that at the moment of death, the individual brain that was the source and wellspring of stupidity, simply became a useless blob of rotting flesh. Or, not flesh exactly, but tissue. Inert and incapable, which, the Director continued, was rather interesting when one considered that for perhaps seventy years, that blob of tissue could have composed a symphony, or developed a New Theory of Everything, or done no more than learn how to make a bowl of porridge – and in the Director's opinion, there were quite a few who hadn't even managed that.

In any event, this fruitful discussion gave way to the Director's consideration of the planning and so forth, of the IsNVLT. The leader of the IsNVLT made clear that because of Israel's unfortunate geographic location and hostile relations with surrounding countries, the launch rocket would take off due west, over the Mediterranean Sea, in order to avoid flying over those hostile territories. Regrettably, this limitation reduced the lifting capability of the Shavit rocket by a substantial, 30 percent. The leader of the IsNVLT said that it would be greatly appreciated if the Director and his team could make clear, when it came Israel's turn to launch, that the bomb that the IsNVLT would fire at the moon, was by no means the largest in the Israeli arsenal. Just so there were no misunderstandings. The Director indicated that he could see no problem acceding to this request, and he indicated that he liked the look of the Shavit. A very business-like looking rocket.

Later, as they strapped themselves into their seats, the Technical Adviser opined that he was most impressed with the television interview in which it had been revealed that the Brainee ads were complete tosh, but in which the Founder, also being the Director of the Nuclear Festival, had shown how ethically motivated they were. The Technical Adviser asked if the Director had seen the headline, "Compassionate

Potts makes laughing stock of TV News." The Director had. The Director said, 'You can lead a horse to water…that's what drives our creative thinking.'

The Technical Adviser said, 'The ends justify the means,' and nodded sagely. He added, 'I believe there was some kind of fall-out, in the studio.'

'Oh?'

'Assault, I understand. Someone was taken to hospital.'

The Director and his Technical Adviser agreed that media people were inclined to be emotional. The Technical Adviser mentioned that he had read that a knighthood was a distinct possibility. The Director gave a little chuckle that denoted how silly that would be – even if it was more than due. But the Director was suddenly afflicted with great unease. A fall-out, in the Studio…and someone hospitalised…perhaps, mused Director Potts silently, a case of mistaken identity…

'You say someone was taken to hospital, then? Not dead, exactly?'

'Not dead at all.'

'But someone was attacked?'

'I don't recall there being any details. It read more like a fracas.'

'A fracas?'

'Yes.'

'With a weapon? Perhaps a gun, or a knife?' The Director brought to mind the hideous assassination of President Ralph. 'Good God! Not…a machete?'

The Technical Adviser cast the Director an odd look. 'Not anything. Perhaps a fist.'

The Director and Technical Adviser settled back and perused the menu delivered by the steward.

The following day, the Director and his Technical Adviser were escorted to the Tonghae Satellite Launching Ground, also known as Musudan-ri. In point of fact, the Director and his Technical Adviser got no closer to Tonghae Launching Ground than 10 kilometres. The leader of the North Korean Nuclear Validation launch Team (NKNVLT) apologised for this inconvenience which was the result of flooding. The Director expressed his sympathy since floods were unpleasant for all involved, and his surprise, since he understood that North Korea was in the grip of a prolonged drought. The leader of the NKNVLT said that he hoped the Director was not making an untoward Western-based insinuation about North Korean weather? The Director said that he had no such intention and that his remark was quite innocent.

The leader of the NKNVLT then said that he may have given a slightly misleading description of the problem, that was better described as a drought. But coming immediately *after* a flood. The Director said that he understood entirely and that there was no need for any further explanation. Drought or flood, it would clearly be challenging to visit the site.

The leader of the NKNVLT asked if that remark, was not the Director making a Western-type insinuation that the NKNVLT had something to hide? The leader of the NKNVLT said that when he said that the Tonghae Launching Ground was inaccessible, due to drought, he was solely motivated by his concern that the Director and his Technical Adviser did not inadvertently find themselves stranded half-way to Tonghae, in which case, heat stress and various other concerns might arise, for which Western-type wrong thinkers would blame the NKNVLT.

The Director said that he was grateful for this solicitude since he had no interest whatsoever in becoming food for the vultures on the road to Tonghae. At which the leader of the NKNVLT became quite heated. Was the Director implying that North Korea would deliberately allow its foreign Western-type guests to become bird food?

The Director said that he was implying no such thing and craved the forgiveness of the NKNVLT if he had even unconsciously alluded to the possibility. His remarks, he added, were of an entirely facetious nature.

The leader of the NKNVLT appeared to be only a little mollified. His eyes became the merest of slits as he examined the Director. He came closer, and closer, until his nose was almost touching the nose of the Director. The Director narrowed his own eyes. Neither man blinked. The leader of the NKNVLT said, in scarcely audible tone, 'Are you thinking that because our bomb test yields have not been very great, that we do not possess much larger bombs?'

The Director said, in a scarcely audible tone, 'Not in the least. I am confident that the NKNVLT has a bomb that will contribute to the great success of the Nuclear Validation Festival. Perhaps even, be the highlight of the Festival.'

The leader of the NKNVLT said, 'We are taking part in the spirit of peaceful collaboration.'

The Director said, 'We expected no less. And that is why our inspection is now completed.'

The leader of the NKNVLT said, 'Thank you for coming.'

*

The Director said they would kill two birds with one stone, since he understood that Pakistan would launch its missile from Kapustin Yar Cosmodrome, near Volgograd and the Russians would launch from the Baikonur Cosmodrome. This led to some discussion about what the expression, "To kill two

241

birds with one stone," actually meant, since there was more or less 2,200 kilometres between the two launching pads.

The Technical Adviser said that the expression surely meant that both birds, metaphorically speaking, were perched sufficiently close together, that one stone would knock them both down. In this case, the two spaceports could hardly be described as being on the same perch. The Director pointed out that no-one expected a spaceport to be on a perch. Although, given that the purpose of a spaceport was to launch things into the air, albeit without feathers, then metaphorically speaking, one might think of a spaceport as being somewhat like a bird. The Technical Adviser said he could not imagine off hand, what kind of bird the Director was envisaging. Even a large bird, such as an ostrich…but the Director pounced and said that in the ostrich one could indeed, see a spaceport. The elongate neck was a very straightforward facsimile of the launching pad, if not the rocket. The Technical Adviser conceded that the neck might represent the launching pad. But what of the legs? The spaceport was not positioned in the air. It sat directly on the ground. Nothing that he could see about a spaceport, bore any resemblance to the legs of an ostrich. The Director accused the Technical Adviser of being overly literal. The Director said that if one thought again of the very rapid locomotion of a rocket – then the large and powerful legs of the ostrich metaphorically, represented that potential for locomotion.

For a time, the Director and the Technical Adviser considered these arguments in silence. Then the Director, feeling that he had gained the advantage, suggested that when one used the expression, as he had, he did not do so in the expectation that he was in discourse with an accountant. An accountant, he suggested, might think that the Director was literally referring to two birds perching on something. The accountant wouldn't even know on what the birds were perching, until the Director, in this case, had said that they

242

perched on a fence, or a twig – and indeed, he would have to describe the fence, or the twig and whether it had leaves, or was an oak versus, say an apple tree. In Spring, or summer or suchlike. The Director added with some finality, 'An accountant would need to be told what kind of birds they are. An accountant might well believe that two ostriches were sitting on a twig. Are you an accountant, Technical Adviser? No. Consequently, I do not expect to have to tell you that I am talking about chaffinches.'

The Technical Adviser was unhappy that he might be compared to an accountant. He said, 'I thought we were talking about spaceports.'

The Director sighed, 'Of course, we're talking about spaceports. Two of them. Which is why I referred to two chaffinches. And speaking figuratively, we are the stone.'

The Technical Adviser said stiffly, 'I can see what you are referring to. But I don't think that figure of speech is altogether the best. The chaffinches are very far apart and we're not going to try to kill either of them.'

*

Shortly, the Director and the Technical Adviser were being introduced to the leader of the Pakistan Nuclear Validation Launch Team (PNVLT) at the Kapustin Yar Cosmodrome. Which, the Technical Adviser had informed the Director, following their discussion about birds and so on, was the Soviet Union's first rocket development centre. In point of fact, Kapustin Yar was of historic interest since during the early years, it was used to test V2 rockets captured from the Germans at the end of World War 2. The Soviets, he added, had also fired quite a number of dogs up to 300 miles and more. For obvious reasons, the dogs did not require much food. This led to a general discussion about how anyone could

243

fire man's best friend into the void with only enough nuts to last a couple of days. Why, in such a circumstance, would you not send along the finest steak, for example? But then, recalling his most recent interaction with man's best friend, the Director mentioned that he could think of one dog, whose name happened to be a palindrome, that he would fire into space without compunction. And its owner also.

The leader of the PNVLT offered his guests a cup of Kahwa, which he said was an excellent tea for 'clearing the mind.' The Director said that was an excellent idea since a clear mind was exactly what was called for in relation to the International Nuclear Validation Festival. The leader of the PNVLT touched his nose knowingly and said that it was the blend of saffron and cardamom that made Kahwa so diabolical. The Director expressed the hope, with a smile, that the INVF wasn't diabolical and the leader of the PNVLT said calmly though with evident disappointment, that it most certainly was and likely represented the End-of-Days.

The reference to the End-of-Days caused the Director and the Technical Adviser some consternation.

The Director said, 'The End-of-Days?'

The leader of the PNVLT remained most doleful. He replied, 'I am afflicted with sorrow.'

The Director found himself thinking that perhaps the PNVLT was an unsuitable participant in the INVF. The Director made a mental note to raise this concern with the Secretary General at the first opportunity. The Director asked lightly, did the leader of the PNVLT have any specific concerns?

The leader of the PNVLT clasped his hands together and bowed his head. Then he took up his cup of Kahwa and slurped, somewhat noisily before saying that the PNVLT was concerned at the apparent mindset evident in the modus operandi of the INVF. This mindset, he said, placed Pakistan second to India. India would go first with Pakistan somewhat later. This was a typical British mindset.

The Director pointed out that he was not British, and if the Festival was to comprise rocket launching in alphabetic order, it was difficult to avoid the coincidence of India coming *before* Pakistan.

The leader of the PNVLT said, 'Ah! There we see the typical British prejudice – knowing full well that by insisting on an alphabetic order, Pakistan must come second. Perhaps,' he added charitably, 'it was an unconscious decision? Perhaps the UN even assumed it was the fairest way forward, but without even being aware that the decision to comply with the alphabet, was a prejudice in itself.'

The Director said that as far as he knew, the UN had decided that the alphabetic order for launching was the fairest way and had done so consciously. Consequently, it could not be properly described as a prejudice. The leader of the PNVLT offered another cup of Kahwa, since it was undoubtedly an excellent tea to help clear the mind. The leader of the PNVLT twirled the end of his black moustache and waved a finger in the air. It was not apparent to the Director what this gesture meant and, in any event, it did not lead to anything, directly. However, shortly, as they sipped their refreshed cups of Kahwa, the leader of the PNVLT said that frankly speaking, he was suspicious of the Indian Nuclear Validation Launch Team. Did the INVLT make any comment about the Launch Sequence?

The Director said that the INVLT had indeed, commented on the Launch Sequence, and specifically, it had taken the view that it was not altogether happy since it had not been put into bat in the proper way.

The leader of the PNVLT leapt to his feet. He said, 'Ah, ha! Not put into bat. That is perfectly true. Did we put India into bat? No, we did not. And why did we not put India into bat? Because we had not even been able to inspect the wicket. We had not even been able to think about the weather and what it might do for our bowlers. Well, well. My colleagues at the INVLT may be smarter than I had thought. So, the Indians think there should have been a toss?'

The Director confirmed that the Indians thought that no-one should be put into bat first, unless the coin had been tossed, after which they either chose to bat first, or, if they lost, the Pakistanis put them into bat. The leader of the PNVLT was evidently well-pleased at this news. He said that surely, this was the proper and clear-headed way forward. There should be a toss, between India and Pakistan, and whoever won the toss would decide whether his own team would go into bat or would take the field.

The Director said, 'But let us return to your remark, in which you described the Festival as diabolical…and the End-of-Days…'

The leader of the PNVLT cried, 'Mr Director, Potts! All I am asking, most humbly, is that we toss the coin, in the proper cricketing way, to decide which of us bats first. If that were done then the Festival would be most perfect and most certainly not the End-of-Days. No. The Festival would be the best way forward. The Festival would be a match to be remembered.'

The Director said that as Director, he was amenable to a toss between India and Pakistan to see who batted first, if that resolved the matter of the Festival otherwise appearing to be diabolical. The leader of the PNVLT clasped the Director's hands in his. He said that that was a wise and munificent British decision and that perhaps – and he hoped he might be forgiven – he had been a little hot under the collar when he suggested that the Festival augured the End-of-Days. He assured the Director that the PNVLT was honoured to be taking part and wished to do so in a spirit of the greatest goodwill and cooperation with the UN and the Indians. He concluded this impassioned spiel by saying that once again, the cup of Kahwa had done its job, with an abundance of clear-thinking abounding.

*

The Technical Adviser remarked as he and the Director landed at Baikonur Cosmodrome, 'Four and a half hours…from Kapustin Yar…' When the Director did not reply, he added, 'One stone would have had to have been more like a very large asteroid…' When the Director did not reply, he continued, 'To kill two birds…'

The Director, who had just awakened from quite a deep sleep in which he had dreamed that Doc Cod had been telling him repeatedly, that the one member of the Nuclear Club was untrustworthy, said 'What?' Then he sighed. 'You really don't understand metaphor, do you? That is why you are a technical geek and not a strategic thinker. I am a strategic thinker, which is why I am the Director.'

Privately, the Technical Adviser thought that he understood metaphor well enough, and that he was quite correct that if a metaphor was to be used, it should fit the circumstance. Two cosmodromes over two thousand kilometres apart hardly seemed to fit the metaphor. However, having made his point, he said that it was worth remembering that on October 4, 1957, the U.S.S.R. became the first nation to put a satellite into orbit. The satellite, which was Sputnik 1, rode atop a rocket called Old Number Seven.

The Director said, 'Did it? My word.' The Director was wondering who Doc Cod was referring to, and then he was admonishing himself for even thinking about Doc Cod.

The Technical Adviser said that Sputnik was only 58 centimetres in diameter. It was a polished metal ball with four radio antennas. Amateur radio operators all over the Earth picked up its signal.

The Director said, 'You don't say?'

The Technical Adviser said that the launch of Sputnik, caused the Sputnik Crisis, whereby Western countries became very anxious that the Soviets were leaving them behind. It was the start of the Space Race, and it started right here, at Baikonur.

The Director said, 'I believe I know where we are. And, I might add, that we are here because the International Nuclear Validation Festival is to help the world avoid a repeat of the Space Race. Levelling up and so forth. Transparency and reassurance about the viability of nuclear weapon stocks and such like.'

The Technical Adviser said that perhaps the purpose was more to avoid an *Arms Race,* rather than a Space Race.

The Director said, 'There we are again. Pedantic. If you were a strategic thinker, which you are not, being a technical geek – then you would be unconcerned by trivial semantics. Fortunately, I have a sound grasp of the bigger picture. You I suppose, have a sound grasp of a microdot.'

The Director said that he had a call-of-nature. The Technical Adviser, who was by now feeling somewhat argumentative, replied that it was his understanding that nature had been declared officially, to be on life support, only this last month.

The Director rolled his eyes 'Piffle!' he cried and hurried to the bathroom where, to his surprise, he espied the man-in-the-mirror. 'So,' he said, 'you've deigned to turn up here. Well, what do you want?'

The man-in-the-mirror looked weary. Indeed, the Director felt that the man-in-the-mirror looked unwell. He said, 'Are you coming down with something? You don't look at all well.'

The man-in-the-mirror gave a wan smile. 'I don't suppose I'm unwell, exactly. But perhaps I'm a little world-weary.'

The Director gave a gesture of impatience. 'World-weary? How pedestrian.' The Director washed his hands. 'Do you see how thoroughly I wash my hands? No comments to make about Nietzsche? I thought not. World-weary? Whoever heard of such a thing. You've hardly been out of the bathroom. Why, I can hardly recall when I last saw you. You certainly weren't in New York. Are you aware that I'm Director Potts, of the International Nuclear Validation Festival? World-weary? How pretentious. You haven't been anywhere.'

The man-in-the-mirror looked mildly pained. 'What about that dream? Weren't you perturbed about Doc Cod – and his warning? I know I was.'

'Pah! Doc Cod! Pah!' Director Potts dried his hands. 'I've work to do. Idle hands – that's your problem. I've no time for it.' Director Potts returned to join his Technical Adviser.

The Technical Adviser, who was still smarting from the Director's dismissive remark about nature, said, 'It's one thing when the elephants are gone, but when the bees disappear, then it is fair to describe that as nature on life-support.'

'You're still on that? We have a very important meeting – in ten minutes, actually, and you're still preoccupied with animals. I've just been hearing from the man-in-the-mirror about that blasted Doc Cod and I can tell you, that's enough. What do you expect? Animals die off. It's happened before and it will happen again. I for one will be entirely happy when ducks are gone. If there's anything that spoils one's enjoyment of the countryside, it's ducks. They eat one's sandwiches and when I was a child, I was pecked by several of them. God! How slow this escalator is.'

Shortly, the Director and the Technical Adviser, who had remained stonily silent for some time following this exchange, were introduced to the leader of the Russian Nuclear Validation Launch Team (RNVLT). The leader of the

249

RNVLT offered his guests a glass of vodka. The Director was about to decline this offer but he changed his mind. The main reason he changed his mind was that the leader of the RNVLT was almost two metres tall and the Technical Adviser had whispered to the Director, as they watched the leader of the RNVLT approach, that the Russian must tip the scales at 140 kg. The second reason the Director changed his mind was that the leader of the RNVLT was accompanied by two fellows whose expressions were as blank as the wall behind them and whose right hands remained permanently inside their jackets.

The leader of the RNVLT raised his glass and said 'Za Zdarovje, comrades!' before emptying the glass in-one. His expression left no doubt in the mind of the Director that this was a firm invitation to do the same. The Director said, 'Cheerio,' and emptied his glass. Which was instantly refilled by the woman who carried a large bottle. The leader of the RNVLT again raised his glass and said, 'Za Vstrechu. To our business, comrades!'

The Director began to say that he very much appreciated the vodka, but he was interrupted by the leader of the RNVLT, who was delighted that his comrades enjoyed the vodka, which he hoped they appreciated, was a Beluga. The leader of the of the RNVLT said that the Beluga was in honour of his guests. He said, 'Comrades, to our successful Festival,' and emptied his glass and waited for his guests to do the same. The leader of the RNVLT held his fifth glass to his eye and said that his love of the Beluga was because of the special scalding technique. No doubt the comrades could perceive the outcome of the triple-distillation, before the Beluga was put through a six-stage filtration process – yes, six stage – and using activated charcoal and quartz sand. And here was the outcome – a sublime vodka that was the perfect way to begin their meeting.

The Director said that he felt privet. The leader of the RNVLT asked what it was to feel 'privet.' This was not a word with which he was familiar.

The Technical Adviser said that he thought the Director meant, 'Provo.'

The Director said, 'No. I meant to say preva. I meant to say I was pritha…'

The Technical Adviser said, 'I thought you meant provink?'

The Director said, 'You should not try to second-grink me. You are a mere…glock. Thas is what I meant.' The Director closed his eyes and in moments, was fast asleep.

The leader of the RNVLT was puzzled. Had they begun their meeting? No, they had not and yet already his guests apparently, had had enough. His guests sagged in their chairs and one of them, indeed, it was the Director, was snoring. The leader of the RNVLT was wondering whether he should feel slighted? Did his guests not like the Beluga Vodka? He signalled for his glass to be topped up and he examined it closely, before swallowing the contents. He pronounced that the Beluga was a most excellent drop. He returned his steady gaze to his guests. They were Westerners, of course. Weak. How it was that Russia was not the leader of Everything, was a mystery to him. Even a Russian loser, that the leader of the RNVLT might also describe as a pigeon, could easily handle a bottle of Beluga without going to sleep. He had at first suspected that his guests had begun to speak in code, but now he was convinced they were simply drunk. It was embarrassing. And he had learned nothing about the plans of the Americans.

The leader of the RNVLT told his two colleagues to keep an eye on his guests, and when they woke, to show them to their room. The leader of the RNVLT hoped that from loosened tongues in proximity to a concealed microphone, he might yet learn something of interest.

The leader of the RNVLT reported to his comrade commandant that the Westerners had been feeble but tight-lipped. They had been arguing it seemed, about ducks and someone called Doc Cod. This was of interest, since the Director had said quite plainly, that this Doc Cod could not know if anyone was trying to sabotage the Nuclear Festival. However, he was confident that they and the Americans were unaware that the only other Tsar Bomba ever made, was now sitting on top of the Soyuz waiting its turn to create a most intimidating and gigantic crater on the moon.

The leader of the RNVLT was silent for a moment, and then he said that the information, regarding Doc Cod, should be passed onto the KGB.

*

You said, "The man-in-the-mirror."

'What of it?'

The Technical Adviser sipped his Gewurztraminer and made a sound of appreciation before adding, quite properly, 'I was wondering to whom you referred?'

'I was referring to the man-in-the-mirror.'

'Yes. But who is he?'

The Director sighed. 'Am I a clairvoyant? Am I an oracle?' He applied a piece of gorgonzola to a wheat cracker and thought that really, he should see if he couldn't obtain another Technical Adviser.

The Technical Adviser replied, 'If you can see him, then surely you recognise him? As,' he added with detectable smugness, 'we all can.'

'How do you suppose you can *all* recognise someone only I see? That's quite absurd. And who is all? That's just as silly. How can I possibly know who, *all* is?'

The Technical Adviser said stiffly, 'I am referring to humanity. I do not expect you to know them all. But I might expect that you would know your own man-in-the-mirror. Just as I do, and she does,' he added with a gesture toward the stewardess.

'I can assure you, Technical Adviser, that she does not know the man-in-the-mirror.'

The stewardess beamed, 'Can I help you gentlemen? Would you care for some more wine?'

The Director declined this kind offer and the Technical Adviser held out his glass.

The Technical Adviser asked, 'Do you recognise the woman-in-the-mirror?'

The stewardess frowned and pretended to consider this ludicrous question. Customers, she thought. Just when you think you've heard it all. She replied gaily, 'I like to think so. Though sometimes, after a long night, I wonder if there's a stranger in my bedroom!'

'There you are,' said the Director with finality, and closed his eyes.

*

The leader of the UK Nuclear Validation Launch Team (UKNVLT) was annoyed. How was it, that the UK had to launch on a French rocket from a French Spaceport? How was it, that an Antipodean, by the name of Potts, was the Director of the International Nuclear Validation Festival? And salt into the wound, the bloody Aussies had nicked British bomb designs, and a piddly company called Rocket Lab had been firing off Kiwi-designed rockets from a New Zealand Spaceport for years. Where were the Brits in all this? Hadn't the Brits been the third nuclear power? Yes, they had. Back in 1952. Hadn't many British scientists contributed to the

Manhattan Project? Yes, they had. Was it not a fact that in 1940, the British nuclear research was ahead of the Americans? Yes, it was. And now what? It was necessary to meet with some trout from the Antipodes who likely didn't know an exothermic reaction from his electric blanket. There were no satisfactory answers. The leader of the UKNVLT suspected it could all be sheeted home to Brexit, or the Tories – or both.

The leader of the UKNVLT asked bluntly, why the Australians, who had apparently pilfered the designs of early British nuclear bombs, were permitted to be involved in the INVF when they hadn't even been admitted to the Nuclear Club? Who else was going to spring out of the woodwork? The Welsh, perhaps? Was it possible these days to simply download the plans of a nuclear bomb from the Internet? And who, by the way, invented the World Wide Web?

The Director of the INVF was a little taken aback, and he was beginning to understand that international diplomacy was much less straightforward than he had first imagined. One thing he had imagined, was courtesy, but here, at the HQ of the UKNVLT, they had not even been offered a seat, let alone a refreshment after a substantial and tiring journey from Khazakstan. And now he was being interrogated, as though the membership of the Nuclear Club was the Director's business. The Director said that as far as he was aware, the Aussies had kept their nuclear programme very much to themselves. But given that they had a nuclear bomb and the means to dispatch it at the moon, they could hardly be ignored. The Director added, hoping that he might mollify the rather prickly leader of the UKNVLT, that speaking personally, he was happy to ignore the Aussies as much as possible. He added that this was somewhat challenging because they lived in a pretty big place, quite close by.

The leader of the UKNVLT was not mollified. He snorted and said that the Australians couldn't claim to have a nuclear programme when the whole thing was stolen. Abruptly, he asked where the Director and his assistant were going next? The Director said that they were returning to New York and Washington DC, to catch up with the American Launch Team.

The leader of the UKNVLT suggested that in that case, he would not waste any more of their time – because the Director and his assistant would find it impossible to move at Heathrow on account of the shambles that was baggage clearance, and that was assuming that any trains turned up, and requested that the butler show the gentlemen to the taxi rank so that they might have some time up their sleeves.

*

Director Potts recoiled in horror. The Enormous Thing was staring in his bedroom window, which mean that the Thing was at least two storeys high. The eye that nearly filled the window was as black as coal and sinister. Director Potts cried out, 'Help!' But not a sound passed his lips. His voice seemed as though it was choked in a sock. Despite his abject fear, Director Potts felt that he knew the Thing. He did know the Thing! It was Mildred Titsman, grown enormous and no doubt filled with malevolence and intent on violence. Here was the assassin! Who would have thought? But of course, Big Pharma would ensure it used someone far removed from themselves. Someone with a known animosity towards the target. Someone with a motive. Doc Cod would forever require a bum-warmer on account of having no hair in that region – courtesy of the Potts. Who could blame this woman from wanting revenge? And here she was, gigantic and peering in at her hapless victim, lying helpless in his own bed.

Director Potts stared with horror at Mildred Titsman's teeth. These were not the teeth of an ungulate. These were the teeth of Tyrannosaurus…Director Potts shouted, 'Help!' But not a sound escaped his sock-filled mouth.

A banging commenced. Titsman was trying to knock the wall in. Titsman intended to break down the wall and then drag the Potts to his death. Titsman clearly intended to dismember the Potts with those bloody sabres…the knocking grew louder.

The Potts stared wildly at the door. The banging was coming from the door! Director Potts stumbled from his bed and crawled to the door. Someone knocking on the door could not be two storeys high. Someone knocking at the door must surely be part of the ring of steel, protecting him from the assassin's machete.

Director Potts unlatched the door and threw it open.

The startled concierge said, 'Good morning, Sir. You requested an early wake-up, but your phone may be off the hook?'

Director Potts blinked at the concierge. He turned to point at his window but dropped his outstretched arm. Director Potts recalled that he was on the nineteenth floor of his hotel.

'Ah. Did I? Yes, I believe I did. Thank you.'

'You're welcome.' The concierge hurried away.

Director Potts could feel the sweat on his brow. It was a very hot night. He looked down. He recalled that that was why he had removed his pyjamas.

THIRTY-TWO

The leader of the Pakistan Nuclear Validation Launch Team agreed to travel to the Shaheed Veer Narayan Singh International Cricket Stadium Raipur, also known as Naya Raipur International Cricket Stadium, in the city of Naya Raipur, Chhattisgarh in India. There he met with the leader of the India Nuclear Validation Launch Team and Director Potts.

For the occasion, they donned cricket whites, and stumps had been set at either end of the cricket wicket. The leaders walked up and down the 22 yards of the wicket, examining the amount of grass and closely inspecting one or two bare patches, and speculating about whether the wicket might take spin, perhaps later in the second innings. They agreed in passing, that this looked like a good wicket on which to bowl first. For an Indian wicket it was remarkably 'green,' and promised some bounce that would favour the fast bowlers.

Shortly, two Umpires approached the wicket. They exchanged pleasantries with the leaders of the Indian and Pakistani Nuclear Validation Launch Teams, and observed that rain was forecast for day three. The leaders expressed surprise, since it wasn't monsoon season, but they would take the umpires advice into their reckoning.

The senior umpire then produced a coin and handing it to Director Potts, gave the honour of calling, to the visitors as was the custom. Both teams were happy with this procedure. So saying, Director Potts flicked the coin into the air, and the Pakistani leader called, 'Heads.' The umpires and Director Potts bent over the coin on the ground, confirmed between them that indeed, the Pakistani leader had called correctly and then advised the two leaders accordingly.

257

The leader of the PNVLT was extremely pleased. The leader of the INVLT was not, but the toss was the toss and the result was what it was. Privately, he hoped that his remarks about how, if he won the toss he would bat first, might cause his opponent to want to bat first. Alas, the Pakistani leader had not been fooled by his opponent's small subterfuge, and flashing a most brilliant smile at the leader of the INVLT, said that he would put the Indian team into bat first.

Coincidentally, of course, this decision meant that there was no change to the alphabetic order for the launching of nuclear weapons at the moon, but the leaders of the INVLT and the PNVLT were no longer agitated since the outcome was the result of the toss, which was the proper way.

*

The Secretary General said, 'The British are annoyed about the Australians. Claim the Australians stole British nuclear bomb designs. What's your take?'

Director Potts said, 'The British never cleaned up after their tests. Seems a fair exchange.'

The SG agreed and observed that where the plans came from, hardly seemed germane. The fact was, the Australians were ready to go. Was everyone set to go? The Director confirmed that everyone was set to go and that the potential for friction between India and Pakistan had been resolved by a game of cricket. Or, the toss at least. The SG asked how the Director had found the Russians. The Director hesitated because he could barely remember the Russians. He did remember a man about half a metre taller and he very vaguely recalled a Beluga vodka. He said that as far as they had been able to ascertain, the Russians too, were all set.

The SG enquired about how he had been received by the North Koreans. The Director recalled privately that he had been unable to get within ten kilometres of the North Korean launch site. He said that the Koreans had been amicable, if a little edgy. The SG nodded and said that that was fairly typical.

The Director said that his Communications-wallah had been advised that preparations for livestreaming of each test were all but complete. There had been a few hitches in Reykjavik where it was reported that a caribou had charged through the outdoor screen. The SG remarked that he was surprised that there was a caribou in Iceland but the Director couldn't help him on that. Might it not have been a cow? No, said the Director – it definitely had antlers. A reindeer, then? But the SG immediately acknowledged that a caribou and a reindeer were one and the same thing. The SG said that it was interesting that it had been a caribou because he was only aware of them being across Siberia and North America. He wondered whether it was a Boreal, or a Porcupine or a Peary caribou? Then he exclaimed that he would bet that the animal was a barren-ground caribou, which was known to inhabit parts of Greenland, which was fairly close by. Did you know, he said to the Director, that Reindeer hooves adapt to the season? Yes, in the summer, when the tundra is soft and wet, the footpads become sponge-like and provide extra traction, but in the winter, the pads shrink and tighten, exposing the rim of the hoof. Clever, isn't it? The rim can cut into the ice and crusted snow to keep the beast from slipping. This also helps them to dig down through the snow to their favourite food – a lichen known as reindeer lichen. Sadly, due to climate change there was no longer any snow to dig through at any season, but there we are.

The Director did not know these very interesting facts and was even more surprised when the SG said that the activity of digging for lichen, is termed 'cratering.' The SG and the Director laughed at this coincidence. You know…said the SG, the INVF is about to embark on the greatest cratering in human history, and here, in Reykjavik, a caribou has been cratering our screen. Perhaps it's a sign? The Director replied that perhaps it wasn't a very good sign.

The SG said, 'Mere coincidence, Director Potts. God's way of remaining anonymous. Although it is a singular thing – about that caribou. Did they shoot it? But never mind. What about the Americans?'

The Director said, 'What can I say? I expect they will provide a suitable finale to the Festival. They were a little miffed that the Aussies wouldn't have them on hand, since it is an American rocket they've borrowed. But the Aussies are playing things pretty close to their chest. No-one really wants to be first-up, do they? Better to see what the other chap is doing. I must say, the Americans are very pleased to be going last.'

The SG agreed that it was an Aussie trait to play it close to the chest. Unless, rejoined the Director, it was a cricket match, when they tended to get everything off their chest, even before the first ball had been bowled.

*

Day One of the International Nuclear Validation Festival could not have gone more smoothly. There had been considerable apprehension in the Nuclear Club and beyond, that a damp squib on the first day would not have reflected well – and given that the first day was given over to a bunch of fairly sneaky Aussies, who had never actually tested their bomb – which was after-all, a British bomb design of some vintage, who knew what might happen? But since the rocket at least was one of theirs, the Americans were confident. The leader of the USNVLF team advised the Secretary General that the rocket was as fail-safe as a rocket could be. And they had gone to some pains to make it more so. The leader of the

USNVLT said they had simplified the rocket control panel so that there was just one large red button, with a sign next to the button saying, 'Rocket takes off.'

Consequently, the millions of people of all nationalities around the world in crowded public places from Reykjavik to Mumbai, counted down to the launch of the Australian rocket. To the annoyance of the Australian Prime Minister, the launch was reported in many countries as the launch 'of a stolen British bomb design atop a borrowed American rocket.'

The PM called the leader of the ANVLT and demanded to know why he and the country were being embarrassed in this way?

The leader of the ANVLT said, 'Prime Minister…all is not quite as it seems.'

'A mystery? We don't need a bloody mystery! We need recognition. Punching above our bloody weight – that's the Australian Way. I tell you, I'm sick of hearing about us stealing big stuff – Phar Lap. Pavlovas and so on…this is time for us to go shoulder-to-bloody-shoulder.'

The leader of the ANVLT said, 'Prime Minister…in around nine hours, we may be the object of a few jibes. A bit of baiting. But that'll be the price to pay for hitting the jackpot…' The leader of the ANVLT went onto explain what the jackpot was and how it would be, that only the little Aussie battler, would hit it. The PM was silent for a few moments and then he observed that though it would be a 'bit-of-a-bastard' in nine-hours-time, he could see that going on to hit the jackpot, was very much the Australian Way.

*

The leader of the Australian Nuclear Validation Launch Team (ANVLT) winked at his 2IC. He said, 'Perfect lift-off, Roger. Right on the nose.'

The 2IC returned the wink and said, 'Bloody oath, Macca. She's a bottler.' By which he meant, yes indeed, and the rocket is performing well.

The leader of the ANVLT looked at his phone and said, 'Ah. Here's a message from the Primo. He says he hopes we're having a cold one and throwing a few snags on the barbie. He says the rocket looks a fair dinkum bottler and the Kiwis will be spewing. And he hopes no stickybeak will take a squiz at anything. Good on yer.' By which the Prime Minister was suggesting the ANVLT should be having a cold beer with some sausages cooked on the barbecue. And the PM was congratulating the ANVLT on the launch, which would likely annoy the New Zealanders, since they didn't have a bomb and no longer had Phar Lap. However, he cautioned the leader of the ANVLT to be on the lookout for anyone who might be curious about any aspect of the launch – such an investigating person being a stickybeak.

Around the world, people watching the launch on an enormous outdoor screen – other than in Reykjavik, which unfortunately hadn't been able to get a replacement for the screen cratered by a barren-land caribou – spontaneously cheered and in some places, dancing and singing broke out.

In the UN, the Secretary General had to admit that the apparent spirit of goodwill and celebration was a refreshing distraction from other difficulties. Only recently, she had felt compelled to describe the world's anaemic response to Global Warming as being tantamount to 'collective suicide.' Oil exploration was continuing. Coal-fired power stations were still being built. The Amazon was all but gone, and entire forests elsewhere were being incinerated by wild fires, whilst in other regions one-hundred-year floods were occurring every two years and farmers were driving their tractors into cities and shouting incomprehensible agricultural slogans. The SG poured herself a dry sherry and decided she must take a break. The burden of trying to be the World's conscience was heavy. And what thanks? A number of national leaders no longer took her calls.

The SG watched the Australian rocket, courtesy of NASA, she understood, speed away from the Earth and armed with the first nuclear warhead to be trained on the moon. It was an impressive spectacle and the SG couldn't help feeling a modicum of pride at humankind's technological prowess. She wondered when some people would get to sleep these next two weeks. The rocket would take a mere nine hours to reach its destination and few would want to miss the moment of impact. The SG had to admit that she was pretty curious herself, about what a nuclear explosion on the moon would look like.

The reporter said that the question being asked tonight, was, would the Aussie bomb actually go off? She said that most agencies were paying around twenty-five dollars for an explosion, and 90 cents for a dud.

The television camera zoomed onto a not insubstantial protest. Hundreds of people were wailing and appeared to be deformed. The SG saw that the deformity was in fact, wings attached to the backs of the protestors. The camera zoomed close and the SG could read a banner held by two of the distracted protestors, which read, 'Innocent Batmen to be fried by Madmen.'

The SG thought, 'My goodness. Those Batmen appear to be fornicating.' She shook her head, sipped her sherry and decided she might read for a while. She took up her dog-eared copy of 'The Idiot.'

THIRTY-THREE

Between five and six hours into the Australian rocket flight, observers at Cape Canaveral, Baikonur and Jiuquan Satellite Launch Center, decided that there was something odd about the trajectory of the Australian rocket. The NASA scientists muttered, 'Goddamn amateurs...' and politely agreed with their Russian and Chinese counterparts, who had also observed the anomaly.

The leader of the USNVLT called the leader of the ANVLT and asked whether the ANVLT was concerned that on its current trajectory, the Australian rocket appeared to be on course to shave the moon and miss? Which would be an acute embarrassment for Australia and the International Nuclear Validation Festival. It would also be an embarrassment to the Americans since everyone knew that it was their goddamn rocket. The leader of the USNVLT said bluntly, 'What are you going to do about it, fella?' The leader of the ANVLT expressed dismay and said that he would take a squiz, and hung-up. He winked at his 2IC.

The leader of the Chinese Launch Team turned to his team and said, 'The Australians have made puck-up.' And he grinned. 'American lackey will look foolish and guilty of wrong-headed thinking and puck-ups.' The CNVLT applauded these words with wild clapping. The leader of the CNVLT said, 'This will mean glorious Zhonghua Renmin Gong He Guo will be first country to strike the moon!' This statement was followed with an even more gleeful round of applause.

Eight hours later, the CNVLT was nearly drunk. This was because the leader of the CNVLT had allowed to be produced a bottle of 'sauce scented' or Moutai Baijiu, which was his favourite Chinese vodka. In fact, it had been necessary to allow several bottles of Baiju to be produced for the purpose of properly appreciating the now imminent Australian humiliation and the celebration that the People's Republic of China would properly open the International Nuclear Validation Festival when it delivered the largest bomb ever made in China. This was a wonderful prospect, said the leader of the CNVLT. For too long, China had not made the Top 10 list of nuclear explosions. This was about to change!

*

The following day, typical headlines read: 'Aussies miss the stumps,' and 'Fortunately the Lucky Country hasn't thrown a boomerang,' and 'Australia lets the side down.'

The Secretary General called the Australian Prime Minister. The SG lamented that in missing the moon, albeit not by much, the ANVLT had gotten the International Nuclear Validation Festival off to a very bad start. Fortunately, the Chinese had just launched and the SG was very confident that order would be restored. Even as she used the expression, the SG found herself wondering, privately, how anything approaching what she had always understood 'order,' to be, could be applied to the nuclear fiasco unfolding. But she had a job to do. It was difficult, the SG continued, to see how the Australians could make amends. What had gone wrong? Was it the American rocket? No, it was not the American rocket. It seemed that the best that could be hoped for was for the Festival to be the resounding success that other nations would undoubtedly make it. Nations that understood the gravity of the situation. Parlous times, said the SG, meant that every opportunity for successful international cooperation had to be seized with both hands. Did the SG need to remind the Prime

Minister that already some lower-lying members of the United Nations now existed only in the abstract? No, the SG was sure that she did not. In Iceland, no-one had been able to stop a rampaging barren-lands caribou from charging straight through their only large outdoor television screen. And now? Now the Australians hadn't been able to hit a very large object, whose location, unlike the caribou, was known precisely every second of the day or night, year-in and year-out. In a moment of considerable exasperation, the SG wondered how it was that a blasted caribou was more accurate than the ANVLT!

The Australian Prime Minister offered little response to this torrent of derogatory headlines and queries. He had decided it was best to simply take it on the chin and bugger off to his holiday home in the Northern Territory. He was ridiculed by the Opposition. Excoriated by the Australian media. And there had been large demonstrations in Sydney and Melbourne. A pub hundreds of kilometres west of Brisbane, in a place he hadn't even known existed, was burnt to the ground in protest. The Prime Minister vowed to himself that if his Launch Team had miscalculated, they would rue the day…

*

In a certain hotel room in New York, the Director of the International Nuclear Validation Festival, was sitting in bed with a supper tray. He had toyed with his pancakes and drunk just half of his coffee before pushing it aside. He had little appetite. The Director was deeply troubled. Doc Cod had warned him, albeit in a dream, but there was no doubt that Doc Cod had known the Aussies were saboteurs. How? The Director poked at his egg with a fork.

266

The Director picked up his phone and called his wife. His wife advised that it was four in the morning.

The Director said that he had dreamt that Doc Cod had warned him that someone would try to sabotage the Nuclear Festival – and what had happened? The Aussies had missed the moon by a mile. He should have expected it. And then, he had received many calls from other members of the Nuclear Club and from the PM and the Secretary General, all asking how it was that the Director and his Technical Adviser had been so easily duped. There were riots in a number of cities. There were new headlines such as, and he picked up one of the many newspapers strewn across his bed, "Nuclear Festival Nuked," and seizing another he read, "World crashes into Depression at Failure of Nuclear Festival."

The Director added, that only the Chinese were pleased. The leader of the CNVLT had said that China would "boots-up" the Festival in a proper way, and that the Australians were an untrustworthy country. Which, exclaimed Director Potts to his wife, was exactly what Doc Cod had said. What did she think about all this?

The Director's wife said that she accepted that dogs were clever animals, but she really doubted that Doc Cod was capable of seeing the future. She advised her husband to drink less coffee at night and suggested that a nice warm bath might help.

*

In Beijing and Shanghai, Xian and Chengdu, on top of the Great Wall and at the Jiuquan Satellite Launch Center, there was great jubilation. The People's Republic of China was the first nation in the world, to strike the moon with a nuclear warhead. The front page of the China Daily proclaimed, 'China shows Aussies how to hit large target with very bigger

267

missile.' The very large photograph showed the very large mushroom cloud from an explosion the Americans assessed to have a yield of 20 MT.

The General permitted himself the slightest smile of satisfaction. He confirmed that this was much larger than anything the Chinese had ever tested. He agreed that it was a considerable spectacle. The flash had been visible with the naked eye. The cloud was certainly very high but as expected, the moon's weak gravity meant the cloud was dissipating into space remarkably quickly. The target area would soon be once again clear, to receive the next missile, launched by the Indians that very morning.

The Secretary of State asked the General for his thoughts vis-à-vis the very large demonstration in Constitution Avenue, protesting against the Nuclear Validation Festival. The General's grave expression became yet more grave. The General said, 'We've got a regiment of State Troopers in the proximity, deployable within minutes and with a full complement of anti-insurrection measures in place.'

The Secretary said, 'Anti-insurrection? This is hardly an insurrection, is it? It's ordinary people concerned about the moon.'

The General's expression became graver still. 'Madam Secretary, we've seen what happens when you let misinformed, ordinary people near the Capitol. In the current situation, we're pursuing a containment strategy.'

The Secretary reached into a draw, produced her mask and fitted it to her face. Then, with a voice that sounded remarkably like Morgan Freeman, she repeated her question. What was the General thinking about the sizeable protest in Constitution Avenue?

The General's grave expression vanished. The General gave a little chuckle. It was the first time the Secretary had seen the General chuckle. It was collegial, but it was not a warm sound. It did not sound like the chuckle her father had given when he was tossing the Secretary on his knee, or when the family dog stole her mother's slipper. It was the kind of chuckle a certain type of man, particularly a middle-aged man made, when in the company of other middle-aged men, having observed a woman back her car into a supermarket trolley. The General said, 'Those airheads won't know what's hit 'em.'

Morgan Freeman replied, also with a chuckle, 'Good to know we're on top of it, General. I suppose you saw the protests in other places? Seems there's a rash of these folks. Every capital in the world, pretty much.'

'Not in Pyongyang. Not in Dhaka – or Brasilia either.'

'True...but Dhaka's underwater right now.' Morgan shook his head, 'Did I tell you I was in Vegas last week and the tyres on my car melted? Never would've have thought rubber could melt.'

The General smirked. 'We use an anti-melt in the tyres of our military vehicles. Damned expensive. But hey – sure there's some protests, but look at the crowds watching the Festival? Bigger than a British coronation. The fact is, Madam Secretary, every society is plagued with a few dumb-asses. Your rank-and-file American knows that the Festival is big. A human milestone. And by God, they're going to whoop and holler when we send Big Boy up.' The General beamed. The Secretary had not previously witnessed or indeed, been the recipient of a beam from the General. The word that instantly came into her mind was 'jackass.' It was unnerving. The Secretary removed her mask and replaced it in her draw. The General's expression was immediately transformed. She believed the term was 'boot-faced.'

The Secretary said, 'General, when this is all over...when we've, as you say, scared the bejesus out of all of them, could it be an excellent time to kick-start the disarmament talks?'

There was a longish pause. 'Madam Secretary. Mutually Assured Destruction has worked for seventy years now. I don't think we'd want to go messing with something that just plain works.'

*

The New Zealand PM asked her Chief of Staff if he had watched. He had. And what did he think? He thought it was a pretty spectacular sight. He was thinking that perhaps his initial misgivings were misplaced. Look at all the people down on the waterfront...some of them camped there for the duration of the Festival, so as not to miss a moment. The Festival was lifting people's spirits.

The PM sighed. 'But what about those people?' She gestured at her window. They could just make out a chant. "Rocket Loonies hear us say! Beautiful Batmen are here to stay!"

The PM said, 'Is he going to jump?'

The Chief of Staff followed the PM's outstretched finger. 'It would appear so. Oh! That doesn't look good.'

'The wings collapsed.'

The Chief of Staff nodded, 'They're upset. They've a right to express their view of course.' He crossed to the window and with a raised finger counted for about a minute. 'Forty-two,' he said. 'There's forty-two people, and a dog.' He added, 'If we take out the batman on the ground, forty-one.'

'I wonder why they think the Batmen are beautiful?'

'I believe they think they have family relatives among the Batmen. Some of them think the Batmen started here on Earth – then flew to the moon. The Batmen were free spirits who wanted to make love, not war, which didn't go down well

270

with the rest of us – hence the fornication in the streets up there.'

The PM said slowly, 'How quaint. But they may have a point about Rocket Loonies.' She tried to smooth what was becoming a persistent frown from her forehead. 'I understand there was a riot in Peapod – Minister Potts's electorate. I believe that protest got out of hand?'

'Oh, that. It seems his neighbour – a woman by the name of Titsman, rioted last night and burned their hedge down. The Riot Squad have taken care of it.'

'He's in New York. My Minister of Foreign Affairs is being fêted for his vision and organisational expertise. I received a message from the Secretary General. She said Potts is making New Zealand proud. She said that despite her earlier misgivings, the global outpouring of euphoria at the Chinese success gave her hope for the future.' The PM continued to massage her forehead. 'But what about the Aussies? A clean miss. Damnably embarrassing.'

The Chief of Staff agreed, with a boyish grin, that indeed, a clean miss was damnably embarrassing. Especially when there was no wicket-keeper.

THIRTY-FOUR

'Nephew,' said Corker Nobody to Verbal Pritchard, otherwise known as the marketing guru of Brainee Ltd, 'Havana's are delicate products...they develop and mature, if kept in the right environment.' He flourished his unlit El Rey del Mundo. 'One must protect the proper cigar from devilish changes in humidity...changes in temperature, light and intrusive odours, Verbal. This is what the connoisseur, such as myself, does. Tut tut.' He added, closing the lid of the humidor against the outstretched fingers, and clearly indicating that the marketing guru was not about to sample the El Rey del Mundo. 'You see, Verbal, the flavour of the El Rey del Mundo becomes rounder and mellower with time.' He clipped the cigar and took up his lighter. 'We must preserve the optimum moisture balance in the cigar, and thus...' he lit the cigar and drew, 'and thus we keep it at the peak of aroma and flavour. And you, my boy, can savour this exquisite luxury by inhaling what I have just exhaled.' And he blew a stream of smoke across his desk, in the general direction of the marketing guru.

After a suitable pause, Corker continued, 'What's on your mind? Of course, I know what's on your mind. Money. That's perfectly natural and you shouldn't feel the slightest bit embarrassed.'

In fact, the marketing guru wasn't feeling in the slightest bit embarrassed. Even when he had discovered that his uncle had been padding his sausages with possums and other vermin, he had not fled Brewster's Neck out of any sense of embarrassment. He had fled out of a finely developed sense of self-preservation. Which fleeing, happened to coincide with the appearance of a most unreasonably vengeful

272

husband, who had discovered that the local radio shock jock, was on intimate terms with his wife. Which discovery had led to the shock jock receiving a very nasty blow to the jaw, with the prospect of more. It was simply time to leave. And soon thereafter, to his new talkback show, 'Flog it with Verbal,' here in Auckland.

'Money,' continued his uncle. 'That's what's on your mind and perfectly understandable. We're rolling in it and you want to dive right on in.' Corker assumed a grave expression. 'I'm a fair man, Verbal. No-one could say otherwise, and you've made your contribution to the Brainee enterprise. There!' He exclaimed, as the hideous carnival jingle marked the sale of another million pills. 'Ha! Ha! Verbal. That's the pure sound of money being made, and a very fine sound it is. Look...' and he retrieved a carefully extinguished cigar butt from the tray, 'You can try this. No? So be it. But gift horse and all that, my boy. So, how much do you want? And don't think that asking means receiving. The wonderful thing about money, is that those who have it do not like to give it away willy-nilly. That's one of the great pleasures of money. Everyone wants it, but only a select few, can have it in indecent amount.' He swung his right foot onto his desk. 'You see there?'

The marketing guru did see. As he had seen many times. As he had admired, many times.

'The shoe is the mark of distinction. The shoe, maketh the man. This shoe is the Louis Vuitton Manhattan Richelieu. That's waxed alligator leather, right there before your eyes. Note the Blake stitching accents and the detailed perforations.' Corker leaned towards his shoe with the intention of better examining the Blake stitching accents but gave up since he seemed to be impeded by his stomach. 'This shoe, Verbal, is so supple...so comfortable, I hardly know it's on. But I don't wear it for its comfort. No, I don't. Why do I wear a shoe that set me back ten thousand smackers? I wear it so that everyone else can see that I am a chap who can roll in cash. I wear it so underlings, such as yourself, I don't mind saying, can see and covet. And why? Because the more you covet, the harder you'll work. That's a business secret I've just imparted, Verbal. I should charge you for it. Indeed, it would be unseemly to ask for more money when you have just received one of Life's most profound secrets. Make the other bugger your beggar. Ha! Ha! I just coined that, Verbal. You should write it down. I am full of pearls today and you are the beneficiary.'

In fact, the marketing guru was thinking, 'My uncle really is a fat bastard. But I'd like those blasted shoes.'

'Well?' Corker said. 'Since there's no other subject worth my time, no doubt you've got some marketing to go do. I liked the new slogan by the way. "Unborn baby begins speaking in two languages." Like it! New market segment, Verbal. And the one we ran last week, "Founder fears Big Pharma conspiracy." Pottso's become a cult leader. Ha! Ha!'

The marketing guru said, 'Uncle...the Department of Health has been sniffing about-'

'Yes, yes. Of course, they're sniffing about. So what? Arm's length – that's where we keep 'em. One step ahead. You see, there I go again. A very important business secret that, Verbal. One-step-ahead. By the time you walk out that door, why, you'll be nearing the end of your apprenticeship. You're on the fast-track, Verbal. Greed-with-care. Ha! Ha!'

The marketing guru said, 'Yes...but they've analysed Brain Booster...' he frowned meaningfully, 'Discovered the secret ingredient...'

Corker removed his Louis Vuitton Manhattan Richelieu from his desk and his eyes narrowed.

'They say,' continued the marketing guru, 'that there is no secret ingredient...' For a few moments silence reigned.

'What do they say?'

'They say that the only plant extract in Brain Booster is broccoli. And they say that broccoli is not typically found in the Amazon.'

'Broccoli?'

'Yes. They say that broccoli is native to the Mediterranean. They say…' and the marketing guru glanced down at the note he now held in his hand, 'That broccoli was originally a relative of the cabbage. It was engineered by the Etruscans—ancient Italians of some sort who lived in what is now Tuscany—who were, they say, considered to be horticultural geniuses. But broccoli is simply a not very nice vegetable and nothing more.'

Corker Nobody squinted at the wall. 'Well, blow me down. Horticultural geniuses? I'm beggared, Verbal, I really am. Etruscans, eh? Well.'

'They say that while broccoli is…' and the marketing guru read, 'rich in calcium and with antioxidant properties, there is no evidence of any kind, that broccoli or any of its constituents could be claimed to boost intelligence.'

Corker opened the lid of the humidor, sniffed and then lifted a cigar. 'Verbal, the simple and reliable way to test the condition of a cigar…is to hold it between your thumb and index finger, like this, and squeeze gently. If it feels firm but springy, as this beauty does, then it is in good condition.' He replaced the cigar and closed the lid. He added, 'If it feels hard and brittle it is too dry. If it is feels soft and spongy it means it is too wet. These are important things for the connoisseur to know. Why do you suppose I share this with you, who, after all is not a connoisseur and nor yet a man of substance – though to your credit you aspire to be? To your credit, you are as greedy a fellow as I've seen, which is the essential prerequisite to being a man of substance. But at this point, you are a man of little substance, despite your pretensions and so forth. But don't take this personally. A mark of the future man of substance is his ability to be told he is a wanker, or a chap

275

of no account, and to simply shrug it off. And you, my boy, have shown on a number of occasions that you have indeed the hide of a rhino, and anyone might have guessed that I was your pater rather than the dunce who was my brother. And when I say dunce, I simply refer to the fact that your pater had no interest in money whatsoever. Which is why you were raised in that most disadvantageous and I must say, degraded and plebian circumstance.' Corker paused with an expression that indicated he was considering a grave matter.

'But, being your actual pater, fortunately, you acquired certain attributes that are standing you in much better stead, you might say.' Having made this astonishing disclosure, Corker added lightly, 'Your mater was wasted on my brother. Are you with me?'

This was one of those exceedingly rare occasions when the marketing guru and host of 'Flog it with Verbal,' was lost for words.

Corker, newly-disclosed-father-of-the marketing guru continued. 'You see, son – I should call you that – you see, your pater was a school teacher, and I'm the first to say that a school teacher has a place in the scheme of things. They do. But the fact is, school teachers, as a class, have no understanding of money. You'll have seen that in your pater. You likely wondered all your life, why it was that you were a naturally greedy chap – and all strength to your bow, but your pater wore those damnable jerseys with elbow patches, and grey shoes. Your pater would never have even begun to appreciate a Louis Vuitton Manhattan Richelieu. Demeaning, that is, Verbal and frankly, a disgrace and a poor example to any young chap. Fortunately...' and Corker stared into the distance at his wall, 'Fortunately, your mater was passably attractive and she saw in me a frigate, you might say, as opposed to a collier.'

The marketing guru had not the faintest idea what a frigate as opposed to a collier were in reality, but he grasped the intent of the metaphor. Finally, he said, 'So...' and he almost said, 'Unks,' but caught himself, 'I'm your heir? Your sole heir?'

Corker replied with enthusiasm, 'There you go! Chip off the old block! But don't go getting any ideas! Here...' and he opened the humidor, 'Perhaps it's time we smoked one to mark an auspicious occasion. The truth is out.' And then with a startling display of sentiment he came around his desk with open arms, 'How about a hug for your pater?'

The marketing guru rose to his feet and returned the embrace of his newly-discovered-pater, whilst wondering whether he should simply acquire the means and then shoot his newly-discovered-pater in order to claim what must be a substantial inheritance. But he quickly dismissed the thought as premature.

'Son,' exclaimed Corker, holding his newly-acquired-son by his shoulders and staring with great magnanimity, 'You can continue to call me Corker. I'm not one to demand the obeisance due to a pater by his gormless progeny. No, and I'm not one to stand on ceremony and so forth. What you and I share is a set of *values,* my boy – I should call you that – and that set of values is *money.* That is what binds us together. More than blood, you might say. More than a name. What flows in our veins, my boy, is cold hard cash. What lubricates the wheels in our minds is not the airy-fairy notions and ideas with which my brother bored one and all to death – but money. Airy fairy ideas and so forth, never bought anyone a proper cigar.' Corker gave his newly-acquired-son a beefy slap on the shoulder and returned to his executive chair. He removed two El Rey del Mundo's from the humidor, cut and lit them and passed one to the marketing guru.

The marketing guru drew on the El Rey del Mundo as he observed Corker draw on his cigar, with the studied expression of a man who truly understands the finer things in life. At once, he understood why his so-called pater, his fake

277

pater as it now transpired, had constantly berated him for his completely justifiable demands for a raise in his pocket money. His fake pater had never comprehended the increased costs faced by his so-called son. When the marketing guru, as a young boy had wanted shoes like each of the heroes he followed – and there were never less than four or five at any given time…or, when he needed to change his hairstyle for the same reason – hairdressers were not getting cheaper – his fake pater had chastised him for his vanity.

The marketing guru reflected that his fake pater, for all his kindnesses, had certainly been a dunce, and as he drew on his El Rey del Mundo, affirmed to himself, that henceforth, no other cigar would suffice. The marketing guru caught the eye of his natural pater and grinned. Corker returned his grin and winked. For some minutes, they smoked in silence. Corker was thinking that his disclosure had gone well. He had assumed it would, but one never knew. Those of a more nervous disposition might have become weirdly sentimental. But Verbal was not of this kind. Verbal was without a doubt, a chip off the old block.

The marketing guru was thinking that Corker properly understood the purpose of money. Which was to have plenty of it and to satisfy one's every whim without restraint. The marketing guru recalled his fake pater's insistence that the world would be better off without money. The marketing guru shook his head in disbelief. The marketing guru wondered whether his fake pater had ever twigged that his so-called son was not in fact his at all? Had he wondered why his so-called son had ginger hair, like Corker? Or why his so-called son had the blue eyes and fair and indeed pinkish complexion of Corker, rather than his own brown peepers and somewhat swarthy cast? The marketing guru suddenly recalled that occasion when his fake pater had been arguing with his mater about something, and his fake pater had cried out that Uncle

Corker was a 'sneaking cock-a-doodle-do…' before slamming the front door on his way out.

Corker said, 'Broccoli…'

The marketing guru replied, 'That's what they said.'

'Personally, I can't stand it.'

'I never liked it.'

Corker pressed the buzzer on his desk. 'Chemical Whizzo,' he said into the intercom, 'Attend.'

Shortly, the Chemical Whizzo entered the office.

'Chemical Whizzo,' said Corker accusingly, 'The marketing guru has a beastly communication in his hand, that insinuates that Brain Booster is in fact, broccoli.'

The Chemical Whizzo was unflustered. She replied in her thick accent, 'In vot sense, Mr Corker?'

'In what sense? In the sense that it is not cabbage, from which it was apparently derived by ancient Italians. Nor is it parsnip. And nor is it from the Amazon. In the sense that some meddling bureaucrat thinks it is a green vegetable shaped like a cauliflower but tasting like compost and called broccoli. In that sense.'

The Chemical Whizzo said, 'In the sense that it is fifty-two percent by weight of the Phase One ingredients?'

'Good God! That much? But it's not from the Amazon?'

'It is from the market garden. Vot, would you like me to add? I could add some piripiri?'

'Piripiri? Is that what I discovered?'

'I sink so. The piripiri plant is that tropical reed that the ancient was eating when you stumbled upon him, doing the brain surgery and you, delirious with jungle fevers. But you, seeing instantly that it was a secret herb that could treat a wide range of conditions.'

'So I did! And obviously, the source of his genius?'

'I believe so. I could add just the hint of the piripiri.'

Corker said, 'And there it is. You see, Verbal? Despite being weak from days without food and water, stumbling in dark and dangerous jungles, as the Chemical Whizzo says, I immediately recognised the significance of what I beheld. Others would not. Others would cry out for food and drink, but did I? No, I did not. Despite my suffering, I enquired of the ancient herbalist, what was the cause of his wondrous skill?'

The marketing guru said, 'And luckily, him being fluent in English.'

'Yes. Remarkable and further evidence, if it is needed, of the magical power of the piripiri. He showed me that reed and said if I wanted proof, then he would produce it there and then.' Corker stared at the wall, visualising again that moment when the ancient herbalist took up a passing dog of some sort and forced the reed down its throat. 'He stuffed that piripiri down the throat of that hound and before my eyes, that hound began walking on its hind legs, reciting verse of some kind! Mother Nature,' pronounced Corker, 'Is truly amazing!'

The marketing guru said, 'The Department of Health hasn't detected the piripiri.'

The Chemical Whizzo said, 'We can add just enough of the piripiri to be detectable only through destructive neutron activation analysis. This will not have been done by the Department people. But if they do, then they will detect it and that will show we have Mr Corker's secret Amazon ingredient.'

'You see, Verbal? Destructive neuron appetiser! That's science! That's what Brainee is about.'

The Chemical Whizzo said, 'Destructive neutron activation analysis. This requires a source of neutrons. Then our pill is bombarded with the neutrons, and this causes the elements to form radioactive isotopes. The radioactive emissions and radioactive decay paths for each element are known, so that means it is possible for us to study spectra of-'

'Yes, yes,' cried Corker, 'Spectra and omissions – yes, yes. That's what happens. Study, Verbal – that's what we're about. Who would have thought that my discovery of pita would have come to this?'

The Chemical Whizzo said, 'Pita is the bread, that you eat. You discovered piripiri. That's the Amazonian reed, which-'

'Yes, yes,' cried Corker, 'Piripiri, Verbal. A reed I discovered deep in the jungle, where I must say I was near to my end. Exhausted! Malnunourished and thirsty! You wouldn't believe how thirsty I was. You probably think it's just a big river with water everywhere, but I discovered – who knows? I might be the first to know, that the Amazon jungles are as dry as a vicar's sermon. I was crying out for water. Crawling I was – along the jungle floor, my arm outstretched, my voice…Verbal, my voice – not the clarion call you hear now, but a hoarse croak – that's all I could muster. I crawled for days. Malnunourished and as wet as a vicar's undies. I crawled into this clearing. For the first time in days – weeks, I saw the sun. I can tell you, I cried out in ecstasy, Verbal, or I would have if I'd been able, but I was reduced to a croak. I was a reduced man. You see this vigorous fellow now, but I can tell you I lost kilos – twenty, more or less. You wouldn't have recognised me. And stark bloody naked! The shirt on my back had been pecked away by some gigantic bird – of prey. And my trousers – eaten by ants. You've never seen ants like these.' Corker shook his head, his eyes closed as he recalled the horrors of the Amazonian jungles and his perilous journey.

'And then…behold!' Corker stretched out a hand towards the ceiling. 'Behold, Verbal, the ancient sage! Right in the midst of brain surgery, but he looked at me and said, now what did he say? He said, "You look like a chap who stops at nothing. You look like a chap seeking the truth…"

that's what he said and before I knew it, I was being stuffed with reeds and suchlike, and that's how I survived and that's how I discovered the poropop-reed, could turn a primitive native into a multi-lingual brain surgeon and so forth.' Corker sat back with a beam and an expression that showed his great satisfaction at having survived the jimjams of the dark and dangerous jungles, but keeping his entrepreneurial wits about him, had also discovered the piripiri.

Throughout this vivid recounting of Corker's adventures, the Chemical Whizzo remained utterly expressionless. The Chemical Whizzo was calculating the volume of piripiri she would apply to the formula, and perhaps at a level it would not need to be declared on the labelling. The marketing guru nodded at the appropriate moments and sometimes at inappropriate moments, because the marketing guru was wondering whether he could find an even more expensive shoe than the Louis Vuitton Manhattan Richelieu. However, it was apparent that Corker was waiting.

The Chemical Whizzo said that she would amend the formula for Brain Booster XL8 with the addition of a minute quantity of piripiri. Jolly good, replied Corker. The marketing guru said how much he admired his pater's courage and fortitude and daring and so forth, in the jungles, and his pater's extraordinary attention to the main chance, despite his ravaged body and all that. But, though the piripiri would answer the question from the Department of Health about the secret Amazonian ingredient, how should they respond to the accusation that there was no clinical evidence of the beneficial effect of Brain Booster on intelligence?

Once again, the alligator skin, Louis Vuitton Manhattan Richelieu, returned to the desk, and the owner of the Louis Vuitton Manhattan Richelieu, leaned back in his executive chair with his hands behind his head. 'Begone,' said Corker, gesturing toward the Chemical Whizzo, 'Back to the lab. Go on, be off and experimentalise the formula.' The Chemical Whizzo departed.

Corker beamed. 'What's that? Clinical evidence? Ha! Ha! Son – I'm getting into the habit of calling you that – son, the horse has bolted. Those dingbats at the Department of Health are no match for your pater...you see? We've already supplied more than...' he glanced at the flashing digital display, 'more than three billion pills. Do you think those punters care about clinical evidence? Most are too stupid to even read the label. There are two kinds of punter, Verbal. The first kind, is earnest and does read things – journals and suchlike. Like your fake pater. You might call this first kind, which understands stuff about the Cosmos and so forth that is entirely useless, you might call them the tormented kind. The Department of Health is full of this kind. The second kind is the basically stupid, which coincidentally, is by far the largest kind. This kind has no idea the Cosmos even exists. This kind is forever thinking about its greedy guts and the footy team. This kind will believe almost any kind of nonsense and once they do, they're yours. Give 'em a slogan and they're happy as Larry. Unless they turn on you. The entrepreneur knows it won't get far with the first kind of punter, so the entrepreneur ignores them. The entrepreneur focuses his bizzo on the second kind, but is alert, Verbal, he's alert to the risk of the second punter turning into a mob. This is another fundamental business truth that I'm sharing with you, because I'm your pater and so forth.' Corker seized a fly swat and thwacked wildly. He succeeded in belting his Golden Goose off the desk. The beak broke off.

Unperturbed he said, 'Now, where are we? We're selling Brainee to half the planet. All those punters believe that Brainee can turn a donkey into a doctor. They're worried, you see? Deep down they know they're as thick as a barn door and the idea that they might get gazzumped by a donkey, is too much. They're thinking – if you could call it that – it's

283

more like a kind of instinct, but we'll call it thinking. They're thinking that they might turn up at the doctor's and it'll be a donkey waiting. And that donkey will ask them to describe their symptomatics and isometrics and pilatemedicals and so forth, and they'll be speechless because they've just got an ache behind their eyes. And you know what that ache is, my boy? That ache is what happens as the brain shrinks. As it shrinks, the brain detaches from the bonce and can shake about, what's more. And then a donkey with a stethoscope asks them about their atmospherics and they're completely lost and even more worried. Do you see what I'm saying? The entrepreneur knows that this punter would swallow a live toad if he thought it would keep him ahead of a donkey with forceps, or some other such medical instrument. And that's Brainee. That's Brain Booster...much better than a toad. And bi-partisan.' Corker fell silent with an expression suggesting that he had just solved for the Meaning of Life.

Confident that he was not the second kind of punter, and yet unenthusiastic about being the other kind that read journals etc, nonetheless, the marketing guru wasn't certain that the problem of the Department of Health had been sorted.

Corker glanced at his gold watch. 'My word, Verbal, It's time to tune into the Festival!' He seized the remote and turned to the large television screen. 'There he is,' he cried, 'Our Pottso!'

The reporter asked, 'Director Potts – is there any risk that public enthusiasm for the Nuclear Festival will wane? The Chinese bomb certainly impressed and made up for the Aussie own-goal, but really, the Indian effort, and the Pakistani? And the Israeli bomb has been described as being more of a Tom Thumb...'

Director Potts pursed his lips, 'Would you like me to comment on that?'

'Yes, if you would Director.'

284

'Would you like me to comment in the specific instance, or more generally?'

'I would love you to be both specific and general.'

'Would you like me to comment retrospectively, perhaps, and vis-à-vis the previous tests, or indeed, prior to that even and back to the historical basis for the Festival? Or would you like me to comment in relation to the Russian test, which even now…' Director Potts glanced at his watch, 'Is a mere minute and five seconds away from impact? I do believe it is important that some consideration is given to both the ontological and epistemological aspects of these issues.'

Corker cried, 'What on Earth is Pottso talking about?'

Seated on his sofa in his own living room, with eyes glued to his television, the Chair of the First Union of Conservative Thinkers said, 'Episto what?'

The Prime Minister was deeply perplexed. She studied the face of her Minister of Foreign Affairs. She observed how unflustered he was – how almost, indifferent he appeared to be. He was neither supercilious and nor yet apprehensive. He appeared to be calm, collected and even slightly amused. How was it, she asked herself, that these things had escaped her? She felt something akin to embarrassment. She had quickly concluded that he was a buffoon, but perhaps he was not. One the other hand, she wasn't sure *what* he was – except that on every occasion he was quizzed by a reporter, somehow, it was the reporter who looked foolish. And here, this ex-mayor of Brewster's Neck, was suggesting that the philosophical nature of the Nuclear Festival might be worth some discussion. It *was* worth some discussion! That it was insane, the PM had little doubt, and yet, all over the world, the great majority of people were celebrating each lunar explosion. The newsfeeds were utterly given over to the Festival. Even this morning, the PM had read, 'Chinese bomb brings new meaning to New Moon,' and 'Batmen Sales Sky Rocket.' The complete subsidence of Holland, the logging truck carried by a typhoon three hundred

285

miles to land on Salt Lake City, and the first sighting of a wild giraffe in eleven years, were mere fillers. The truck driver said, "What a helluva ride! Have I missed one of the bombs?" And the Prime Minister of the Netherlands said that the loss of his country was to be regretted, but when all was said and done, no-one had ever really thought they'd keep out the sea forever.

Then, the countdown to the impact of the Russian missile began.

THIRTY-FIVE

Nuclear Festival Director Potts was not called upon to discuss the ontological or epistemological aspects of the Festival. Director Potts held up a finger as the crowd chanted, as they did prior to every bomb, 'Five, four, three, two, one...' and he turned to look at the huge screen. The audience was stunned to silence by the truly gigantic detonation in the Sea of Tranquillity – as indeed, within moments, the Sea of Tranquillity simply disappeared. Indeed, momentarily, the entire screen – all four hundred square metres of it, seemed to be consumed by blinding light. Eyes cast towards the moon saw only purple dots for several minutes. All around the world, public screens appeared to be blank, but only for seconds before the brilliance resolved into a roiling of darker colours outlining a mushroom cloud of stunning size and acceleration. All around the world, a collective gasp of astonishment and delight might have been heard on an adjoining planet, had there been one. But there wasn't. There was only the moon. And deep in the jungles of the Amazon, people fell to the ground and writhed and cried out in their existential pain at the desecration of the sacred moon, and no-one heard.

And all around the world, people of many countries were chanting hysterically, 'Russia! Russia! What a mother f******!' And they danced spontaneously and vowed to never forget this day. And in Reykjavik, a caribou dodged hundreds of bullets as he raced dementedly through the public screen on his way back to the barren lands.

*

The General commented that it was pretty much as he had expected. The Russians had spun a line of bullshit from the beginning. His analysts had confirmed that they had secretly upgraded the Tsar Bomba from a yield of fifty to seventy-five megatons.

The Secretary of State couldn't take her eyes off the unfolding scene in the Sea of Tranquillity. She wondered that the General was apparently indifferent to the fact that the Apollo 11 landing site no longer existed. Indeed, how could the Sea of Tranquillity retain its name when it was now so altered by the gargantuan crater left by the Russian explosion? She wondered what it meant that the General could smirk with evident satisfaction, at this stupefyingly large detonation…but she also experienced a quite contradictory emotion. The Russians would be celebrating. The Russians would likely be quaffing a large quantity of vodka and thinking they had done the Americans in the eye. The Tsar Bomba Mk II was impressive. The mushroom cloud all but caused the moon to disappear. The flash when the gigantic bomb exploded was quite the most remarkable thing she had ever seen in the sky. The new crater in the Sea of Tranquillity would accommodate a city. But the Secretary of State knew what the Russians did not…the Americans had Big Boy…and the Secretary couldn't repress a sense of pride and even triumph. The Secretary could not avoid imagining just how big the detonation of Big Boy would be. And she imagined how it would be in Russia – and China – and indeed everywhere around the world – but most especially in Russia, when Big Boy made the Tsar Bomba effort look like a pothole!

The Secretary confirmed that Big Boy would launch at 0900 in two days. The Secretary mused silently that then at least, it would be all over. The International Nuclear

288

Validation Festival would have run its course. The fireworks would come to an end. The demonstrations would also, hopefully, come to an end. The Secretary was sympathetic toward many of the protesters, though she kept this view to herself. She agreed entirely that nuking the moon was a terrible idea from every possible perspective. The lunar landscape would need to be re-mapped. She was aware that it was already proposed that the Sea of Tranquillity was to be re-named, 'Paramount Potts.' Did it really matter? Who bothered to consult a map of the moon? A handful of astronomers and those intending to mine for rare earths…a name she found most whimsical. And indeed, the press was already opining how the fresh new craters would be helpful in discovering the best places to mine. Perhaps the craters may have made it very easy to begin extraction? But the wailing had yet to subside and she supposed, would reach a crescendo when Big Boy did its thing. How could anyone ever explain to people who regarded the moon as a goddess, that the Nuclear Festival was of no consequence?

The Secretary was also aware of the large demonstrations in Sydney and Melbourne and a much smaller protest in a place called Cunnamulla. The Secretary enquired about those demonstrations, that were protesting the ineptitude of the government and its space agency, and not to mention the embarrassment caused to the little Aussie Battler, when the Australian rocket had clean-missed the moon.

The General said tersely, 'We don't believe they missed.'

The Secretary was nonplussed. 'But there was no explosion. Did their bomb not go off?'

'We believe they never intended to hit the moon.' The General's expression hardened. 'We don't like allies who aren't straight-up. The Brits, you can make some allowance for – and the French – we're always making allowances for the French. Flaky, as far as military strategy goes. But the Australians? We thought they were straight-up. It seems not.'

The Secretary was most surprised. 'Why would they want to miss the target? Who would want to look that hopeless?'

'You haven't missed the target if you were always aiming at something else. NASA has informed us that there's a certain planetary alignment at present. A certain circumstance that means that a missile that bypassed the moon on the day that the Australians bypassed the moon, will go onto hit Venus. It is our view, though the Australians will not admit it, that they aimed at Venus.'

The Secretary was even more astonished. 'Why?'

The General's complexion darkened. 'Because,' he replied with a rasp, 'They will be the first nation in history, to nuke another planet. Big Boy will be the biggest nuke in history, but it's the moon. The moon,' he added unnecessarily, 'is not a planet. And every other bastard has hit it. The Australians are still claiming, officially, that they made a mistake with their trajectory calculations. We're certain this is bullshit – excuse me Ma'am.' The General continued, 'Our man in the Australian PM's Office, has told us that the PM and his top brass, were celebrating their moon-shot, after it apparently missed. Our man tells us that they were singing a song…a very old and I have to say, horrible pop song by some Dutch group, called, 'I'm your Venus.' The General's expression displayed considerable distaste. 'We're confident that Australian headlines will come out after Big Boy, confirming they will be first to nuke another world.'

'Upstaging us?'

The General nodded dourly. 'Unreliable.'

'And with an American rocket?'

'One of ours. We should have realised when they refused us entry to their Launch Pad. We assumed it was because their Launch Pad is that refurbished milk factory.

Now, we know they didn't want us to see their launch plan. Goddamn untrustworthy.'

The Secretary nodded slowly. 'We can't overtake them?' The Secretary wasn't sure why she asked this.

'I'd like to see their balls caught in the door.'

'Yes,' said the Secretary without enthusiasm. More controversy, she thought. How would the Russians and the Chinese respond? Especially the Chinese, to this considerable loss of face? In point of fact, how would the Russians and the Chinese respond to Big Boy? The Secretary sighed. She asked the General to keep her abreast of developments.

*

The caribou did not make it to the barren lands. It was reported that three hundred and twenty-four bullets were recovered from the animal's corpse and that at least two hundred and fifty firearms had been involved. Unfortunately, sixteen people had died and forty-seven were wounded, with eleven now in intensive care. The article said that the good news was that America was gifting an even larger screen, so that Icelandic Festival goers would not miss the ultimate explosion on the moon – the American bomb.

The Secretary General said, 'Look at it…' Her staff looked at the photograph of the dead caribou. It was surrounded by men with high-powered weapons. Several beamed at the camera, one foot set upon the bloody remains. She added, 'Is it even a caribou? How would you know?' The caption above the photograph read, "Rogue brought to heel."

*

The Governor of Texas shook his fist at the sky. He cried, 'We're coming! God will soon be with you!'

291

A small crowd began chanting, '10, 9, 8, 7…1!' At which an ancient Redstone rocket, purloined by gubernatorial decree from the Texas Space Museum, lifted-off the temporary launch pad erected on the Governor's ranch west of Houston. As the rocket soared into the blue sky, the reporter asked, 'Governor, some people are saying you are too late. The moon is already nuked?'

The Governor smiled grimly. 'God doesn't care about timing. God makes time, and He listened. And we said, God, we're onto it, because what God wants most, is a fighter!' And he raised his square jaw a little and gazed into the sky at the disappearing rocket, and held his pose long enough for a decent photograph to be taken of God's Fighter. Then he added, 'It would be good if you used those words.'

The reporter said, 'About time?'

'No, about God wanting a fighter.'

'Yessir.'

The reporter asked why the Governor cared about the Batmen. The Governor replied that it didn't matter that the Batmen fornicated in the streets, or even, as had been said, that they practised abortion. They were disgusting, clearly, but they were still part of God's Work. And God's Work was the Governor's work. And the Governor knew that God wanted someone to get up and fight for those fornicators, whose only crime was that they had never received the Word of God. Which is why the Redstone, speeding toward the moon, carried one thousand copies of the New Testament – with certain tracts highlighted painstakingly by Texas Women Saving Lunar Bestials.

The Reporter asked why the TWSLB hadn't acted much sooner. Hadn't the Batmen's plight been known since 1835, when their presence and bestial characteristics were described in the pages of the New York Sun?

The Governor said grimly, 'The Federal Government. The Federal Government has been deliberately concealing the

292

existence of the Batmen…as it has many other things. But no more. God won't allow it. I won't allow it.'

'Because you're God's Fighter?'

'God wanted someone who'd get up early, wash his teeth and kiss his wife goodbye, as he went out to do God's Work. A Fighter, who'd bring His Word to the Batmen while there's still a chance. It's all we can do,' he added humbly.

*

The Director General of the WHO waited until the last of his expert advisory team was seated. The DG held a copy of a certain international newspaper. The DG glanced at the headline dominating the front page. "Venus to be nuked by little Aussie Battler." The DG cleared his throat and then read aloud: "It was confirmed today that the Australian Space Agency (ASA) expects its nuclear missile to hit Venus on the 19th of September this year. The Prime Minister denied that the ASA had deliberately aimed at Venus and thereby flagrantly contravening the rules of the International Nuclear Validation Festival. The PM said that a slight trajectory discrepancy was due to 'technical error,' but that despite the obvious embarrassment, Australia was proud that it would be the first nation in history to nuke another planet."

The DG shook his head wearily. He read, "The Governor of Texas said today that when the Redstone hit the moon, the Word of God would be bestowed on the bestial Batmen and they would soon see that their cavorting in the streets and so forth, must come to an end. The Governor said that of course, the Apollo astronauts hadn't seen the Batmen. The Batmen lived predominantly on the Dark side of the moon – in very deep craters and caves. And because they didn't wear a stitch of clothing, with skin the colour of moonstone, they blended with the lunarscape. Nonetheless, the Governor believed that the Federal Government was well-aware of the Batmen for decades, but had chosen to conceal their existence from the common man. God wanted someone to stand up and fight for all his creatures, despite their primitive and obnoxious habits. This was the Christian Way."

The DG paused as various conversations broke out. 'On the Dark Side of the Moon?' And, 'That makes sense. But what about the Chinese? Haven't they landed on the Dark Side?' It was agreed by some that the Chinese had indeed landed on the Dark Side, but their Government being even more duplicitous than the Federal Government, it would be no surprise that they would say nothing. Indeed, one might expect the Chinese to be trying to secretly annex Batmenia, as their territory had come to be known.

At the end of the table an earnest conversation weighed the pros and cons of the Australian mission to be the first nation to nuke another planet. The DG gathered that there were those who admired the Aussie initiative and those who thought it exhibited a typical hubris and lack of trustworthiness.

As these various erudite exchanges continued, the DG's eye was caught by a minor heading at the bottom of the page. 'Bangladesh gone.' He read silently, 'It was confirmed yesterday by The Intergovernmental Panel on Climate Change that Bangladesh has followed Holland in being overtaken, or at least submerged, by rising sea levels (more on this story on page 26).' The DG contemplated the front page of the newspaper. Somehow, it seemed out-of-plumb. He could see that being the first to nuke another world, was quite a big deal, and something that some might be proud of. It could only be done once – nuking another world, and so, one could admire the Aussie initiative, or misadventure. And he could see that if there was any possibility that Batmen, if they existed, were indeed in danger of being exterminated by the International

Nuclear Validation Festival, then getting them the Bible before they disappeared, might be good for their eternal souls or at worst, irrelevant. But the loss of Bangladesh? The DG frowned and massaged his brow with his right hand. He said, 'Does anyone think that the submergence of Bangladesh might rank above Bibles for Batmen?'

But no-one replied. A heated disagreement between a devout Texan doctor and a supercilious Australian physicist had gotten out of hand, and blows were being traded.

*

The Director of the International Nuclear Validation Festival was invited to the Office of the Secretary of State to witness the lift-off, of the truly enormous rocket that would carry Big Boy to the moon. Director Potts was accompanied by the Secretary General of the UN and several of her senior staff. Director Potts was very pleased when the General's Aide immediately approached him and with a most winning smile, slipped her arm through his and welcomed him to this auspicious occasion, which, she said, was entirely due to the foresight and vision of a man, albeit from a small and insignificant nation, who had seen that this Festival was necessary for the good of humankind.

The General said, 'Director Potts? Of course. We dined together – unforgettable.' And then he moved on. The General's Aide remarked that her boss was a man of few words and that for him to have remembered their dinner – given the weighty military matters that were constantly on his mind, was an enormous compliment. Director Potts was happy to accept the General's abrupt words as a compliment.

The Secretary of State asked if Director Potts was happy at the outcome of his most persuasive speech to the Security Council. The Secretary of State was still pondering the possible correlation between a thickened neck and reduced critical thinking faculties. She had opened a conversation on the subject with the Secretary of Health, but nothing had come of it. The Secretary of State had mentioned, in passing, that she had been wondering – that is to say, she had had the thought that perhaps a very thick neck might be due to either the thickening of the brainstem, or perhaps, the more solid neck simply acted like a tourniquet on the flow of blood and hence oxygen, to the brain. In both cases, the Secretary of State said offhandedly, it might cause one to wonder whether this in some way explained why the Pandemic of Alta Stultitia seemed to affect older men the most...and had anyone looked at correlation and possible causation? Unfortunately, before she could hear the views of the Secretary of Health, the President rose and rapped a glass until the room was still, and then proceeded to talk for an hour and fifteen, by which time the Secretary of State and many others, were reduced to a stupor, and one White House official slumped from his chair and was later pronounced a victim of Torpor.

What was it about the sound of Director Potts's voice? The Secretary heard Director Potts saying that he was indeed proud to have played some small part in this wonderful Festival, though he took little credit for it himself. But she was listening to the tone of his voice and she believed she recognised a similarity between this voice and that of the General. How could she describe it? Deep, certainly...measured, it seemed...and monotonous? Yes. Monotonous. It reminded her of a farm tractor, such as she had heard many times in her childhood. A kind of lower register, pugnacious growl, filled with the certainty of a full tank of diesel and an ample supply of air, that brooked no resistance. Discreetly, the Secretary studied the neck to head ratio of Director Potts. She decided that it was very nearly one-to-one. The General's neck, on the other hand, definitely out-sized his head. The Secretary heard Director Potts agreeing with one of her staff, that whilst one admired the fact that the Australians might be first to nuke another planet, the *Australian affair* as it was becoming known, did not reflect terribly well on that country. The Secretary heard Director Potts saying that he was not altogether surprised, since, as he recounted, the Baggy Greens had once won a cricket match by bowling an underarm delivery on the very last ball…

The Secretary of State took another glass of champagne and reflected on the purpose of this gathering. Shortly, the countdown would begin. The huge rocket on the huge screen would belch flames and would begin its brief journey to self-destruction. In a few hours, no doubt this same group of people, drunk with patriotic fervour would cheer wildly as Big Boy created the crater of all craters. Speeches would be made about the peoples of the World coming together in a spirit of cooperation and shared progress. There would be barely concealed delight that Big Boy had put the USA head and shoulders above its rivals and taught the World a lesson. In some quarters, there would be wailing and self-flagellation that the Batmen, for all their barbarism, had been exterminated before they ever had the chance to read the Texan Bible.

Indeed, at that moment, the countdown did begin, and just as the Secretary had imagined, the crowd roared out the count until their voices were drowned out by the roar of the rocket. 'I don't know…' thought the Secretary, and despite herself, detected in herself a thrill of pride that America was still well able to be biggest and best.

THIRTY-SIX

'Unfortunately,' said the head of NASA, 'we have encountered a technical hitch.'

*

The Prime Minister in Aotearoa New Zealand watched the American rocket rising into the deep blue sky with a feeling of resignation and mild interest. Soon, she thought, unconsciously prescient, it will be all over. She wondered why the flame seemed to have gone out.

*

The Head of the Chinese Nuclear Validation Launch Team cried jubilantly, 'The Americans have make the stuff-up!' Then instantly, he fell silent.

*

The Director of the International Nuclear Validation Festival had returned from the bathroom. He was still pondering the apparent demise of the man-in-the-mirror. He turned to the General's Aide. 'Is it supposed to do that?'

The General's Aide had suddenly released the arm of Director Potts. Her golden complexion was drained of colour. Her mouth was open but she remained wordless. Director

298

Potts asked, 'Shouldn't the rocket still have a flame? Coming out the back?'

*

The Secretary of State asked, 'How long have we got?'

Uncharacteristically, the General had loosened his tie. Momentarily, the Secretary wondered whether a strangulating tie, worn for hours on end, might not have a deleterious effect on blood flow to the higher regions of thought...

The General glanced at his watch and seemed mesmerised. Finally, he said, 'I would estimate...three minutes and twenty seconds, give or take.'

The Secretary said, 'It can't be restarted?'

The General shook his head.

The Secretary said, 'Where will it hit?'

The General closed his eyes. The Secretary had never beheld the General's face with its eyes closed. Somehow, it seemed to strip away many years. For a few moments, the Secretary wondered whether she could see a hint of the boy, which gave her to wonder further, how a harmless but gormless boy, as they all were, could transform into a General with a military mind. But she dismissed this thought also, as superfluous and repeated her question.

The General said, 'I am advised that the point of impact will be just north of Bozeman.'

The Secretary said, 'Bozeman, Montana...' The Secretary of State had a most vivid vision of her family's farm and a most unpleasant lurch in her chest. She said, 'Shouldn't we be heading for a bunker?'

The General didn't seem to hear.

*

The President bellowed, 'What the F***!' In fact, he bellowed these words five times. Then he shouted, 'How could anyone forget to open a fuel valve on a f****** rocket? What the F***! It's down in three minutes? Are we safe? Are we safe down here? How many will be killed? Millions? Is this place safe?'

It seemed, advised the Vice President, that the engineer whose job it was to open fuel valves, was experiencing brain fog. Normally a top man, he was a victim of the Pandemic. Instead of doing his job he'd gone for a coffee.'

The President stared at the Vice President incredulously. 'Fire that f***! Fire him now, today!'

The Vice President replied that there probably wasn't much point, or time. Given that Big Boy would impact Bozeman, Montana, in about two minutes.

The President gazed for a moment at the wall of the Deep Bunker. 'Do we hold Montana? But what the f***? How much will be left? Will any of our States be left? Or theirs? Who'll come out on top?'

The Vice President said that he thought it probably didn't matter much which states were red and which blue, since Big Boy would largely take out the USA.

The President was stunned. 'And Mar a Lago? Gone? F*** me...but what about the Chinese? They'll take over everything. Manhattan will be full of f****** dim sim. Are we safe down here?'

The Vice President glanced at the clock on the wall. 'Less than a minute, Mr President. Can I suggest a prayer?'

The President gaped, and shouted, 'F*** the prayer. Have we got enough food?'

THIRTY-SEVEN

Henry Simpson heard it before he saw it. A roaring sound high above his hog farm. Henry looked up and saw a light that seemed, even in the blue sky to be as bright as a star. He guessed it must be a comet or something like that. He stood transfixed as he watched the roaring star descend from the Heavens towards the farm on which he had raised hogs all his life – on the land his pappy and his grandpappy had raised hogs on before him. The land he had planned would become the hog farm of his eldest boy, Henry III. Henry Simpson was a devout man. 'Sweet Jesus,' said Henry, 'protect your humble servant from calamity. Amen.'

Henry barely had time to think about his hogs or his family. It crossed his mind that he must have transgressed badly. It crossed his mind that the thoughts he had entertained about Lucy Vincent at the service just this last Sunday, had been intercepted by the Lord, and the Lord, as he knew well, could be an unforgiving SOB. And here it was. Punishment swift and uncompromising. Henry fell to his knees. The bright star hit his bottom field and there was a shocking explosion and a mushroom of dust and dirt.

'Sweet Jesus!' Cried out Henry as he was knocked flat by the blast. Then all was silent. Henry spat dirt from his mouth. Henry raised himself onto all fours and peered down at the bottom field. There was a crater – about ten metres across, where there had for a century, been a fine walnut tree. A thin stream of smoke came from the crater. Henry rose and heard the voices of his wife, Mildred, and their three sons. He couldn't make out what they were saying. He shouted to his sons to each fetch a bucket of water, and then he made his way resolutely down the slope to the crater. Henry peered cautiously into the hole, that was more-or-less, a man's height in depth. Mildred ran to join her husband and seized his arm.

'Lord save us!' She cried. 'What is that thing?'

Henry didn't wish to think too much about the Lord at that moment, given that he was pretty sure that his thinking about Lucy Vincent *in that way*, was likely the root cause of this disaster. 'I'm danged if I know,' he replied. 'Give me those,' he said to his boys and taking each bucket of water in turn, he sluiced the large object that sat in the centre of the crater. The large object resembled a kind of feed silo of a rather sinisterly dark kind.

'Salute you neighbour!'

Henry saw that they had been joined by Hank Simmons. Hank Simmons also ran hogs. Hank had one glass eye that happened to be blue, whilst his natural eye was brown. Unfortunately, Hank's vision was about 20/200, which in medical terms meant he had been rendered legally blind by his own shotgun on the occasion he was attempting to dispatch a chicken-raiding coyote.

'Salute you, neighbour,' replied Henry. 'Danged if I haven't lost a good bit of this here field to this…whatever it is.'

Hank stood alongside and peered into the crater. 'So that's the varmint caused all that noise and so forth. I was thinking, so here it is. Judgement Day. The Lord has finally decided to wreak His vengeance on the sinners. And lookee here. The Lord has chosen the field of Henry Simpson. But it's danged close to the fields of Hank Simmons. So, I was thinking to myself, perhaps it was just the Lord missing His true target by a mite and there's no satisfaction to be gained from thinking that he just tired of the sinning of Henry Simpson.'

Henry Simpson replied, 'Hank. There's no need or justification for you calling me a sinning man, though God knows I am. But that's up to God.'

Hank said, 'You know danged well enough, Henry Simpson, that you let your dawg come through the fence to carry off my fresh-cooked Thanksgiving turkey. If that ain't a sin, Lord strike me down this moment.'

Henry made an expression of exasperation. 'That dawg has been dead some twenty years gone by, neighbour. If ever a man was going to bear a grudge, why, I declare it's you.'

'The leopard don't change its spots, Henry. You knows that well enough. Every year since, I've been waiting by that winder with my shotgun in case one of your varmints comes sneaking by on Thanksgiving. Vigilant.'

'Hank. Down there is something I don't like the look of. None of us do.' He gestured at his gaping boys and his wife. Then he shouted at his eldest, 'Don't you even think about climbing down there, boy! Or you'll feel the wrath of your pappy on your sinful butt.'

For a minute or two, the small group gazed at the dark and sinister silo in the hole. At last Hank said, 'Well, Henry. It's your field so it's your hole. Which means that that there thing, is also yours. That's just common sense. But if you look at it another way, your field is right alongside your neighbour and so, your neighbour should like as much, have something to say about it.'

'Well, neighbour, what do you have to say about it?'

'Well, Henry, if that hole and that thing, whatever it is, is part of the Lord's Wrath, then I'm danged if I know what He is fetching to say. That's my honest opinion.'

Henry nodded and replied, 'But what if it's not a message from the Lord? What if it's nothing to do with the Lord because the Lord is busy elsewhere? In which case, it's a message from someone else. Aliens…'

'Aliens?'

'I read not so long ago, Hank, that the Federal Government has been hiding aliens in the desert, over in Nevada or some place like it, which as the crow flies is not so far. What if this here hole and this thing, are aliens finally breaking out of their secret prison?'

'Lord save us.'

Henry added, 'Could be aliens. We'll go call Sheriff Mosely. But someone should stay. Just in case it's the Lord and He's not ready to impart His words at this point. Someone should be standing by. Just in case.' He looked meaningfully at Hank, and then because Hank was legally blind, he slapped him on the shoulder and shouted in Hank's good ear, 'You better stay here, Hank. Whilst we go and fetch up Sheriff Mosely.'

*

The President shouted, 'What the f***! It didn't go off? What the f***! Where is it?'

The Vice President said that the rocket had landed – or at least, crashed, into a field on a farm just north of Bozeman, belonging to Henry Simpson. The rocket, apparently was completely destroyed, as one might expect, but Big Boy was intact.

The President stared at the VP incredulously. 'Intact? How can the nuke be intact? What the f***? If it hit the f****** moon, it would be intact?'

The VP winced. 'It would appear so. Apparently, the bomb wasn't triggered. It appears that the engineer who failed to open the fuel valve to stage two of the rocket, also overlooked the switch that triggered the bomb.' The VP added that it appeared that the engineer was badly afflicted by Alta Stultitia – but no-one had noticed. That was the thing about

304

Alta Stultitia – a person who was also a Vector, could look quite normal even though they were afflicted by severe brain fog and in the worst cases, clinical stupidity.

The President's colour had changed from orange to puce. The President shouted that America would be a laughing stock. The President shouted that at least if the f****** bomb had gone off, hardly anyone would be around to blame Americans. But for the f****** bomb to be stuck in the field of a hog farmer was a disgrace. And a horror. The President demanded to know if the engineer was a Democrat. But whether or not, they must quickly and immediately make sure Americans understood that he was. Instantly, the President tweeted, 'Failure of our bomb a NATIONAL DISGRACE caused by a faulty DEM engineer. DEMS should leave America ASAP.'

The VP advised that the military was on its way to Bozeman.

*

Ever since he was a small boy, which was many decades gone by, Hank Simmons had been an obedient servant of the Lord. Indeed, Hank Simmons was an obedient man. So, when his neighbour said that he must remain by the hole and the mysterious Thing, in case the Lord was fixing to explain Himself, then Hank didn't for a moment think of arguing, despite that he found the Thing, pretty unnerving. And not for a moment did he imagine that his neighbour, whose dawg had stolen his Thanksgiving Turkey twenty years gone by, would be saying to his wife, 'If aliens are going to come out of that Thing, it's best they find Hank rather than us, close by.'

Overhearing this observation, Henry's middle boy cried, 'Do you think Hank will be skinned and eaten alive, Pappy? Do you think the aliens suck blood?'

305

'Hush your mouth, boy!' remonstrated his mother. 'Lest those aliens decide they prefer a cheeky boy to that stringy old Hank Simmons.'

Then the Simpson family retreated to the safety of their house and Henry took to phoning.

Beside the hole, Hank squinted with his brown eye but as always, whatever that Thing was, it would not look like any more than a dark, fuzzy Thing. After a while, Hank sat down on the edge of the hole with his legs dangling, and considered the morning and how things were, before the hole. He had fed his hogs. He recollected that he had given his hogs a good measure less than normal, because he couldn't be bothered taking his wheelbarrow to fetch more grain. That was because of his back, which he recollected had bothered him through the entire night. Consequently, he had thought at the time, 'You danged hogs will have to make do with a bit less, today. And it's no use complaining.' Now, he wondered if that uncharitable thought was the cause of the hole in Henry Simpson's field. Perhaps the Lord had overheard that uncharitable thought and decided that His servant, Hank Simmons was an undeserving son-of-a-bitch. Perhaps the Lord had thought, 'Take notice, Hank Simmons, that when you short-change your hogs, you short-change Me, and you might get smitten to the ground.' But at that precise moment, the Lord was distracted by some other sinner, someplace else and likely in DC, and consequently, His aim had gone a tad off. That was one way of looking at the Thing. The other way, was as his neighbour had surmised, that the Thing was actually the aliens breaking out of the secret Federal prison. Perhaps those aliens had been looking to get off into space, but through years of imprisonment and torture, most likely, they simply didn't have the energy and had managed to get only as far as Henry Simpson's farm. At this thought, Hank felt quite sympathetic. After-all, wasn't that just how he had felt that very morning when he got up to feed his hogs. If Hank had gotten up this morning and had it in mind to fetch himself into outer space, he doubted if he would have had the energy to get up higher than his chimney.

Hank mused on these matters for quite some time and wondered why Sheriff Mosely was taking so long. Perhaps Sheriff Mosely was on a call-out someplace else. Perhaps the Sheriff had to attend to police business across-State…in which case, the whole thing rested with Hank Simmons, for Lord knows how long. Hank looked toward the Simpson house, that was quite a long ways off. But apart from a fuzzy blob, which he knew was the Simpson house, he couldn't make out anything else. If a man was unrepentant after his dawg had stolen his neighbour's Thanksgiving turkey, Hank contemplated, might not that same man leave his neighbour alone, with the Thing? Might not that deceptive neighbour be thinking that if in fact the Thing was the Lord fixing to bring His wrath on Henry Simpson, that Henry Simpson might be banking on the Lord mistaking Hank Simmons for the true object of His wrath?

This was an uncomfortable thought. And if the Thing was, on the other hand, escaped aliens, might not that truly untrustworthy neighbour be hoping that Hank Simmons would be a suitable sacrifice to placate the aliens? This too, was an uncomfortable thought and occupied Hank for some time. And once again, he could detect no movement from the direction of the fuzzy blob that was that untrustworthy man's house.

After a time, Hank heard something. It was, he noted, a lark, high above and singing its heart out. Right up above the hole in which sat the Thing. 'Dang!' Hank thought. 'Is that sweet sound the word of the Lord?' It occurred to Hank that the Lord was unlikely to take the time or to demean Himself to the extent that He would actually speak directly to His humble servants. What would the Lord do? The Lord would, likely as not, send one of His minor messengers to speak on

307

His behalf. And if ever a creature could be said to be a messenger of the Lord, why, it would be a lark, high in the sky! And if that lark was singing the Lord's message to Hank Simmons, what would he be saying? He would be saying, 'Strike out those uncharitable thoughts, Hank Simmons, about your neighbour. Think about what lays before you. Think about creatures trapped in the Thing at your very feet, and crying in their misery for release. Think about what you can do, to do the Lord's Work!'

Hank looked down at the dark, fuzzy Thing, and pictured how inside, there was a bunch of small innocent creatures, quite possibly like his own dawgs. And what, if not a dumb dawg, was an innocent servant of the Lord?' At this notion, Hank peered up into the clear blue sky from which the Thing had descended, with not the slightest hope of seeing the Lord's messenger singing its heart out up there, and he cried out, 'Lord, I'm a coming!' He clambered down into the hole and slid right into the side of the Thing.

THIRTY-NINE

Corker Pritchard stared at the digital sales display. He said, 'Percy, this gives me the creeps.' Percy rose and reaching up the digital display, he gave it two good whacks. But the digital display was frozen. It read, 5,362,874,540.

The Chemical Whizzo said, 'Vot is the matter with that?' But she was not referring to the digital display. She was watching the large screen that was live-streaming the International Nuclear Validation Festival.' The Chemical Whizzo was referring to what seemed to be the American rocket, turning slowly in the sky until it was pointing back the way it had come. 'That rocket is not going,' she added.

Corker shook his head in disbelief. He said, 'There's no sales. Stopped. Just like that. Has the world gone mad? Verbal – we need a new campaign and we need it fast.'

But Verbal had gone pale. 'It's coming back.'

Corker replied, 'That won't cut it. "It's coming back?" Do you think the average punter will understand that? We need something with punch! What about, and I've been giving this some thought, 'Brainee brings hope to mothers of Democrats?' Could give us a big boost in the States.'

Percy said evenly, 'We're f*****.'

'What,' shouted Corker, 'that's worse than "It's coming back!"'

The Chemical Whizzo said, 'You know, it's been nice to know you.'

Corker removed a waxed alligator skin, Louis Vuitton Manhattan Richelieu shoe and hurled it at the digital display, which blinked out.

The Director of the International Nuclear Validation Festival stared balefully at the man-in-the-mirror. 'So, you've bothered to some over? I wonder you could find the time.'

The man-in-the-mirror replied, 'I thought you should like to know that Doc Cod passed away last week.'

Dimple said, 'Is that all? He was an old dog. I suppose Mildred is blaming me for that?'

'Mildred said that everything is your fault. She's started a new movement, against middle-aged men. She calls it Poop.'

'Poop?'

'People Opposed to Old Progenitors.'

Dimple scowled. 'I don't have children. Stupid woman.'

The man-in-the-mirror said, 'She is speaking figuratively.'

Dimple sniffed. 'Who cares? You know I'm in isolation? I'm a Vector, it seems. If you're not careful you might go down. It seems I'm one of those exceptional types who can hit someone with Torpor from a long range. I'm wondering whether I might not be able to direct it. I wonder if I might not be able to target the founder of Poop? Even cooped up in this hotel.'

The man-in-the-mirror said, 'You know the American Nuclear Validation is a complete disaster?'

'Of course, I know! I'm the Director. Monumental embarrassment. Second stage didn't work and now its landed somewhere and didn't go off.' He shook his head. 'You start to admire the Aussies. Who's going to remember a few craters on the moon? Everyone is going to be waiting for the Aussies to hit Venus.'

'The bomb is on a farm in Montana.'

'Is it? But so what? I'm done with this Festival. I'm resigning. When I get out of isolation, I'm going to demand the Finance portfolio. Brainee is paying far too much tax. The Chair was right. I'm over all this diplomacy. It's not me. I'm a straight shooter and all this mealy-mouthed stuff goes against the grain. You wouldn't believe the tripe I've had to put up with. Russian vodka. British condescension. North Korean wrong-headed thinking; French fries…I've got to get back to my entrepreneurial roots. I'm thinking beyond Brainee. I've been thinking for some time about a system for streamlining the whole funeral thing – doing away with pall bearers and so forth. A balloon for moving the coffin.'

*

The Head of News was thinking. What would make the better angle? 'American Big Boy makes piddly crater in Montana pig farm?' Or, 'Aussies steal show with stolen bomb?' Or, 'Batmen saved by American Bungle?' Or, 'Dimple Potts is #1 Poop?'

He said, 'I'm leaning towards the last. Who cares about international cooperation? It's overworked. People are bored. The Festival was supposed to bring people together but look what's happened? American embassies attacked everywhere because they didn't deliver a decent finale. People are disappointed and who can blame them? But is that news?'

The Senior Reporter considered Ridgy's words carefully. She was still nursing a black eye. 'No-one cares very much about any festival, after it's finished.'

'Forgotten in about a day,' agreed the Head of News.

'And only a few Texans actually believe there are Batmen on the Moon.'

'True.'

The Senior Reporter continued, 'It might be better we bring the focus, closer to home?'

'You're on it. That's my thinking. Bring the news back where it belongs. Local stuff. But link it to the Festival fiasco. Now, there's a thought. 'Potts number one Poop, presides over Festival Fiasco.'

The Senior Reporter nodded admiringly. 'That's smart. Two birds with one stone.'

Which occasioned a prolonged exchange about what the metaphor actually meant, in this context.

*

The Chair sat in his favourite chair, staring at the television screen. He had seen the leader of the First Union of Conservative Thinkers in the glittering assembly in the Whitehouse, watching the failure of the American rocket. He had to give it to Potts. From Brewster's Neck to magnate to habitué of the corridors of power. Who would have thought? And who was that glittering thing with her arm through his, who had suddenly clapped her hand over her mouth and fled in the direction of the rest room?

The Chair listened on and with great relief to the update from CNN, which said the world was safe because 'Big Boy,' as the American bomb was apparently called, had failed to detonate on impact with a hog farm near Bozeman, Montana. The American President was quoted as saying that this was just as his administration had intended. To show the world that despite having the biggest nuke ever built, the Americans chose to show the world the meaning of restraint.

FORTY

The Thing was not hollow. Hank was accustomed to checking on the contents of a feed silo with a quick rap of the knuckles and a finely tuned ear. When he rapped on the Thing, there was no sound whatsoever. It was even more silent than a full silo. It was as if he was rapping on granite. But it was smooth. He ran his hand cautiously across the surface. It felt somewhat warm, because it was a sunny day. He decided it felt like spun steel, with which he was familiar from his days in the steel mill. But it felt a little different from any steel he'd previously encountered. That difference added to his feeling that the Thing was not of this Earth. In which case, it could only be alien.

Hank circumnavigated the Thing. It was nearly two metres across and stood three metres high. But part of it, and he guessed perhaps another metre or two, was buried in the Bozeman clay beneath his feet. On the top of the Thing, appeared to be a kind of spike and though it was hard to make out, Hank pondered that something might have broken off. Otherwise, the entire Thing was smooth and intact. But the top was a little different and Hank felt behoved to investigate this further, but on account of its height, he couldn't reach it. He climbed out of the crater and stared toward the Simpson house, but there was no sign of Henry or Sheriff Mosely. Hank shook his head and then trudged across to the boundary, clambered over the fence and made his way down the slope to his shed. He located his short ladder and carried it back to the crater. He let it down and then slid back into the hole. He said, 'Them others might not be coming to help, but Hank Simmons is on hand.' Hank was pretty confident he didn't need to say stuff out loud in order for the Lord to know his thoughts, but it seemed a good precaution at this point, when the contents of the Thing were as yet unknown. It could be that it did not contain friendly small creatures. It could be it contained something unpleasant. How was a man to know? But a man could know that the Lord was on hand, in some capacity and despite His many other concerns across Bozeman. Likely as not, the Lord was simultaneously addressing that idiot Horace Walpole who only last week was found guilty of re-labelling chickens with a new use-by date and had poisoned quite a few folks in west Bozeman.

Hank placed his ladder gingerly against the Thing and listened. There was no sound anywhere in the hole. He climbed the ladder and squinted at the top of the Thing with his good eye. He was right. Something had broken off. But as he ran his hand across, he felt something. Like a lever, or a handle of some sort. A thrill of excitement ran down Hank's entire being such as he had not experienced since he saw President Ralph dispatched in that movie, whose title he could not recall.

Hank climbed onto the next rung so that he could bring his eye to bear on the lever. There were words! The aliens wrote words! Hank brought his eye closer and made out the word, 'Turn.' He blinked several times. 'Turn,' was an English word. Unless by some peculiar coincidence, the aliens used a word he knew, but which meant something else entirely. In Alien, the word 'Turn,' might mean 'kill...' How could a man know?

Hank looked up into the sky and said, 'Lord, if this alien word is in English, it is telling me to turn. But does that mean I should be turning around, until I'm facing back the same way? Or, does it mean I should turn-back? Or, does it mean, it's my turn? And where is Henry Simpson and Sheriff Mosely?' Of these three turning possibilities, the first was easily dealt with. So, Hank turned himself around on the ladder until once again he was peering at the lever. He moved his good eye closer to the Thing and espied another word coming into the edge of his 20/200 vision. 'Dang me…' he muttered, 'if it ain't another word…' He made out that word to be, 'to.'

Hank scratched his head because he hadn't thought of this notion of turn. 'Turn-to.' He was very familiar with those words. When he was in the Army, those umpteen years ago, he'd always been turning-to. Whenever he figured he was going to catch up on a few winks of sleep, the Drill Serjeant was bawling at the platoon, 'Turn-to!' Hank stood back and reflected. Was this the word of the Lord? Was this the command of the Lord? Perhaps the Lord was saying, 'Hank Simmons, you just turn-to!' But if that was what the Lord had in mind, what did the Lord want him to do next? When the serjeant bawled turn-to, a man knew what he wanted. He wanted a man to get his boots on real quick and to shape up with his rifle to hand. But here, in the hole with the Thing…

Hank brought his good eye down close to the words and let out a small gasp. Danged if there wasn't another word! The new word was longer and it began with the letter 'A.' Hank squinted and moved his head about until he could spell out the letters of that word. A-c-t-i-v-a-t-e. Hank raised his head and said, 'Turn to Activate. Well, I'll be.'

Here, clearly, was The Answer.

Also by Greg Billington

She Sings

Vote Dimple Potts

Songs of the Other Man

The Ghost in the Aspens

The Lavender Man

The Trials of Max Pipe

Oystercatcher (Reed NZ 2003)

Spindrift (Reed NZ 2000)

Manufactured by Amazon.com.au
Sydney, New South Wales, Australia

13743469R00179